Truly, Madly, Deeply

**A heart-melting collection of the best
romantic fiction from Mills & Boon and
the Romantic Novelists' Association**

Truly, Madly, Deeply

EDITED BY SUE MOORCROFT

&

INTRODUCED BY JILL MANSELL

MILLS
BOON

Published in Great Britain 2014
by Mills & Boon, an imprint of Harlequin (UK) Limited,
Eton House, 18-24 Paradise Road, Richmond, Surrey, TW9 1SR

TRULY, MADLY, DEEPLY © 2014 Harlequin Books S.A.

A Rose By Any Other Name Would Smell as Sweet © 2014 Adele Parks
A Sensible Proposal © 2014 Anna Jacobs
The Corporate Wife © 2014 Carole Matthews
The Art of Travel © 2014 Elizabeth Buchan
The Rough with the Smooth © 2014 Elizabeth Chadwick
Living the Dream © 2014 Katie Fforde Limited
True Love © 2014 Maureen Lee
Love on Wheels © 2014 Miranda Dickinson
Clarion Call © 2014 Catherine King
Puppy Love © 2014 Chrissie Manby
Third Act © 2014 Fanny Blake
A Real Prince © 2014 Fiona Harper
The Fundamental Things © 2014 Heidi Rice
Summer '43 © 2014 India Grey
How To Get A Pill Into A Cat © 2014 Judy Astley
Life of Pies © 2014 Kate Harrison
Head Over Heart © 2014 Melanie Hilton
The Marriage Bargain © 2014 Nicola Cornick
Shocking Behaviour © 2014 Sue Moorcroft
Feel The Fear © 2014 Alison May
The Eighth Promise © 2014 Jenny Harper
A Night To Remember © 2014 Nikki Moore
The Truth About The Other Guy © 2014 Rhoda Baxter
The Fairytale Way © 2014 Sophie Pembroke

ISBN: 978 0 263 24561 5

097-0314

Harlequin (UK) Limited's policy is to use papers that are natural, renewable and recyclable products and made from wood grown in sustainable forests. The logging and manufacturing processes conform to the legal environmental regulations of the country of origin.

Printed and bound by
CPI Group (UK) Ltd, Croydon, CR0 4YY

ACKNOWLEDGEMENTS

Thanks to all the many wonderful contributors to this book for their fantastic stories and to the Harlequin team for making *Truly, Madly, Deeply* possible.

The Romantic Novelists' Association was formed in 1960 to promote romantic fiction and to encourage good writing. Its membership comprises many successful writers, agents, editors and other industry professionals. These stories showcase the wonderfully diverse work of its writers.
www.rna-uk.org/

Dedication

To every member of the Romantic Novelists' Association, past, present and future

CONTENTS

&

Introduction by Jill Mansell

Well, guess what? The last compilation of short stories by RNA members was such a dazzling success that they were asked to do it all over again. And this time they managed to do it *even better than before*. Really, is there nothing these brilliant writers can't do? (And I say this as an RNA member who finds writing short stories the hardest thing in the world, which is why I'm providing the foreword again. Those who can, do. Those who can't, provide introductions...)

Someone asked me the other day where was my favourite place to read. And having given it some thought I decided the answer was: wherever I happen to have a book. Because it really doesn't matter where you are – in bed at night, on the beach somewhere exotic or under the desk at work – if you can lose yourself in another world, you're winning. Trapped on a train that isn't going anywhere? A book will help you through it. Waiting in the car for a small child to finish their karate lesson? Escape to a better place through the pages of a novel and time will fly by. Just so wrapped up in a story that you keep sneaking off to read a few more pages, leaving the family to wonder where on earth you've got to? Ah well, never mind. If they're your family, they're probably used to it by now.

To love reading is a gift and I feel genuinely sorry for those who don't have it. We're the lucky ones. And as long as we have books like this one to entertain, enthrall and engage us, we need never be bored. I've said it before and I'll say it again, I am so proud to be a member of the Romantic Novelists' Association, surely one of the friendliest and most supportive groups anywhere. We work hard, play hard and have an amazing wealth of talent among us. Best of all, we will make you laugh and cry and think about love, life and all it entails. It is our aim to entertain.

I really hope you enjoy reading the carefully selected stories in this anthology. And if you do, please do let us know on Facebook and Twitter. Most of us are on there and we love to hear from our readers. Plus – sshh, don't tell our editors – it's always good to have an excuse to stop writing the books and have a little online chat instead!

Adele Parks

Adele Parks worked in advertising until she published her first novel, *Playing Away*, in 2000; she's since published thirteen novels, including *Whatever It Takes* and *The State We're In*. All her novels have been top ten bestsellers; she's sold 2.5 million copies of her work in the UK alone, and has been translated into twenty-five different languages. Adele is known for writing unforgettable heroes and lovable (although sometimes cheeky!) heroines.

She has spent her adult life in Italy, Botswana and London until 2005 when she moved to Guildford, where she now lives very happily with her husband and son. Adele believes reading is a basic human right and good for your health! Therefore she's an Ambassador for The Reading Agency, a charity that encourages the love of literacy in all.

Visit **www.adeleparks.com** to learn more about Adele. Find her on Facebook **www.facebook.com/OfficialAdeleParks** and follow her on Twitter **@adeleparks**

&

A Rose By Any Other Name Would Smell As Sweet

'I'm thinking of throwing a Valentine's party this year,' said Katie, dishing up a big, innocent grin.

'You're kidding, right?'

'More partying is in everyone's interest.'

Jane sighed and looked at her sister with a blatant mix of accusation and incredulity. 'You've hosted three birthday parties this year. Why would you even think of having another party?'

'They were for the kids. I want to throw a party for grown-ups? I mean adults.' Katie corrected herself. The adults she knew were not all grown up; that was her point.

Jane felt sick. This was the most ridiculous and painful idea her well-intentioned, but woefully misguided, sister had come up with yet. Valentine's Day! Jane's own private hell. These were the two words most likely to strike fear into her heart; crueller than 'facial hair', more uncomfortable than 'smear examination'.

Jane, unlike her sister, did not have children to throw birthday parties for. Nor did she have a husband or even a boyfriend. She had been engaged once, in her early twenties. They'd split up before the wedding. On Valentine's Day. To coin an old-fashioned phrase, she'd jilted him. Sometimes, when she looked back on her actions, she struggled to remember them with absolute clarity; she laboured to justify them. She remembered feeling panicked that the wedding planning was cutting into far too much of her studying time – she had her exams to think of – and she remembered thinking that Mark was a nice enough guy but that nice enough wasn't enough. Although it wasn't clear exactly what might be enough for Jane. It was all such a long time ago. She'd since dated various men on and off but she'd never committed. Sexy, bad boy types disappointed her, she ridiculed and distrusted devoted romantics and she dismissed any one in between as, 'Boring, far too normal.'

'What are you looking for?' Katie often asked, exasperated.

'Just someone who understands I have a career and friends of my own. Someone who has that too but wants to share.' Jane didn't think this was too much to ask. It seemed practical and sensible so it should be possible. Jane was all about the practical and sensible; admittedly she gave less thought to what was possible.

Her mother had never quite forgiven her. 'What sort of girl calls off her wedding on Valentine's Day?' she'd yelled. 'You've ruined your one chance of happiness.'

Jane thought her mother was wrong about her ruining her one chance of happiness. It simply wasn't true. Jane was happy. At least, she felt very content, which was a lot like happiness. She had a full life. She was a solicitor and would probably make Partner next year; all her studying and hard work had paid off. She went to gigs with the frequency of a teenager, she had good friends, two dogs – not cats, she'd resisted becoming a cliché – and a stylish home. A home in which she was free to eat whatever she liked, whenever she liked and to watch anything she pleased on TV. Microwave meals for one and uninterrupted viewing of *The Walking Dead* were sufficiently compensatory. The only time that she found being single difficult, and contentment illusive, was on Valentine's Day.

On February 14th, Jane's life felt like an enormous black hole. No matter how many computer literacy or yoga classes she fitted in, committees she sat on or hours she spent in the office, she could not fill that day. She found herself dwelling on the fact that every other woman in the United Kingdom was wearing silky lingerie under her new, fabulous dress, eating a delicious meal by candlelight and drinking vintage champagne while her husband or boyfriend serenaded her and threw red rose petals in her path. Jane told herself that it was actually, simply a materialistic, manufactured, almost grotesque commercial enterprise but the image of a more beautiful and romantic version of Valentine's Day, largely manufactured by glossy, glorious magazines, always chewed its way into her consciousness and, secretly, she longed for it.

Not that she'd ever admit such a thing. If there was one thing a single girl understood the importance of, it was saving face.

'Well, count me out,' declared Jane.

'Have plans do you?' asked Katie.

Jane glared at her. 'No one will come anyway. Don't couples want time by themselves on Valentine's Day? Isn't that the point?'

'I don't *just* know couples.' Actually, Katie's friends were mostly couples but she thought they would rally when they heard her plan; all her friends were aware of Jane's singledom.

'Why would you want a bunch of drunks staggering around your house and throwing up in the cloakroom?'

Katie laughed at Jane, obviously unwilling to be put off. 'It won't be like that. I'm going to have a romantic theme and ask everyone to wear pink.'

'Even the men?'

'I'll serve salmon canapés and rosé cava.'

'You'll find it spilt on your new cream sofa.'

Katie ignored her. 'I'll have a chocolate fountain.'

'Chocolate is not pink, it's not theme appropriate,' pointed out Jane churlishly.

'Don't be such a spoilsport, Aunt Jane. A party is a marvelous idea. You might meet someone and find luuurvvve?' Isobel, Katie's eldest, interrupted the conversation. She had a habit of sneaking up on her aunt and mother when they were chatting. She'd found eavesdropping a tremendous source of information since she was an infant.

'No, I won't,' said Jane. 'I believe in "luuurvvve" less than I believe in Santa Claus or the Easter Bunny.'

'Don't let George hear you. He wavered in his belief this year.'

'At least George is eight. Your mother told me Santa didn't exist when I was three!' The outrage in Jane's voice was as crystal clear now as it had been back in 1979 when the truth was first revealed.

Katie cringed inwardly. She'd only been seven when she blurted out her discovery that the man who filled the stockings was their dad and that the elves that produced the gifts didn't exist, it was their mum who spent from November

trailing the stores for treats. Katie had spent her life trying to
make up for the faux pas that robbed her sister of her inno-
cence. Sometimes, Katie worried that the early disillusion-
ment was the reason behind Jane growing up to be such a
pragmatist. She was so sensible, rational and logical which
was, in Katie's opinion, the real reason she'd never fallen in
love. To do so, you had to give a little. In fact you had to give
a lot. You had to trust, hope and lose control.

Katie didn't think that being married was the only way to
find happiness, but it was the way she'd found happiness.
She, Graham and their three children already had 'it'. They
were healthy, loved and loving. Between them they formed
that enigmatic and enviable thing – a happy family. Of
course, they squabbled, snapped and snipped at one another
from time to time. There had been that very worrying period
when Isobel became secretive and dated unsuitable boys.
George was dyslexic, which had its challenges, and Sarah,
the middle child, had started to cuss this year, repeatedly and
ferociously, just to see if she got a reaction. But most of the
time they were one another's heart ease. Magic dust. Happiness. Call 'it' what you will.

Katie wanted more of the same for her sister. Jane had the
bigger home in the smarter part of town, a career, foreign
holidays, a wardrobe to die for and Katie had a demanding
family whose needs had long since drowned out her own
desires. Unfashionably, she had no problem with that. She
believed it to be the natural order of things. Her own mother
had always made Katie and Jane a priority. Katie had suggested that her sister try blind dating once.

'I don't know anyone who knows anyone who's single
anymore! Who could fix me up?'

'Well then, internet dating.'

'I'm not in the market to meet psychos.'

'Speed dating?'

'I have to enter into enough high-pressure pitches at work, thank you. I don't want that sort of nonsense intruding into my private life.'

So Katie had decided to go back to basics. The good old-fashioned method of meeting people at parties.

Katie made a huge effort with the party. She blew a silly amount of cash on rosé cava and she baked and cleaned for hours. She nearly passed out blowing up pink balloons and she decked the kitchen, living room and hall with enormous red crêpe paper hearts. She was very strict about the entrance policy. Not only did she insist that her guests wear red or pink, she also explained that, instead of having to bring a bottle, every couple had to bring a spare man.

Her friends were surprised but after a little cajoling, they agreed to the stipulation. After all, it was Valentine's Day, generally, most women are secret matchmakers and delighted in the possibility of being responsible for new love blossoming even if it did mean they had to sacrifice a romantic meal in the local restaurant.

Finally, the big day arrived; Katie could not have been more excited. It was, as she'd expected, lovely to see her friends discard their coats, hats, scarves and gloves and melt in the warmth that her home oozed. But it was especially exciting to see the number of single men that had been brought along. She quickly assessed them, as though it was a beauty contest. At least two were especially handsome men, four had friendly smiles, the rest were passable. They probably had lovely personalities. Only one chap stuck out like a sore thumb. He was sitting on his own, drinking tap water instead of the frothy cava, he wasn't wearing so much as a red tie or pair of socks, he was dressed in jeans and a grey jumper; he was not even faking an interest in the conversations around him, the only person he deigned to speak with was Isobel.

Jane was late.

'The invite said 7.30 p.m.,' scolded Katie as she took her sister's coat. She noticed that Jane had ignored the dress code too. She was wearing black as though she was at a funeral. Katie shoved her towards the kitchen, where the party – like all parties – was thriving. 'Ta-dah.'

'What?'

'What's different about this party?' prompted Katie.

Jane looked around the kitchen. It was heaving. There were a lot of men, which was a bit odd; normally at parties the women stayed in the kitchen and the men hung around the iPlayer.

She hazarded a guess. 'Decent food?'

'Men!'

'What?'

'These are all single men. I asked my guests to bring a single man rather than a bottle. I asked them all to play cupid for you.' Katie beamed. 'Most of them know about your broken engagement and everything, so they were really sympathetic.'

Jane starred at her sister in horror. How could she have been so cruel? So thoughtless? The humiliation was intense; a hot blush was already forming on Jane's neck. Valentine's had always been ghastly when Jane was privately fighting her demons – the lack of a picture perfect scenario: flowers and hearts, hubby and kiddies – but it had been bearable. Now,

Katie had outed her and the mortification was overwhelming.

Jane turned, grabbed her coat and ran. She didn't notice that she'd dropped her glove. She had to get out of the stifling house full of pitying and patronising couples.

Jane nearly slipped on the icy path. She stopped at the gate; fighting angry tears, she had never felt so alone.

'Excuse me.'

Oh God, that was the last thing she needed. Someone had followed her out of the house. Jane pretended she couldn't hear him calling to her and she began to walk along the street.

The man jogged to catch up. 'You dropped a glove,' he called.

Normally, Jane loved her soft, beige buckskin gloves. Right now, she hated them.

'Thank you.' She refused to meet his eye.

'I saw your dramatic exit. Very Cinderella.'

'I don't believe in fairy tales,' she said stiffly. 'Not even on Valentine's Day.'

'Nor do I. *Especially* not on Valentine's Day. I hate it. The sickest day of the year.'

Jane looked up startled. It was refreshing, although somewhat surprising, to find someone else who was equally vitriolic about the day. She'd always found that there was a deep and dark silence surrounding the gloomy reality of the day. Single women simply dared not roll their eyes at the torturous nylon basques that seeped from every shop window, even though it seemed that the sole purpose of such garments was to humiliate flat chested and saggy bummed women, aka normal women.

'Do you know what I most hate about it?' he asked.

'The pink, plastic "I Love You" stamps for toast and similar plethora of tack that are no doubt mass-produced by children working in illegal conditions?' Jane wondered whether she sounded bitter and defeatist.

'Ha! No, although that is offensive. It's my birthday too.'

'You're kidding?'

'Wish I was.'

Jane took the glove.

'So why do you hate it then? I'd have thought it being your birthday made it tolerable. At least you're guaranteed cards.'

He smiled wanly but didn't answer her question. 'I'll walk with you, if you're going to the tube station.'

Jane stole a glance. The guy didn't look like a psycho. 'Where are you going?'

'Err, embarrassing thing is, nowhere. So I've got time to squander. It's my birthday *and* Valentine's Day and yet I have some time to kill until my sister-in-law and brother emerge from the party. Then I'm staying with them for the weekend. I think they thought that if they took me along to the party, then all their duties towards me, in terms of celebrating my birthday, were null and void. It's always such a disappointing day.' The man grinned as he made this awful admission.

Jane noticed he had nice eyes. Particularly attractive when he grinned.

'Isn't it?'

'What were you hurrying from?'

'All of it.'

'I see.' They both fell silent. It was a comfortable silence. Jane realised she was enjoying the peaceful company of her fellow anti-romantic.

He sighed deeply; his hot breath clouded the cold night air.

'I know you think you are having a bad night but somewhere in that house, something truly awful is happening.'

'What?' Jane asked.

'I was talking to this teenager. Her mother has set up this whole party to try to off-load some maiden aunt.'

Jane gasped. 'How terrible.'

'Isn't it? I told the girl her mother shouldn't be so interfering and pushy. Just because it's Valentine's Day doesn't mean the maiden aunt is suddenly going to find love or even want it. It's such an imposition.'

Jane nodded, mute with shock and embarrassment. She couldn't let this cute guy know that she was the spinster aunt. Because he was, well, a cute guy. He had full lips and lovely curly hair. And a cynical side that she appreciated.

'What did the teenager say?' Jane knew that the forthright Isobel would have expressed an opinion.

He grinned at the memory of the bolshie teenager dressing him down. 'She said I was a miserable devil. She said her mother was only trying to help and that she *did* believe things were different on Valentine's Day; that there is a little more magic everywhere and, of course, the aunt wanted to find love.'

'Teenagers,' said Jane with a tut. 'So damned optimistic.'

They both fell silent again.

'Look, would you like to go for a drink? No bubbles though, anything but that.'

Jane considered it. Maybe. She quite liked him. She liked his sensible attitude to Valentine's Day. She was so fed up of people insisting that it was a romantic, enchanted time. It's just another date on the calendar. And it was his birthday, after all. No one wanted to be alone on their birthday.

'I'm Jane.' She held out her hand, he shook it.

'Pleased to meet you, Jane.'

Jane waited for him to volunteer his name. He didn't.

'And you are?'

'OK, well, this is it, I suppose. Crunch time. So it's my birthday today, right.'

'Yes, you said.'

'I'm Valentino Lovelass.' Jane snorted with laughter. 'What's funny?' he asked with mock incredulity.

'Nothing, nothing at all,' Jane was practically choking on her laughter. 'Are you joking?' she asked eventually.

'I never joke. I'm eminently sensible and practical. I'm always serious.' There was a glint in his eyes that belied the fact that he was always serious so Jane insisted he produce his driving licence to prove he wasn't making up a ridiculous alias.

'I do at least understand why you hate Valentine's Day,' she said as they set off towards the pub.

'And my parents too, don't underestimate how much I hate them,' he joked.

'Oh get over it.' Jane laughed. Teasingly she added, 'It's not like they destroyed your belief in Santa Claus at an early age.'

'True, that would be really bad. Very bad indeed.'

Katie and Isobel were watching from Isobel's bedroom window. Katie winked at her daughter. 'Perfect,' she sighed.

'You are a regular cupid, Mum. Congratulations. You do know his name though, right?'

'Oh yes. And how I'm going to enjoy hearing my sister introduce him!'

Anna Jacobs

Award-winning author Anna Jacobs writes both historical and modern romantic novels about families and relationships. She's had over sixty novels published, with more in the pipeline, and she's the sixth most borrowed author of adult fiction in the UK. She and her husband live half the year in Australia and half in the UK.

This story is a spin-off from her Swan River Saga series, set in Lancashire and Western Australia in the 1860s. If you'd like to read more about the group of young women sent to Australia as maids, try her three novels *Farewell to Lancashire*, *Beyond the Sunset* and *Destiny's Path* and the spin-off series The Traders (starting with *The Trader's Wife*).

You can find out more about her books, each of which has a separate page on her website, where you can read the first chapters and find about what gave her the ideas for the various stories on her website: http://www.annajacobs.com

&

A Sensible Proposal

1

1863, Lancashire

Sarah Boswick had been hungry for so long she couldn't remember her last full meal. She stood quietly in the queue, not expecting more from the soup kitchen at the church than a bowl of thin soup and a chunk of stale bread. It would be her only food of the day.

None of the mill workers had realised that the war between the states in America would affect Lancashire so badly, cutting off supplies of cotton and therefore putting people out of work. Sarah's husband had been delighted to think of all the slaves being freed. He'd been such an idealist, poor Daniel. He'd died a year ago, weakened by lack of food, and she still missed him.

The line of women shuffled forward and someone poked Sarah to make her move with them.

When a gentleman with silver hair stopped nearby, Sarah didn't at first realise he was speaking to her.

Mrs Foster, one of the supervisors, said sharply, 'You, Boswick! Step out of the line and answer the gentleman. He's spoken to you twice already. Where are your manners?'

Sarah moved quickly, not allowing herself the luxury of

resenting the scolding – it didn't pay to cross the supervisors, not if you wanted to eat here regularly. 'I'm sorry, sir. I'm afraid my thoughts were miles away.'

'It's partly my fault. I should have waited to be introduced to you before I spoke. I'm Simon Marville, from the town of Swindon in the south, and I'm here because my church has raised some money for the relief fund in this area.'

She tried to pay attention but the smell of food nearby was intoxicating. Sometimes gentlemen or ladies came to the north to stare at the poor starving cotton operatives. It was annoying to be treated like a wild animal on display and it did little good that she could see. There would still be no work for those in Lancashire after the visitors had gone back to their comfortable lives.

'Could we talk for a few minutes, Miss Boswick?'

'Mrs I'm a widow.' Sarah couldn't help looking towards the food and as she did, her stomach growled.

'Have you eaten today?' he asked, still in that same gentle tone.

'No, sir. The only food I'll eat today is what's offered here at the soup kitchen.' She saw Mrs Foster looking at her and added quickly, 'For which I'm very grateful.'

He turned to the supervisor. 'Do you think we could have some food brought for this poor woman, ma'am? It'll be hard for her to concentrate on what I'm saying if she hasn't eaten anything yet.'

'Of course. If you sit down over there, I'll bring some across for you both.'

'None for me, thank you. Save it for those who need it so desperately.' He led the way to the table indicated, pulling out a chair for Sarah.

At least this visitor was treating her courteously, she thought as she sat down.

He took his own seat and was about to speak again when Mrs Foster brought her a big bowl of soup and two pieces of bread.

Sarah's mouth watered at the sight of the larger bowl and extra bread. Clearly the lady patronesses were out to impress. She looked at him, wondering whether to start eating.

He waved one hand as if giving her permission and she could hold back no longer. She didn't gobble down the food, because that would make her ill, but chewed slowly, spooning up soup in between each dry mouthful of bread. As she finished the first slice, she looked round and whispered, 'Would you mind if I put this other piece of bread in my pocket, sir? I have a neighbour whose child isn't thriving.'

'No, of course not. Though you look as if you need it yourself. You're very thin.'

'I'm managing but it's harder on the little ones.'

When she'd finished, he asked, 'How long have you been hungering?'

'Since my husband died last year, before that even.'

'May I ask what happened to him?'

'Daniel came down with a fever and hadn't the strength to resist it. He was low in spirits, took it very badly not to be able to earn a living.'

Mr Marville's expression was so genuinely sympathetic, Sarah felt tears rise in her eyes. She tried to change the subject. 'What do you wish to talk about, sir?'

'You, my dear. I'd like to find out more about your life.'

That puzzled her. What had the ladies been telling him?

'I've been charged with helping select a group of cotton

lasses to go to Australia, where there is plenty of work for those willing to become maidservants. The supervisor has suggested you. What do you think?'

She gaped at him. 'Go to Australia? Me?'

'Yes. Do you know where Australia is?'

'On the other side of the world. I saw it on the globe at school. But I don't know much else about it. I'll have to see if there's a book in the library.' It had saved her sanity, the new free library had. If you could lose yourself in a book, you could forget the gnawing hunger for a while.

'A ship going to the Swan River Colony will be leaving in two weeks. How long will it take you to decide whether to go?'

She looked round and laughed, though it came out more like a croak. 'I don't need any time at all, sir. If there's work there, I'll be happy to go because there's nothing for me here, not now.' Only Daniel's grave, and beside him in the coffin a tiny baby who had not lived even one day.

'How long will you need to get ready, pack your things?'

She looked down at herself and grimaced. 'I have very little beyond the clothes on my back. I regret that. I'd keep myself cleaner if I could.'

'A complete set of clothes can be supplied.'

'I'd be very grateful.'

He hesitated and asked again, 'Are you quite sure?'

She wasn't sure of anything but to do something was surely better than doing nothing. 'I shan't change my mind, sir.'

'Then you may as well travel south with me when I return. I'm sure Mrs Foster will provide you with clothes for the journey and we have other clothes in my church.'

'Thank you.' Poor box clothes. She knew what those were like but beggars couldn't afford vanity.

'Do you have *any* family here, anyone you should consult?'

'No, sir. I'm an orphan.' She'd only had Daniel. At the moment she was sharing a room with five other young women to save money. The others would be jealous of this chance she'd been given, so the sooner she could leave the better.

When Mr Marville had gone, she took her platter to the clearing up table and went to thank Mrs Foster for recommending her.

The other woman nodded then reached for a small, cloth-wrapped bundle. 'You'll need better food to face such a long journey. There's more bread here and a boiled egg. Eat it all yourself.' She held on to the cloth. 'Promise you'll not give this to anyone else like that bread in your pocket.'

She blushed in embarrassment. 'I promise. Um, could I ask why you recommended me?'

'Because you're still trying to help others, sharing what little food you have. You deserve this chance.'

'Thank you.' Tears welled in Sarah's eyes at these unexpected words of kindness.

'Come back at four o'clock and we'll go through the clothing in the church poor box to see what else we can find for you.'

She'd look a mess, Sarah thought, but at least she'd be decently clad. And warm. She'd been so cold during the winter.

2

Ellis Doyle stood by the rails, his back to Ireland, staring out across the water towards England. He and his wife had planned to go to Australia, and now it seemed the only place far enough away to escape the anger of his employer, an arrogant, spiteful man.

After the funeral he'd overheard Mr Colereigh gloating to his wife that Doyle would make a fine new husband for Mary Riley and get the expense of her and her children off the parish – well, he'd better marry her if he wanted to keep his job.

Mary was a slovenly woman with a nasty temper and three whining children of her own. Ellis wasn't having his sons raised by such as her, nor did he want her in his bed.

He and Shona had made such plans for their boys and saved their money so carefully. As he saw her splintered wooden coffin lowered into the ground, he'd sworn that somehow he'd still make her dreams come true.

Ellis had heard good things about Australia. A man had come back to the next village to take his family out there to live. Ellis had spent hours talking to him.

He watched the massive buildings of Liverpool show on the horizon in the chill grey light of dawn, then went to wake Kevin and Rory, who were huddled together on a hard wooden bench below decks. 'We're nearly there and it's light already. Come and look at Liverpool, boys.'

He helped seven-year-old Rory straighten his clothes, and checked nine-year-old Kevin, annoyed that however hard he tried, he couldn't keep the lads looking as neat as his wife had.

He wondered what Mr Colereigh would say when he found that Ellis had run away while the master was visiting friends. Would he come after them? Surely even he wouldn't go so far to get his own back?

* * *

By the time they arrived in Southampton, after a long rail journey from Liverpool, the boys were bickering and complaining. Ellis was exhausted but didn't dare take his eyes off his sons.

The emigrant hostel consisted of large rooms full of bunk beds: families and single women were housed in one, single men in another. After they'd eaten, he put the boys to bed, warning them sternly that if they moved away from their bunks without his permission, they'd be in big trouble.

In the middle of the night he woke with a start to find Kevin standing beside him, tugging his sleeve.

'I need to go, Da. You said not to go on our own.'

'I'll come with you.'

They used the necessary, then Rory said, 'I don't like it here, Da.'

'It's just a place to stay till we go on the ship.'

'There's nowhere to play.'

'There's a yard outside. They'll let you out tomorrow after

we've seen the doctor.' He knew they were all three healthy, so didn't fear failing the medical – well, not much. But they couldn't leave the hostel now until they went on the ship. The supervisor had been very clear about that.

Ellis didn't care. He didn't want to go anywhere in England. All he wanted was to make a new start in Australia.

3

Passage was booked for the group of sixty female pau-
pers from Lancashire on a ship called the *Tartar*. Sarah
hated being called a pauper but it was just one indig-
nity among many. They were sent to the emigrants' hostel, which was crowded with people waiting to board the
ship.

She was dreading the medical examination. Her new
underwear wasn't ragged or dirty but it was an older woman's
sensible flannel clothing, washed until it was grey and matted. She should be glad of it but with better food, vanity had
returned. She hated to see her gaunt face and dull hair in the
mirror. She looked years older than her age.

Most of the other women were haggard and some didn't
look respectable. A few even had the cropped hair of women
coming out of prison.

Sarah saw a young woman from their group beckoning to
her from the corner where there were four bunks. She hesitated but soon went across to join the woman and her two
companions. They looked better fed than most and proved to
be sisters.

'I'm Sarah,' she said to the one nearest.

'I'm Pandora Blake. These are my sisters: Maia and
Xanthe.'

Maia was weeping, mopping up the tears with a handkerchief, then having to use it again.

From what she overheard during the next few hours, Sarah realised the sisters had been forced to go to Australia by an aunt and were leaving behind a much loved older sister, for whose life they feared.

'I have no one,' she said when they asked about her family.

But she had hope now, shining brightly in her heart.

* * *

The medical examination took place the next morning: quick but still embarrassing. Then Sarah was sent to wait in the yard.

Some lads were there waiting for their father, and when two of them got into a fight, she took it upon herself to separate them.

'What will your mother say if you tear your clothes?' she scolded. 'You want to look your best when you board the ship.'

'The Mammy died,' the older boy muttered. 'And Da's taking us to Australia. I don't want to go.'

'I do,' the younger boy said

'Well, I don't! I won't have any friends in Australia.'

A man came across to join them. 'I hope my boys weren't giving you any trouble?'

'No, but they were quarrelling and needed settling down.'

He turned to glare at them. 'Did I not tell you to behave yourselves?'

They scuffed their feet and stared at the ground.

He turned back to Sarah, sighing. 'Thank you for your help, ma'am.'

Just then there was a disturbance by the gate. As he turned to see who it was, his face turned pale. 'Dear God, the master's sent his bailiff after us.'

Sarah looked at him quickly. 'What did you do?'

'Left the estate after my wife died instead of marrying a woman the landowner chose.'

Sarah saw the desperation on his face. She knew how arrogant some employers could be and her heart went out to him. 'You could pretend I'm your wife. He won't have any use for you then.'

He stared at her. 'Are you sure? Thank you.'

'My name's Sarah Boswick.'

'Mine's Ellis Doyle.'

'Put your arm round my shoulders and look affectionate. Rory, in this game I'm your new mother. Come and stand next to me.'

'I want to go back,' Kevin said.

'And have Mary Riley for your mother?'

Kevin hesitated then went to his father's side.

By the time the constable got to them, they were standing as a family group.

'This is Doyle,' the bailiff said. 'He's running away from the woman he promised to marry. Mr Colereigh wants him back.'

Ellis seemed to be fumbling for words, so Sarah spoke for him. 'Well, he *can't* marry anyone else. He's married to me.'

'There hasn't been time.'

'We bought a special licence.'

'I'd not have come back, even if I hadn't married Sarah,' Ellis said. 'And there's no law that says I have to.'

The bailiff leaned forward. 'What if the master said you'd stolen some money? You don't have enough for a special licence.'

'You never said anything about stolen money,' the supervisor said, looking suspiciously from the bailiff to Doyle.

'It was my money that bought the special licence,' Sarah said. 'It took every penny I had. He had none left from paying the fares.'

Ellis put his arm round her and pulled her close. 'Even if you forced me to go back, I couldn't marry Mary Riley now, could I?'

Everything hung in the balance for a moment or two, then the bailiff stepped back. 'I'd not marry her either. It'd be better if I tell him I couldn't find you. Don't ever come back, though.'

They watched him walk away, then Sarah realised Ellis was still holding her close. She didn't dare move until the bailiff was out of sight. And she didn't want to move either. She'd missed the feel of a man's strong arm round her shoulders.

Ellis moved away. 'Your quick thinking saved us. I can't tell you how grateful I am.'

'He didn't ask to see the marriage lines. He could have proved us wrong.'

'No. He's not a bad fellow but if he wants to keep his job and home, he has to do as he's told.'

Rory tugged at her skirt. 'Are you really our new mother?'

'No. We were just pretending. But I can be your new friend.' Her eyes sought Ellis's for permission and he nodded.

4

As they stood there, Ellis cleared his throat. 'Um, I probably need to go and see the supervisor and explain to him that we aren't really married. Will you keep an eye on these two rascals for a few moments?'

'Of course.'

But suddenly the supervisor came striding back into the yard. He walked across to Sarah and Ellis, scowling. 'I want the truth now. Are you two married or not?'

'No, we're not,' Ellis said in his lilting Irish voice.

'Well, you'll need to get married if you want to travel as a family.' The supervisor studied the children. 'Looks to me as if these two need a mother's care.'

Sarah could feel her cheeks burning because she'd had a sudden fervent wish that she was married again. She was so tired of being alone, fending for herself.

The supervisor looked at her disapprovingly. 'We don't allow any hanky-panky on board, Miss. They're very strict about that sort of thing.'

'I'm a widow, not a "Miss".'

'It's not hanky-panky to be courting someone,' Ellis told him. 'And that's what we're doing, courting.' He put the arm back round her shoulders.

It felt good.

The supervisor's voice softened. 'Oh, it's like that, is it? Well, I'll have to report this but no one can stop you talking to one another on deck.'

He walked away and Ellis turned to Sarah. 'I had to say something to save your good name.'

'I'm really grateful. But…we'll have to meet and talk to one another or they'll be suspicious.'

'I know. I hope you don't mind.' He looked at her as he spoke but not the way a man looks at a woman he desires. Pity.

There would be other women on the ship who were nicely dressed, who would attract and keep the attention of a man like him. Such a nice-looking man.

She sighed and told herself not to be stupid. But she wasn't used to being ignored. She'd been told many times she was a fine-looking woman. Other men had wanted to court her when she was younger, not just Daniel.

She wasn't fine-looking now, wouldn't have been even if she had been dressed nicely. Haggard was the best way of describing her, and she knew she looked years older than her age.

Perhaps one day she'd attract a man again, even if not this one. She'd like to marry, have children, live a normal life.

In the meantime, she had an adventure to face: a journey by ship to the other side of the world.

She had new friends: Ellis and his boys, and the Blake sisters. They were well-read and always had something interesting to say. She envied them their education. They must have read many more books than she had. She would enjoy their companionship on the ship.

5

Sarah was glad when it was time to board the ship but sorry to find herself lodged with another group of single women – widows like herself – instead of with Pandora and her sisters.

Her cabin was large. It had a long narrow table down the middle and cubicles down the sides, each sleeping four women in two pairs of hard, narrow bunks. They were placed in messes of eight with a leader appointed to take care of the food for the whole group. Why they chose Sarah as leader, she couldn't work out. She didn't want to be singled out in any way, just wanted to build up her health.

When they went up on deck, the matron kept a careful eye on the single women. That amused Sarah. Did they think any of the men would want women who looked like starvelings?

She didn't see the Doyles the first time on deck, but on her second outing little Rory came running towards her smiling and she found herself sitting there talking to him, telling him stories as her mother used to do with her.

Kevin stood to one side pretending not to listen.

Ellis came across to join his sons, speaking politely about

the weather, not staying long. He didn't waste words, that was for sure.

* * *

At first time hung heavy on their hands. Everyone feared for the three months the voyage would take, but to her delight the ship's passengers organised classes to help pass the three month journey to Australia. She joined groups for reading and sewing, went to the regular weekly concert. She'd have joined the choir, because she loved music, but she was a poor singer, often making people wince when she did join in.

She noticed that Ellis was in the choir and found the boys coming to sit with her during the concerts. Afterwards he would always hurry them away.

There was no pretence of courting. Well, it wasn't real, was it? He probably found her ugly, with her scrawny body and horrible old clothes.

Only once did they have a real conversation.

'What did you do in Ireland, Mr Doyle?' she asked.

'I was a stable hand. I'm good with horses. But I'll work at anything to make a good life for my lads in Australia. It must be hard for you, going so far away on your own.'

'Yes, but I have a job waiting, as a maid.'

'Will you like that?'

'I'll like eating regularly and being paid. And it'll give me a start.'

'I don't have a job waiting. But I'm hopeful. People always need help with horses, don't you think?'

He stood as if trying to think of something to say, then walked away abruptly.

* * *

Although the journey was long and the confines of the ship so stifling, Sarah found enjoyment in reading and sewing classes.

In the reading class, the Blake sisters were the best speakers. Sarah could have sat and listened to them all day.

Ellis was also a member of the reading group but when he was asked to take his turn, he read so haltingly and looked so embarrassed that he wasn't asked again. The teacher was tactful like that.

A very short woman called Miss Roswell was the best at sewing. It was obvious that she didn't need lessons, just wanted the company. She soon began helping the teacher, who could get a bit impatient if people were clumsy in their work.

When the teacher claimed exhaustion and gave up running the class, Miss Roswell took over, which was all to the good.

One day she asked Sarah to stay behind. 'I hope you don't think I'm being too personal but I know what it's been like for the people of Lancashire. I can see that your clothes were made for other women and I wondered if you'd like me to help you alter them?'

Sarah felt ashamed but wasn't going to miss an opportunity like that. 'Would you have time?'

'I have all too much time on my hands at the moment. You'd be doing me a favour.'

Gradually, Sarah's hand-me-downs were transformed into

well-fitting and even stylish clothes. Oh, that made her feel so much better.

But out of perversity, she didn't wear the best of them, even though Miss Roswell had hinted that Ellis kept looking at her when he thought no one would notice and she should encourage him.

Sarah knew her face had become rosier, could see for herself that she was getting her shape back under her newly altered clothes. But if he had to have her wearing new clothes to want her, then he wasn't worth it. Was he? Or was she being too proud?

* * *

Ellis joined the reading group to while away the long hours of doing nothing. He sent his lads to a class for children, relieved that they wouldn't see how poor he was at reading. Well, when had he ever had the chance for a proper education?

He saw Mrs Boswick in the class but when he made a mess of his first reading and heard how well she could read, he felt too ashamed to do anything but sit at the back and try to escape everyone's notice.

He was glad to see her looking better, filling out a little, getting nice rosy cheeks. She must have been short of food for a long time. She wasn't the only woman whose appearance had changed since they set off. Quite a few of them had blossomed. But the others didn't interest him. She did.

After the second reading group meeting the teacher asked him to stay behind.

'Would you like me to give you some extra help with the reading, Mr Doyle?'

'Why would you do that, Mr Paine?'

'Because I have too much time on my hands and because reading is such a joy to me that I like to share it with others.'

'Oh. Well. If you don't mind, I'd be grateful, I would so.'

'You can come to my cabin for the lessons. We can be private there.'

But what was he going to do with his boys? They were so lively, they needed someone to keep an eye on them. He didn't want them falling overboard.

After some thought, he asked Mrs Boswick if she'd mind watching them because she seemed to enjoy their company. He was too embarrassed to explain why, but she didn't ask, just said in her usual quiet way, 'I'd enjoy that. We can play games or I can read to them.'

Rory in particular seemed very attached to her. Ellis wasn't sure whether that fondness for her was a good or bad thing. After all, they might never see one another again after they arrived in Australia and Rory had already lost one person he loved. But learning to read better was so important, Ellis took the risk of her finding out what he was doing and looking down on him.

6

The men talked quite a lot, sharing what they'd heard about life in Australia, revealing their hopes for a better life. A few knew what it was like because they had relatives there. A man called Martin had lived there for a while and was going back, along with his new wife. When he talked about Australia, people hung on his every word.

'Couldn't you find a wife there?' one man teased.

'No, I couldn't. There are ten men to every woman in the Swan River Colony, so I went home and let my aunt find me a wife. And she did very well by me. A fine, sensible woman, my Dora is.'

'Do you think being sensible matters?' Ellis asked.

Martin looked at him as if he was utterly stupid. 'Of course it does. Women are much more practical about marriage than people give them credit for.'

That gave Ellis a lot to think about. He wanted to marry again. And it hadn't taken him long to realise Sarah would suit him well because she made him feel so comfortable and...Oh, just because!

But if there were ten men to every woman, she'd have other suitors. She could choose someone better than him, someone who could read and write fluently, who didn't already have a family.

And even if he asked her, she might say no. She could be very sharp when annoyed

But…Ellis did like her. A lot.

So he had to be sensible about this and do it quickly, before someone else beat him to it. He chose a moment when he could get her on his own, planning to ask her straight out. 'I've been thinking…' He couldn't get the words he'd rehearsed out. They sounded stilted.

'Thinking what?'

'Thinking we should…get married.' He couldn't bear to look her in the eyes. If she looked scornful, he'd shrivel up and die.

Her voice was cool. 'Why should we do that?'

He summoned up the main argument, the one he thought would appeal to a woman most. 'Because the boys need a mother and I need a wife. It's the most *sensible* thing to do.'

'Is that all?'

Words stuck in his throat. 'Isn't it enough?'

She shook her head. 'No, it's not enough. You didn't say you cared for me.'

Someone came along just then and he turned to look over the rail, screwing up his courage to try again.

But when he turned back to say of course he cared for her, Sarah had gone.

* * *

After his failed proposal, Ellis tried several times to catch Sarah on her own but she seemed to be avoiding him. Maybe that was her way of saying no.

He didn't know what to do. He couldn't sleep at night for thinking of her.

Then he heard two of the other men joking about a bet they'd made: they were competing to see which of them could get Sarah to marry him. Pete and Jim had also listened to Martin, it seemed.

Ellis got up the next day determined to have it out with her even if he had to shout out his feelings for the whole ship to hear. He wasn't going to lose her now.

After breakfast he saw her at the other end of the deck and hurried along. This was it. He'd do it. As he got closer he saw Pete on his knees in front of her and he knew what that meant.

Ellis would have turned away but she looked across at him. It seemed to him that she was pleading with him, that she was trying to pull her hand away from Pete's.

Something snapped inside him and Ellis ran across the last few yards of deck, pushing between Sarah and Pete. 'Don't do it! Don't marry him. He won't love you half as much as I do. I can't *bear* it if you marry him.'

'Oi!' Pete tried to pull him away.

He shoved Pete aside but the man came barrelling back.

Sarah stepped between them. 'Go away, Peter Millton!' she yelled. 'Or you'll spoil it for me.'

She turned back to Ellis.

He smiled, his anxiety past now, at what her words had revealed. 'I love you, Sarah Boswick. I can't think of anything else but how much I love you. Will you marry me?'

'Of course I will, you fool. I'd have said yes last time but you were so horridly sensible.'

He laughed and wrapped her in his arms, kissing her soundly. It took him a while to realise that someone was tapping his shoulder. He swung round, ready to punch Pete if he had to. But it was the matron of the women's quarters. So in his joy, he gave her a big hug too. 'She's just agreed to marry me.'

Then he turned back to finish kissing his Sarah properly.

Author's Note

They really did send sixty starving cotton lasses from Lancashire out to Western Australia in 1863. I've written a whole series based on this fact, the Swan River Saga (*Farewell to Lancashire*, *Beyond the Sunset* and *Destiny's Path*). But that wasn't enough to get those young women out of my mind. When I was asked to write a story for this anthology, I immediately thought of using this scenario again. My heroine may be imaginary but the background is as true to life as I can make it.

Carole Matthews

Carole Matthews is a bestselling author of twenty-four hugely successful romantic comedy novels. As well as appearing on the *Sunday Times* and *USA Today* bestseller lists, Carole is published in thirty-one different countries and has sold over 4 million books. Her books *Welcome To The Real World* and *Wrapped up in You* have both been short-listed for the Romantic Novel of the Year.

Previously unlucky in love, she now lives happily ever after with her partner, Lovely Kev, in a minimalist home with no ornaments or curtains. She likes to drink champagne, eat chocolate and spends too much time on Facebook and Twitter. Her latest book is *A Place to Call Home*.

For more information visit her website
www.carolematthews.com

&

The Corporate Wife

I was a trophy wife when Ethan married me, you know. Oh, yes. I could have had my pick of anyone. Men buzzed round me like bees round a honeypot: they were irresistibly drawn to me. I was showered with gifts morning, noon and night. I was wined and dined on private yachts from Antibes to Antigua. That was the life I had.

I was a model, a bloody good one too. I'd done *Vogue*, *Harper's*, *Vanity Fair*: all the glossies. I didn't do catwalk though. My breasts were too luscious, my hips too curved. It was all heroin chic in my day and they wanted six-stone skeletons for that. I'm a woman and have always been proud to look like one. I was never going to be just a walking coat hanger. Which meant that I wasn't ever quite as big as someone like Elle or Naomi. But I never minded that. Not really. I *did* get out of bed for less than ten thousand dollars a day though not that often. And, let me tell you, I'd been offered far more than that to get *into* bed too. Not that I ever did. I was very choosy. There were no scandalous pictures of me falling drunk out of nightclubs, wrapped round a different man every night, or snorting cocaine with some unsavoury, unwashed rock star. I always kept myself nice. Held myself well.

I'd had more marriage proposals than you could shake a

stick at and had batted them all away. But when Ethan asked me, I said yes straightaway. Ethan was different. He didn't fawn over me like other men. He was secure in his confidence. We met at a polo match in Windsor. I was presenting the prize and he was the captain of the winning team. His smile lit up my life in a way that nothing had before and made me weak at the knees. I gave him my number and he didn't call me for weeks. I liked that. Not too eager. It continued like that throughout the whole time we dated. My phone was never deluged with texts and calls from Ethan. *I* had to ring *him*. That was a new experience for me. Sometimes he'd leave me sitting alone waiting in restaurants for him – how the press loved that. When I called he'd simply say that he'd forgotten about our arrangement. I thought he was playing a game with me. I guess I learned the hard way.

Ethan was rich, even then. Not as ridiculously wealthy as some of my suitors, of course, but we were never going to be on the breadline. He was from good stock with a family pile in Hertfordshire, a solid, handsome house where we eventually lived. I had my own money too, at one time. But it was expensive being me – looking like that doesn't come cheap, I'm sure you can imagine – and soon there was very little of it left. Plus, once we were married, Ethan didn't like other men looking at me. Not in magazines, anyway. The shoots were getting raunchier, less and less clothing. I could have had a big contract with a line of very racy underwear but Ethan didn't like the idea of that either. He didn't think that it would be good for my image. On his advice, I turned down so many bookings that eventually, I slipped off the radar. As soon as I hit thirty-five, the agency stopped calling at all. The paparazzi didn't wait outside our London apartment or chase after me when I came out of restaurants. Ethan said that he was relieved. And I was too. In a way. Plus there were always the hungry young things snapping at your heels: nineteen-year-olds with more confidence and attitude than experience. I was one of them once.

* * *

'Are you ready, darling?' Ethan asks as he swings into the dressing room. He glances impatiently at his watch and does that tapping thing with his foot. 'We're going to be late.'

He's still handsome, my husband. There's a smattering of grey in his hair, but it only makes him look more distinguished over the years. It's so terribly unfair that men grow more beautiful with age whereas women, inevitably, do not. He looks so smart in his hand-tailored charcoal grey suit and crisp white shirt.

'Is that a new tie?' I usually bought all his clothes and I didn't recognise it.

He looks down. It's grey silk with a faint black line through it. Very stylish. 'Yes.'

'You bought it yourself?'

Ethan rolls his eyes. 'I am perfectly capable of buying my own ties, Lydia. I don't see why you should be so surprised.'

But I am surprised. That was my role: I looked after the house, I looked after Ethan, I shopped for him.

'It's nice,' I offer.

Even after all this time, I still love him. We' recently celebrated our fifteenth wedding anniversary. Well, when I say 'celebrated' I mean that Ethan was away on business somewhere – Denmark, I think – and I opened a bottle of fizz on my own and watched re-runs of *Wallander*. When he was less busy we were hoping to hop off for a week somewhere warm.

It's a party tonight. Another one. This one at The Dorchester. A thank you for five hundred of Ethan's staff for hitting their targets in these terrible times of recession. Some of them will be made redundant next week, but they don't know that yet. Tonight, they'll still be blissfully unaware of their fate and on a high.

I take one last look in the mirror. The last time I appeared in the *Daily Mail* it was a shot from our beach holiday in Barbados pointing out the cellulite on the back of my thighs. I was mortified. That was the day that my unswerving attachment to the sarong started. Of course, that was years ago. I'll be forty-five next birthday. Not a milestone birthday, as such, but one that takes me another step further away from my prime. None of the newspapers care what I look like now. But I do. My skin used to be like porcelain, white and flawless. There are wrinkles now – fine ones, thanks to Crème de la Mer and some well-aimed Botox. But they're undeniably there. Perhaps I'll have some of the lights taken away from around this mirror. It's too bright, unforgiving. I might like myself better if I were perpetually in soft focus. I ease back my cheeks with my fingertips and watch my jawline tighten. That's how I used to look. Once when I was young and desirable.

'How much longer, Lydia?' Ethan presses. 'The car is waiting.'

'I just want to make sure that I look my best.' I clip on my diamond studs, then stand up and check myself in the full-length mirror. This dress is cut on the bias and flatters my figure, which is fuller than it used to be despite the hours I spend in the gym and the hours that I spend looking at food rather than eating it. It's sapphire blue and emphasises the colour of my eyes.

'No one will be looking at you,' my husband says. 'I'll see you downstairs.'

It's not just the newspapers who don't care what I look like anymore, it seems.

It wasn't always like that. Obviously. Ethan used to love having me on his arm at his corporate functions. Mouths used to gape when he introduced me. I knew what they were thinking. That Ethan had punched above his weight. That he had married well. My husband might not have wanted me to carry on with my career, but he liked men to look at me. He liked their mouths to water when they saw me with him. He encouraged me to dress in the skimpiest of clothes. And I was happy to oblige. He couldn't keep his hands off me then. At the most inappropriate moments, I'd feel his thumb graze my nipples, his fingers inching up my thighs. I've lost count of the corporate dinners where his hand would be between my legs under the table before we'd even reached dessert.

There was a photograph of me in the tabloids. We're on a yacht in the Med – I can't remember whose now – and I'm standing at the bow alone in impossibly high heels, the tiniest of gold bikinis that barely contains my breasts, a gold chain accentuating my slender waist, the scant thong exposing my tanned buttocks. My long blonde hair streamed behind me. It was my natural colour then. I look like the cat who's got the cream. It made page four of the *Sun*. I remember exactly the day it was. We were with a party of businessmen who we were entertaining for lunch. I was the only woman on board and yet Ethan insisted that I wore the bikini and nothing else. He even picked it out for me. Even after we'd spotted the paparazzi on another boat, he'd come behind me and slipped a finger under the thin fabric of my swimsuit and inside me. The other men were all lounging on the deck with champagne just behind us, but he didn't care. Then Ethan took me down below, lifted me straight onto the counter in the galley, pulled down my bikini bottoms and made love to me right there. At any moment, any one of the men, or all of them, could have walked in. I thought he'd done it because he was overwhelmed by passion, because he loved me so much.

I'm older and wiser now.

I slick on my lipstick, smooth down my dress and plump my cleavage. It's all still my own but it needs help now from well-cut and ferociously expensive underwear. Picking up my diamanté purse, I make my way down the stairs.

* * *

The Dorchester is one of my favourite venues and this is from someone who has been to the Burj al Arab on a regular basis. But that is tacky in its opulence whereas The Dorchester is all about understated elegance. Mind you, every five star hotel thinks that they're far better than they are. We like the Terrace Suite here, which has the most marvellous view over London, and we were booked in overnight. I'm hoping to do some shopping in town tomorrow and perhaps have some lunch at Harvey Nics. Ethan, of course, is going into the office even though it's Sunday.

The Ballroom Suite is already thronging with Ethan's colleagues. They're all bright young things, university educated with degrees in such things as philosophy and politics. They have conversations where they all shout over each other about the FTSE and the Dow Jones and I have no idea what they're talking about and have no desire to. I stand and sip my champagne and try to look interested.

The room is beautiful, stylish, all cream and gold. We stand at the top of the sweeping staircase so that Ethan can greet his staff. We shake hands endlessly with the damp, the sweaty, the cool, the dry, the over eager, the bone-crushingly aggressive and the limp-wristed. No wonder the Queen always wears gloves. How could she bear to have all those strangers touch her?

'Hello, Lydia.' I look up to see one of Ethan's managers, Colette, standing in front of me, smiling widely. I think she's one of his favourites as she always seems to accompany him to his business meetings. 'Beautiful dress. You look lovely.'

'Thank you.' She's visited the house several times too, so we are familiar enough with each other to air kiss cheeks. 'You look simply divine too.'

She's slender, Colette. Sickeningly so. Self-consciously, I pull in my tummy. Tonight she's dressed in a black, clinging number with a perilously plunging neckline that leaves little to the imagination. It must be held on with tit-tape and I'd bet a pound to a penny that she's not wearing any underwear. It makes the brightness of my blue look garish in comparison. Like I'm trying too hard. She's young. Twenty-six at most and has a boyish figure with a washboard stomach and no hips. For work she power dresses in crisp white shirts and pencil skirts with vertiginous black patent heels. She looks like a woman who wears stockings to the office. Her skin is soft and coffee-coloured. Her corkscrew curls – the height of fashion – bounce onto her bare shoulders.

I feel I should ask her a question but I don't know what to say, so she moves on and turns her attention to my husband. 'Ethan.' Her eyes brighten.

'Good evening, Colette.' His hand slips onto her hip and his thumb traces the arched curve of her bone. Very few people would notice, but I do. She wets her lips and leans into him slightly as her kiss lingers too long on his cheek. 'Great tie.' Her fingertips stroke it lightly and a glimmer of a smile plays at her mouth.

And I know instantly who bought it. Of course, I do. Does Ethan think that I'm gullible enough to believe that he would ever trouble himself with his own shopping? Colette moves on and I watch Ethan's eyes as they follow her. I feel sick to my stomach. If she thinks she is the only one, the first, then she is sadly mistaken.

It's hot in here, stuffy and I wonder if they've forgotten to turn on the air-conditioning. The rest of the line snakes past us and soon we make our way down the staircase into the ballroom below. I always used to like this dramatic entrance, felt as if I was in a movie, *Folies Bergère* or something starring Fred and Ginger. I liked the heads that turned to look at me. Now I can't wait to rush down to my seat and my legs shake as I take the steps.

'Are you all right?' Ethan snaps. 'Do pull yourself together, Lydia.'

I trail in his wake until we reach the top table. 'I need to talk to Colette and Brad Walker,' he says over his shoulder, pulling out his own chair. 'I've sat them either side of me.

Hope you don't mind entertaining Canning. He's a bit of an old bore, but he'll love you.'

What he means is that he's old enough to remember the photograph of that wretched gold bikini and will leer at me all night. I take my place next to Stuart Canning halfway down the ballroom. He pulls out my chair for me and kisses my hand. There's spittle at the corner of his mouth.

I have no idea what's served for dinner, my stomach is too knotted to be able to consider eating. At the top table, there's much banter and laughter and I have to drag my attention back from Ethan and listen to the man droning on at my side.

After dinner, the music starts. The dance floor starts to fill. Ethan kicks back his chair, unbuttons his collar, loosens that tie. The laughter doesn't stop. Soon, I hope he will remember me and ask me to come to his table. But the minutes stretch on, the songs continue and, still, he doesn't make a move. Eventually, I make my excuses to the extremely dull Mr Canning and weave my way through the tables to Ethan's side. I wait until he finishes his conversation and then I kiss his cheek. He looks at me in surprise. Perhaps he had forgotten that I was here at all.

'Dance with me, darling,' I say brightly.

'Have to keep the wife happy,' he jokes and stands up. I take his hand and lead him to the dance floor. I risk a backwards glance and see that the laughter has gone from Colette's lips.

Ethan takes me in his arms and we sway to whatever's pounding out. His face is flushed with drink and he's a bit unsteady on his feet. Trying to keep to the beat is pointless. I want to speak to him, be witty and bright, but my brain is frozen and nothing will come to my mouth. I hold onto him tightly for three songs but, already, he's looking bored and his gaze starts to wander.

'Is this a ladies' excuse-me?' Colette asks over my shoulder. Before I can answer or register a protest, she manoeuvres her way in between me and my husband with such breathtaking impudence that I have to give her credit for her audacity. 'You don't mind if I do, Lydia?'

I do mind, but how can I make a scene? These are Ethan's staff, his colleagues. He would be embarrassed if I made a stand against her. And what if I lost? What if, publicly, he brushed me aside for her?

She sweeps Ethan away from me and he brightens instantly. Now I stand on the dance floor, alone, abandoned and I don't quite know what to do. In days gone by, there would be a dozen men clamouring to take his place. But not now.

Gathering my senses, I hold my head high and walk from the dance floor. I may not have graced the catwalk, but I can still strut my stuff like a model. I'm not sure where I'm going, but my feet take me to the grand staircase again and I climb them on auto-pilot. When I reach the mezzanine floor, I lean on the balcony and watch the revellers below me. I'm breathing heavily, sounding as if I've exerted myself when I haven't. It's just that my body is having difficulty processing this. My heart is beating erratically and there's a thrumming in my ears, the rush of blood. My cheeks blaze. I know that there have been others in the past. No one travels so regularly on business without finding some female company. I've been on the receiving end of enough male attention to be well aware of that.

I watch Ethan and Colette twirl round the floor, moving in unison. Ethan is a good dancer, something else that I used to love about him. I dig my nails into my palms and push the tears away with pain. A woman comes and stands next to me, leaning on the rail.

She nods at my husband below us. 'He's a slimy bastard,' she says, casually. 'He's shagged his way through half of the office.'

My mouth goes dry.

'He might be the President, but that doesn't stop him from trying it on with just about every woman in the place.'

I turn to her. She is also young and pretty. 'You too?'

'Groped me in the lift after a long night in the bar at a conference. I should have slapped him with a sexual harassment complaint. But you don't, do you?'

'No,' I agree. 'You don't.'

'I got off lightly really.' She swigs at the drink in her hand. 'He's married too.'

'So I understand.'

'I've heard she was a model. A real beauty once.'

'Yes. I'd heard that too.'

'She must be a bloody idiot. Or a saint.'

'I think idiot.'

The girl laughs. 'Yeah. You're probably right. Poor bitch.'

Poor bitch, indeed.

My husband twirls Colette again and she tuts her disapproval at them. '*She's* a bloody idiot too. She's thinks she's special. Her sort always do.'

And she's right because I once was that sort too.

'He'll tire of her and move on.' She points an accusing finger in Ethan's direction. 'He always does.'

She sounds too bitter and I wonder if their encounter went further than she's admitting or whether her prospects suffered because it didn't. The girl raises her eyebrows at me and lifts her glass. 'Bar calls again,' she says. 'Can I get you one?'

'No, thank you. But it's very nice of you to ask.'

She leaves and it's all I can do to hold myself upright. Bile rises to my throat. I thought that they respected him. Above everything, I thought that Ethan was held in high esteem by his co-workers. It seems that I was wrong about that too.

Reeling, I make my way to the powder room. Thankfully, I'm alone in there and I run my wrists under the cold tap. I'd like to splash water on my face too, but I can't risk ruining my make-up. People would know that there's something wrong and for the last ten years or more, I've been pretending that there isn't. I rinse the sour taste from my tongue and stare at myself in the mirror. If I could will myself to be twenty years younger, then I would. I would do things differently, make different choices. But no matter, how hard I wish, it's still resolutely the older me who looks back.

When did he last make love to me, my husband? When did he last tear the buttons from my blouse in his haste, rip my underwear from my body, consume me with hunger in his eyes, take me on the marble floor of the hall or in the leather seats of the Aston. Not for a long time. It has even been months since he grunted above me in the darkness of our bedroom.

When I feel that I can hide in here no longer – surely Ethan will be missing me now – I go back out onto the balcony. My chatty companion hasn't reappeared and I take up my position again. The dance floor is crowded now. The party in full swing. My eyes search the gyrating bodies, but there's no sign of Ethan or Colette. I swivel my gaze to their table, but they aren't there either. Perhaps I should make my way down to the bar, grab some champagne, drink and be merry.

I can't make another entrance down the main stairs. I can't face it. I want to slide anonymously back to the party, so I make my way down the quiet side corridor and the back stairs. When I open the door, I see them there and I stop in my tracks, the shock making me stagger with pain as surely as if I've been stabbed in the heart.

Colette is pressed against the wall, the weight of my husband pinning her there. Her dress is hitched up to her thighs and I would have won my bet regarding her lack of underwear. The top of her dress is pulled down, exposing her breasts. With one hand, Ethan toys with a nipple. The other is between her legs and she squirms against his hand, head thrown back, eyes closed, lips parted in ecstasy. I remember that feeling. But only just.

I back out of the stairwell before they see me and I lean on the wall too, but not in ecstasy. My heart is hammering in my chest and I only know that I need to get out of here fast. Blackness threatens the edge of my vision. Biting down my panic, I walk to the foyer, smiling as I go. When I was a model I learned how to smile even when my feet were cold, or my back hurt or my head pounded. I developed my very own technique and now I've found that it also works when your heart is broken.

Retrieving my wrap from the cloakroom, I head out into the night. It's a summer's evening and London is muggy, heavy with exhaust fumes. I glance at my watch and see that it's nearly midnight. The trees on Park Lane sparkle with white lights. I always think that they look Christmassy, somewhat strange in August. I slip off my shoes and hold them in my hand. High heels hurt my feet now and I think I have the beginnings of a bunion.

I make my way down Park Lane. Even at this hour the traffic is still busy. I wonder where they're all going, where they've been. I wonder do they think of me. A middle-aged woman wandering alone in the middle of the night. I wonder do they realise, do they care that I might be suffering or in need of help. But I forget that I'm only bleeding inside.

I could have done so much with my life. I went to grammar school, I could have gone to university. A good one. In the days when not everyone went. But I chose to use my body and not my brains. It was on a rare day out to London that the model scout handed me a card. My parents were against it, of course. No one in our family had ever earned a living in such a frivolous way. I wonder where they are now, my mother and father. I haven't seen them in years. Ethan was always reluctant to go to the small terraced house that they lived in and so we drifted apart. I didn't want them uncomfortable in their own home. I've a sister too, similarly estranged.

We never had children either. Ethan isn't much for families and I was always terrified of losing my figure. Can you imagine it? How could I waddle onto parties on yachts heavy with child in voluminous pregnancy dresses? Ethan would never have allowed it. That wasn't what we were about as a couple. And I was frightened that he would want me to stay at home, out of sight, go off alone and leave me. Ironic really. I used to long for a daughter. Someone who I could bring up to be strong and independent. Someone who would find a man to love her for who she was, not how she looked.

I thought I would always be beautiful, always be wanted.

Now my husband looks at younger women, the way he looked at me. His eyes and his hands tear the clothes from them too. The cars whoosh past me, billowing my dress. I pull my wrap tighter round me even though it isn't cold. I walk the entire length of Park Lane, past the glitzy car showrooms, the lavish estate agents' windows, the glittering hotel entrances. A few people pass me, but this is London, and they don't look twice at the barefooted woman in their way. Eventually, I find my way back. There are tables outside The Dorchester, closed up for the night, patio heaters cold. I sit there watching the lights, letting my mind roam free. What will I do? Where will I go? Who will look after me? How will I live? What do you do when you are forty-five and have nothing to show for your life beyond a marvellous wardrobe and a hoard of designer shoes? I can't hold a conversation. I can't bake a cake. I can't arrange flowers. For my entire marriage, I've been nothing but a shadow. A pretty, empty shadow.

When I next look at my watch its gone two o'clock. The night is cooler now, the traffic has slowed to a constant trickle and I'm shivering. I should reach inside myself and find anger, but all that's there is fear. I'm afraid to confront Ethan. Afraid to confront my future. Afraid that if I cry or scream I will never stop. My feet are numb and my head throbs, but still I stay in my chair. I don't know how long I wait, but eventually I notice that's there's a refreshing breeze. I can taste autumn in it, a subtle change, a freshening. I like autumn – a time when the old dies away heralding in the way for the new. I feel something in my heart gently settle. When I can put it off no longer, I pick up my shoes and head back into the hotel. The party is over. Streamers from party poppers litter the floor and weary, heavy-eyed staff tidy up and rearrange the tables. Soon there will be no sign of the party at all.

I make my way back up to our suite and let myself in, tossing my designer shoes to the floor. I can't face the discomfort of them any longer. Ethan is sprawled out on the bed, naked, face down. He's snoring heavily. His charcoal suit, his white shirt, his traitorous grey tie are scattered on the floor. The tie catches the moonlight and shines up at me. One by one, I pick them all up and put them on the clothes horse at the foot of the bed, folding the trousers carefully, smoothing down the lapels of the jacket as I have done for many years.

My suitcase is on the stand, still unpacked. Could I leave? Just walk out on my life? I pour myself a brandy from the decanter and go to the terrace. Looking out over London, the lights of the city beckon. It's a place of infinite possibilities. I could lose myself here. I could start again. Learn things. Do things. Believe things. Look at my face in the mirror and like myself again. I had dreams. Once. I could have them again.

I take the last sip of the brandy and it burns down my throat and sizzles in my stomach like acid. The cut glass makes a clink when I put it back on the sideboard and I'm worried that it will rouse him. But he snores on, oblivious. He grunts and twitches, but doesn't wake. Standing at the bottom of the bed, unmoving, I watch Ethan breathe, deeply, evenly. Nothing can disturb his sleep. Is this what I have to look forward to?

Quietly, I undo the zip of my overnight case-one from a matching set of Louis Vuitton. Inside my cosmetics bag, there's a pair of nail scissors. I cross to the clothes horse. Carefully, meticulously I cut the bottom half from the grey silk tie and let it fall. It lies on the plush carpet, torn. There is hope in that severed tie, I think. Just a glimmer. But hope nevertheless.

I put the scissors away and zip up my case. It's quite heavy but I don't want to ring the concierge. I can manage by myself. I can manage everything by myself. I know I can. With one last lingering look at Ethan, I pull my wrap around me. When I leave, still barefoot, I softly close the door behind me.

Elizabeth Buchan

Elizabeth Buchan began her career as a blurb writer at Penguin Books and moved on to become a fiction editor at Random House before leaving to write full time. Her novels include *Light of the Moon* and the prize-winning *Consider the Lily* – reviewed in the *Independent* as 'a gorgeously well written tale: funny, sad and sophisticated'. A subsequent novel, *Revenge of the Middle-Aged Woman*, became an international bestseller and was made into a CBS Primetime Drama. This was followed by several other novels, including *The Second Wife*, *Separate Beds* and *Daughters*. She has just finished a novel about SOE agents operating in Denmark during the World War II.

Elizabeth Buchan's short stories are broadcast on BBC Radio 4 and published in magazines. She reviews for the *Sunday Times*, has chaired the Betty Trask and Desmond Elliot literary prizes, and has been a judge for the Whitbread (now Costa) awards. She is a past Chairman of the Romantic Novelists' Association, and is currently a patron of the Guildford Book Festival and The National Academy of Writing.

&

The Art Of Travel

Polly consults the ferry timetable. Having puzzled over it many times during the past seven years, she knows its little ways.

Buried in its print, is the key to the vessels which skim over the sunlit Greek seas and plough through the stormy ones. And, yes, there is one due to sail from Piraeus at 11.30 the following morning. This gives Polly plenty of time to arrive at the port and to find a coffee and sandwich. She is sometimes sea-sick and copes better being so on a full stomach.

Dan used to tease her about that.

In Athens, she checks in at her usual hotel – discovered quite early on in her travels. It is cheap and central and nobody bothers about her there. In her room there are the familiar blue-and-white striped ticking window blinds and the matching bedspread.

The mirror is new though, and Polly peers into it. She has left London in a rush – working in the office until the very last-minute, which meant there had been no time for leisurely preparation. *She* doesn't much care what she looks like but others do. If you're travelling on your own, it's best to make an effort.

She phones Nico at the salon.

'Ah Polly, Polly. Please come at once.'

Nico owns a chain of hairdressing salons but is always to be found in the one near Avidi Square. He is waiting for her when she walks in.

'Hallo beautiful Polly,' he says in his mixture of Greek and English. 'Very, very good to see you.'

Polly replies in a similar mixture of language–only, in her case as she often teases him, her Greek improves each year.

Nico sits her down and wraps her up in a gown. 'Your hair is good.' Their eyes meet in the mirror. 'You have kept it well.'

She has. She has. Shoulder length and still blonde with touches of honey and toffee, Dan loved her hair.

Nico examines a lock in a professional manner. 'A small trim?'

'Please.'

He cuts it wet and gives Polly his news. The fifth grand-child arrived. The family is well. Times are hard.

He knows that Polly will not respond with similar informa-tion. Polly's lack of family always shocks him.

The scissors emit a faintly metallic sound and, despite her-self, the hairs on the back of Polly's neck rise.

No, she lectures herself.

'And where are going to this time, Polly?'

'Skopolos.'

Nico cuts a meticulous half inch of hair across her back. He knows that, after his ministrations, Polly is unlikely to visit a hairdresser for weeks and he has a professional reputation to maintain.

'Why Skopolos?'

'I've never been there.'

'When are you going?'

It's a question Nico has asked seven times before and he knows the answer. He sighs and puts down the scissors. 'Helena is expecting you at seven-ish. Is that alright?'

Polly grins at them both in the mirror. 'Your wife is a very good woman.'

* * *

Helena never changes. Never looks a day older. Her hair is still as dark and her olive-y skin still as smooth.

'You're thinner,' she says. She gives the once-over to Polly's tamed, shining hair and her skinny jeans and jacket. 'But very smart.'

Polly kisses Helena and gives her the selection of expensive teas she has bought from England. 'I gather another grandchild has just arrived. I hope I'm no trouble.'

'Trouble? My role is to deal with trouble. Nico earns our money. I arrange the important things.'

The new mother, Andrea, is sitting in the garden feeding the baby. Her other two children wheel like starlings around the adults who sit and gossip until Helena calls them into eat.

Halfway through the meal of rice and meatballs, Nico rises to his feet. 'We are so glad to have you with us again, Polly. Nothing can take away the circumstances of how we met but the friendship which has come from them…well, there is something good.' He raises his glass. 'Let us meet for many, many more years.'

Towards midnight, Polly gets up to go. 'How can I thank you both?'

The new baby cries and Andrea catches it up with a great deal of cooing and shushing. They are happy sounds.

Helena rests her hands on Polly's shoulders. 'Tomorrow is the anniversary…'

'Yes.'

Walking hand in hand with Dan along a crowded Athens street. The car veering out of control. Body and bone impacting on it. Dan sprawled on the pavement outside Nico's salon. Bright red blood. Too bright to look at.

Scissors in hand, Nico running out and shouting, 'Get back everyone.' Nico cutting Dan's shirt away with the scissors.

Polly cradling Dan and begging him. 'Don't die.'

Nico holding Polly.

'What time?'

'Mid-morning.'

Helena looks long and hard into Polly's eyes. What she sees evidently does not please her. 'Spend it with us,' she says. 'It's Sunday tomorrow and the whole family will be here. I keep telling you that you should be with family and not travelling alone.'

Polly says. 'I think it's what I do best now.'

She kisses them all fondly, thanks them over and over again and returns to her silent room in the hotel.

Emerging from the Metro the following morning, the warmth hits her. It's 22 or 23 degrees which is normal for late spring. Knowing what to expect, she is dressed in linen trousers and good quality cotton T-shirt unlike many of the sweating, overdressed tourists who are arriving from the airport.

She makes for the coffee shop adjacent to departure gate E8 and queues.

'I'm worn out,' says the woman directly in front of Polly.

Her companion, a woman with white hair and bright pink lipstick, looks alarmed. 'We've only just got here.'

'And my feet have swollen.' The woman points to her unsuitable leather shoes. 'See.'

Polly has some sympathy. She remembers the early years of her annual pilgrimages. The decision to go, but where? What to wear? What to pack? How to live without Dan? The unknown *is* tiring and mistakes are made.

Coffee in hand, she moves off to join the queue for the ferry – and spots that the handsome local hustler dressed up in a fake uniform is back in business. She watches him size up an affluent looking older couple with copious amounts of luggage and slip into his routine. He is so charming. So persuasive. Within minutes, they will allow him to carry their bags to the head of the impatient queue...'the captain would wish it'. Only then, would he demand a hefty tip.

She listens to the subsequent row, which she can rehearse, almost word for word. Should she have intervened? Perhaps she should have done. Yet, the most useful experience is the most hard-won and Piraeus is a tough, chaotic place.

The queue moves forward. Embarked, Polly will head forward, which allows her to manoeuvre between sun and shade, her book for the trip easily accessible in a rucksack pocket. This year it is *Anna Karenina*, and she anticipates biting down on Tolstoy's combination of story and philosophy. The idea of reading only one book on her travels is to ensure that its text becomes second nature. In this way, she has tackled seven classics, each one soldered imaginatively to the place she read them. *Great Expectations* is Rhodes. *A Portrait of a Lady* is Crete.

At the front of the ferry, she would watch the sea, with a touch of heat haze layering above it. At Skopolos the ferry would lumber into its berth with the usual noise of arrival in any port. Then, she would search for a bed and breakfast. Check for insects. Check the water ran properly. Check for an extra blanket. She would be loose in time and space, her past discarded as easily as tossing old bread crust into the water.

Dan.

Seven years ago, he died. Her new husband. Each year, on the anniversary, she travels alone, for three weeks or so, and always around the Greek islands. It is something which is now second nature. Cyclades, Dodecanese…there were as many as there were years in which to face life without Dan.

The sun was growing hotter. The queue is undulating. She swings her rucksack up onto her back. Her foot is on the gangplank…

Dan.

Dan?

She feels his hand grasp her hair. The smell of him which she loved.

She needed him. He needed her.

His warm skin.

He is living in her, and she suspects he always will.

Polly, he says. *Don't do this*.

Why tell me now? she cries silently. I am about to go in pursuit of the memories.

Because Polly…

Suddenly, she swivels on her heel and, pushing her way through the hot, cross tourists, retraces her steps. In the Metro she is forced to balance her rucksack on her knees. Dense with odours of discarded food and bodies crushed too tight together, it is impossible to read.

It is late afternoon when she reaches Nico and Helena's house. The front door is open and in Polly walks.

The kitchen is very warm, steamy and filled with good cooking smells. Nico is chopping onions and Helena is stirring a pot on the stove. The table is piled with vegetables and cheeses wrapped in waxy paper. Since yesterday, someone had strung dried peppers over the door leading to the garden and they make a necklace of blood red drops.

'Hallo.'

Helena drops the spoon into the pot. 'Polly...'

'Do you mind? I have come back...like you said.'

Helena gestures to the garden where the table has been laid. 'We allocated you a place.'

'How did you know?'

'We didn't. But each year Nico and I hope.'

Polly licked her fingertip and caught up a grain of sea salt on a chopping board and put it in her mouth. The insides of her cheeks pucker.

Nico continues with his chopping. 'You can only go on so long, Polly. The time comes...'

'You are good to me,' she says with a rush of emotion.

Helena wipes her hands on her apron and grabs Polly's hand. 'Do you remember...afterwards that you came to stay with us and we looked after you? That makes you family.'

The onions were making Polly cry. She holds on to Helena's hand. 'I suddenly thought I didn't want to be alone today. And Nico...'

Nico stopped the chopping.

'Nico, you knew Dan. For just a few seconds, but they were important ones. You shared the moment of his death.'

Nico frowns and Helena shakes her head at him. 'Go on Polly.'

'I can't go on thinking about it. I can't go over, and over the details any more.'

'At last,' says Nico.

'It's as if I am travelling over the same ground, over and over again, and never getting anywhere.' She pauses. 'I never arrive, however carefully I prepare.'

Helena extracts a clean knife from the rack and hands it to Polly. 'The tomatoes need chopping. Can you do that?'

Polly smiles. 'In slices?'

'If you like. They're for the sauce.'

'But I must do it right.'

'You do it the way which suits you,' said Helena.

Polly sets to, the red flesh falling away from the knife blade and the seeds spurting onto the board in a crimson gel. *Just like blood.* She hesitates.

'Go on Polly,' urges Helena. 'It's getting late.'

Polly smiles at them both to show that she is perfectly in control. Her movements gather speed and dexterity.

Helena adds a handful of thyme to the saucepan. 'A bed is made up,' she says. 'No need to go back to the hotel.'

She glances at her watch. At this moment, the ferry would be berthing at Skopolos and a brief, but intense, regret flits through her mind. Then it is gone.

She glances up at the laid table where her place is waiting to be occupied. The image of Dan, held so long and violently in her mind, dims and softens into the bearable.

'Thank you,' she says. 'Thank you.'

Elizabeth Chadwick

Born in Bury, Lancashire, Elizabeth Chadwick began telling herself stories as soon as she could talk. She is the author of more than twenty historical novels, which have been translated into sixteen languages. Five times shortlisted for the Romantic Novelists' Association Major Award, her novel *To Defy A King* won the historical prize in 2011. *The Greatest Knight*, about forgotten hero William Marshal, became a *New York Times* bestselling title, and its sequel *The Scarlet Lion* was nominated by Richard Lee, founder of the Historical Novel Society, as one of the best historical novels of the decade. *The Summer Queen*, the first novel in her new trilogy about Eleanor of Aquitaine was published in June 2013.

When not at her desk in her country cottage, she can be found researching, taking long walks with her husband and their three terriers, reading, baking, and drinking tea in copious quantities.

She can be contacted at her website www.elizabethchadwick.com At Twitter @chadwickauthor On Facebook https://www.facebook.com/elizabeth.chadwick.90

&

The Rough With The Smooth

May 1164

Isabel Countess de Warenne was smiling as she supervised the flurry of activity in her chamber. Spring sunshine spilled through the open shutters, flooding the room with light and drawing in the garland scent of tender greenery. It was time to wash and scrub the linens, to beat the old season out of blankets and hangings, and to let new air into the room.

She and Hamelin had married seven weeks ago, and the sky had done nothing but rain ever since. Not that they had noticed at first, being too caught up in discovering that sometimes, against the odds, arranged marriages were very compatible. However, emerging from their cocoon of mutual delight, the constant rain had been a source of nuisance and concern; it was a relief to see the sun.

Hamelin was the King's half-brother and had needed an inheritance to bolster his standing at court. She was the means of providing that inheritance – a wealthy widow, just over thirty years old with castles and vast estates to her name. They had known each other for several years from a polite distance that had not allowed any room for intimacy: glance and a bow at court; a curtsey and move on. That was until the King had given the command that they wed, and without recourse to refusal.

The potential for disaster had been huge but the opposite had happened. It was a long time since Isabel had felt so happy and fulfilled. Indeed, after the death of her first husband while on campaign in Toulouse, she had not expected to ever feel whole again. But now the sun had emerged and the world was glittering and new, like a golden chalice sparkling with pale green wine, waiting like a loving cup to be shared.

Hamelin had ridden out on the King's business and she had decided to use the time to spruce up their chamber so that she could surprise him on his return.

Her steward, Thomas D'Acre, entered the room and bowed. 'Madam, there are men at the gate craving entrance,' he announced, his expression screwed up and doubtful. 'Their leader claims to be a close friend of my lord Hamelin, but I have not heard of him before and he is dressed like a ruffian. He gives his name as Geoffrey of le Mans.'

Isabel had not heard Hamelin speak of such a friend, nor had she encountered anyone of that name at court. Although England was at peace these days, common scoundrels still abounded and with Hamelin away it would be the height of folly to admit someone lacking credentials. Perhaps there was a good reason for their arrival while her husband was absent.

'I will come and look,' she said, and bidding her women continue with their task, she followed Thomas to the gatehouse where she climbed the tower to look down at their prospective visitors. They were as Thomas had stated: a rough looking group, mud-spattered and clad in rough woollens, scuffed and disreputable. Their leader, red in the face, was bellowing at the gate guards, calling them turds and idiots, and waving his fist. Isabel could see a sword hilt poking out from beneath his cloak.

'Tell him to come back when my husband is at home,' she told Thomas, looking down her nose at such uncouth behaviour. 'They are not dressed like noblemen or anyone he would know. If they are mercenaries looking to be hired, they can go and bide their time in Lynn.'

'I thought that too, Madam.' Standing tall and expanding his chest, Thomas went off to deal with the situation.

Feeling like a bird with ruffled feathers, Isabel returned to her spring refurbishment, chivvying the maids and immersing herself in the task until she began to feel less perturbed. Incidents such as this brought back disturbing memories of the violent war for the throne that had engulfed England for fifteen years; when strangers at the castle gate meant danger of attack and no one could be trusted.

The exquisite whitework embroidery on the new coverlet, the jug of spring flowers on the polished coffer, and the honey scent of beeswax permeating the room eventually worked their spell and Isabel was able to put the visitors to the back of her mind. She went to sit at her sewing frame in the embrasure, where she could look out on the lovely spring day while working on the tunic hem she was embroidering for Hamelin. Selecting a warm red silk, she threaded her silver needle and began work on the lion she had outlined yesterday.

It was early afternoon when the horn sounded at the gate again. Isabel looked up from her work, her stomach lurching with anticipation and anxiety. When Thomas sent a squire to tell her that the Earl had returned, she abandoned her sewing and flew down the stairs to the hall, arriving to greet him just as he walked in from the yard.

Her heart opened wide at the sight of him; his height, his thick tawny-gold hair and warm brown eyes with smile creases at their edges. She greeted him with a proper formal curtsey to his bow, and although she was past thirty years old, she felt like a girl in the first flush of new love.

'Husband,' she murmured.

'Wife,' Hamelin responded, the word full of intimacy and amused affection.

Blushing, she took him up to their chamber so that he could refresh himself, and because she wanted him to see the changes she had made. She watched his reaction as he paused on the threshold and gazed round the fresh, refurbished chamber. 'You have been busy,' he said with approval. 'Very restful indeed.'

'Do you like it?'

'I like everything you do.' He pulled her to him, nuzzling her throat and kissing her softly on the lips. 'I have to say the bed looks very inviting.'

Isabel laughed and nestled against his broad chest. 'Indeed it is, but you need to take your boots off before you try it. And are you not hungry?'

'I'm ravenous but not necessarily for food.' Giving her a wicked look, he sat down swiftly on the box chair at the bedside and began tugging off his footwear.

Isabel dismissed the servants with a peremptory wave of her hand, and as the door closed behind the last one, knelt to help him with the task. With gentle fingers he removed her headdress and unwound her braids, letting her hair tumble around them in waves of heavy brunette silk: a sight and a privilege reserved only for a husband. He was indeed ravenous but he wanted this particular banquet to go on for ever.

* * *

'We had some disreputable visitors while you were gone,' Isabel said some considerable time later as they lazed in the aftermath of their lovemaking. 'But Thomas saw them off.'

'What do you mean "disreputable"?' He had been stroking his forefinger up and down her bare arm but now he pulled back slightly, alert to the suggestion of danger.

'Mercenary types looking to hire their swords but it might be wise to send men out to see if they caused troubled in any of the villages. Their leader claimed to know you but I doubt it. I told them to come back when you were home and that there was accommodation in Lynn should they wish to wait: I had no intention of allowing them under my roof.'

'Did their leader give a name?' There was a frown between Hamelin's brows as he reached for his discarded shirt.

'Yes, Geoffrey of le Mans. He was not the sort of person I would want to admit through my gates the way he looked and behaved. What's wrong?'

Hamelin had stiffened as she spoke the name and his frown had deepened.

'Geoffrey of le Mans,' he said. 'What did he look like?'

'Red hair, red beard with a white streak in the centre. Not a young man and dressed like a common peasant with manners to suit.' Isabel bit her lip. 'Surely you don't know him?'

'Very well indeed,' Hamelin said grimly. 'He's my

mother's cousin and was one of my father's most trusted knights, not to mention my tutor in arms and horsemanship when I was a boy.'

Isabel swallowed. 'He was dressed like a common hired soldier. Anyone looking at him would think he had mischief in mind!'

'Life is not like a tale spun by a troubadour,' he said curtly and began dressing rapidly. 'If a man has been on the road for a while or met with difficult circumstances, he may not arrive at your door looking as if he's about to dine at a court banquet.'

'And what if I had admitted him and he had turned out to be a thief and cutthroat? How was I to know?' Tears prickled her eyes at the injustice of his words.

Hamelin sat on the edge of the bed and pulled on his boots. 'Would you say that if the Christ Child came calling dressed in rags? Would you turn Him away because you were not to know?'

Her own anger began to rise. 'So by that rule do you expect me to admit every beggar and vagabond that arrives at our gates and sit them at our table?'

'By that rule I expect you not to judge people by their appearances. You have offended not only my kin but a very fine and old friend, and this might cost me that friendship.' He stood up, his face flushed with anger. 'Go and consult your mirror and your etiquette concerning the matter of true courtesy. You will greet all guests as my guests, not just your own.'

Isabel watched him, a lump of misery in her stomach that felt like a lead weight. 'Where are you going?' she asked as he stalked towards the door.

'To find him and atone where I can, because I doubt he will want to come back this way after the treatment he received.' He clattered from the room and she heard him calling to his men.

Isabel gave a soft gasp and pulled the covers over her head. She was angry at the way he had spoken to her but she was chastised too. She should have investigated further and not been so swift to judge. She had been too involved in sprucing up the bedchamber and too wary to consider further. Refusal had been the easiest road to take.

It was the first argument of their marriage and her heart was bruised in a way that it would never be bruised again.

* * *

Riding on the Lynn road, Hamelin encountered a large ale-house that had recently brewed a fresh batch as denoted by the bunch of evergreen hanging on a pole outside the door. Dismounting, he handed his horse to his squire and entered the establishment. The trestles were full of drinkers; Dame Agatha's brew was famous and when the sign of the bush went up outside her dwelling, men flocked to taste her ale. Seated around a table at the back of the room was a motley group of men, muddy from travel. They looked weary but well able to handle themselves, especially one with a beard of rust and silver, and sharp grey eyes.

Hamelin signalled to the pot boy and walked over to them. 'I hear you have been creating mayhem over at Acre, cousin,' he said, as he sat down on the bench. 'My good wife thought you were up to no good.'

Geoffrey of Le Mans raised his brow. 'I came to wish you

well of your marriage,' he replied. 'I did not expect to be turned away from your gate like a common vagabond.'

'I am sorry for that. Had I been home, it would have been a different matter. It is a pity no one was there who would recognise you, but they were my wife's attendants. After all the troubles of Stephen's reign, the Countess is wary – and justly so.'

'You make excuses?'

Hamelin gestured at his friend's rough tunic. 'You must admit that you are hardly dressed to announce your rank.'

Geoffrey narrowed his eyes. Hamelin met his gaze steadily, feeling like the youth he had once been, training under the knight's stern scrutiny. 'Well, that is true,' Geoffrey said after a long moment. 'But we had suffered a difficult sea crossing and I thought we could make ourselves presentable at your fine castle – but we were turned away.'

'I am sorry for that, as I have said, and so is my lady, and I have come to make amends. You are very welcome at the castle, although I will understand if you choose not to ride back my way.'

Geoffrey gave him another long look. 'Perhaps I shall ride your way, and look forward to a welcome, but it will be in my own time.' He leaned forward on the trestle. 'Now, since you have a full pitcher in front of you, let us catch up on old times, and then move on to new.'

'I'll drink to that,' Hamelin said with a smile.

* * *

It was very late, and Isabel had given up on Hamelin when he finally returned to Castle Acre. She ran to her chamber door but immediately thought better of it. Whatever was said was probably best done in private, not in the hall.

Her heart started to pound as she heard footsteps on the stairs. Hamelin opened the door and walked in. His tread was steady; he was not drunk but as he came to her she could smell drink on his breath.

'I am sorry,' she said. 'I should not have been so swift to judge.'

He touched her face. 'I am sorry too. I should not have been so swift to castigate you for your prudence. There has been no harm done. Geoffrey saw the humour in the situation and agreed that he could have arrived better presented. He swears he will wear his best robes next time he comes to visit.' He gave her a large embrace. 'You must not mistake me if I ever come home in muddy boots!'

She gave him a little push, feeling giddy with relief that the awkward moment was over and all seemed to have been resolved. 'I thought you might not come back,' she admitted.

'Why would I do that? Geoffrey is good company, but you are more beautiful and I would rather sleep in my own bed than on an alehouse mattress.'

That made her feel guilty for a moment, thinking of the troop she had turned away, but Hamelin's evident good humour made her cheerful enough to set it aside.

'Come,' he said. 'Bring your cloak and walk with me.'

Strolling at his side, with his arm around her waist, and the world to themselves, Isabel felt the last of her unease slip away and was supremely content.

Standing on tiptoe, she murmured in Hamelin's ear, and when he turned to her with an exclamation of delight, she smiled and drew his hand to her womb and kissed him in the moon-silvered night.

* * *

Hamelin was out riding when the troop of horsemen arrived at the gates of Castle Acre. Isabel was inspecting a new horse in the stables when Thomas came to her with the news. 'Sir Geoffrey of le Mans is back, my lady,' he said wryly.

'Bid him enter and be welcome,' she replied in a calm voice, although her heart had begun to pound. She decided she had better follow Thomas to the gate and greet them herself.

She was in time to see the great wooden doors creak open and a band of riders trot through the gateway, clad in rich garments and furs that would not have looked out of place at a tournament parade. The horses had been groomed until their hides shone. Harness gleamed and sparkled, sunbursts dazzling on bits and stirrups. Even the pack ponies were spruced, with smart saddlecloths and scarlet ribbons plaited in their manes.

The leading rider swung down from a glossy black stallion and knelt to her, elegantly flicking his blue woollen cloak out of the way. The cuffs of his tunic were embroidered in red and gold, banded with small seed pearls. Behind him his men dismounted and knelt too in a jingle of harness and shiny equipment. 'Geoffrey de le Mans, your servant, Madam Countess,' he said. 'I trust I meet your exacting standards today.'

Isabel curtseyed and knew she was blushing because her cheeks were hot. 'I have no complaint sire,' she said. 'Please accept my apology for the previous occasion and be welcome at Castle Acre. Will you come in and take refreshment?'

Before the kneeling man could reply, Hamelin rode through the gate at a canter, his garments and horse mud-spattered from a swift ride over moist ground.

A smile lit in Geoffrey's eyes. 'Who is this vagabond?' he demanded. 'Shall I see him off for you, Madam?' He set his hand lightly to his gleaming sword hilt.

Isabel laughed, 'I can do that for myself if I so choose,' she said, entering into the spirit of the teasing.

Hamelin clapped Geoffrey on the shoulder and then turned to his wife. 'I would far rather be taken hostage to good food, fine wine shared with friends and kin, and then a warm bed shared only by my wife.'

'I am sure that can be arranged,' Isabel said demurely as he slipped his arm around her waist.

The company entered the castle together. Once inside, Geoffrey formally presented Isabel and Hamelin with a wedding gift of a set of silver gilt spoons for the high table, wrapped in a valuable purple silk cloth. Once they had thanked him and marvelled at the exquisite workmanship, he produced another set and presented them to Isabel with a flourish. This time the spoons were fashioned of rustic, crudely carved wood, standing upright in a plain earthenware jar.

'For any eventuality you may come across,' he said with a twinkle in his eyes.

Isabel thanked him. 'You are very thoughtful,' she said gravely. 'I promise that I shall always hold them both in equal esteem.'

Author's Note

Isabel de Warenne was a wealthy widow who married King Henry II's illegitimate half-brother Hamelin in 1164. Hamelin took her name as his as far as the family line went and they seem to have had a long and happy marriage blessed by a son and three daughters.

Castle Acre in Norfolk was the core castle of Isabel's estates, but Hamelin went on to build a magnificent fortress in Yorkshire at Conisburgh. The couple will feature significantly in my forthcoming trilogy about Eleanor of Aquitaine, *The Summer Queen*, *The Winter Crown* and *The Autumn Throne*.

Katie Fforde

Katie is currently the President of the RNA and the author of twenty books. She lives in the Cotswolds with her husband, some of her three children, and three dogs. Her hobbies include being a member of a choir and Lindy Hop, a new hobby which may or may not be continued.

She declares herself to be the RNA's biggest fan.

&

Living The Dream

Isobel had always been a fan of those books set in Cornwall, where the sea roiled (there was never a book when it didn't) and the sun danced like stars on the waves. Either the sun shone like it hadn't done for years in real life, or the sky brooded and storms blew, lightning highlighting the passion of secret lovers, or murders, or books containing the dark secrets of the ancient family.

There was always a matriarch, always beautiful, and either with an amazing talent for something – opera singing, poetry, painting – or with a secret. Every man she met fell in love with her, even when she was in her seventies.

Life was not like this for Isobel. She had a perfectly happy life but as she had got older, her confidence had begun to wane and she longed to be the sort of powerful, charismatic older woman who starred in those books.

She also wanted the beautiful house in Cornwall. Instead of the large, detached house with plenty of garden on the edge of a very pleasant town, where she had brought up her children and where she and her husband still lived, she yearned for a wild cliff top, or the bottom of a wooded valley, either an ancient farmhouse, a large Victorian mansion, or even an architect-designed modern house with spectacular views. All of these imaginary houses would have some sort of dwelling in the grounds. Her favourite daydream was a boathouse; there was something very sexy about a boathouse.

One year, she decided to make her dream real. She searched the internet exhaustively and eventually found the perfect house. It didn't have another dwelling in the grounds but it was right on the river and the views were sensational. She went to find her husband who was working on a model ship in his shed. He was always working on a model ship in his shed, apparently finding this more absorbing than the company of his wife, now the children had all left home.

'Darling, I want to take the whole family on holiday. Jenny said the other day they couldn't afford to go away this year and I suddenly thought what fun it would be to get together.' She glanced at him and then went on. 'It would be good for the grandchildren to spend quality time with each other.'

Rather to her surprise he didn't grunt when she said 'quality time'. Instead, he nodded. 'And we pay for it all?'

'Yes,' Isobel said firmly. The children would never give up their holiday allowance to go to Cornwall if they had to pay.

'OK,' he said, and went back to his scale model of the *Cutty Sark*.

Isobel went back to the house, half annoyed that he hadn't said, 'But I wanted to take you to Antibes,' and delighted that he'd agreed to her plan.

Her husband's early retirement had been a bit disappointing. She'd imagined lovely days out and meals in pubs now they had time to be with each other but mostly he made models. And nowadays, if she asked him if she looked all right, he always said 'fine' but never glanced in her direction.

Her three children, two sons and a daughter, all married

or with partners, were all keen on the idea of a paid-for holiday in a luxury holiday home. 'Lovely to have built-in baby-sitters,' said one son. 'Good to have time to catch up with the sibs,' said another.

Isobel made the booking. Now she would live the dream. She would become charismatic, beautiful, in spite of her nearly sixty years. She wouldn't just be 'good old Mum'.

* * *

What she hadn't envisaged when she'd been searching for the perfect house was the amount of cooking and washing up a family holiday with grandchildren entailed – all in a kitchen a lot less well organised than her own. It was not so much 'living the dream' as 'living the washing up'. What had seemed such a good idea in January, when she booked the house, now seemed a terrible idea. As for her transformation into the heroine of one of those books, she felt more like the faithful family housekeeper than her employer.

The men all loved cooking – that wasn't a problem – except they used every implement in the house and while they sloshed water around quite a bit, they somehow never actually cleared up. Considering they had cooked this seemed sort of OK, but it was the same when she cooked. Her husband wiped half washed saucepans with clean tea towels, which meant very soon none of the tea towels were clean.

She realised sadly that she was not a matriarch, she was a woman who was a member of a book group, shopped in Waitrose and had to travel with her own pillows. And while, during the holiday at least, she had some trappings of the Yummy Mummy – the pale marks on the shoulder of every garment, the faint odour of sour milk, and Babybels loose in her handbag ready to feed a hungry toddler at a moment's notice – she didn't feel remotely yummy. And she didn't even have a wicked past to look back on either. She'd married young, had children and stayed married. Her life was completely free of delicious memories of past loves. What had always seemed something to be admired now seemed plain boring.

At least the holiday was going well. Everyone seemed to be enjoying themselves. Days on the beach with the children, with Grandpa willing to go rock pooling, buy ice creams and carry small children for miles. And later, meals cooked and served at the huge table with ample quantities of wine. Yet somehow she still found herself doing most of the donkeywork. Everyone was happy to fill the dishwasher but no one wanted to empty it, carrying the clean things to a cupboard across the kitchen. It was a job Isobel hated too but still found herself doing it several times a day.

One morning, when she'd got up early to do the washing up that the men had sworn they'd do, she went on strike halfway through. She made herself a cup of tea and took the visitors' book out onto the terrace. The sun was shining and no one else was up. She felt entitled to a few moments not looking after people. These moments were hers.

Earlier, when they'd first arrived at the house and were reading the instructions to the Aga and the telephone number of the woman who 'did' plus the way to the nearest beach, which was several miles through traffic-filled lanes, Isobel had looked at the visitors' book. In it had been a name she'd recognised. A man she'd known briefly and rather fancied – Leo Stark – had obviously stayed at the same house with his family. They'd both been married when they met but she was fairly sure there'd been some sort of spark.

On impulse she went to find her phone and emailed him. After all, there were no other ways she could rebel that wouldn't impinge unpleasantly on someone else. This was a little private thing that would go no further.

'Dear Leo, I'm sure you won't remember me, Isobel Dunbar, but we met at the McCreadys' once. We're staying in the house where you stayed last year. Such a coincidence, I had to get in touch.'

Feeling very slightly naughty, and so cheered up, she went back into the house to finish the clearing she had abandoned.

Very much to her surprise she had a reply from Leo. She sneaked a look, feeling wonderfully teenage, while supervising the two-year-old's porridge consumption.

'Isobel! Of course I remember you! How could I forget? And by an amazing coincidence we're down here too! Do you think you could manage a lunch? Not the whole family, just us?'

She was so shocked and delighted she couldn't even think of replying. She just held her glorious – and guilty – secret to herself. She whizzed through the chores and even made up some batter for pancakes for breakfast. She almost ran down the lane to the little shop that stocked everything a holidaymaker might require and was open almost continuously. She panted back up the hill clutching croissants and maple syrup.

'Mum!' said her daughter, a plump baby on her hip. 'You

didn't get any nappies while you were in the shop, did you? We're nearly out.'

'Sorry, darling, I didn't know about the nappies and just thought it would be fun to have pancakes.' The adrenalin shot of the email protected her from resentment. 'Now, shall I take Immi so you can start frying?'

All day she was superwoman. She packed a picnic of homemade pizzas and sent the whole lot off to the beach. 'I'll meet you at lunchtime. There are just a few things I want to do here!' she said, as she waved them off.

Then she ran to her phone. 'It's as if I have a lover!' she told herself, slightly breathless, as she switched it on. The thought of having a lover was like being submerged by a huge wave and then being lifted up by the same wave. She couldn't decide if the feeling of exhilaration matched the feeling of utter doom. It was while she was feeling ridiculously happy she wrote a quick reply: 'That should be possible. When did you have in mind? Not today,' she added hurriedly.

She doubted if Leo had had to tidy the kitchen, go shopping and make pancakes – not to mention the picnic – in order to have a few moments to send an email, but was very pleased to hear the ping of a reply while she was clearing up sodden towels from the shower. It was him. He mentioned a pub in a little village a reassuring distance from the house: 'Tomorrow any good? We're going back at the end of the week.'

'Lovely,' she wrote back, not giving herself time to think further. If she passed up this opportunity it wouldn't happen and she'd regret it for ever. 'One o'clock?'

Feeling as guilty as if she had made a pact with the devil, Isobel made her way to the beach, bringing chilled bottles, extra cardies and some sunscreen with her.

'Oh great, beer,' said one of her sons, taking a couple of bottles out of her bag, which had been very heavy.

'That's fine, darling,' Isobel muttered. 'It was no trouble bringing it at all…'

* * *

The following morning Isobel got everyone's attention at breakfast time – as far as one could, given that they all had separate distractions. 'I'm going out for the day,' she said. 'I'll be taking the car.'

'What do you want to do that for?' asked her husband, utterly bemused.

'Oh you know. I just need a bit of time on my own. "Me time".' She bit her lip to stop herself adding 'because I'm worth it.'

'Will you be back to help with bath-time?' asked one daughter-in-law. 'You promised to read Otto a story!'

'I'll be back in plenty of time for that.'

'This is a bit out of left-field, isn't it?' said a son.

'Yes, and what about supper?' asked her daughter. 'What are we having?'

'Why don't you decide?' she asked. She turned to leave but before she had got out of the room her daughter stopped her.

'Don't you think you ought to at least wash your hair first?'

Isobel laughed. 'Oh no, my hair is just fine.'

She managed not to spray gravel as she drove away, feeling as if the family car had turned into a getaway vehicle. In her Cath Kidson shopper, like stolen goods, were as many of her clothes that she felt she could get away with taking, and her entire make-up kit. Her holiday packing had not included control pants or a sexy dress but she had bought a couple of new tops and some new linen trousers that were quite flattering. She knew of a public lavatory with quite big cubicles, she'd do her changing there.

Her hair would be sorted by a quick wash and blow-dry at a local salon. It couldn't go too wrong and if it did, she could gussy it up with some products that the local Boots would provide. She was going to enjoy every minute of this.

But in between the wonderful excitement came troughs of guilt. She was struggling into her new trousers in the public convenience, giggling at the ridiculousness of it all, when she suddenly pictured her husband. What would happen if he found out? She suddenly felt sick. It would be too awful. He would be so hurt. Her mouth went dry and for a moment she couldn't move. After a few minutes she collected herself and carried on getting dressed in a more sombre manner. She walked out of the cubicle in two minds. Should she cancel?

A glance in the mirror decided her. She was looking good. Well, as good as she could look given the circumstances. The local salon had done a good job on her hair and her new clothes were nice. She would meet an old friend for lunch, she would do a bit of shopping and then go back in time to bathe the babies and cook supper. After she'd had her few hours of intrigue would she go back to her humdrum role of wife and mother and not care that no one seemed to appreciate her, let alone treat her as the sort of goddess who starred in her favourite sort of reading material. She would have her secret, even if it was a very small one.

She felt so sick with nerves when she arrived at the pub that she nearly turned round and went back to the holiday house. But she knew she'd regret it if she did that – and it was only lunch, for God's sake. She and Leo might wonder what on earth they had ever seen in each other. She would more than likely go home wondering what on earth she'd gone to all that trouble for – but she had to find out.

Leo was waiting for her, watching the door for her to come in, and stood up the moment she appeared. She recognised him instantly, and going by the smile on his face he recognised her too.

They hugged briefly, and then Isobel sat down. Her knees were shaking.

'What can I get you?' Leo asked.

'A white wine spritzer,' she said. She needed at least some alcohol to get her through this. And if she stuffed herself with sandwiches when she was alone again, after the salad she would have in front of Leo, she should be OK to drive back.

'So, Isobel. This is so nice.' His words were bland but the expression in his eyes was anything but. She may have forgotten some of the signs but she was fairly sure she saw a twinkle of admiration. 'I've often wondered what would have happened if we hadn't both been married when we met.'

Isobel took a sip of her drink – she wouldn't have been able to talk if she hadn't. 'But we were both married and still are.'

He smiled ruefully and nodded. 'So there's no point in suggesting we get a room then?'

She started to laugh. It was so ridiculous. He laughed too and then they were both chuckling away. Isobel knew it was a release of tension – for her anyway – but whatever the reason it was lovely.

'All I can say,' he said, when they had recovered themselves, 'is that your husband is a very lucky man. Now what would you like for lunch?'

* * *

When Isobel drove away from the pub she was on a cloud. Her self-esteem had rocketed and she felt powerful and attractive. Nothing untoward had happened during the lunch but she knew Leo had fancied her. She may not be a matriarch, adored by all, but she now had a secret, even if it wasn't really a wicked one.

Rather to her surprise, the family was all in the kitchen when she arrived. As they all had slightly odd expressions she wondered for one ghastly moment if she had been discovered.

'Mum!' said her daughter, coming forward and kissing her. 'You look great! Got your hair done?' Isobel nodded. 'Which is good because we've got a plan!'

'We're going out for dinner,' said her husband.

Isobel beamed, her happiness and relief when she realised she hadn't been discovered having lunch with another man. 'How lovely!'

'We realised you've spent most of the holiday looking after us, so today I'm taking you out,' her husband said. 'And Adam has kindly offered to take us and pick us up so we can drink.' He smiled at her and she recognised the man she had once been madly in love with.

All she really wanted from life was with her right now. She didn't really need a secret or a luscious Cornish house.

'Lovely, I'll go and get ready then.'

'The table's not booked until seven,' said her daughter. 'You can still help with bath time…'

'I'd love to,' she said.

Maureen Lee

Maureen Lee has had twenty-seven novels published, most of them family sagas, one of which won the Romantic Novel of the Year Award in 2000. In an earlier life she sold about 150 short stories to magazines all over the world. Her musical play, *When Adam Delved and Eve Span*, had a three-week run at the Mercury Theatre in Colchester. She is married to Richard and has three grown up sons. After writing, her main interests are politics and reading other authors' books.

&

True Love

The sun came out, flooding the room with brilliant light. Although his eyes were closed, the man turned restlessly on the bed and uttered a little moan. The sudden light had disturbed him. His wife rose and hurriedly pulled the curtains together, then returned to her chair beside the bed. She smoothed his brow.

'There, there, darling,' she murmured.

'Where are we?' he asked in a deep young voice that surprised her.

'Why, at home, Robert,' she replied. 'On the farm. It's morning, the sun's just appeared, and two of your grandsons have already telephoned to ask how you are.'

His son, their only child, had enquired merely from a sense of duty. He'd been a strict, unforgiving father, not at all well-loved. But with his grandchildren he'd been openly fond and caring.

He was old, in his ninetieth year, and he was dying. Everybody knew that, his wife most of all. She'd loved him since they'd first met: she had been sixteen and he more than twice her age. Her father had been a parish councillor and he'd come to the house about a planning matter. He was a farmer; sternly handsome, smiling rarely. He'd proposed within six months and she'd accepted gladly.

'I'll make some tea,' she said, not that he would understand. He'd heard nothing for days apart from internal voices he would occasionally converse with, voices that belonged to people she had never known. She left the dining room and went into the kitchen – he'd been brought downstairs and the dining room had been turned into a bedroom.

Through the window, the modern bungalow – built for their son when he took over the management of the farm – throbbed with life. Her great grandchildren, two little girls, were spending the summer there, and were already playing on a swing in the garden. Dorothy, her daughter-in-law, was hanging washing on the line and Francis, the 'Crown Prince' as Robert sometimes called him in a rare moment of humour, was staring at the house where he'd been born as if wondering how his father was today. At some time this morning, he'd come over and enquire about his health.

She was tempted to wave, but Francis would come immediately out of a sense of duty and she would sooner he didn't. He would argue that his father should be in hospital.

'He loathes hospitals,' she would insist. 'He'd far sooner be at home.'

She made tea and took two digestive biscuits out of the tin – she'd make herself a proper breakfast later – and took them into the dining room where, to her utter astonishment, her husband was singing an old war song.

'There'll be bluebirds over...' he sang, followed by unrecognisable murmurings.

'The white cliffs of Dover,' his wife offered. Then she sang the line in full, 'There'll be bluebirds over, the white cliffs of Dover.'

She was even more astonished when he opened his eyes and smiled at her, a brilliant, open, truly gorgeous smile that was totally unfamiliar.

'Hello,' she said, taken aback, overwhelmed by the feeling of aching sadness that she would shortly lose him.

* * *

'Hello,' Robert MacEvoy exclaimed, almost exactly seventy years earlier. It was late September, the war was just over a year old – it had only been predicted to last six months. He'd just woken from his afternoon nap in the hospital of an RAF camp on the Essex coast and she was standing beside his bed with a cup of tea. She wore a blue and white uniform. A new nurse!

She laughed and put the tea on his bedside cabinet. 'Hello,' she cried, adding, 'You've got a lovely smile.'

'You've got a lovely everything.' She was outstandingly pretty, with dark curly hair and eyes the colour of forget-me-nots. He was twenty-one and had never spoken so frankly to a girl before – flirtatiously almost. 'What's your name?'

'Moira. Moira Graham.' She made a face, squinting her eyes and wrinkling her nose. 'What's yours?'

'Robert. People call me Rob.'

'Well, I shall call you Robert, if you don't mind.'

'I don't mind a bit. Will you be at the dance tonight?' Another first for him; virtually asking a girl for a date.

'I will indeed. Shall I save the last dance for you?' She

spoke in a deep sultry voice like Marlene Dietrich while fluttering her eyelashes.

He nodded. 'As well as the first and all the dances in between.'

'There's just one thing, Robert,' she said.

'And what's that, Moira?'

'Have you forgotten you have a broken leg? It's why you're in hospital.'

He looked down at his feet protruding from under the blanket. The right one was heavily plastered, leaving only his toes bare. His ankle was also broken and his knee shattered.

'I hadn't forgotten, no. I thought we could sit the dances out. You can take me in my wheelchair.'

She looked serious for a change. Perhaps she felt the same as he did; that something remarkable and truly wonderful had occurred.

'Oh, all right, so we'll sit the dances out.'

* * *

The dance was being held in the canteen, the tables folded in a corner, piled on top of one another. He could limp a bit, his wheelchair was outside, and they were holding hands and sitting on one of the benches tucked against the walls. He was keeping his leg well out of the way, not so much bothered that someone would fall over it but that they would stand on his unprotected toes. The big room was crowded and the band played ear splittingly loudly.

'What happened to you?' she asked.

'My plane crashed on landing,' he said simply. 'I was the rear gunner and thrown forward. Broke half a dozen bones.

We'd taken a few hits over Berlin. It had needed a wing and a prayer to get us home.'

She shuddered and squeezed his hand. 'Poor Robert,' she whispered. 'It must have been terribly painful.'

Robert shook his head. 'I was knocked unconscious straightaway. I woke up in hospital, pleased to find I was alive and all in one piece. They sent me here to recuperate. Apparently, the hospital has a great reputation – it's bound to improve with you there.'

'I only recently passed my final exams. This is my first week as a nurse.' She laid her head on his shoulder and began to croon 'There's A Boy Coming Home On Leave' along with the band's singer, a blonde in a tight red sequin dress.

Couples shuffled past locked in each other's arms, even though they may have only met that night. There was a war on: Dunkirk was still painfully fresh in their memories, bombs were dropping all over Britain, Germany occupied several European countries, ships were being sunk. Life was cheap and thousands had already died. It meant that people lived for today and to hell with tomorrow.

It was hot in the canteen and his leg was itching madly. He wriggled uncomfortably.

'What's the matter?' she asked.

'I'd pay five quid to be able to scratch my leg,' he groaned.

'When's the plaster due to come off?'

'Another three weeks.'

She stiffened. 'Will you be sent somewhere else?'

He shrugged, unsure. 'I'm supposed to spend three months convalescing. Whether they'll leave me here, I've no idea.' He still suffered excruciating headaches.

His hand was squeezed again. 'Let's hope that they will.'

* * *

He'd been born in Kent when his mother was in her late forties and her other children had grown up and left. He'd been an unpleasant surprise and she had no love left for him. His father, a farmer, spent little time at home. Robert had sometimes wondered what life was for.

And now he knew. It was to meet Moira. She was meant for him and he for her. Both realised that after just a few magical, dreamlike days.

What good luck it had been that his plane had crashed when it had and with him as the only one seriously injured. He wouldn't have wanted his good fortune to come as a result of a tragedy for others. He was in love, *they* were in love, and every day was a miracle.

'Will you marry me?' he asked when they'd known each other a fortnight.

'Of course,' she smiled back. 'But do we really need a piece of paper to prove we love each other? We're already married in spirit, if not in law.'

She was so familiar to him it was as if they'd known each other all their lives.

* * *

The day after the plaster was removed from his leg, they made love. For both it was the first time. Moira laughed a lot and cried a bit at their initial fumbling attempts to do it properly.

They chose the private ward of the hospital, the one with only two beds reserved for officers, empty now. The door was locked but they still worried. There were only three patients in the main ward: the other two were asleep. But Moira had been left in charge and if someone came and there was no sign of her, there'd be hell to pay. And if someone came and discovered what they were up to…!

'We'd be shot at dawn,' she said soberly.

'Not before they'd pulled our fingernails out.'

'Don't joke, it's not funny. We'll have to find somewhere else.'

* * *

Night after night more bombs fell on more British cities. Sixty miles away London was being pounded ceaselessly. The war was spreading as the weather became colder and winter drew in.

As if in defiance of the misery being wrought upon them, the atmosphere in the camp became quite joyful. It was impossible to walk far without hearing a song being sung, a mouth organ being played, someone whistling. The dances got quite wild, but they finished with couples clinging to each other as if they never wanted to part. Groups of people would suddenly burst into song but likely end in tears as the lyrics touched hearts in a way the composer had never imagined. 'Kiss the Boys Goodbye', 'We'll Meet Again', 'Somewhere Over the Rainbow': it was the language of love and loss, of words easier to say in song than spoken.

Robert was transferred from the hospital to a single room befitting his rank of Flight Sergeant. He needed a stick to get about so, for now, there was no mention of him being sent elsewhere. He was given a part-time job in the stores filling out order forms. Otherwise nobody bothered him.

When advised he could go home on leave, he replied he'd sooner stay on the premises.

'Strange chap,' commented the clerk who'd made the offer, eyeing him suspiciously.

Robert shrugged and said nothing. He just wanted to be with Moira. Nothing else mattered.

Three times a week, when Moira wasn't working nights, they stayed in an old pub in Mersea, a watery village five miles from the camp. It was reached by a rambling bus usually full of RAF and Army personnel. Their attic room had a sloping ceiling, and was clean, comfortable and cheap. They were committed to sign in at the camp before eight o'clock next morning.

'I don't want us making love in a doorway,' Moira said wrinkling her nose.

'Or behind the canteen,' said Robert. Some nights there'd be a whole row of couples.

Moira giggled. 'Or in a lavatory!'

'Oh, God, no.'

Other nights they sat in pubs or walked arm in arm on the flat sands where the moon was reflected over and over in the little pools that shimmered like diamonds, pausing to kiss and say, 'I love you,' for perhaps the hundredth or the thousandth time.

Sometimes, a German plane would fly over on its way back from London, occasionally dropping the odd bomb there hadn't been time to release on its intended target.

They knew one day it would have to end. Robert's health

was improving, the headaches fading; he no longer needed a stick. They thought it unlikely both would still be there by Christmas.

'What shall we do then?' Moira asked.

'Write to each other. See each other as often as we can – *if* we can.' He could be sent abroad. So could she.

* * *

December came. Time was short. Each day began as if it was their last together. The weather worsened and it became icily cold. They spent as many nights as they could manage in the pub, making love full of wonder as well as sadness.

They were there one Saturday when the bar was crowded with military men and women, and locals. Songs, old and new, were sung, as well as Christmas carols.

Upstairs in their attic Robert and Moira made love. It was a surreal experience. The songs filtering up through the floorboards and sounding as if they were being sung in the room with them. As the night wore on, the music slowly faded until all that could be heard were faint voices, still singing, on their way to the bus stop.

They were lying in each other's arms when they heard the plane approach. Moira got out of bed to watch it passing over.

'Stay here,' Robert implored. Had he sensed the danger he was to wonder afterwards?

She was at the window when the bomb plunged through the roof, taking away half the room, leaving him safely in bed on a shelf of severed floorboards. Robert watched, horrified, as she disappeared from sight amid tons of debris and a thunderous whooshing sound.

For a long time, it was like the end of everything.

* * *

Many years went by until the time came when he met a woman who loved him. They were married and she bore him a child. A day never passed when he didn't think of Moira. Nor did a day come when he was as happy as he'd been with her: his one and only love.

And now, seventy years later, he knew they were about to meet again. He could see her more clearly than he'd ever done. She drifted in and out of his mind, she was foremost in his thoughts; singing, always singing. And now here she was, coming towards him, smiling, holding out her arms ready to embrace him.

'I love you,' he cried, opening his own arms to greet her. 'Did I ever tell you how much I love you?'

* * *

The wife knew that he had gone. She wept, not just at his passing, but at the words he'd never said, not once, throughout their long married life. Still, it was wonderful to know that all that time he had really loved her.

Miranda Dickinson

Miranda Dickinson is the author of five *Sunday Times* Bestselling novels, two of which have been international bestsellers in four countries. She is published in six languages and to this date has sold over half a million books world-wide. She is also the founder of the New Rose Short Story prize. She has been nominated for two RNA awards – the RNA Romantic Novel of the Year award 2010 for *Fairytale of New York* and the RONA for contemporary novel of the year in 2012 for *It Started With a Kiss*. Her fifth novel, *Take A Look At Me Now*, is available now, published by Avon (HarperCollins).

Miranda publishes regular vlogs at her website: www.miranda-dickinson.com and blog: coffeeandroses.blogspot.com. You can follow Miranda on twitter @wurdsmyth and on Facebook: www.facebook.com/MirandaDickinsonAuthor.

&

Love On Wheels

I love my job.

It's not glamorous or particularly well paid, nor is it anywhere near what my careers advisor had in mind for me when I left school, but it offers magic that few people looking in would see. The van I drive and company sweatshirt I wear may be emblazoned with SUNNYSIDE MEALS ON WHEELS, but my job is so much more than that. I might deliver affordable, nutritionally balanced ready meals to elderly customers, but what I receive in return is priceless. For I am a collector of stories, a sharer of nostalgia, a confidant of dreams.

Not that my boss – who, awkwardly, also happens to be my mum – understands this. She would much rather I limit my conversation with customers to 'Hello' and 'Goodbye', or maybe 'See you next week', if it's a quiet day on my round.

'We don't pay you to be their *friend*, Emily, we pay you to deliver their food,' she lectured one morning, clearly imagining herself to be the female incarnation of Lord Alan Sugar. 'If they want company I'm sure their families can oblige.'

'Mum, have you ever met the customers on my round?' I protested, knowing full well that she hadn't and that my argument was futile. 'I'm the only other person some of them see all day.'

Mum cast a disapproving eye over my dyed hair – this

week a fetching shade of blue. 'What a treat for them! The point is we are not a charity or a befriending service. First and foremost, we are a business. Now, I need you to read this time and motion study Trevor's written. And *act* upon it.'

As she passed me the sheet of paper, I inwardly groaned. *Trevor*. Repulsive, fifty-something boyfriend of my mother and the kind of man so boring even paint drying would mock him. Since Mum had met him at a business breakfast six months ago, he had fast become the balding, beige-faced bane of my life. What Trevor Mitchell didn't know about health and safety, workplace law and mindless business jargon simply wasn't worth knowing. In fact, he seemed to think it was his God-given right to comment on anything and everything, regardless of how much he actually knew about it. And, judging by his latest intrusion, Trev was on top form.

I cast my eyes over his calculations, unimaginatively typed in Comic Sans font – the childishness of which only served to make the whole document more insulting. Well, he could shove this exactly where all his other advice could be deposited. I knew that effectiveness in my job couldn't be measured by miles covered per hour or minimum amount of time spent with each customer. It was in how I could share a conversation, spend a little time with someone lonely and maybe make a difference to their day. Unfortunately for me, Trevor saw our lovely elderly clients as nothing more than aged donkeys on a conveyor belt, good only for parting with their pension and having food chucked at them.

'Trevor says you've been spending too long with each client,' Mum continued, oblivious to my disdain. 'By his calculations it should take no more than seven-point-five minutes to make a delivery. Now, there's a new gentleman on your round today, so Trevor says you should begin the new timings on this one.'

I rolled my eyes and this time she couldn't ignore it. 'Oh well, if *Trev* says…'

Mum gave me a stare that could freeze the Sahara. 'His name is *Trevor*, Emily, and I'll thank you not to disrespect him. That man could well be your next stepfather.'

On that cheery note I left, glad for the peaceful sanity of my company van when I climbed into it. I wasn't surprised by boring Trev's intervention, but it still annoyed me.

'Idiot!' I grumbled aloud, pulling out of the gravel car park by the small industrial unit Sunnyside Meals on Wheels called home, to turn left onto the busy coast road. 'Well, it shows how much *you* know, Trevor Mitchell! Our customers are more than ticks on your ridiculously timed list. And, I'm sorry, but who actually says "seven-point-five minutes" anyway?'

My indignation brought a wry smile to my face, not least because if boring Trev could see me ranting to myself in the van he'd probably accuse me of wasting company oxygen.

I glanced across at the small clipboard attached with a suction pad to the windscreen. Mrs Clements was first today – and straight away proof that Mum's boyfriend was completely wrong.

I've delivered meals to Mrs Clements since my first day on this job, eight years ago, and she is one of the most fascinating people I've ever met. When she was only seventeen years old she made the biggest decision of her life: to move to Canada to look after her nephew and brother-in-law after her older sister's untimely death. She had been a promising student and dreamed of being a teacher but she left it all to go to another country and live the life her sister had left behind. Eventually, she married her brother-in-law and adopted her nephew as her stepson, only returning to England after her husband's death in the mid-1970s. Mrs Clements was the first Sunnyside customer to share her memories with me and since then I have always taken time to listen when someone on my rounds wants to tell me about their past.

So yes, maybe I did take longer than the other two drivers to complete my deliveries but how else would I have learned about Mr Cooke earning his Distinguished Service Order medal by saving four of his Army comrades under intense enemy fire; or when Mrs Trellawney met the Queen; or about Miss Atkinson's secret dream to be a champion ballroom dancer?

None of this mattered to my mother and boring Trev, of course. But that wasn't important: it mattered to me.

Mrs Clements met me at the door already armed with a time-battered photograph album and the sound of the kettle boiling from the tiny kitchen of her retirement bungalow.

'Oh good, you're here, Emily. Come in, come in!'

I swung the box I was carrying into her hallway and closed the door behind me. 'You're chirpy today, Mrs C.'

'That I am,' she replied, leading the way down the hallway to her kitchen. She shuffled along in her favourite nylon skirt, polyester jumper and tartan bobble slippers and I imagined the static she created could be hooked up to the national grid to power her house. She made a pot of tea while I unpacked her week's worth of meals, knowing her kitchen cupboards better than I did my own. It's true what they say about trades--people: at the end of my working day the last thing I ever want to do is to cook a meal. If Mum knew how many takeaways and ready meals I consume each week, I'd be excommunicated for certain.

When her cupboards were filled and the teas were made, she ushered me through to the tropical heat of her living room. She sat in her favourite chair as I allowed her too-squashy sofa to attempt to eat me alive.

'I found these at the weekend,' she said, turning over the yellowing photo album pages with her blue-veined fingers until she found what she was looking for. 'There – look at this.'

She swung the album to face me and prodded at a photograph. It was a black and white image of an opulent-looking hall filled with a huge crowd of couples, each one solemnly face to face in stiff ballroom holds.

'This is The Rialto Ballroom in Truro,' she chuckled. 'It's long gone, of course. But believe it or not, this was the happening night spot when I was young.'

'When was this picture taken?'

'July 1951. Two months before I left for Canada.' Her smile carried the wistfulness of many years. 'I used to dance there twice a week: Wednesday nights when they taught old-time ballroom to a hall full of girls and, of course, Saturday nights when you got to practice with the *real thing*.' She winked at me. 'Saturdays were when the magic happened.'

I looked at the girls with their almost identical dresses and the men looking awkward in ill-fitting suits. 'So who danced with you?'

She flushed slightly, a wicked glint in her watery blue eyes. 'Anyone who'd have me.'

'Mrs C! You little scoundrel!'

'We-ell, I was young, we'd not long come out of the war

and suddenly a lot of young chaps were back on the scene. It would've been rude not to indulge.' She tapped the side of her nose with her finger. 'But it was only dancing, mind. None of that heavy petting nonsense you see young kids doing today.'

I took a sip of tea and felt the high caffeine content clunk against my teeth. 'I'm sure you were the perfect picture of virtue.'

She nodded. 'I was back then. It was only when I came home after Alfie died that I gave *proper* hanky-panky a go. Couldn't believe what I'd missed out on…'

I was still reeling from the revelation of Mrs Clements' late-flowering libido as I drove to my next customer. The warm September sun bathed the villages and fields whizzing past my window in a beautiful light, and I thanked heaven that I was lucky enough to work in such a breathtaking part of the world. After ten miles, the road rose steeply as I approached one of my favourite views: a sudden expanse of Cornish coastline appearing on my left; jagged cliffs falling away from the lush green above, with the wide sweep of perfect blue ocean beyond.

Inevitably, the scene brought bittersweet memories as Isaac's face flashed into my mind. My Isaac. Until last summer the one and only love of my life. When we were together we would park not far from the road here and stride across the thick, waving grass down to the cliff path, while Django – our over-excitable Jack Russell – bounced around our feet.

I had dealt with a lot of my feelings for Isaac Pemberthy since he'd unceremoniously dumped Django and me, but somehow this single memory refused to budge. Even my dog had something of Isaac he couldn't let go of. He refused to be parted from one of Isaac's old socks even though it was now more chewed hole than knitted acrylic. At least Django understood. Maybe that was why I loved spending time on my rounds rather than with my friends, who still saw Isaac occasionally. Maybe I was as lonely as some of Sunnyside's customers...

Mr Arbuthnot was in a bit of a hurry when I arrived with his delivery, so I quickly unpacked his meals and said good-bye, accepting an old Roses tin full of stodgy homemade flap-jacks as his apology for not being able to chat longer. It's so sweet when my customers make me something, which many of them do. And I'll always eat it, even if it means I sub-sequently keep Gaviscon in business for the next few days. Placing the tin carefully on the passenger seat of the van, I set off again.

Mrs Wilson was next. A formidable former headmistress whose husband Eric was apparently so terrified of being in the same room as her that he almost always hid in his shed. Today, he appeared just long enough to pass a lightning-fast comment about the pleasant weather before scurrying back to the safety of the blue larch-lap hut at the bottom of the garden.

'Always under my feet,' Mrs Wilson tutted, at which I had to pretend to cough so that she wouldn't see my smile. 'Now, how's your love life, young lady?'

Being quizzed by Mrs Wilson was a little like facing an Eastex-suited firing squad, so I felt compelled to answer. 'Still quiet, I'm afraid.'

'I have somebody in mind for you,' she barked, and the appearance of what I have learned is her version of a smile flashed across her face. 'My daughter's boy. Lawyer. Sen-sible. Probably good-looking. Thoughts?'

'I'll certainly bear him in mind,' I replied, not wanting to hurt her feelings but terrified by the thought of Mrs Wilson as a grandmother-in-law. 'But I'm not sure I'm ready yet.'

'Nonsense!' She stirred her tea with military precision. 'There's no such thing as being ready when it comes to court-ship. When Eric told me we were getting married I wept myself to sleep for weeks. But he was right. And here we are.'

Eric Wilson *told* his wife they were getting married? Today was certainly the day for revelations. The thought of the timid, pale-faced old man doing his best Rhett Butler impres-sion amused me all the way to the next address on my list.

The address belonged to a Mr Timothy Gardner – a name I wasn't familiar with. Smiling to myself as I parked beside a small, whitewashed fisherman's cottage at the head of a tiny fishing village, I set the stopwatch on my mobile phone.

Seven-point-five minutes with the new customer. We'll see about that, Trev.

I knocked several times before the door opened, revealing a tall, slender-limbed man with stunning blue eyes and a dra-matic sweep of white hair forming an impressive quiff. He was dressed in a faded granddad shirt over corduroy trousers with bare feet, and immediately stood out from my other cus-tomers because I found it impossible to guess his age.

'Good afternoon,' I said. 'I'm Emily from Sunnyside Meals on Wheels?'

He pushed his reading glasses up onto the top of his head and jutted out his hand in a hurried handshake.

'Lovely to meet you,' he said, a blush creeping across his tanned face. 'I must confess this is the first time I've done this. Since my hip trouble I've been finding it difficult to get out. Can't drive, you see. Doctor's orders. I've only just moved back to the area after living in the States for thirty years, so I'm still finding my feet in the village. And those online delivery things scare me to death…Oh.' His eyes fell on the heavy box in my hands as I waited politely on the doorstep and he quickly invited me inside. 'I'm dreadfully sorry, do come in.'

His walk was stilted and painful, leaning heavily on a polished mahogany walking cane in his left hand as he made slow progress towards the kitchen at the rear of the cottage. I followed at a respectful distance, not wanting to pressure him or draw attention to his snail-like pace.

The kitchen was bright and airy: teal painted bespoke units, a Belfast sink and a large Aga-style stove nestled around a central island illuminated by halogen spotlights embedded into the low ceiling. I could imagine Hugh Fearnley-Whittingstall cooking with uncontrolled glee in a room like this and Mr Gardner appeared quite at home in it. He opened a large cupboard door, which concealed a full-height fridge.

'If you could pop the meals in here, that would be wonderful.'

'No problem.' I opened the box and began to stock his fridge with Sunnyside's finest meal selection, noticing that he had opted for the 'deluxe' menu. Not many of our customers could afford this top-of-the-range option. In fact, only Mrs Clements had ever ordered it before, and that was after she won a couple of hundred pounds from a bet on the Grand National last year. No wonder Mum and Trev were keen for me to impress our new customer.

Closing the fridge door, I turned back to Mr Gardner and smiled. 'You're all stocked for the week, Mr Gardner.'

'Tim, please. Mr Gardner makes me sound like my father and he's been dead over twenty years. Look, I don't suppose you have time for a cuppa? I've not long boiled the kettle and it'd be lovely to share it with someone.'

I thought about the stopwatch on my mobile monitoring the precious Sunnyside seconds being wasted in the name of good manners. *Sod it.* Mum and Trev weren't to know whether I was delayed by illegal conversations or backed-up traffic caused by a farm tractor.

'That sounds wonderful.'

He appeared both genuinely shocked and delighted at once. 'Great. That's great!'

We sat on stools at the wide kitchen island and I thanked him as he passed me tea in an Emma Bridgewater mug. 'How long have you been in St Merryn?' I asked.

'Four months. My son brokered the deal for me while I was still in California selling my house and wrapping up the business. I sold it for a song,' he grinned and I found myself grinning back.

My mobile phone began to ring and I glanced at the screen: Trevor Mitchell calling.

Honestly, the nerve of the man! Barely six months with my mum and suddenly he was muscling in on her business. Well, until the odious busybody was paying my wages, he could stick his opinions right up his...

'So what made you decide to return?' I asked Tim, even more determined now to smash boring Trev's seven-point-five minute target.

'Nostalgia, I suppose. I'm a Cornishman: it was inevitable Kernow would call me back eventually. And I wanted to be close to Ethan, my son. I've always loved St Merryn and thanks to the success of my business sale I can finally afford to live here.'

My phone buzzed angrily: New message from Trevor Mitchell.

I ignored it. 'Well, you have a lovely home.' Remembering my job, I added, 'Let me know if there are any changes you'd like to make for next week's menu. Here's my number.'

He accepted my business card. 'Thank you. Hey, I don't suppose you know anywhere that does old-time ballroom dancing around here, do you? Call it nostalgia but I was remembering my misspent youth today and suddenly had a hankering for a dance. I know The Rialto Ballroom in Truro closed years ago.'

I stared at him, amused. 'It's funny you should mention that. One of my other clients showed me a photo of The Rialto this morning.'

'Well I never. Do you know when it was taken?'

I thought back to my conversation with Mrs C. '1951. July, I think.'

His smile vanished. 'Really? How – *strange*…' He was quiet for a moment. 'Look, I don't know if this breaks any confidentiality rules but is there any way your customer would lend it to me? Just to have a look?'

I hesitated. 'I'm not really sure…' It was Mrs C's personal memory she had shared with me and I didn't think I could promise something that wasn't mine to offer.

'I'd be really interested to see it again. The time it was taken – Well, it's uncanny. There's a reason I loved that place: a very good reason…'

He looked so sad all of a sudden that I felt I had to say something as I rose to leave. 'Look, I can't promise anything. But I'll ask.'

'That would be wonderful, thank you!'

I thought about the odd coincidence all the way back to Sunnyside HQ. My job has always surprised me but this was something new. Mr Gardner had appeared so startled when I mentioned the date of the photo and that made me wonder if perhaps he had been there at the same time as Mrs C. Would he have seen her there? Or been one of the many young men she had enjoyed dancing with before Canada called her away?

Boring Trev and Mum were waiting with uniform disgust for me as I walked back into the unit. It irked me that Trev was even here, but more that Mum allowed his interference.

'Mum, Trevor, how lovely to see you!' I chirped, enjoying the flush of fury this invoked in my not-so-welcoming committee.

'Cut the attitude,' Trev snapped, making even Mum stare at him in surprise. 'You *had* your orders for the new client and you *deliberately* disobeyed them.'

'*Excuse me?*' Even for Mum's horrible boyfriend, this was a step too far. Angrily, I whipped the now crumpled sheet of paper out from my back pocket and brandished it. 'You mean this? I think you'll find, Trevor, that this is a *suggestion*, not an order. It's a suggestion because you don't actually work here or employ me, therefore I'm not obliged to obey it whatsoever.' I turned to Mum. 'And I would have hoped, Mum, that you would have just a little more faith in your daughter. For your information, I was *investing* time in our new client in order to ensure he received the best service from Sunnyside and kept ordering from us. I happen to think that's more important than impressing your boyfriend.'

Mum looked from me to her fuming other half and back. 'Well, I…I think it's good to protect our client list…but really the time on your round is quite a bit longer than the other drivers…not that I think you're doing a bad job, obviously.'

'Thank you.' Ignoring the daggers of death Trev was now willing at me with his stare, I calmly handed my clipboard to Mum and walked into the staffroom to collect my things.

* * *

The more I considered Mr Gardner's request that weekend, the more intrigued I became: so much so that by Monday morning I could bear it no longer and took a detour at the end of my round to visit Mrs C.

'Emily! What a lovely surprise. Come in, dear.'

When we were sitting with china mugs of tea and large slices of homemade ginger cake, I broached the subject of the photograph.

'I have a favour to ask,' I began, studying her expression carefully. 'Last Friday, I went to see a new client who has recently returned to the area and he mentioned The Rialto Ballroom.'

'Really? How funny.'

'I know. I said as much to him and then I happened to mention that I'd been shown a photo of it that morning. With hindsight, I realise I shouldn't have said anything, but it took me by surprise and I mentioned the photograph before I thought better of it. The thing is he reacted very oddly when I told him the date the photo was taken. I think he might have been there the same time as you. And I know I probably shouldn't ask, but I wondered if I might borrow the photo, just to show it to him?'

Mrs C observed me quietly and stirred her tea.

Instantly, I regretted asking. 'Obviously if you say no I'll completely understand,' I added.

'How old is this gentleman?' she asked, her expression giving nothing away.

'To be quite honest, I don't know. It's difficult to tell.'

'Hmm.' I watched the silver spoon make several more rotations. 'The photograph is very precious to me, Emily. When I was in Canada it was the one thing that reminded me of home, of who I really was. Of the life that might be waiting…' Her eyes were very still, focused a thousand miles away. 'You have to understand that when I went to Canada I had to become somebody different: someone's mother, someone's wife. And for many years, I felt like my life wasn't my own. Remembering who I'd been in England gave me strength enough to return years later. The photograph was a big part of that.'

Her candidness hit me like a fist to the stomach. I knew she hadn't had an easy life in Canada but I'd never appreciated how much of herself she'd been asked to give. 'I'm sorry, I shouldn't have asked. Forget I did, OK?'

She shook her head. 'No, it's lovely that you asked. I know how precious my memories are: if this gentleman wants to see the photograph to bring back his, I see no reason why he shouldn't.' She reached for the photograph album by the side of her armchair, turned its pages and gently removed the picture. 'There. Take good care of it.'

My hands were shaking as I accepted. 'Thank you, Mrs C. I promise I will.'

I called Mr Gardner as soon as I returned to my van, but there was no reply. Disappointed, I placed the photograph carefully in my work diary and drove back.

* * *

For the next three days, none my attempts to reach Mr Gardner were successful. By Friday, my anticipation was at bursting point and my delivery round seemed to take an age before I was finally driving down the steep streets of St Merryn.

Waiting on the doorstep of his cottage, my heart was thudding against the cardboard box I held. I wanted to see his face when I produced the photograph, excited to see him reunited with a piece of his past.

The door opened and a young man appeared, taking me completely by surprise. It was as if I was meeting Mr Gardner over fifty years ago: his eyes were the same sapphire blue, his frame as tall and his hair as thick, albeit a dark mass of black-brown rather than silver.

'Hi,' he smiled, and my world seemed to spin momentarily. 'You must be the famous Emily. Come in.'

As I shakily entered the hallway, he shouted over his shoulder. 'Dad! Delivery!'

Tim appeared at the far end of the hall. 'Ah, Emily! I see you've met Ethan. You see, son? I told you she was beautiful.'

Flushed, I hurried past him and began to unpack the meals.

'I'm sorry I missed your calls,' Tim said, as Ethan joined us.

'That's OK. I have a surprise for you.' I closed the fridge

door, opened my work diary and handed him Mrs C's photograph.

For a moment, Tim appeared to wobble and Ethan rushed forward to steady his father. Sitting on a kitchen stool, he stared at the photo.

'Dad?'

'I'm fine, son. This just takes me back…' He looked at me. 'Can I ask the name of the person who gave this to you?'

'I'm not sure I should say.'

He nodded. 'Of course. But it looks so familiar. If I didn't know better I'd swear…' Slowly, he turned the picture over and closed his eyes. '*T.W.M.A.*'

Ethan and I watched helplessly as Tim's loud sobs filled the kitchen.

* * *

'What if she says no?'

'Dad, you can't think of that. You said it yourself, you had a connection once.'

'I don't know. What did you tell her, Emily?'

I smiled at Tim. 'I said I had a surprise for her and that I was taking her out for afternoon tea.'

Tim Gardner's face was pale as he hovered in the lobby of the hotel, wringing his hands. 'I didn't think she would come. What do I say to her after all these years?'

'You start with, "Here's the photograph that I gave you."' Ethan grinned at me and I found myself grinning back. Like father, like son…

'When I handed Genevieve that picture my heart was

breaking,' Tim said, gazing through the glass door that separated him from the girl who walked out of his life sixty-two years ago. 'She was leaving for Canada the next day. I penciled "T.W.M.A" on the back to remind her I was waiting: Till We Meet Again. I told her to keep it as a reminder of the woman I knew she was.'

I put my hand on his shoulder. 'She said it was what kept her strong during all those years in Canada. And what made her come home. I think you might have been an important part of that. Why don't you just go in there, say hello and see what happens?'

His blue eyes glistened as he looked at me. 'Thank you. For finding the love of my life again.' Shaking hands with Ethan, he turned, took a deep breath, and walked into the hotel restaurant.

And that's when I knew: I knew my job was more than time slots and ready meals, more than delivery rounds and menu plans. It was a gift, in the truest sense of the word.

Would Mrs Clements and Mr Gardner rekindle their romance after most of their adult lives spent apart? I couldn't say for sure. But learning that Genevieve Clements had made the ultimate sacrifice – to leave her sweetheart behind – to do what she thought was right for her family, made me wonder if maybe she had waited all her life to put right the decision she had regretted most.

'I think they'll be OK.'

I looked up to see Ethan Gardner smiling at me. 'I hope so. She might never forgive me for setting her up.'

'Maybe. But you made Dad smile and I haven't seen him look that happy for years. I'd take that as a good sign. So, do we wait?'

'I suppose so.' I peered through the glass door but couldn't see their table.

'Well, I think I should get a coffee while I'm waiting.' He held out his hand, his blue eyes – so like his father's – intent on mine. 'Shall we?'

Heart racing, I reached out and felt his warm fingers close around mine. And as we walked through the doors, I smiled to myself.

I *love* my job.

Catherine King

Catherine King was born in Rotherham, South Yorkshire. A search for her roots – her father, grandfather and great-grandfather all worked with coal, steel or iron – and an interest in local industrial history provide inspiration for her stories.

&

Clarion Call

The Yorkshire Dales, Spring, 1905

Bright sun streamed into the warm kitchen and Meg felt her excitement bubbling. She hoped Jacob would be at the Mission today and she looked forward to spending time on her appearance before she went out. She could hardly wait to see him again.

'My, that was a grand dinner, Meg.' Her father scraped back his chair and stretched out his legs.

'Thank you, Father.' Roast beef and Yorkshire pudding with fresh greens from the garden was his favourite Sunday dinner and she hoped it had put him in a good mood. He wouldn't be happy when she told him she was going out. She stood up and said, 'I'll get on with the washing-up now. Would you like a cup of tea?'

'We'll have it later, love. My roly-poly pudding hasn't gone down yet.'

That meant tea in the middle of the afternoon and Meg wanted to be at the Mission Hall by half past three.

Meg loved her father. He was a good parent to all of his six children, even though they were scattered across the county. As youngsters, they never went short of shoes or night school fees for the boys, and he still worked hard at the quarry all week. But she was the youngest and the others had grown up and gone.

Meg had helped her mother cook Sunday dinner for years and had run the household since Mother had been taken from them two years ago. It had been just before Meg's eighteenth birthday; her elder sister had married and only two of her brothers had been living at home then. Now the boys were young men and had good jobs and lodgings in Bradford and Sheffield. So there was only Meg left to look after Father.

He was wedded to his routine. Meg thought she had done the right thing by keeping it going when Mother died. But recently she had noticed that he was becoming more set in his ways and dependent on her. She didn't want to grow old as a spinster looking after her aging father. She was already twenty and her friends were beginning to marry.

Meg cleared the table and washed up in the scullery while father enjoyed a pipe of tobacco in his easy chair by the kitchen fire. The casement clock in the hall chimed. She dried her hands and said, 'Well, that's all done for today. I said I'd meet Sally to help out at the Mission Hall this afternoon.'

'Don't you want to give me a hand in the garden?' Father sounded hurt. 'Your mother used like sowing seeds on a sunny day.'

I'm not Mother, Meg answered silently. She felt disloyal. Her mother and father had been close and had brought up their six children to support each other. She had loved Mother as much as he had. A tear threatened and she pulled herself together. *Why don't I tell him about Jacob?* she thought. *Because there's nothing to say yet, and there never will be if I can't get out and meet him on a Sunday.*

'Isn't Sally stepping out with a young man?' Father queried.

'She is. Robert's a clerk in an office now.'

Father nodded with approval. 'She's done well for herself.'

Meg cheered up at this comment. At least Father would approve of Jacob. He'd been at the grammar school with Robert and he worked in a lawyer's office in Leeds. But he came out to the Dales every Sunday on the railway train even when it rained.

'They won't want you tagging along, will they?' Father added.

'Robert will be cycling with the Clarion Club until teatime.' *So will Jacob*, she thought, and dreamed for a moment about seeing his tanned smiling face and bright blue eyes when he returned.

'There'll be a Clarion Club in every town soon,' Father commented.

'Well, so many folk have bicycles nowadays. Sally and I have been asked to help with teas at the Mission Hall. They're busy on a Sunday with all the cyclists as well as the ramblers.'

'Haven't you enough to do here, after a week at the mill?'

More than enough, Meg thought. She never grumbled, as a rule. She had gone to work in the mill as soon as she left school. The hours were long but the money was good and sometimes she and Sally got best quality cloth cheaper than from the market because the loom had produced a flaw in the bolt and it couldn't be sold to a warehouse. She made most of her own clothes and looked forward to wearing her new blouse this afternoon.

'We are raising money for the chapel roof,' she explained.

He couldn't argue with that, she thought, but he sounded disgruntled. 'I see. What time will you be back?'

Meg's heart sank. She decided to stand her ground. Father would have to get his own tea today. 'I don't know. We might go for a walk by the river afterwards.' *With Robert and Jacob*, she added silently.

Father made a grunting noise in his throat and Meg hoped he wasn't going to be difficult. She stifled her mounting impatience and went on, 'I've made your favourite lemon curd tarts. I'll leave them on the kitchen table under a tea cloth. There's a full kettle on the range and I've put the tea in the pot ready for you.'

'You've made up your mind then.'

'Don't be like that, Father. I don't go out in the week. By the time I've walked home from the mill, cooked a meal and tidied round, it's too late to do anything.' *Not that there was anywhere to go in their small market town*, Meg thought. Her life revolved around working at the mill and looking after Father.

Nonetheless, she felt guilty. Father was lonely without Mother and he suffered more on a Sunday because it had been their family day together for over thirty years. He saw no reason to change the habit of a lifetime, and neither had Meg until Jacob came along.

'It'll be Sunday afternoon on my own again,' he muttered.

Meg didn't know what to say to cheer him. She stood up before she weakened. 'I'll just go and get changed then and I'll be off.'

She put on her Sunday best skirt in a lovely maroon grosgrain and shoes with heels, then piled her long fair hair up under a jaunty little hat adorned with a maroon ribbon, sticking it firmly in place with a couple of her mother's hatpins. She had wanted to look like a Gibson Girl since she had seen a sketch and article in a journal. It was a popular fashion with all the young women at the mill. Meg had spent her evenings making an intricate white blouse with a high neck, a pleated tailored bodice and full sleeves with deep fitted cuffs. Satisfied with her appearance she went down to the kitchen, picked up a tin box tied with string and called, 'Cheerio,' to her father in the back garden.

Sally was waiting for her outside the Mission Hall. Until this year, Meg had not been to the Mission since before she started work. When she was little, her elder sister used to take her and her brothers every Sunday afternoon for an hour's Sunday school. Now, her sister was married with three children of her own and lived miles away in York. Two brothers had also married and settled away from home where they had found employment. There was only the quarry here for men and Father had been firm that none of his sons would be quarrymen like he was. Father believed in education and was proud of his boys working in offices for town corporations or railway companies.

Sally wore a Gibson Girl blouse too, but her skirt was dark blue. 'The Hall isn't open yet. What's in the tin?' she asked.

'I made a few tarts for Robert and – and Jacob, if he's here.' He'd said he would be but, even so, Meg was nervous; or was it excitement that churned her stomach?

'Oh he will be. Robert says he's quite taken by you.'

'Really?' Meg felt a thrill of anticipation run down her back. Jacob belonged to a different Clarion Club from Robert, but this little market town in the heart of the Yorkshire Dales was popular with cyclists escaping grimy cities for fresh air.

In summer, the early train from Leeds was packed and the guard's van full of bicycles.

'I saw a notice in the post office about setting up a Clarion Club for girls,' Meg commented. 'Are you interested?'

'I was going to tell you later. I'll be moving to Leeds. Robert's landed a job with the Corporation and found us a house to rent so we're definitely getting married this summer.'

'Oh, how exciting! You are lucky.' Meg was really pleased for Sally and Robert, but she would miss her friend at the mill. First her family and now her friends were moving away.

'You should join, though,' Sally suggested.

'I haven't got a bicycle.'

'I'm sure you can find one rusting away in somebody's wash house.'

Meg warmed to the idea. 'And I can easily run up a divided skirt with that wool worsted from the mill.'

'Like Mrs Dawson,' Sally giggled, 'pedalling along the High Street.'

'Sssh, she'll be here in a minute.' Meg looked around for the lady in charge of teas at the Mission Hall on Sundays and commented, 'She's late with the key this week.'

Sally wandered away scanning the fells basking in hazy sunshine for a sign of the cyclists on their way back. Meg lapsed into thought and wondered what her father would think. Lady cyclists were considered, at best, to have independent ideas or at worst, be radicals or suffragists. But a bicycle would be really useful to her. She could get home from the mill quickly and be able to carry home end-of-the-day bargains from the market. She wondered how much she would have to pay for one. She caught up with Sally and said, 'I think I might see if I can find a second-hand bicycle. Will you ask around for me?'

'Robert might know somebody'

'Where have they gone today?'

'Swallowdale.'

'Oh, not too far, then. Here's Mrs Dawson at last. She's pushing her bicycle; she must have a flat tyre.'

A group of Mrs Dawson's Mission ladies had gathered and waited patiently while she wheeled her bicycle round the back, unlocked the back door to stow it safely in the scullery and returned to open the front entrance. Mrs Dawson was limping, Meg realised, as she followed the last of the ladies into the Hall and placed her tin box on the floor by the small stage. She and Sally set to work arranging trestle tables and wooden benches in long rows ready for the ramblers and cyclists. It was hard work so the older ladies were glad of their help. Besides, Mrs Dawson wouldn't let them near the food and drink. Meg heard her giving orders to her helpers. One of the older ladies came over with cleaning cloths to wipe down the tables.

'It's not like Mrs Dawson to be late,' Meg commented.

'She's got a bad knee,' the lady said. 'She had to push her bicycle all the way here. The doctor says she got to ease up a bit.'

'Do you mean she will give up her Mission work?' Meg thought that Mrs Dawson was a permanent fixture on the ladies committee.

'It's time somebody else had a chance to run things.' The lady's tone was critical. 'We felt sorry for her. She came back home as a widow to look after her ailing sister. When the sister passed away she had empty days to fill so we invited her on to the committee and now she's taken over. We were glad to have her at first but you can have too much of a good thing.'

'I suppose she's lonely,' Meg said. 'Where are her children?'

'They all emigrated when they married, so she doesn't get to see them.'

'Oh, that's a shame.'

Mrs Dawson had taken up her position at a small table by the door to take the money when walkers and cyclists clattered in, hungry and thirsty from their outing. Her selected servers stood behind a wooden counter making up the enamel plates of potted meat sandwiches, buttered scone and fairy cake or jam tart, baked by Mrs Dawson and a select few.

When the Hall was ready, Sally went outside to look for Robert. Meg followed her to the door and asked, 'What shall I do next, Mrs Dawson?'

'Go and help with the copper in the back. If the water's ready you can fill the teapots.' She stared at her for a moment before adding, 'You don't want to be spoiling that nice blouse. You'll find a clean pinny in my bicycle basket.'

'Thank you, Mrs Dawson.'

The big enamelled teapots were so heavy when full of water that they had extra handles above the spout for lifting. Meg put wood on the fire underneath the copper and added more water from the pump at the sink. Then she took off her apron and went to stand with the other ladies behind the counter in the Hall.

She scanned the benches for Jacob. Sure enough, he was

sitting with Robert, enjoying his tea. He noticed her and waved. Meg's heart somersaulted and she waved back.

Sally sidled up beside her and murmured, 'He's here, then.' Meg felt a tingle of pleasure run down her spine. She remembered their first meeting outside this very hall.

Robert had introduced him to his fiancée and her friend, and Meg was immediately attracted to Jacob. They had chatted about the villages he'd cycled through and he had told her about his position in an office. Jacob was handsome and sociable with dark hair and bright blue eyes that crinkled at the corners when he smiled. He had told her about his position in an office but that was all she knew about him, except that she'd taken an instant liking to him. He'd said how much he loved the Dales and they had discussed whether the railway was a good thing or not for the villages.

Mrs Dawson distracted Meg from her dreaming as she arrived at the counter with her cash box ready to take money from those who were hungry enough for a second round of tea.

Jacob rose to his feet and came over. He handed payment for two more teas to Mrs Dawson and scanned the remaining plates. 'Any more with lemon curd tarts?' he asked.

'Lemon curd tarts?' Mrs Dawson queried. She appeared to be offended. 'I didn't ask for lemon curd tarts. We don't do them as a rule.'

'Oh!' Meg exclaimed. 'I left them in a tin…' She looked around quickly for her tin which she spied under the counter, opened and empty. 'Oh,' she repeated, 'they were mine, Mrs Dawson. I made them for my father's tea and – and – I brought some with me.' She looked at Sally who had put her hand over her mouth to stifle her giggles.

Jacob smiled at the row of ladies in front of him and went on, 'They were very good. We both said so. May we have them again next week?'

'We'll see,' Mrs Dawson replied, handing him two plates with sandwiches, scones and jam tarts.

'I'll bring your mugs of tea over,' Sally volunteered, and went to talk to Robert.

'The lemon curd tarts did look very nice,' one of the Mission ladies commented.

'I made the lemon curd myself,' Meg added.

'I suppose you want paying for them?' Mrs Dawson answered.

'Well no, not really, they were for…' She stopped.

'You have to be paid for the ingredients now they've been sold,' Mrs Dawson stated. 'How many did you bring?'

'A dozen.' Jacob was in lodgings and she thought he might take them on the train back to Leeds.

Mrs Dawson opened her cash box and began to count out coppers.

'No, honestly, Mrs Dawson, I don't want paying for them.'

'The Mission always pays its way.'

'Well – Er, well,' Meg's mind was racing. 'Well, actually you could do me a favour instead.'

'What kind of favour?' Mrs Dawson sounded defensive.

Meg looked at her expectant face. 'I'm looking for a second-hand bicycle. Do you know anybody with one for sale?'

'For you?' Mrs Dawson asked.

'Yes, we're having a girls cycling club here.'

'Indeed?' Mrs Dawson appeared to approve. 'I'm thinking of selling mine. The doctor says I have to get rid of it.'

'Can I have a look at it, Mrs Dawson?'

'It's worth more than a dozen lemon curd tarts, my girl.'

'Oh yes, of course. I didn't mean – ' Meg began.

'You'll have to wait until I've had my committee meeting after we've done. Go for a walk or something.'

Oh, dear, she would be late home and Father would be wondering where she was. But she wanted a bicycle. 'All right, Mrs Dawson,' she replied and went over to join her friends.

* * *

Later, Jacob suggested that he and Meg take a different path from Sally and Robert. He leaned his bicycle against a stone wall and turned his face to the sun. 'You're lucky to live in these parts.'

'There's not much work though,' Meg commented.

'I know, but I wish I still lived here.'

'Where are you from, then?'

'My father's a gamekeeper up on Ferndale Moor. I used to help him in my school holidays.'

'Ferndale's a long way from the grammar school.'

He smiled at her – she adored his smile – and continued, 'I had lodgings in the week. I'd won a scholarship, you see.'

'Good for you.' Meg had inherited her father's admiration for learning. 'They said that I could have gone on to the girl's high school if I wanted.'

'Didn't you want to?'

'I did actually,' she realised suddenly. She hadn't bothered too much at the time but now she experienced an unusual pang of disappointment. 'But I have four brothers and they came first.'

'That's a pity.'

Yes it was, she thought, and liked him for saying so. She said, 'But I wouldn't have met Sally in the mill,' and smiled.

'Or me,' he added seriously.

'I have to go back to the Hall before Mrs Dawson locks up. She might be selling her bicycle and I want one.'

'Is that so? Which model is it?'

'I don't know.'

'Well, how much does she want for it?'

'I don't know.'

'You'd better let me take a look at it for you.'

'Would you?'

'Of course I would. Although, I reckon Mrs Dawson will have bought the best, don't you?'

'Probably,' she agreed with a grin.

'Come on then, let's go back.' Jacob pushed his bicycle with one hand and offered Meg his free arm. She linked hers with his and it felt comfortable.

Meg stopped suddenly when they approached the Mission Hall as she recognised her father talking to a couple of the Mission ladies' husbands. They were waiting for the committee meeting to finish.

'Oh dear,' Meg muttered with a sinking heart. Surely her father could have spent his Sunday afternoon without her? She hoped he wasn't going to make a fuss just as she and Jacob were getting on so well. 'My father's here,' she said.

'Really? Where?'

'Over there with the others.' Reluctantly she unhooked her arm from Jacob's and said, 'Wait here.'

'Why? I'd like to meet him.'

'He doesn't he know about you yet.'

'Don't you think he should, then?'

Jacob looked hurt so she rushed on. 'He's – he depends on me so much since Mother died. He doesn't like me going out on a Sunday and I – I don't want him any more upset.' Neither did she want her father to blame Jacob for keeping her out. It was very important to her that Father liked him. 'I'll see what he wants,' she said, and quickened her step.

Thankfully, Jacob didn't follow her. It wasn't that she didn't want Father to meet him. It's just that she didn't want Father to think she was deserting him. Well, not yet anyway. But there was no sense in avoiding it now, because everyone at the Mission Hall had seen her with Jacob so she ought to tell Father about him before anybody else did.

'Hello, Father.'

Her father turned round and his face brightened immediately. 'Hello, love.'

'Is everything all right?'

'The house is empty without you. I wondered where you were.'

Meg suppressed a sigh and raised a smile. 'I'm on my way home now. I was just waiting to have a word with Mrs Dawson. She's the lady in charge.' Meg looked around for her and saw Jacob approaching slowly. He stopped a few yards away, caught her eye and began to examine his bicycle chain.

One or two ladies wandered out of the Hall, called, 'Cheerio,' and left. The next one headed straight for her husband and said, 'Mrs Dawson's giving up the chair at last.' They linked arms and walked off with their heads together.

'Where is this Mrs Dawson, then?' Father asked.

'She'll be locking up. She wants to sell her bicycle and I was thinking of buying it for going to the mill.'

'You want a bicycle now? You're full of ideas you are, just like your mother.'

'Here she is.' Mrs Dawson came round the corner with her bicycle.

Father frowned in the sunlight. 'Who did you say she was?'

'Mrs Dawson.'

'I know that face.' Father gazed at Mrs Dawson. 'Don't I know you?'

Mrs Dawson stared back. 'Albert Parker?'

'Edith Braithwaite?'

'Edith Dawson now. Well I never. Albert Parker.'

'I thought you lived in Leeds.'

'I did. I came home after my husband passed on.'

'I'm sorry to hear that.' Father looked flustered and went on quickly, 'I mean I'm sorry about your husband, not about you coming back.' After an awkward pause he added, 'I know how it is. I lost my wife a year ago.'

'It's two years now, Father,' Meg added.

'Is it, love?' He seemed surprised.

'Is this your daughter?' Mrs Dawson asked.

'She's my youngest.'

'Well I never,' Mrs Dawson said again. 'Mine are all married. Are you still at the quarry?'

'I'm foreman now,' he answered proudly.

Mrs Dawson looked impressed and her father smiled. Meg hadn't seen that smile in a long time and her tears threatened again.

She heard Jacob cough behind her. 'Is this the bicycle?' he asked, stepping forward.

Meg took a deep breath. 'Father,' she began, 'Father, this is Jacob. He's with the Clarion Club from Leeds.'

Father looked at him thoughtfully. 'Yes, I thought there was a lad involved somewhere.'

Jacob held out his right hand. 'Jacob Wright, sir, how do you do?'

Meg's father took it in a firm grip. 'I'm pleased to meet you, Jacob. From Leeds, you say?'

'Ferndale Moor, actually. My father is a gamekeeper up there.'

'Ferndale? I know the mason at Ferndale Lodge. He comes to the quarry for his stone.' He glanced at Jacob's bicycle. 'That's a fine machine you have there, young man.'

Now it was Jacob's turn to look proud. 'Thank you, sir. Do you cycle yourself?'

'Not these days.'

'Meg is thinking of buying Mrs Dawson's bicycle. I said I'd take a look at it for her.'

But Meg had been watching Mrs Dawson and her father's cheerful reaction, and she had a much better plan in her head. 'Oh you don't really have time now, Jacob. You mustn't miss your train.'

'It's not until – ' Jacob started to protest. Meg shook her head slightly and he stopped.

'Father, I'm going to walk to the railway station with Jacob. You know all about bicycles, so why don't you have a look at Mrs Dawson's for me?'

'Mrs Dawson doesn't have time to stand about waiting for you – ' her father began.

'Yes, I do,' Mrs Dawson said. 'It's a lovely afternoon, Albert – I can call you Albert, can't I? Let's go and sit on the wall.'

'All right then, Edith.'

Chrissie Manby

Chrissie Manby is the author of sixteen romantic comedies including *Getting Personal*, *The Matchbreaker* and *Seven Sunny Days*. She has had several *Sunday Times* bestsellers and her recent novel about behaving badly after a break-up, *Getting Over Mr Right*, was nominated for the 2011 Melissa Nathan Award.

Chrissie was raised in Gloucester, in the west of England, and now lives in London. Contrary to the popular conception of chick-lit writers, she is such a bad baker that her own father threatened to put her last creation on www.cakewrecks.com. She is, however, partial to white wine and shoes she can't walk in.

Chrissie's new novel *A Proper Family Holiday* will be published by Hodder in summer 2014.

&

Puppy Love

Fiona Griffiths was not having a good day. Of the team of four people she managed at the Candlewick Café on Cathedral Green, only one had turned up for the busy Bank Holiday Monday. The others had claimed various chronic ailments but would all be spotted later that evening at the free concert in the town park.

So Fiona had slaved over a sandwich toaster all day long with only cross-eyed Sarah to assist her. Actually, 'assist' was not the word for it. Sarah spent most of her shift standing in front of the open fridge door, complaining of a debilitating flush. She couldn't go out into the café dining room, not looking as red as she did, she said. In the end, Fiona sent Sarah home early and thus had to shut the café early too.

If she hadn't had to close early, none of this might have happened. But shutting the café had meant that Fiona was home a good hour before she was expected. It meant that she was putting her key in the door just as her best friend Lucy was reaching new heights of passion. With Fiona's live-in boyfriend.

'Oh, er, Fiona,' said Lucy, when they met at the top of the stairs. 'Greg was just showing me…'

Fiona knew exactly what Greg had been showing her.

'Really quite small, isn't it?' said Fiona.

Lucy left in a hurry. Greg stayed to make his excuses, but, really, there were none that Fiona wanted to hear. There were certainly none she believed.

'I'll move out at the weekend,' Greg muttered.

'Yes,' said Fiona. 'I think that's for the best.'

* * *

All four members of Fiona's team were back at work the next day. Fiona was so miserable she completely forgot to tell the 'festival three' they were sacked. And, in a way, she was glad that she didn't because, perhaps driven by the guilt of having skived the previous day, they were all extremely kind to her. Having heard about Greg's infidelity, they would not let Fiona out into the dining room, insisting instead that she sit in the tiny office where she usually did the paperwork. They kept her supplied with tea, cake and sandwiches all day long. If only she'd felt like eating.

There was only one customer that Fiona left the office for that afternoon. Jackie Spring was the most regular of the café's regulars and she noticed at once that Fiona was not there to pass the time as she waited for her latte. Cross-eyed Sarah explained the situation in a theatrical whisper. Jackie told her to go and fetch Fiona out from her hiding place at once. Then Jackie ordered an extra latte – she knew Fiona had a soft spot for them too – a large slice of carrot cake and two forks. She insisted that Fiona take off her apron and join her at the dining room's quiet corner table. She made Fiona tell her everything. She even offered to put a jiffy bag of dog mess through Lucy's letterbox.

Jackie Spring had easy access to a ready supply of dog

mess. Jackie was well known about the town as the proprietor of the local dog shelter – Paws For Thought. Every Saturday afternoon, Jackie and a selection of her most photogenic puppies would position themselves outside the supermarket to raise funds to keep the shelter going. Jackie lived like a bag lady to ensure that no dog that ended up in her care was put down for lack of money. She may have eaten baked beans six days out of seven but the dogs at Paws For Thought ate like royal corgis. Lattes at the Candlewick Café were Jackie's only indulgence, though there had been a time when she couldn't even afford those and Fiona had secretly given Jackie freebies and dropped off unsold sandwiches on her way home every night.

So, Jackie was well loved and respected by the softhearted animal lovers of the town, of which Fiona was a fully paid-up member. Fiona loved dogs. She simply adored them, but she'd never been able to have one because Greg, who'd lived with her for the past eight years, was horribly allergic to dog fur.

'Good riddance,' said Jackie when she heard that Greg would be leaving that weekend. Jackie didn't trust anybody who could resist tickling the velvety nose of a puppy. Naturally, being allergic, Greg had always recoiled from Jackie's pups in disgust. But it was more than that. He had always recoiled from Jackie too. When Fiona raved about her friend and her devotion to dogs, Greg would respond, 'She's a witch. I tell you. The way she looks at me. The way she smells.'

It was true that Jackie did sometimes smell somewhat funky, but Fiona didn't think that was a reason to dislike her.

'It's joss sticks,' said Fiona. 'She burns a lot of joss sticks in her bungalow to cover the smell of the animals.'

'It's not joss sticks, it's her potions,' Greg insisted. 'She's a wicked old witch. Just look at the wart on her nose.'

Now, as she sat in the corner with Jackie, who was being so very kind to her, Fiona felt ashamed that she had not defended Jackie from Greg's insults rather more vociferously. She was certain that there was at least one occasion on which Jackie had overheard Greg being cruel about her looks and smell. At the same time, she sort of wished that Jackie were a witch. If she could just have Greg turned into a frog…

'It won't last,' said Jackie, when she heard that Greg and Lucy were an item. 'She'll only have wanted him in the first place because he was forbidden fruit. She's always been jealous of you, has your friend Lucy.'

'Really? I thought she was my best friend,' Fiona said. 'You know, I used to think it was a load of rubbish when I read about my sort of situation in magazines and the wronged woman always said she missed her friend more than her man. But it's true; I'm going to miss Lucy way more than I'll ever miss Greg.'

Jackie squeezed Fiona's hand. Both of them knew that Fiona was going to miss both Lucy and Greg like hell.

'Perhaps you should take one of my puppies for company,' said Jackie. 'While you get used to having an empty house. I've got a new lot in this week. Collie-Lurcher cross. Four months old, I reckon. A bit boisterous but ever so lovely with it. There's a female. She's got the kind of eyes that make you certain she's lived before. She knows things. She's a wise old soul. Morgana, I've called her, after Morgan Le Fay.'

Jackie was big on her Arthurian legends. She was big on

reincarnation too. She once told Fiona she'd had a past life as a nun, which was what had brought her back to work in a café opposite the cathedral. 'Your name began with a T,' Jackie added.

The thought of a celibate existence didn't especially resonate with Fiona but a couple of days after Jackie mentioned it, as she was shutting up shop for the evening, Fiona discovered a prayer card decorated with St Theresa in a nun's habit tucked under a sugar bowl and was more than a little freaked out.

'Coincidence. A customer left it,' said Greg. 'Your café is opposite a cathedral. It's going to attract religious types.'

But Fiona couldn't help paying closer notice to Jackie's pronouncements after that. The other girls in the café were all over Jackie when she was in one of her psychic phases. Jackie told Sarah that in her past life she had been killed by an arrow that went right between her eyes, hence her eyes now staring inwards. Sarah was slightly insulted until Jackie elaborated on the circumstances of the fatal arrow wound.

'You were a warrior princess, riding into battle in defence of your clan. You rode alongside the great kings of ancient Britain. Your name is inscribed on King Arthur's throne.'

'Oh,' said Sarah. She felt a lot better about being cross-eyed after that.

That afternoon, Fiona told Jackie that she felt stupid for having put up with Greg for so long.

'Not stupid,' Jackie insisted. 'Perhaps you had some karma to work through. Perhaps Greg was meant to teach you a lesson about not taking yourself and your own needs so lightly. Not giving your power away.'

So far, so Oprah.

'You do have the power, my love,' Jackie continued. 'You can have revenge if you want.'

'I don't want revenge,' said Fiona calmly. 'Revenge is for the weak.' She sipped her drink. 'No, hang on,' she began again. 'I do. I want my bloody revenge. I want Lucy to become repulsed by that arrogant little idiot. I want her to be unable to spend ten minutes in the same room as him without wanting to be sick. I want Greg to come crawling back to me on all fours. I want him to be devoted to me. I want him to follow me around, trying desperately to make me notice him…'

'You want him as your boyfriend again?' Jackie asked her.

'No,' said Fiona. 'I don't want him as my boyfriend. But I do want him to worship me. I want him to howl at the moon if he can't be by my side.' Fiona took a deep, stuttering breath. 'Oh, I only ever wanted him to be faithful.'

Jackie nodded. 'If you want faithful, my darling, get a dog. Will you take my puppy?'

'I can't,' said Fiona. 'The lease on my flat says "no pets". I didn't think it would matter while Greg was still in my life.'

'You're starting a different life now,' Jackie reminded her.

* * *

Fiona's new life got off to a slow start. It was almost a year later that she was able to get out of the lease on the flat that did not allow pets. During that year, Fiona did her best to alter the flat so that she was not reminded of Greg the moment she opened her eyes in the morning and saw the walls that he had painted and the pictures he had hung. Changing the decor of her flat was easy enough, but unfortunately, Lucy's flat was just two streets away and Fiona often saw them walk past her building, arm in arm, with no care for their broken-hearted former friend. Sometimes Greg even wore the fisher-man's jumper that Fiona had knitted for him their first winter as a couple. She remembered how happy she had been, as she thought about her handiwork keeping her lover warm in her absence. Seeing him wearing it, as Lucy snuggled against him, doubtless making the heavy wool smell of her chokingly strong perfume, Fiona only wanted to cry.

So Fiona was hugely relieved when she was able to move to the other side of the town, to a little terraced house where she would be able to keep pets if she wanted to. Fiona knew it was just a matter of time until she did.

On those days off which she would once have spent watching Greg play Grand Theft Auto on the Wii while tipping bar-becue flavour Pot Noodles straight into his mouth from the pot, Fiona now volunteered at Paws For Thought. Morgana and her siblings had quickly found new homes, but there were always new puppies coming in.

'It's just a matter of finding the perfect match,' said Jackie. 'I'll know it when the right dog comes in.'

Then something strange happened: Greg disappeared. Cross-eyed Sarah heard the gossip from her cousin who worked with Lucy at the council offices. Apparently she had come home one evening to find all his stuff gone. There was no trace of him. Not a single stray sock. He hadn't left a note and he wasn't answering his mobile. Lucy went to the police but they were of the opinion that there was nothing sinister afoot. He'd done a runner, hadn't he? Simple as. He'd got fed up of the relationship and didn't know how to tell her, so he cleared out his stuff while she was at work. At least two of the constables at the station had done the same. If he'd left his stuff, now that would be suspicious.

Fiona tried to feign disinterest but she was absolutely intrigued. Where had Greg gone?

'He'll turn up,' Jackie said, when Fiona told her. 'Blokes like that always do. Give it a couple of weeks and you'll hear from him, mark my words.'

Though she pretended she didn't care if she did, Fiona was secretly thrilled by the prospect. Would Greg come back to her? Exactly how long would that take?

'Though of course, I wouldn't want him if he did,' Fiona assured herself.

Fiona tried not to be disappointed when Greg didn't rush to rekindle their relationship after leaving Lucy so abruptly. Perhaps, she told herself, he thought he had no chance of getting back together with her. If only there were some way she could let him know that the door was still open. Perhaps if she told a few people…

'For heaven's sake,' said cross-eyed Sarah. 'What do you want him back for? He's a cheat and a liar. And he's been a cheat and a liar in all his past lives, I'm telling you.' Sarah had been taking lessons in past life divination from Jackie. 'He's going to keep on lying and cheating until he works his karma out. Forget about him. Get a puppy. Walking a dog is a great way to meet a new man.'

So everyone kept telling her.

Perhaps it was time. The following day, Fiona wasn't working in the café so she went to the dog shelter instead. It was a cold day. Jackie was in the kitchen of her bungalow. When Fiona saw her, Jackie appeared to be dandling a baby on her knee. As Fiona got closer, she realised that the bundle wrapped in the tatty old fisherman's jumper was a dog. Of course.

'Staffy Labrador cross, I reckon,' said Jackie. 'Three months old. Found on the council tip. He was all on his own, wrapped up in this jumper.'

As Fiona drew nearer the puppy scrabbled at its old jumper swaddling to get a sniff of her. Fiona let him lick her hand.

'He definitely likes you,' said Jackie.

'He's got a sweet face,' said Fiona.

'I think you may have found your dog. What are you going to call him?'

'True-Love,' said Fiona all of a sudden, without having the faintest idea why.

* * *

So True-Love became Fiona's puppy and he was certainly as devoted as his name implied. It was no trouble at all to train him. While she worked in the café, he sat quietly in the office. Well, most of the time he sat quietly. If True-Love felt that Fiona had left him for a little too long, he would start to howl, a heaving, mournful song that would silence the chatter in the café and make everyone think of the loves they had lost and friends they'd long forgotten.

It was about six months after True-Love came into Fiona's life that Lucy reappeared. She surprised Fiona as she was locking up one evening. Fiona almost jumped out of her skin. She was glad to have True-Love beside her until she realised she had been accosted by her former friend and not a mugger.

'I wanted to apologise,' Lucy began. 'And to tell you just

how much I've missed you. Greg was never worth losing you for.'

Fiona nodded. She knew from the gossip around town that Lucy had found Greg's departure hard. She certainly didn't look as cocky as she had done the last time Fiona saw her, snuggling into Greg's fisherman's jumper.

'I know what I did to you doesn't deserve your forgiveness but…'

Fiona remembered the old days when Lucy would sit at the kitchen table and bemoan her single status while Fiona lectured her on the way to find and keep a man. Had Fiona's smugness at being part of a couple contributed to Lucy's unsisterly decision to go after Greg?

'Come to my flat and we'll have a cup of tea and talk it over?' Fiona suggested.

Lucy looked incredibly happy at the idea. But once inside Fiona's flat the tears started, as Lucy apologised a thousand times and both girls admitted their friendship was the greater loss than Greg Whitehouse's disappearance. Once the apologies were over, however, Lucy kept right on crying.

'I can't seem to stop,' she said. 'I think I must be allergic to your dog.'

'To True-Love?'

At the sound of his name, True-Love raised his head from the fisherman's jumper that lined the inside of his basket. He wouldn't be parted from that jumper, though it was a filthy rag by now.

'I must be,' said Lucy. 'My nose is streaming. But I've never been allergic to animals before.'

Lucy and Fiona had called a truce but their friendship never really recovered. Especially when Lucy let slip to cross-eyed Sarah that she found True-Love rather repulsive: 'The way that he slobbers. Just…ugh.'

Not that Fiona had much time for her friends anyway. Jackie had been right about dogs helping bring people together. One sunny spring morning, Fiona was walking True-Love in the fields behind the estate where they lived. True-Love caught sight of a rabbit and made a run for it. Fiona called after him but it was in vain.

'True-Love. True-Love! Come back here.'

She had to walk home without him but later that day, a responsible citizen returned the dog, having read the address engraved on his collar tag.

'I don't know how I can thank you,' said Fiona.

'Well,' said the handsome stranger. 'You could start by letting me take you out for a drink.'

One thing led to another, of course.

* * *

Years later, when Fiona and the handsome stranger, whose names was James, were married and twins were on the way, Fiona took True-Love to stay with Jackie so that she and James could have one last weekend away alone.

Though Jackie had a magical way with most animals, Fiona couldn't help noticing that True-Love would tuck his tail between his legs as they turned into the driveway of Paws For Thought. Fiona put it down to bad memories of his puppy-hood and abandonment on the council tip.

Jackie opened the door.

'Hello, Fiona. Hello, True-Love.'

She enveloped Fiona in her arms for a hug: the scent of

Jackie's peculiar perfume would follow her about all day. She remembered Greg's cruel comments but had to admit there was something a bit witchy about Jackie's very individual scent.

True-Love looked up at Fiona, his eyes imploring her to take him on holiday too.

'Sorry, True-Love.' Fiona scratched the top of his head. 'This is the last chance James and I have for a holiday before the babies come.'

Fiona quickly headed back to her car. She didn't want a long goodbye.

Alone in the bungalow, Jackie arranged True-Love's scrappy old jumper on a cushion by the fire.

'We're going to have a lovely weekend, you and me,' she said. 'I've got in all your favourites: minced beef, roast chicken, barbecue flavour Pot Noodles...'

True-Love took up his spot by the fire and laid his head on his paws. Deep in his doggy brain, stirred some very peculiar memories. He used his claws to scrunch the fisherman's jumper into a more comfortable pile and remembered the day he first wore it.

Fanny Blake

Fanny Blake was a publisher for many years, editing both fiction and non-fiction before becoming a freelance journalist and writer. She has written various non-fiction titles, acted as a ghostwriter for a number of celebrities, and is also the books editor of *Woman & Home*. She has written three novels, *What Women Want* (Blue Door), *Women of a Dangerous Age* (Blue Door), and her latest *The Secrets Women Keep* (Orion) is out now.

You can visit www.fannyblake.com to find out more or contact her at http://www.facebook.com/FannyBlakeBooks or on Twitter @FannyBlake1.

&

Third Act

Inside, the old car was stifling. Beth lowered the window. In wafted exhaust fumes fused with the scent of hot metal and melting tarmac. She glared at the line of traffic stretching ahead of her and, in frustration, banged the steering wheel with her fist. Being stuck on the M11 had not been part of her planned journey to Norfolk. Especially not on the first decent day of the summer.

If only Gerry had taken dear old Betty, the battered people carrier in which she was sitting now, with him. In their other car, she would have sped out of London and missed the worst of the traffic heading north. But, of course, along with his half of their joint assets, he had taken the convertible, assuming its ownership even though he'd bought it with their money in the year before he'd left her.

She'd imagined them sharing their mid-life crises: speeding through Europe, her wearing a headscarf, Grace Kelly style, dark glasses, arm dangling in the rushing air. Him, bronzed and – well, not beautiful perhaps, but beside her. He had, it turned out, shared her dream but was busy fulfilling it with Tina from accounts.

The period of mourning her marriage was long over. Gerry had been gone for more than eighteen months and Beth was in control of her life again. She pressed the horn just to demonstrate the fact. Other drivers turned and stared. She ignored them. With the traffic at a standstill there was nothing anyone could do, bar hurtle down the hard shoulder as if there was an emergency. But Betty couldn't be relied on to get up the necessary speed so Beth could only resign herself to the wait. She channelled her thoughts towards Stephanie, her older daughter: the actress of the family.

That night Steph was opening in a summer production of Noël Coward's *Private Lives* in Sheringham. Beth was on her way to play the role of proud parent, which she was. The niggling concern that her daughter might have invited Gerry too was not making the long journey any more bearable. He wasn't mentioned the last time they spoke and Beth certainly hadn't wanted to seed the possibility of his coming by posing the question. She would only have provoked a row. Nothing must spoil Steph's moment of glory in this, her first professional engagement in a leading role.

'You'll probably have heard of the director, Mum. Rafe Starling? He's an actor who's been around for years.' Steph dismissed him with the disregard of youth. 'But this is his first directing job.'

Beth sat up immediately. Of course she had heard of him. She and Ralph – as he'd been known back then – Starling had been at university together; members of the same drama society. A shared history.

'But how funny,' she'd said. 'We starred in our final year dram soc production together. And believe it or not, it was *Private Lives*.' She had wanted to reminisce with her daughter, marvel at the coincidence, share her memories of her own days treading the boards but, full of excitement with her own achievement, Steph had cut her off.

'How weird.' She hadn't wanted to know more. That was ancient history. She just carried on talking about how lucky she was to have got the lead role of Amanda, after the months of getting nowhere since drama school.

For Beth, however, it felt genuinely weird and sent her reeling back to the past. Until that university production she had barely known Ralph Starling, being, as she was, on the very periphery of the theatrical in-crowd. He was one of the stars of the society whereas she had only ever been given the most insignificant parts the group could offer. But two weeks before the first night their leading lady had gone down with glandular fever and Beth, the understudy, again, was asked to step in. 'It's time you had a chance to shine,' said the director. Despite feeling ever so slightly patronised, Beth grasped the challenge, and that's how she and Ralph had finally met.

She was already engaged to Gerry at the time, a promising young lawyer, who encouraged her involvement with the 'amateur thesps', as he irritatingly termed them. She had believed unconditionally in him then, admired his ambition and longed to be his wife. He was her first real love she reminded herself, staring out of the window past the stationary traffic into the distance.

What Gerry hadn't understood was the thrill Beth experienced acting alongside Ralph, who, incidentally, boasted a university-wide reputation as a heart breaker. With Beth, he had been different. Throughout the rehearsals and three performances, he was professional to the tips of his shiny ponytail, but when the curtain came down for the final time and they were basking in the success of the production, he had turned to her and said, 'Now the show's over, come back to my flat. I've been wanting to ask you ever since you took the part.'

'But what about Gerry?' she replied, knowing full well the implications of the invitation and of her acceptance. 'We're getting married in a month.'

'Don't marry him,' said Ralph, at his most dramatic as he leaned towards her. 'I know that deep down you're a free spirit like me. You need to spread your wings. See the world. Marriage isn't for you.'

He gazed into her eyes, and for that moment, she knew he was right.

Gerry wasn't around that evening, having been invited to London for an interview with a top law firm. If he got the job, his future would be assured. He had no alternative but to miss her last performance and go.

She had never told anyone what happened that night. But the following morning, despite Ralph's attempts at persuasion, she was less sure about her future as a free spirit and her need to spread her wings. Besides, the invitations had been sent out weeks earlier. It was too late: she and Gerry were married a month later.

She had never quite forgotten Ralph and, in the drearier moments of her life as devoted wife and mother, had even occasionally been moved to wonder, 'What if...' But she had dismissed those possibilities and thrown herself into her teacher training course and the business of being Gerry's ideal partner. After that, the girls and her career had taken up almost all her time. She was now deputy head of a highly regarded secondary school.

Over the years, she had tracked Ralph's career, as he changed his name and starred in a couple of West End shows and turning up regular as clockwork in *Midsomer Murders*, *Casualty*, *Lewis* and the like. There had even been a flirtation with Hollywood that had lasted over several films in which he would be so reliably British. On Saturday afternoons, while Gerry was playing golf, Beth would sneak into the local cinema alone to watch Rafe. She loved the way he camped it up in Wilde, stiffened his lip for Rattigan, smouldered in Austen. When she saw his name on the celebrity gossip pages, Beth's pulse would accelerate with the memory of their night together. Perhaps she saw those events in greater technicolour than was their due but certainly, as years went by, they made a stark contrast to the black and white of her marriage.

The frustrated drivers in the queue were getting back into their cars. Engines were being switched on again. She put Betty into gear and jerked forward as the file of traffic slowly moved off.

Two long hours later she was in Norfolk. The lanes were narrow, flanked by the rural landscape. Above her, a vast bowl of blue sky: 'Very flat, Norfolk.' She couldn't help smiling as she remembered the words from Coward's play, spoken out loud for the last time by Ralph when they were in bed together. His hand lay on her stomach when he'd given his finest imitation of Gertrude Lawrence, the original Amanda. And she'd followed the script, in her plummiest Noël Coward: 'There's no need to be unpleasant.' They'd thought it was the funniest thing.

She was nearing Sheringham and the modest country house hotel where Steph had booked her in for the night. Steph had been very plain that she didn't want to see her mother until after the show. 'You'll make me too nervous,' she'd said. Beth glanced at the clock. Only an hour until curtain up. She would just have time to check in and change before racing down to the theatre.

She had chosen her dress carefully, the blue one that Lucy, her older daughter had insisted she bought shortly after Gerry left. 'We can't have you going round in sackcloth and ashes for ever,' she said, her attitude in robust contrast to her mother's miserable self-pity. The choice and the way the dress made her feel about herself had marked the beginning of her climb back to normality.

As she neared the theatre, Rafe crossed her mind again. After all, wasn't he was the real reason she had chosen to wear the dress? As she walked past the parade of shops, she wondered if their paths would cross on the way to the theatre. What a ridiculous thought. Of course he'd be with his jittery cast, calming any last-minute nerves.

She picked up her ticket from the box office and ordered herself a glass of wine for the interval, feeling nerves of her own for her daughter's performance. She rebuked herself. There was no need. Steph would shine as she always had in the unfortunately few leading parts she'd managed to land at drama school.

The theatre itself was charming. Beth climbed the steep rake of the compact auditorium; sorry that Steph had got her a seat quite so close to the back. She settled in, angling herself to get the least interrupted view of the stage and waited for the show to begin.

From curtain up, she found herself echoing the words in her head; able to remember them as if she'd last recited them only yesterday. 'Very flat Norfolk.' She laughed with the rest of the audience, but wondered whether somewhere back-stage, Ralph was sharing her memories.

Steph made a wonderful Amanda – glamorous, funny and sympathetic – as her character discovered she and her new husband were staying in the adjoining hotel room to Elyot, her ex, and his new wife as the marital merry-go-round turned.

During the interval, Beth sipped her drink, listening to the audience chatter. Everyone seemed to be enjoying the play and, to Beth's pleasure, praising the two leading actors and their evident rapport, just as they once had admired her and Ralph. She was about to return to her seat when there was a tap on her shoulder. At last. She spun round, her stomach knotting, wondering what they would say to each other. She felt herself smile, then stopped. In front of her stood Gerry.

'Thought I might see you here.' He'd grown a goatee since they'd last met and was sporting a golden tan. *Europe*, she thought bitterly. Tina was nowhere in evidence. At least he'd had the decency to leave her behind.

'I wouldn't miss it,' she said, trying not to show her disappointment.

'Nor me,' he agreed. 'But, don't worry, I know you're taking Steph out after the show, so I'll make myself scarce and see her tomorrow. I'm sure you've got lots to talk about.'

'Thanks.' Beth had nothing to say to him, the man who had once meant everything to her.

'Perhaps you and I could have a drink later on, after you've eaten?' He sounded tentative but hopeful. 'It's been a long time.'

At that moment the bell rang for the audience to return to their seats. Beth hesitated. 'I don't think that would be a very good idea.'

'Pity. I suppose it would be rather late.' He let her lead the way into the auditorium. From her seat at the back, she could see his thinning hair where he sat in the second row. She tried not to feel hurt that Steph had got him a seat nearer the stage than hers.

After the final applause had died down, Beth headed for the foyer bar where they'd arranged to meet. She was relieved to see there was no sign of Gerry. He had obviously kept to his word and beaten a retreat. As she waited, she looked around, still hoping to catch a glimpse of Rafe Starling. The rapture in Steph's eyes as she took one curtain call after another had been a powerful reminder of her own emotions after her own performances, nearly thirty years ago.

And then, there was Steph, pushing through the waiting crowd towards her, looking radiant and thanking people for their compliments. At last, she reached Beth. They hugged tightly.

'You were wonderful, darling,' Beth congratulated her.

'You really think so? Not too shrill?'

'Not at all. You judged it perfectly.'

'Well, Rafe seemed pleased and that's the main thing.' Steph waved at someone across the foyer. Beth followed her gaze. Her stomach flipped as she realised she was looking at Rafe himself. Whatever damage the years had done, she would have recognised him anywhere. She raised a hand towards him but he looked straight through her then turned away. Her wave quickly transformed into a rearrangement of her hair, hoping no one had noticed her mistake. Of course he didn't recognise her. How presumptuous to think that he might. Concealing her disappointment, she turned back to Steph.

'So dinner. Where would you like to go? I saw Dad. He said you were meeting him tomorrow.'

'Yes, *if* Rafe allows us a moment of free time,' she laughed as she spoke, obviously not really minding that he might not. 'I've booked you and me a table in the pub. But, Mum, I haven't had a chance to tell you. I've asked Jack to come along too. Is that OK?'

Still smarting from her rebuttal, she only half heard what Steph had said. At that moment, the young actor who had played Elyot came up beside them, grinning as he tucked his arm around her daughter's waist. The penny dropped. The evening that she'd anticipated as a rare opportunity for mother and daughter bonding wasn't going to happen. Instead there would be the three of them and, judging by the way they were gazing into each other's eyes, she was to be cast in the dual role of credit card and gooseberry. Suddenly ashamed of her attitude, she pulled herself up short. Whatever the evening threw at her, she would make the most of it. She hadn't driven all this way for nothing.

As they left the theatre, she glanced over towards Rafe Starling again. He was holding court to a small circle of admirers. He looked briefly in her direction again, nodding at something someone said, but keeping his eyes fixed on her. Then he returned to his conversation. Had that been a glimmer of recognition? She doubted it.

She followed Steph and Jack to the pub. Steph was firmly entwined around her leading man and occasionally threw the odd remark over her shoulder towards her mother. The kitchen was closing and the specials board was rubbed clean so they ordered quickly from the menu. Beth had another glass of wine despite their refusal. Heady with their success, they could only talk about the play, their performances and the rest of the cast. Beth tried to keep up as she tackled her fish and chips, but was soon lost in the blizzard of unfamiliar names, except, of course, for that of Rafe.

'Did you see him talking to that agent, Hope Fletcher, afterwards? He must be hoping she'll take him on even though he hasn't been on TV for ages.'

'Maybe he fancies her.' Jack laughed as if he was talking about a pair of dinosaurs. 'Bout time he tried it on with some-one his own age.'

'Tell me about it,' said Steph, taking a mouthful of scampi. 'He can be so gross.'

All of a sudden, Beth was rather relieved that she hadn't been recognised. 'He hasn't tried anything with you, has he?' she asked, dreading the answer.

'Christ, no.' Steph's eyes widened.' He wouldn't dare. It's just his sense of humour, that's all. You'd probably think he was funny.'

'Thanks, darling. I'll try to take that as a compliment.'

They all laughed. Steph had obviously completely forgotten about her mother's foray into amateur dramatics with the object of her scorn.

As their evening drew to a close, Beth couldn't wait to get back to her hotel. The hellish drive to Norfolk had taken it out of her and, despite her pleasure in seeing Steph and her success, her daughter was now so caught up with Jack she felt decidedly superfluous. By end of the meal, she'd have needed a crowbar to prise them apart. Not that she begrudged Steph her love life, not at all. She just didn't want to be quite such a close spectator. They would meet the next day after Gerry had left and talk together then. *If* Rafe allowed it. Making her excuses, she paid the bill and left them, to their evident relief.

The lights of the hotel blazed a welcome. Walking through the car park, Beth spotted Gerry's convertible parked near the door. She cursed under her breath. Steph must have booked him here too, without any consideration for the friction it might lead to. The last thing Beth wanted was to have to spend the next twenty-four hours avoiding her ex-husband.

She collected her key and went upstairs. Her room was cool and quiet, overlooking the large garden at the back of the hotel. Having made her break from the lovebirds, she felt less tired so took her book from her case and went out to enjoy the still balmy night on the veranda. Switching on the outside light, she sat on one of the two chairs at a small round metal table. From the room to her right came the sound of voices. From the room to her left, silence.

She turned her attention to her novel, a thriller set amid the frozen wastes of Norway, but she couldn't concentrate. Her mind kept returning to Rafe and the look they'd exchanged across the crowded foyer. Could he really have forgotten her? She couldn't believe that their night together had meant nothing to him at all when it had remained so real to her. As she looked up to the stars, brilliant in the velvety blackness, the door of the room to her left slid open and its occupant stepped out. A man. He pulled out one of his two chairs from the table, scraping it over the concrete, then sat, mostly hidden by the rambling rose covered trellis between them.

Beth looked up as a ghastly thought struck her: she wouldn't put it past Steph to have booked her parents into adjoining rooms. A misguided way of bringing them together again – not that there was any chance of that happening, however conciliatory Gerry had shown himself to be earlier in the evening. She sighed quietly, reminded momentarily that her ex did possess some good qualities. Better to return inside, rather than risk meeting again.

Determined to do this without alerting him to her presence, she stood up gingerly, but her chair repeated the noise of his. She froze, watching as he stood too but walked to the front of his veranda where he paused, a silhouette in the darkness, to stare across the garden.

She dared not move in case any more noise drew his attention. She heard him sigh as he turned back to his table, then stopped dead, having noticed her at last, standing in the spotlight on her veranda.

She tried to make out his features but they were hidden in shadow.

He cleared his throat and raised his glass in a toast. 'Very flat, Norfolk,' he said.

Her heart leaped. Definitely not Gerry. She would recognise those dark, chocolaty tones anywhere.

'I thought it was you in the foyer,' he added as he took a step towards the dividing trellis.

Rafe! He hadn't forgotten her. All she could feel was the thudding of her pulse.

'There's no need…' But she couldn't finish the line. Was this coincidence or fate that had brought them together?

'…To be unpleasant.' He finished it for her. They laughed as he moved out of the shadows towards her side of his veranda.

'A nightcap?' he asked, head tilted to one side. 'I've got some very good brandy in my room. I'm assuming you're still the free spirit I remember?'

'I'm not sure,' she said but crossed to where he stood. 'I think I could be. Marriage wasn't for me, in the end. You were right.'

He smiled at her. That smile.

She took his proffered hand and held her breath, wondering briefly what Coward had really thought about Amanda and Elyot. Lovers who could not live together but neither could they live apart. Did it really matter? She glanced across at the waiting Rafe. She was free and had all the time in the world to make up her mind. Perhaps, as he had once suggested, the moment had come for her to spread her wings at last.

Fiona Harper

Award-winning author Fiona Harper writes fun, flirty, heart-warming romances for Harlequin Mills & Boon. Her books are sold round the world and have been translated into over twenty different languages.

As a child, she was constantly teased for two things: having her nose in a book and living in a dream world. Things haven't changed much since then but at least in writing she's found a use for her runaway imagination. Fiona lives in London, England, with her very patient husband and her two wonderful daughters. She loves good books, good films and good food – especially anything cinnamon-flavoured – and she can always find some room in her diet for chocolate. Her new novel *Make My Wish Come True* is available now.

&

A Real Prince

Some women spend their whole lives looking for their prince. I'm standing right next to mine. He's tall and good-looking and he's very dashing in his red and gold uniform. He smiles lovingly at me before we both turn and face the hundreds of people pressing themselves against the metal barriers, leaning forwards and madly waving their plastic Union Jack flags.

I wave and the cheers increase in volume. Cameras and smartphones point in our direction, capturing every nanosecond of our public interaction. I know this is my job now and I shouldn't mind their presence. I also know I have to put on a good show, that I can't let my nerves work their way to the surface, so I smile and flick my long dark brown hair back off my face with my fingers, careful not to disturb the heavy waves or the crimson fascinator perched on top of them that matches my suit.

'Duchess!' someone calls. 'Over here!'

I turn, keeping my smile bright, and wave my hand from the wrist like I've practised.

More shouts now, coming from all directions.

'Prince William!'

'Kate!'

We stand united and smiling beside the rest of our family.

Well *his* family. Mine don't usually generate such a fuss.
His parents. His grandparents. His little brother…The whole
gang is here.

In a minute we'll have to go down the steps and into the
vast building and walk down the wide path carved out by
dull grey metal barriers. Right now I'm happy to be a little
distance away, waving so hard I'm surprised my hand hasn't
fallen off my wrist.

Once again I'm struck by the sheer absurdity of it all. Why
should these people turn up to wave and cheer at me? I'm one
of them, really. An ordinary girl, from an ordinary family. A
girl who, by sheer stroke of fate or luck or whatever you call
it, has ended up with this life.

I'm woken rudely from my musing by the feel of the
prince's hand sliding round my waist, pulling me closer.
I freeze. This really isn't appropriate, and I know the hand
isn't going to stay there. He proves me right, sliding it lower
so his fingers curve around my bottom and gives it a little
squeeze. My smile goes rigid.

I manage to hiss at him through my teeth, while still beaming demurely at the gathered crowds. 'If you don't move that
hand right now, Gareth, I'm going to use that sword of yours
to do a little impromptu surgery.'

'I'd like to see you try,' he whispers. 'It's fake.'

And so is he. My lookalike Prince William leaves his hand
just a second longer on my backside then drags it away, main-
taining contact as long as he can, then lifts it to wave at the
people who have gathered outside the entrance of a south
London shopping centre to see us.

'Not nearly as good as Pippa's anyway,' he mutters. 'That
new girl at the agency – Hannah, or whatever her name is –

she might not have the sister's face exactly, but turn her round and she's spot-on.'

Ugh.

What a prince.

And I had stupidly believed my new career as a Kate Middleton lookalike was going to help me meet a decent man. Fat chance. Gareth Parsons, my faux prince, is like all my rotten ex-boyfriends rolled into one. It wouldn't be so bad if we didn't always get booked as a couple, and demand has been sky-high since the wedding and the Jubilee. I have to put up with his wandering hands at least three times a week. Sometimes more.

Why can't he be more like the real Wills? There's a man who knows how to behave, who clearly adores his wife. The strange thing is that Gareth is such a good match for the prince that at first I willed him to change, waited for him to pick up some traits from the man he emulates, but I've been working beside him for more than a year now and there hasn't been the slightest sign of improvement. If anything, he's got worse.

How hard can it be? To find a good man. I'm not even asking for royalty. Just a Y chromosome and a basic grasp of how to behave like a human being. Knowing how to make a girl *feel* like a princess would definitely be a bonus, but I'm starting to realise how unlikely that is. I used to think I was just unlucky, but now I think finding a man like that is about as probable as getting married to a prince for real.

Damn Kate for getting there first!

I look just like her. I could have done it. With a bit of luck and a following wind…

Three years ago I was working as a waitress for a pizza

restaurant. A few people commented that I looked like Prince William's girlfriend, but only if I did my hair a certain way or dressed up – like at my cousin's wedding. I just used to make a joke about it and say no, I wasn't her, but I wouldn't complain if my very own Prince Charming swept me off my feet.

But then Kate and William got engaged and suddenly people were staring and pointing at me when I went to the supermarket. When I went up to the West End once a couple of Japanese tourists started following me and wouldn't leave me alone until I'd posed for a picture and signed the London street map they were clutching fiercely. I tried to tell them the truth, but they just thought I was trying to put them off the scent.

I went home and told my flatmates about it over takeaway curry that evening, and it was Becky who came up with the idea of approaching a lookalike agency. 'Come on, Sophie,' she said. 'It'll be a laugh.'

And that wasn't the only perk. Extra money in the bank. Meeting interesting people, dressing up, going to glamorous locations. I gave up waitressing eighteen months ago. And it has been fun – at least until Gareth started to believe he had groping rights on my dèrriere.

The rest of the 'family' aren't so bad. Pam, who's the Queen, is a retired schoolteacher and uses her lookalike work to fund her trips abroad with her sister. She's off to Peru next. Steve and Annie, who are Charles and Camilla, are actually married. They never stop laughing with each other and they've invited us all to their silver wedding anniversary party next month.

I don't know much about Harry. He's new. The agency

only took him on a couple of weeks ago. I sneak a look across at him. He's pretty good, actually, even though his hair is a shade darker and I think he's broader than the real Harry. But he's obviously decided to embrace the bad-boy side of the prince, because he's eyeing up all the pretty girls in the crowd and showing off.

Shame. The two brothers are a matching pair. I was hoping he wouldn't be cut from the same cloth as Gareth. One of *him* was plenty.

Thankfully, it's time to start the 'walkabout' and it's going to be much more difficult for Gareth to get a surreptitious squeeze in with eyes staring at us from every angle.

We descend the stairs and walk through the main entrance of the shopping mall. I smile. I shake hands. I pose for photos. I don't talk much. I've been having voice lessons, but I can only manage a few select phrases before the tinge of cockney in my London accent gives me away.

The walkway gets narrower as we head towards the vast department store, where we're all supposed to gather for a publicity photo shoot before Pam can cut a ribbon, declare the shop open and we can all go home and have a nice cup of tea. I can't wait.

I wonder if the real Kate feels like this during public engagements? I think it must be even harder for her. I can dress down, look like me if I want to. She's got no choice but to be her. But having Wills to go home to must be all the compensation she needs. If I took Gareth home for a cuppa – shudder the thought – I'd have to disinfect the place afterwards.

I keep walking and waving, slowly heading to the bright lights of the department store at the other end of the mall, but things start to go wrong. The crowds are pressing closer, all trying to get a glimpse of us. I still find that a bit surreal, but I suppose I can understand it. I stood in the rain for five hours to get a glimpse of the real Her Majesty when she did her Jubilee tour and all I saw was the back of her hat. It's all of us together today, so maybe we're a good second best?

But then I realise that the barriers here nearer the shops aren't as sturdy as the metal ones outside. Near the department store they've gone for looks rather than functionality, opting for those posts with ropes clipped between them. All it takes is one over-excited child to lean on one section, causing the posts at either end of the rope to come crashing to the floor, and the crowds surge towards us, holding their iPhones aloft and yelling our fake names. Pole after pole goes down and suddenly royals and commoners are just one big mix.

Bodies are pressing in close, hands grabbing. Someone tugs at my hair. 'Ouch!' I say and spin round, but I can't tell who did it, or even if it was deliberate.

The Queen and Prince Philip were leading the way farther ahead and the shopping centre security guards leap into action, steering them inside the department store entrance and lowering the shutters until they're a couple of feet above the floor. Charles and Camilla manage to duck underneath just after them. I see Harry only a couple of steps behind.

My heart starts to gallop. Gareth and I have managed to lag behind, mostly because everyone seemed to want a photo of us together, and the crowd now fills the gap between us and the half-closed shutters.

No one is nasty; they're all smiling and jolly, pleased to see us, but that doesn't stop the people who were at the back of the crowd pushing in behind, crushing us all into one mass of torsos. I'm reminded of my one ill-fated experience of a mosh-pit, when I had to be rescued by a nice St John's Ambulance man and missed half the concert. I start to wish I hadn't kept up with Kate and lost those extra ten pounds last year, because I start to feel fragile and alone in the crush. The bodies around me are packed so tightly together now that I lose one crimson stiletto as I'm lifted off my feet and transported a few steps sideways.

'Gareth!' I croak. I thought I'd seen him a little ahead of me and I twist to see if I'm right. He's taller and stronger than I am, and he might be faring better. I never thought I'd voluntarily ask him to put his hands on me, but I'm coming pretty close. Where the hell is a close protection officer when you need one?

I manage to catch sight of Gareth, heading towards the department store. I call out again and he looks right at me. With a rueful expression on his face, he shakes his head and turns before carving an easy wake through the enthusiastic shoppers.

I hop as best I can, in one stockinged foot and try to follow him, but I'm not quick enough. The crowd closes in behind him and if I make a few paces headway I just get swept back again. My other shoe disappears. Not good for all sorts of reasons, but mostly because I'm shorter without my heels and it feels as if the crowd is starting to close in above me too.

I'm not her! I want to yell. Leave me alone! But my breath is stuck in my throat and all I can manage is a pathetic squeak. I elbow the seven-foot lump of lard next to me in the ribs and when he jumps back and shouts 'Oi!', I suck some much needed oxygen into my compressed ribcage and yell for help. I don't care at all if my Catford vowels are giving me away.

A firm hand grabs mine and I scream, but when I look down I see the sleeve of a uniform and some gold brocade. Thank goodness! Gareth has finally come good. About blooming time he lived up to the man he impersonates!

He pulls me through the crowd. People seem to part and melt before his more substantial frame. I just keep my head down, pressed almost against the back of his jacket and do my best to follow him.

I squeal in pain as someone stamps on my shoeless right foot. My prince pauses briefly, turns to see what the problem is, then lifts me into his arms in one swift motion he picks up his pace to a swift march. I stop rubbing my damaged toe and clasp my hands around his neck to stop me tumbling back down to the floor as, and it's only then that I realise my rescuer isn't Gareth the Groper.

It's fake Harry.

He's the one carrying me effortlessly through the thinning crowd. I change my mind about those ten pounds, glad I lost them now.

'Are you okay?' he asks, frowning a little. His voice is deeper than I expected and close up I can see his face is leaner than the real Harry's and his eyes are green, not blue.

I nod, still unable to find my voice.

When I look over his shoulder I see people starting to follow us. I tap 'Harry's' shoulder and point. Rather than breaking into a run and heading down the main drag of the shopping centre he ducks into a menswear shop and heads towards the back. He doesn't stop until we're in the – thankfully – empty changing rooms and he's pulled a curtain across a cubicle to hide us. Then he lowers me gently to my feet.

My heart is still thumping, even though there are no sounds in the shop outside and it seems Harry's quick thinking has saved us. Although the cubicle is spacious – maybe six feet by six feet – I find I'm still pressed up close to him, right where he deposited me, and my hands have slipped from his neck and are now splayed on his uniformed chest.

'Thank you,' I stutter, and then I let out a little laugh. 'It got a little crazy back there for a second.'

He smiles back and my words die away. 'I'm afraid you're looking a little dishevelled, princess.'

I put my hand up to my hair to discover my fascinator, once held fast by a million hair grips, is at half-mast and my lovely glossy waves are a little matted. When I look down I discover there is a ladder in my sheer nude stockings.

I must look a little disoriented, because he asks, 'Are you *sure* you're OK?'

I nod again. I seem to be doing that a lot. 'My foot's a little sore, but other than that I think I'll survive.' And I'd better. I'm booked for a *What the Young Royals Should be Wearing This Season* fashion shoot the day after tomorrow.

He nods too. Neither of us moves.

There is a discreet cough from the other side of the changing cubicle curtain. 'Can I help, sir? Madam?'

Harry blinks and breaks eye contact. I feel my chest re-inflate and I step back. He pulls the curtain aside and we watch as the store manager's eyes widen as he takes us in.

'We're lookalikes,' Harry explains, and goes on to tell him about the grand plan for the department store opening gone wrong. 'The crowd got a little…enthusiastic,' he adds.

The store manager, bless him – who is all of twenty-two, but obviously has been styling himself after Captain Peacock in *Are You Being Served?* – regains his composure in a heart-beat.

'Well, if Your Highnesses…I mean, sir and madam, require any assistance – or the continued use of our changing room until the mob disperses…'

Harry sends him a smile that would turn my knees to chocolate if he'd directed it at me. 'What would be really helpful,' he says, 'is if we could borrow something to put over these clothes. Dressed as we are, sneaking away unde-tected might be a little tricky.' He reaches inside his pocket and brandishes a credit card. 'I can leave a deposit, if need be?'

The store manager waves the rectangle of plastic away.

Ten minutes later we've found a trench coat to cover my red suit and my hair is piled up and hidden under a base-ball cap. We've tried every pair of shoes in the shop, but the smallest are at least three sizes too big for me. Harry, meanwhile, has been transformed into not-so-Harry, just by switching the uniform for a T-shirt and a pair of chinos. Like that, he doesn't look like a prince at all.

He looks even better.

'Stay there,' he tells me seriously and dashes out the shop. I exchange glances with the manager then fiddle with the belt on my coat. It's only a moment or two until Harry is back again. He has my shoes, one in each hand, and he kneels so I can slide my feet into them. I shiver as the nylon of my stock-ings grazes his fingertips.

The stilettos look a little odd with the coat, but they'll have to do. It's either that or flapping around in a pair of over-sized brogues like a clown.

He stands up and grins at me. 'Ready?'

I smile back at him. Not Kate's demure one. The cheesy one that's all my own.

That just seems to make him grin harder.

And then he grabs my hand and we shout our thanks to the store manager before jogging out of the shop and heading for the nearest exit. We don't stop until we're in the sunshine, round the corner of the park outside, our backs pressed a wall, chests heaving in unison. We turn to each other and laugh.

'Welcome to the family,' I say.

'You make it sound like the mafia.' His voice is serious but his eyes are twinkling.

'It kind of is,' I tell him. 'After all, this is it for us now. We look like them and they look like us. I'm never going to be able to switch jobs and do – oh – Angelina Jolie instead.'

'Neither am I,' he says, and we both start laughing again.

He opens his mouth to say something, but both our phones go off simultaneously. An email from Celebrity Doubles, our agency. Caroline at the office is livid about the situation and will be tearing strips off the shopping centre security team shortly. In the meantime she says Pam and the others can carry on without us and we can go home if we want. Full pay. I discover I'm almost sad the day has to end.

'Are you okay to get home?' Harry asks me.

I nod towards the bus stop. 'I'm a local girl,' I say. 'Only fifteen minutes away on the two-five-seven.'

He insists on coming with me to see I get there safely, even though he lives in completely the opposite direction. I'm still dressed as Kate, he reasons, and he wouldn't want there to be a repeat performance of the shopping centre mob. I'm pretty sure I'll be okay with my trench coat and my baseball cap, but I don't put him off.

If this was Gareth, I'd think he had some ulterior motive, that he'd find an excuse to get inside my flat – like pretending he needed to use the loo or something – and then I'd never be able to shove him out again, but Harry walks me to my gate, smiles at me then stays on the pavement side while I take a couple of steps down the path.

'This is me,' I say brightly, even though I already told him the address and my key is in my hand.

'See you at the Young Royals thing in a couple of days,' he says and lifts his hand, half in salute, half in farewell gesture. He takes a step backwards. The perfect gentleman, damn him.

'Harry!' I call out and he stops. I shake my head. 'I can't keep calling you that. It's stupid.' I take a breath. 'I'm Sophie. Sophie Gale.'

He walks back towards me, even comes inside the gate. 'Tom,' he says smiling.

I twist the knot in the belt of my raincoat. 'Thanks for today,' I say and I feel my cheeks heat. I'm blushing. How very Kate. 'I don't think I'd have made it out alive without you.'

He shrugs one shoulder and smiles. I step forward and kiss him on the cheek.

I pull back, just a little, and he doesn't move.

And then his arms slide around me and he kisses me properly. So properly my baseball cap falls off and lands on the path, and my hair unknots itself and tumbles down my back.

Not *too* much of a perfect gentleman, thank goodness!

Two old ladies walking past do a double-take and stop.

'Isn't that…? And isn't she…? Well, I never!'

I just smile against Tom's lips and kiss him back.

Maybe, just maybe, there's something in this prince thing after all. It just turns out I had my heart set on the wrong one.

Heidi Rice

USA Today bestselling author Heidi Rice lives in London and is married with two teenage sons – which gives her way too much of an insight into the male psyche.

She was working as a film journalist when she joined the RNA's fabulous New Writers Scheme in 2006. She got published through it the following year and is currently writing sexy contemporary romance for Mills & Boon's new Modern Tempted and Cosmo Red Hot Reads series. She loves her job because it involves sitting down at her computer and getting swept up in a world of high emotion, sensual excitement, funny feisty women, sexy tortured men and glamourous locations where laundry doesn't exist. Then she turns off her computer and does chores – usually involving laundry.

You can find her at www.heidi-rice.com or on Twitter @HeidiRomRice, where she likes to natter about romance, books and hot movie stars (not necessarily in that order).

&

The Fundamental Things

Unbelievable. Of all the lifts, in all the office blocks, in the whole of London, the biggest mistake of my life has to walk into mine.

Elizabeth Ryan sent up a silent prayer for invisibility as she inched behind two suited executives. Her back bumped against the mirrored wall in the executive elevator at Stokes and Company's brand new twenty-eighth storey tower in Canary Wharf. Unfortunately, someone up there wasn't listening, because she failed to disappear.

Lorenzo Kelly.

The name whispered across her consciousness as heat crawled up her neck and flared across her scalp.

Twenty-two years since she'd last seen him and yet recognition had blasted her in the sternum as soon as he'd edged into the crowded lift. Which was surprising, because that fitted steel-grey designer suit was one heck of a departure from the wrecked jeans and third-hand leather jacket he'd lived in at Hillbrook Secondary.

Thank God he was absorbed in the lift monitor and hadn't looked her way. One glance at those heavy-lidded bedroom eyes a moment ago had been more than enough to make her heart swell up and stop beating for several crucial seconds. Funny how even after more than two decades, and what looked like a major *GQ* make-over, those slightly slanted emerald green eyes still made him look as if he'd just got out of bed – or was about to lure her back into one.

The lift glided to a halt on the mezzanine level. And her two-executive shield, as well as most of the rest of the lift's inhabitants, shot out, making a beeline for the Starbucks™ queue. Her shoulders tightened and she stared straight ahead tuning out the chatter about a press launch from the three young women who'd deliberately positioned themselves next to Ren.

She risked another glance. He seemed taller and more muscular. She didn't remember his physique being quite this over-powering. But from what she could see from this angle, little else about him was different. He still had the dramatically high cheekbones. Although now expensively styled and with a wisp of grey at the temples, his thick dark hair still had those curls that skimmed his collar and made her fingers itch to caress them. And even in his expertly tailored suit, he had maintained that laid-back-to-the-point-of-insolence stance that said loud and clear he didn't give a toss about anyone or anything.

Oddly enough, it had been that stance rather than his spectacular looks that had lured her to him back then, giving him the dangerous attraction of forbidden treasure.

She let out a shaky breath. Ren Kelly *had* given her treasure, however unintentionally, that was one thing at least she hadn't been wrong about. The sucker punch had been her idiotic belief that a tender, tortured soul existed beneath Ren's bad boy exterior.

The lift bell pinged, zapping Liz back to the present as the trio of PR women exited on eighth. All three checked Ren out as they passed.

Liz's stomach tightened as he sent them an impersonal smile and hooked his hand into the pocket of his trousers. One of them blushed prettily in response.

Liz scowled. *Watch out, girls. Wolf in Gucci clothing.*

The man might look dreamy but she knew he was every woman's worse nightmare. Her gaze dipped to the bottom edge of his jacket, which rode up over his backside, revealing the same tight orbs she had once spent entire lunch hours admiring framed in battered denim.

Resentment flared. Was there no justice in the world? While her boobs now required a bra underwired with tungsten to stop them heading south, and her face took at least thirty minutes to apply every morning, maturity had only enhanced Ren Kelly's megawatt sex appeal. Surely for a man as shallow and self-absorbed as he was, there had to be some sort of deal with Beelzebub going on for him to still be this gorgeous?

She shifted further into the corner, as the lift stopped on the eleventh floor and let out a freckle-faced office boy – the last person left sharing the lift with them.

She counted to five but no one else entered before the lift doors slid closed, sealing them into the metal box alone together.

Bugger.

The lift rose, and the weightlessness in her belly was suddenly accompanied by an odd flare of heat, relaxing the muscles of her abdomen. The heat spread up her chest and reignited her scalp.

Terrific, thirty-eight years old and my body chooses this precise moment to have its first hot flush.

She slung the strap of her laptop bag over her shoulder, crossed her arms over her boiling chest and studiously ignored the man in front of her – who, thankfully, had yet to look her way.

Only five more floors to go until she could make a dignified exit at Human Resources and reassign the biggest mistake of her life to his rightful place in her past.

The overhead light flickered and a sudden jolt had them both gripping the railing. Ren straightened first. The lift stuttered to a halt, the panel light fluttering ominously between twelve and fourteen – there was no thirteenth floor, even though they appeared to have stopped there.

'You OK?' His gaze wandered over her, as if checking for injuries. And her heart beat into her throat, the harsh fluorescent lighting picking up the flecks of gold in his irises, which Josh had inherited.

'Fine.' Her stomach muscles tangled into knots as her knuckles tightened on the rail. She tried to recall the breathing technique she'd learned at the ante-natal classes before Josh was born. As her son was now twenty-one and she'd ended up having every drug known to man by the time he was actually delivered, it was a fairly vain hope.

Relax. Don't panic, maybe he won't recognise you.

After all, she'd changed completely since that long ago afternoon in the clinic waiting room, the last time she'd seen him. She had cheekbones these days. Her once long, dyed black hair was now its natural chestnut trimmed into a sleek bob. The thick Goth eyeliner and nose ring had been replaced by make-up in subtle autumn hues, which enhanced her pale skin rather than making her resemble a close relative of the Addams Family.

A shudder ran down her spine at the memory of how much effort she'd put into looking atrocious at sixteen. No wonder Ren – the unnaturally beautiful lost boy whom every girl in Form 10B had flirted with mercilessly – had only asked her out on a bet.

His gaze returned to the lift panel. And her breath eased out past gritted teeth. But the gush of relief was tempered with a tiny flicker of regret, which she ruthlessly quashed.

Don't be a ninny. It's good that he doesn't recognise you. It shows how far you've come from that sartorial disaster zone.

A loud metallic clanking sound filled the lift, which inched upwards and then stopped again with a juddering bump.

'Jesus, what the hell was that?' Ren murmured.

'It's only teething problems, they've had a few in the last couple of weeks.' Liz squeezed the sensible words out past the ticking bomb lodged in her throat. 'It'll move again in a moment.' *Or I shall throttle every single member of the premises support team with my bare hands.*

He stabbed the emergency call button and shouted into the intercom: 'Hey, anyone out there? We're stuck in here.'

A crackling sound came over the line followed by a disembodied and remarkably relaxed voice: 'Sorry, folks, give us a couple of minutes and we'll have you rolling again.'

'Thanks,' Ren replied, as he took his finger off the button. Propping his butt against the wall, he dropped his briefcase and raked his fingers through his hair.

Liz stared at the panel above his head. Anywhere but at those disturbingly familiar green eyes. She sent up a silent prayer, this one as fervent as the one she'd once made while standing by her newborn son's crib in the neo-natal care unit of UCL hospital. Although, this time, instead of praying for Josh's father to magically appear, now she prayed for him to disappear as quickly as was humanly possible.

'So, Lizzie, when did you cut your hair?'

She raised her head, the blush spreading like a mushroom cloud. 'You recognised me.'

The quirk of his lips sent a dimple into his cheek. Her pulse-rate accelerated. As a boy, he'd used that dimple on women like a lethal weapon. Age and maturity hadn't dimmed its power.

'Like I could forget you,' he said, the tone sardonic. 'You're the only woman I've ever kissed who kneed me in the balls.'

A dart of shame pierced her consternation, at the memory of him tumbling off the bed with his hands cupping his groin, tears of pain squeezing out of his eyes.

'As I recall we did a lot more than kiss.' Her spine stiffened as she refused to remember how much more, and instead concentrated on the furious argument they'd had before she'd sent him rolling onto the floor. Yes she'd hurt him, but he'd deserved it at the time. 'And I didn't get *that* much leverage. You made far too much of a fuss about it.'

'I remember very well how much more we did.' The low tone sounded oddly seductive. 'But even my ex-wife only ever kicked me in the balls metaphorically speaking,' he continued. 'And when it comes to leverage, believe me,' he shuddered theatrically, 'you got enough.'

She saw the quirk of self-deprecating humour on those sensual lips and wanted to kick him in the balls all over again. Seriously? Wasn't he even going to mention why she'd kicked him? Or was he just being coy?

'All credit to your ex-wife,' she replied, dismissing the hollow knowledge in the pit of her stomach that he had been married and divorced in the last twenty-two years, and probably had other children. 'The woman must have had the forbearance of a saint.'

He grinned, the flash of white teeth in his tanned face disconcerting. 'She certainly thought so.' His head tilted to one side as his gaze drifted up to her hairline. She resisted the urge to smooth her hand over her bob or acknowledge her thundering heartbeat.

'It suits you.' He nodded. 'The hairstyle. I can see more of your face.'

'Thanks,' she said caustically, not quite able to keep the bitterness at bay. Wasn't he even going to mention Josh, or ask after him?

She'd thought the worst thing that could happen would be that he might recognise her. She had been wrong.

'You look good, too,' she added. 'Although it does make me wonder what state the painting in your attic must be in these days?'

Instead of looking offended by the barb, he laughed. 'There's no painting. Yet. But Dorian was definitely onto something. If I could swap a magic painting, however grotesque, for having to sweat my nuts off in the gym four times a week, I'd do it in a heartbeat.'

A satisfied laugh escaped her lips at the gratifying thought that even he had to work hard to look good these days.

She glanced at her wristwatch. 'You should ask them what's going on. I have a meeting and we've been stuck in here for five minutes now?' she added. She wanted to make it clear she wasn't enjoying their trip down memory lane.

He hitched his shoulder, then buzzed the intercom again. After a brief talk with the services team, an engineer came on the line. 'I'm sorry, sir. We're having to override the trip switch, there's been a short in the…'

'Save me the tech jargon, pal,' Ren interrupted. 'All we're interested in is how much longer we're likely to be in here?'

'Definitely not more than ten minutes,' the engineer replied. 'Twenty tops.'

'What?' Liz yelped. No fricking way was she going to be able to survive another twenty minutes of small talk without having the enormous elephant crammed into the lift with them rear up on its two hind legs and crush her to death. Or worse, tumble out of her mouth. And if that happened she'd never forgive herself.

She'd made a promise to herself on Josh's first birthday that she wouldn't contact Lorenzo Kelly again – finally letting go of the immature hope that he'd never received the letters she'd sent. His disappearance had spoken volumes right from the start, but she'd refused to see it for over a year. And the result had been lots of pointless tears and sleepless nights when she should have been devoting herself to her son.

Once she'd let go of that delusion, everything had got easier. Slowly but surely, she'd gone from being a heart-sick teenage drama queen expecting Ren to return and sweep away all her problems – while leaving her mum to do most of the childcare – to being a single mother ready to face up to her responsibilities. Not to say that it had been easy, because that had been one hell of a steep learning curve, but she'd survived and eventually prospered.

But she didn't think she could stand here for another twenty minutes and have this man continue to pretend Josh didn't exist right to her face without reverting to a bit of teen-age drama, and quite possibly murdering him.

Taking the three steps to Ren's side, she elbowed him aside and stabbed the intercom button herself. 'Listen, buster, I have a meeting. A very important meeting.' *Not to mention a man's life in my hands, which I cannot be held responsible for if you don't get a move on.* 'So you need to stop mucking about and get me out of here.'

The young engineer coughed guiltily. 'Do you want us to tell them you'll be late, Miss?'

'Are you a complete moron…?' She stopped, tried to drag her temper back from the brink as Ren's dark brows launched up his forehead at her outburst. 'No, I don't want you to rearrange the meeting…' She struggled for calm but her whole body was starting to shake. He was standing so close, she could smell him. The far too familiar scent of laundry soap and man – no longer masked by the aroma of Golden Virginia tobacco – brought back all sorts of heady memories. She'd thought the scent of his roll-ups was incredibly sexy at sixteen. Unfortunately, the clean scent of him was much sexier now.

Stop right there. You're not attracted to him, you're just a little stressed.

Her tongue darted out to moisten her lips as she turned away from the beautiful mouth that had once kissed her with such longing, and now belonged to a stranger.

Make that a lot stressed.

'I simply need to get out of here…' She finished, feeling hideously exposed.

'Are you all right, Miss?' came the engineer's concerned voice.

'Yes, of course.'

Give or take the odd nervous breakdown.

But then Ren's warm palm covered the fingers that she hadn't realised had begun to tremble on the intercom button.

'The lady's fine,' he said into the intercom as his warm grip eased her fingers off the button to replace them with his own. 'Just get us out as soon as you can, OK, buddy?'

'Twenty minutes, tops. I promise.'

As Ren broke the connection, she yanked her hand out of his grasp, and walked back across the lift, her legs now as shaky as the rest of her.

Twenty minutes, she could keep it together for twenty minutes. Surely?

'I never knew you hated me that much,' he murmured.

She looked up, to find him studying her, his hands braced on the rail and his expression heavy with regret. She shook her head. Now he wanted to talk about it? Was he trying to send her right over the edge?

'I don't hate you, Ren,' she said. Although given the way her heart was battering her chest wall she was forced to admit she still had strong emotions where he was concerned. 'I simply don't want to be stuck here.'

'With me,' he added.

So he'd finally got the message. Although she couldn't quite believe how self-absorbed he was being. Hadn't he matured at all in the last twenty-two years? Did he honestly still believe this was all about him?

'Yes, with you. What on earth did you expect, Ren? I was sixteen and pregnant and you abandoned me. Of the top ten people I would least like to be stuck in a lift with, you're right up there with Adolph Hitler and Gary Numan singing "Are 'Friends' Electric?".'

He sent her a wry smile. 'Adolph I get, but please tell me I at least rank below Gary.'

She sent him a rueful smile back, devoid of humour. 'I can't. It's a very close run thing.'

He let out a long sigh. 'That bad, huh?'

'Yes, that bad.' She should probably resent the fact that he had managed to turn even this into a joke. But somehow it didn't seem to matter anymore.

'You're right,' he said, the serious tone surprising her. 'There's no excuse for what I did that day. It was unbelievably selfish and pretty damn unforgiveable.' He pushed upright, slung his hands into his pockets. 'But I was seventeen and scared to death and if it's any consolation at all, I regretted it for months afterwards. And if I'd been able to, I would have come back and apologised.'

She laughed the sound hollow. '*You* were scared.' She placed a hand on her breastbone, desperately trying to hold back the angry recriminations that she had never been able to voice. '*You* were scared. I was bloody terrified.' She clamped her mouth shut. There were so many other things she could say. But she stopped herself.

In eighteen minutes, if the engineer kept his promise, they'd be out of here and this would all be nothing more than a bad dream.

'Jesus, Lizzie. I know you were terrified.' He threw up his hands with an exasperation she didn't understand. What right did he have to be exasperated? 'And I know you were doing the right thing. For both of us. And as I'd been man enough to get you pregnant, I should have been man enough to support your decision and stand by you, instead of running away. But…' His shoulders slumped and he stared down at his feet, the dark hair falling over his face – she strained against the knee-jerk reaction to reach up and push his fringe back off his forehead, just as she always did with Josh. 'But I kept thinking about the baby. Our baby. And what was going to happen to it. And I just couldn't…'

She frowned, the boulder in her throat making it hard for her to decipher the words properly. They swirled round in her head like the lame excuse they were, but something about them didn't quite fit. 'What are you talking about?'

Those deep emerald eyes met hers as he swept the hair back from his forehead, his expression bleak. 'All I'm trying to say is, I couldn't bear to be there when you had the abortion.'

* * *

Ren Kelly felt something shrink inside him at the look of shocked disbelief on her beautiful face. Her pale skin had gone so white it was almost transparent, the subtle brown shading on her eyes making them look as big as dinner plates.

He shouldn't have tried to explain. He should have known this would be her reaction. Stupid to expect her to give him the benefit of the doubt twenty-two years after the fact. Why should she? Why would she? No one else ever had when he was growing up. And anyway, what had he ever done to make amends in all the years since that day? How would she know that he had always regretted being such a gutless coward?

He'd been unable to even find her, once he'd returned to the UK?

'It was a cowardly thing to do,' he continued, even though the justification sounded weak to him now too. 'I should have been there with you, helped you through it, and I know I didn't.' He sucked in a breath and hoped to hell she would at least believe this much. 'And I would have come round to visit afterwards, I swear, if I'd been able to. But my stepfather found out I'd nicked the money for the abortion from the garage's petty cash and beat the living crap out of me when I got home that night.' She still looked shocked rather than accusatory, so he soldiered on. 'I didn't want you to see me in that state. Not after what you'd already been through. But before the swelling went down, my mother shipped me off to Italy to stay with her family.' He buried his hands back in his pockets, glad at least to finally have got the explanation out. 'I think she was worried he'd end up killing me, or calling the police. When I got back six months later, you'd moved away with your family.' He shrugged. 'And I figured it was probably for the best.'

Who was he kidding? He'd spent months trying to track her down. Had even had some stupid idea that she'd forgive him, even though he knew he didn't deserve it. But he'd been forced to give up eventually. Because every dead end, every missed lead, just felt like another kick in the balls. Telling him he was worthless, and stupid and he had never deserved her in the first place.

She'd been smart and chatty and a total dork, who he'd taken out on a bet, and ended up falling hopelessly in lust with. And then he'd got her pregnant. But worse than that, the night she'd told him, he'd blamed her for it – because he'd skipped all the sex education classes in school, and his best friend Tom had assured him contraception was the girl's responsibility. Hence the famous kick in the nuts, which he'd richly deserved. And then there was the day when he'd arrived home from Italy and raced round to her house only to find the place deserted, and the window he'd once climbed into so they could make love on her single bed, boarded up. That was the moment when he'd finally figured out he'd fallen in love.

Classic Kelly timing, in every respect.

'Didn't you get any of the letters I sent?' Her voice cracked on the words, confusing him. 'To your mother's house?'

'Letters? What letters?'

'I sent letters, Ren. Loads of letters and I called too. And she told me she'd get you to call me back, but you never did.'

'My mother never gave me any messages,' he said quietly. If she hadn't been dead for ten years, he would have given her hell about it. But then, knowing her, she probably thought she was protecting him. 'I'm sorry for that too, then Lizzie. She didn't like you much. I didn't tell her why I'd stolen the money but I guess she figured out it was something to do with you.'

'Oh God.' She swayed.

'Hey.' He shot across the lift and wrapped his arms round her waist to keep her from falling. 'Are you OK? It's getting a little hot in here.' He looked down at her, stupidly pleased that she was letting him hold her. 'Hopefully they'll have us out soon,' he said, hoping no such thing as he took in a deep breath of her hair. The subtle summery scent was completely different from the candy-coated shampoo she used to use, but it still smelled like her, triggering a predictable reaction in his groin. His fingers slid over the cool silk of her blouse, the rise and fall of her breasts giving him a tantalising glimpse of cleavage.

How could he have forgotten how good she had always felt in his arms?

She lifted her hand, placed it on his forearm, and he tensed, waiting for her to shove him away. But instead, her slim fingers fisted on the sleeve of his suit and she clung onto him, so tight he could feel her digging into the sinew. Then her eyes lifted to his, the rich caramel wet with unshed tears.

'What is it, Lizzie, what's the matter?'

'Ren, I didn't…' She swallowed, her voice raw with emotion. 'I didn't have the abortion. I couldn't go through with it in the end. Any more than you could.'

'I don't understand?' His voice echoed off the lift walls and reverberated in his head.

'I had the baby, Ren. Your baby.'

'You didn't,' he whispered, the words so jagged they scoured his throat.

She nodded furiously, the tears rolling down her cheeks and splashing into the valley of her breasts.

'You had our baby?' So many emotions were racing towards him – joy, shock, awe – he couldn't catch his breath.

'Uhuh. Although he's not a baby any more. He's a grown man.'

'How old is he?' he asked, everything inside him too raw, too real, to be able to do the maths.

He had a child. A son. With Lizzie. The child he'd wondered about often, dreamed about even, but had always believed had been lost long ago.

Was he nineteen. Christ, twenty. Not a child. A man.

'He's twenty-one and his name's Josh. And he's an amazing human being. Although I would say that because I'm his mother.' She gave a soft laugh, like the shy, sweet ones he remembered, and it felt as if he had skipped back in time. And taken a different path.

And then everything went dull and ragged and disjointed. The long, sickening roll of grief hitting right under the joy, because he hadn't taken that path. Lizzie and Josh had taken it. Without him.

He'd had a child. For twenty-one years, he'd had a son and he'd never had any idea. And because of a misunderstanding, bad timing, his overprotective Italian mother, and his own cowardice, he'd missed everything.

His child's first smile. His first step. His first word. He'd never given his son a piggyback. Or shown him how to tie his shoelaces, or held his bicycle while he learned to ride, or helped him with his homework – not that he would have been much good at that. But he could have told him all about girls, he knew a heck of a lot about…

His hands dropped from her waist and he stepped back. Sick with longing and regret and a blunt, futile anger. For all the things he'd lost that he could never get back.

* * *

'Sit down, Ren, before you fall down,' Liz whispered as she guided him to the lift wall, and watched him collapse. She sat next to him, brushed her own tears away. He looked shell-shocked. Even more shell-shocked than she felt.

'I'm sorry, I shouldn't have told you straight out like that,' she said, touching his arm, worried he might pass out. He looked so fragile.

'I don't think there's an easy way to tell someone that.' He gazed at her, his eyes so full of pain her heart wrenched.

She'd spent years exorcising all her memories of him but now they came flooding back, like water breaking through a dam. The taste of tobacco and need, the first time they'd kissed. The smile in his eyes when he teased her. Sinead O'Connor playing on the radio the first time they'd made love. Her elation when he'd told her it was his first time too. The excitement whenever his head appeared at her bedroom window after dark. The world of wonders they'd discovered under her Fresh Prince of *Bel Air* duvet. The bone-numbing agony when he'd gone.

Over the years she'd persuaded herself those memories didn't matter, that he wasn't important to her or to Josh. To realise now all that pain and denial had simply been the result of a terrible mistake was too much to contemplate, almost too much to bear.

He drew his legs up, draped his wrists over his knees. 'I've missed everything,' he said, the words so forlorn her heart hurt.

She pressed her palm to his cheek, her hand trembling against the hint of stubble. She wanted to say something, to make the pain go away. But what could she say? He had missed so much. And so had Josh.

He blinked, and his Adam's apple bobbed as he swallowed. 'Do you think I could meet him?'

She nodded. 'I could speak to him. Tell him your name, who you...'

'He doesn't even know my name?' He swore softly.

'Didn't he ever ask about me?' His head dropped back against the carpeted wall, his distress palpable.

Shame engulfed her.

'He did ask when he was little, but I think he knew I found it too painful to talk about and so he stopped.' She threaded her fingers through his, gripped his hand tightly. 'I'm so sorry, Ren, I didn't know you wanted to be...'

'Don't, Lizzie.' His fingers tightened around hers, and he turned towards her. 'Don't apologise. It's not your fault. You were just a kid, we both were.' He held onto her, their joined hands swinging lightly.

But the guilt still lingered. At the thought that she'd allowed her own resentment, her own heartache, to rob her son of his father during all the years of his childhood.

'I don't suppose you've got any pictures of him with you?' The tentative words ripped through the fog of recriminations.

'Oh my God. Yes, of course.' She scrambled across the lift on her hands and knees, pulled her iPhone out of her briefcase. Rushing back to sit beside him, she switched on the phone, opened the photo app and flicked to the album of photos she'd uploaded a year ago, the day after Josh had left for university, and she'd been suffering horribly from empty nest syndrome.

'Here.' She flicked to the first set: Josh's early years. 'You can start there and then just flick through them. I've put all my favourites of him in there.'

As Ren held the phone and scrolled through the photos, they were able to share at least a small part of their son's childhood together: Josh blowing out the candles on his Thomas the Tank Engine cake at his third birthday party. The gap-toothed grin on his face on his first day of primary school. His arms draped over his teammates shoulders when his football team got to the final of a local tournament. Holding his new boogie board one hideously wet summer in Cornwall. And a fifteen-year-old Josh looking a little too fondly for Liz's liking at his first girlfriend, Andie the punk.

Ren peppered her with questions, engrossed in every moment, and she answered every one, her heart bursting with pride and love but aching with sadness and regret at the same time – she couldn't turn the clock back and give Ren more than just the pictures.

At last they came to the most recent photo: Josh and her leaning against his third-hand Fiat Panda, the car packed to the gunnels with his stuff for college.

'He's handsome, he looks like you,' Ren murmured, his thumb stroking the picture.

Liz smiled, but enlarged the photo so it was magnified on Josh's face. 'There's a lot of you in there, too,' she murmured, her voice hoarse as she acknowledged all the things about Josh she had forced herself to deny for so long. 'He's got your eyes, and the shape of your face, and that deadly dimple.' She laughed. 'And girls follow him around, just like they used to do with you.'

He took a deep breath in, let it out and then handed her back the phone.

'Wow, this is kind of intense.' He raked his hands through his hair, driving it into furrows. Then he turned and smiled, the deadly dimple winking at her, despite the bittersweet emotion she could see in his eyes. 'You did an incredible job, Lizzie.'

The words without me' seemed to hang in the air, torturing her.

But then he cupped her chin, and shifted round. 'Thank you,' he whispered, and his lips touched hers.

At first the kiss was sweet and tender and sincere. She kissed him back, desperately grateful that he didn't blame her for what he'd lost. But then his tongue touched the seam of her lips and gratitude wasn't all she felt. Opening her mouth, she let him in. And suddenly, all those long-forgotten memories – the heat, the excitement, the longing – shimmered across her skin.

He drew back, his breathing as ragged as hers as he framed her face in gentle palms. 'Please tell me you're not married, or attached.'

She shook her head, her hands covering his on her cheeks. 'Not at the moment. Are you?'

'No.' A slow, steady smile spread across his handsome face.

'Do you…' She hesitated. 'Do you have any other children?'

The smile faltered as he shook his head and let go of her face. 'I wanted them, Annie didn't. It was one of the things that split us up.'

'Annie's your ex-wife?'

'Yeah.'

'How long were you married?' Silly to feel jealous of this woman, but somehow she did.

'Ten years,' he said, the dispassionate tone going some way to assuage the green-eyed monster. 'Which was six years too long.' He jerked a shoulder. 'She got remarried five years ago to an accountant. I didn't get an invite to the wedding.'

And just like that the monster slinked silently away.

The lift jolted and began to creak upwards.

He stood up swiftly and held out his hand. Tugging her to her feet, he settled his hands on her waist. 'Listen, Lizzie. I'd really like to see you again, tonight. Would you…' His voice faltered. 'Would you like to go out after work?'

She nodded, the thrum of excitement, of possibilities almost too intense to contemplate. Maybe they couldn't make the past right… But what if there was a chance to have a future? 'Yes, I'd like that. I'll ring Josh this afternoon. Tell him about…' She sighed, more than a little overwhelmed by the events of the last twenty minutes. How did you cope when your life changed so fundamentally in such a short space of time? 'I'm not sure he's going to believe it.'

'I'm not sure *I* believe it.' Ren chuckled, the sound incredulous and yet pleased.

'He's coming back this weekend,' she continued, trying not to read too much into that breath-taking smile. 'Maybe if you're available?' she stumbled to a halt. This was such a massive step. For all three of them. And it wasn't going to be easy.

'I'm supposed to be flying to New York on Friday on business,' he said. 'But let me know if Josh wants to meet up and I'll cancel.'

'Oh, right, OK.' She nodded around the choking feeling in her throat.

'Hey, Lizzie, don't cry.' He brushed the moisture from her cheeks with his thumbs. 'I won't put too much pressure on him, I swear.'

'It's not that,' she stuttered. 'I think he'll be excited and…'

'Then what is it?'

'It just feels so huge, that something I never thought would happen – could happen – is going to happen…' She hiccoughed, knowing she wasn't making a lot of sense. 'And when it does, we'll always have to face the fact we could have had so much more.'

His hands rubbed her arms and she realised it wasn't just Ren's relationship with their son she was talking about.

'I know.' He kissed her lightly, drew her close. 'And I'm sure it's going to make us both angry and resentful at times.' He stroked an open palm down her hair. 'But right now, I don't want to think about any of that. I just want to start from here and see what happens.' He pulled back, smoothed his thumbs over her cheeks. 'You've given me a child, Lizzie. Something I never thought I could have. Knowing that and having you in my arms again, makes me feel like anything is possible.'

She gulped down the emotion closing her throat, and smiled into those beautiful emerald eyes as the lift doors swished open.

'Hi, folks, sorry to keep you waiting so long.'

Liz glanced round at the short, sweaty young man standing outside the lift, beside two men in blue overalls.

'Don't be sorry.' She dropped her head back onto Ren's chest, circled his waist and felt his arms wrap tight around her shoulders. 'We're not.'

India Grey

India Grey's qualifications for a writing career include a degree in English Language and Literature, an obsession with fancy stationery and an inexhaustible passion for daydreaming. She grew up – and still lives – in a small market town in rural Cheshire with her husband and three daughters, loves history and vintage stuff and is a firm believer in love at first sight. She's written eleven books for Mills and Boon's Modern series.

You can visit her website at www.indiagrey.com, check out her blog at www.indiagrey.blogspot.com or find her on Twitter@indiagrey.

&

Summer '43

'One pound forty-four? But I only want half a dozen stamps!'

Beneath their heavy dusting of powder Mrs Partridge's cheeks quiver with indignation, but the currant-like eyes glaring at me through the glass partition are confused. I swallow my impatience as the bell over the shop door rings again.

It's always busy on a Friday. These days a good proportion of Whitbourne's cottages are second homes for weekenders, who park their BMWs on the double yellow lines outside and nip in to buy lightbulbs and pints of milk. Today it's even busier than usual, which is unfortunate as I'm here on my own and having to serve behind both the shop and post office counters. Ivy Partridge, who thinks it's 1929 rather than 1992, is holding up the queue.

'I'm afraid that's how much they are these days, Ivy. Twenty-four pence each.'

Although I've pitched my voice at a volume that can be heard by deaf old Mrs Partridge, I'm aware of someone else talking just as loudly. It's the American accent that gets my attention and makes my heart lurch, even now. Of course, it's the re-union this weekend. Fifty years since the USAAF rolled into Norfolk and changed it forever.

I slide Mrs Partridge's stamps through the little slot beneath the glass with a hand that isn't quite steady. I've been trying to ignore the event, although it's been harder than ever this time as the annual low-key commemoration has been turned into something altogether more ambitious in honour of the special anniversary. From behind my glass screen I've heard the plans being discussed for months; a new memorial to the 429th Bomb Group is going to be unveiled and – aware of time catching up with them, perhaps – more veterans than ever are predicted to attend.

Lips pursed, Mrs Partridge finally manoeuvres herself and her shopping trolley out of the way, enabling me to see the loud American lady. She is standing beside the rack of postcards, and as I watch she picks up the spectacles that are resting on a gold chain against her lilac angora pullover and perches them on the end of her nose. Even without the accent I'd know straight away that she wasn't from Whitbourne from her expensive jeans and superbly cut hair, tinted a shade of ash blonde not on the colour chart at Salon Valerie. I suppose she must be about my age, but she might as well be a different species.

'Oh, look at these, aren't they darling?' she announces to the shop at large, picking up a card bearing a black and white image of Whitbourne, before cars were parked alongside the cottages and when Jim Brook's garage was still a forge. 'Lyle, honey, we must send some of these home! They're so quaint!'

My next customer moves up to the window but I don't see who it is because darkness has gathered quite suddenly behind my eyes, like it does sometimes when I stand up too quickly. *Lyle*. Did I hear that right? I have to grip the edge of the counter until I know I won't pass out, and when the darkness dissolves again it's the American lady who is standing in front of the glass, laying the postcards in a fan before her.

'I think there was a queue,' I croak.

She looks around, genuinely surprised. 'Oh I beg your pardon – '

'You go ahead.' It's Dan Lockett who moved aside for her. I hadn't noticed him come in. He looks at me now and gives me the ghost of a smile. 'I don't mind waiting.'

The lady beams, like a child that's been given its own way. 'Well now, I'd to send these to the United States. Six of them – one for each of our grandchildren. I can't believe I found such perfect postcards! Lyle, honey, come and see.'

There's no mistaking the name this time. The worn lino on which I've stood almost every day for the last fifty years seems to dissolve beneath my feet and I feel like I'm spinning down through thin air. I'm aware of her husband coming over but I keep my head down, concentrating hard on opening up the big book of stamps and tearing carefully along the perforations. *It might not be him*, I tell myself. Lyle must be a common enough name in America, and since there were two thousand Yanks up at the base back then it's possible there were dozens of Lyles. The stamps are torn out. I brace myself to hit the ground and look up.

It's him.

He is holding one of the postcards, studying it at arm's length, the way I do myself these days. My first thought, as my heart clenches painfully, is that he hasn't changed, not a bit. It's ridiculous of course, since no one looks the same at – what, seventy-four? – as they did fifty years earlier, but he is instantly, achingly familiar. The same heavy-lidded, laughing eyes; the same tanned, hollow cheeks.

'Well, look at that – Just how I remember it.'

The same voice, which used to make goosebumps rise on my arms.

'My husband was with the 429th,' the lilac lady – *Lyle's wife* – explains proudly. 'He was based here during the war.'

'I know.' I force the words past the lump in my throat. 'I remember.'

Her eyes widen and her face splits into an incredulous smile. '*No*? Lyle, d'you hear that, honey? This lady thinks she might remember you!'

He lowers the postcard and through the glass his eyes meet mine. The same faded blue as I remember – a precise match, I used to think, for the washed-out blue squares on my mother's checked tablecloth. I kept that tablecloth after she died for that reason. Have it still, somewhere.

'Hope?' he says with a slow-spreading smile. 'Well I'll be…Come out here and let me take a proper look at you!'

And so, like a sleepwalker I leave my glass enclosure and go through into the shop. There, amid much laughing and oh-my-goshes from his wife, Lyle takes hold of my shoulders and kisses me on each cheek. Then, with his eyes still on me, he puts his arm around his wife's lilac shoulders and says, 'Hope, I want you to meet Nancy. Nancy, this is Hope Riley.'

'Oh Lyle, she might've been Hope Riley fifty years ago but I'm sure she has a different name now!' Nancy Johnson laughs as she too kisses me on both cheeks. I breathe in her perfume with a pang of masochistic fascination.

'No.' Pulling away awkwardly, I tug my cardigan down

over my tweed skirt, eating him up with my eyes. 'No, that's still my name. I never married.'

'Oh, well fancy that!' Nancy's hands flutter to the glasses around her neck. For a second she looks a little flustered but rallies quickly. 'Well, it sure is nice to meet you, Hope. We're staying up at Alford Hall – do you know it? You must join us for dinner one evening, mustn't she Lyle? Then you two can reminisce about old times.'

Dear God. My hand goes to my mouth to hide an involuntary and wholly inappropriate burst of laughter. I look at Lyle, expecting to see my own horror at the idea of reminiscing about old times in front of his wife mirrored on his face, but he just smiles that smile that makes my bones melt.

'That sounds like a fine idea. How 'bout we say tomorrow? Seven o'clock?'

Seven o'clock. I hear myself repeat it, as if that might make it seem less surreal. It's only after Lyle and his wife have left the shop that I remember my other customers. I look around for Dan Lockett, but he's already gone.

* * *

Alford Hall used to be home to the Pemberton family and a staff of thirty until the war changed their fortunes and robbed them of both their sons. These days it's one of a discreet chain of carefully-styled hotels, frequented by businessmen and groups of women on spa weekends. I haven't been near the place for years.

Lyle and Nancy are waiting for me in the lobby, sitting on an overstuffed sofa beside the empty fireplace, drinks on the table in front of them. Nancy sees me first and gets up, her hands outstretched. She's wearing a narrow two-piece of dull gold silk, a thousand times more elegant than my Laura Ashley shirtdress, or indeed anything else I've ever owned.

'You look a picture,' she says kindly. 'Doesn't she, Lyle?'

'She sure does.'

His voice is warm and approving and his eyes move lazily over me like they used to, even though his wife is watching. He seems perfectly at ease, but then he always did. It was one of the things that thrilled me; that in the midst of all the chaos and danger he should be so completely relaxed. 'What can I get you to drink, Hope? We're having gin and tonics.'

My skin prickles. I shake my head. 'Sherry, please.'

I long to follow him to the bar but Nancy pats the sofa beside her, inviting me to sit.

'So, tell me all about yourself, Hope,' she says, and gives a peal of silvery laughter. 'I was going to ask if you've lived in Whitbourne long, but I guess I already know the answer to that.'

'I was born here,' I say, struggling to match her vivacity and failing entirely. 'My father was the vicar. I started work in the post office when I was seventeen, the year the US Army arrived. The men from the base used to come in all the time, although in those days there was precious little to buy.'

It became a joke between us, Lyle and me. Once he'd spent his plentiful GI pay on more string and ink than any man could reasonably need he began to think up increasingly ridiculous errands as an excuse to come in. He'd ask for a refill for the air in his bicycle pump, camouflage paint, a tube of elbow grease; all the time looking at me with those lazy blue-sky eyes that told me what he really wanted. Me. *Me*.

When he comes back with my sherry he tells us that our

table is ready. As we go into the dining room I try to meet his eye to see if he too is remembering the last time we went out to dinner together. The first and only time.

Ten missions down his crew got forty-eight hours leave; time too precious to waste on crowded trains bound unreliably for London. We went to Cambridge, where he checked us into a hotel as Mr and Mrs Johnson. On honeymoon, he told the stony-faced receptionist, and got away with it too, thanks to the uniform, the accent, the smile. I kept my hands rammed into my pockets because I had no ring. In the lift on the way up to our room he made easy conversation with the prehistoric porter, while all the time his hand was beneath my jacket, his fingers tracing circles of ecstasy down my spine.

It was my first time but I wasn't scared. Lyle was different from the undernourished English boys I knew. *I* was different. Since I'd met him I'd been filled with a kind of energy, almost violent in its intensity, and as he kicked shut the door of our sparse little room and pressed me against it, I suddenly understood what it was for.

I still remember every detail of that room, from the pattern in the gold rayon curtains to the cigarette burns on the bedside table. We didn't leave it much, except to dash down to the icy bathroom at the end of the corridor, and for dinner that night in the echoing dining room.

As he pulls my chair out I am back there. The modern-day opulence of the 'Pemberton Restaurant' fades and I can smell over boiled greens, sense the curious stares of other diners rapidly souring into disapproval when Lyle slides his hand up my thigh under the tablecloth and I let out a yelp of laughter and lust.

'I expect you dinc here a lot,' Nancy says now, looking at me over the top of the leatherette folder that holds the menu.

'Not often, no. My goddaughter's son got married here, but other than that—'

'You have godchildren? Oh, how wonderful.' Her face lights up with relief at this conversational lifeline. 'How many?'

'Four. Plus two nieces and five great-nieces and nephews. Far easier and more enjoyable than having any myself.'

It's a line I've used so many times over the years that it trips off my tongue automatically. Nancy laughs and reaches for her handbag.

'You're right about that. That's why I love being a grandma – you can spoil 'em like crazy and give 'em back before bedtime. Here, let me show you ours.' She's taken a Kodak envelope from her bag and is shuffling prints like a croupier with a deck of cards. 'Three fine sons and six adorable grandchildren. There's Tiffany and Madison – they're Michael's girls – and Casey and Lyle Junior…'

Their tanned, smiling faces blur into one, but I notice their eyes. Blue eyes. Lyle's eyes, staring out at me from every photograph, accusingly it seems, although I'm prepared to accept that's my own paranoia. Or guilt. Even so, after a few more snaps I have to look away.

'Forgive me, I'm boring you.' Briskly Nancy gathers the photographs together, smiling to disguise the fact that she's hurt. 'I guess you never wanted kids yourself then?'

It's very hot in the dining room. My mouth is dry. I pick up my glass and drain the last of the sherry.

'I didn't want to be like my sister, Joy,' I say quietly, looking straight at Lyle. 'I didn't want to spend my life washing nappies and mashing up carrots.'

He is studying the wine list as if he really is interested in it. As if he genuinely doesn't remember. But perhaps he can sense my eyes on him because he shuts the folder with a snap and smiles widely at both of us.

'As this is a special occasion, whaddya say I order us some champagne?'

* * *

I can't sleep. Too much champagne, probably. My heart is racing and my mind is trying to keep pace with it.

It's 3.30 am, and I've taken the box in which I store things of sentimental significance down from the top of the wardrobe. I can't stop thinking about the photographs Nancy showed me; the children's faces have been flickering in a jerky slideshow behind my eyelids as I've been trying to sleep. I move aside invitations to long-ago weddings and yellowed snippets from newspapers, delving down through the strata of my life until I find what I'm looking for.

It's the only photograph I have of myself and Lyle, the only one that exists. His arm is around me and we're both laughing, which has made our faces blur slightly. Dan Lockett took it when we came across him in Whitbourne woods one day – his father was a forester on the Alford estate and they had a cottage up there. Dan was turned down by the Army, on account of a weak heart, apparently. He had a desk job in some department or other, but he'd broken his ankle – God knows how, in an office – and been sent home to recuperate that summer.

I look at the photograph for a long time, then close my eyes and let the colours bleed back into the faded black and white scene. It's late afternoon; the sun is warm on my face and there are bits of leaves in my hair. My hips ache pleasantly, and the tops of my thighs are damp because today Lyle forgot to bring a French letter. He didn't discover this until he had unbuttoned my dress and kissed me all the way up from my navel to my mouth, by which time both of us were way past caring. One time, he says afterwards. One time'll be fine.

It better had be, I say lightly. I am seventeen and hungry for life beyond the vicarage and the post office; the life we've talked about having together once the war is over and he has broken it off with Nancy. I don't want to end up like Joy, and spend my days washing nappies and mashing up carrots.

Laughing into the camera, we have already forgotten about the gamble we have taken. It is getting late and Lyle has to get back to the base. Tomorrow, although he doesn't know it yet, he will fly his sixteenth mission, to Regensburg; a mission that will go down in USAAF history as one of its most ill-fated. Sixty B-17s will be lost, hundreds of men killed, including the navigator and tail gunner in Lyle's crew. Lyle, in the top turret, will be hit in the shoulder and elbow. He'll be taken to hospital in Lincoln, but it will be two frantic weeks before I find this out, by which time he will be on a Red Cross ship halfway across the Atlantic.

We have shared our last cigarette, our last shivering orgasm, and are down to the last few of our numberless kisses, but we know none of this as he puts his arm around my shoulders and pulls me against his body and we squint into the afternoon sunlight and laugh.

I turn over the picture. On the back Dan Lockett has written Summer '43.

* * *

I don't intend to go to the unveiling of the memorial but in the end I can't keep away. The ceremony takes place around the village war memorial, beside which – after lengthy debate – the monument commemorating the 429th has been sited. I deliberately arrive a little late so I can stand at the back of the small crowd, unnoticed.

The mayor is giving a speech, welcoming the USAAF veterans back. There are perhaps twenty of them, recognisable by their smart brass-buttoned blazers. I spot Lyle straight away. He's holding a wreath of paper poppies and his face shows a solemnity in remembrance that I never saw back then. Nancy is standing beside him, wearing a beautiful dark blue coat and an expression of beatific calm, which almost looks like triumph.

The vicar – an earnest youth with a chumminess of manner that would horrify my father – is speaking now. A sharp-edged autumn wind hurls leaves onto the steps of the war memorial and snatches his voice away, tossing back the words sacrifice and loss. Nancy tucks her arm through Lyle's and bitterness shrivels my insides. What does she know about those things? With her husband and her three fine sons, her six blue-eyed grandchildren. *What does she know?*

The vicar lifted his hands, palms upturned. 'Friends, let us share a moment of silence, to remember…'

There is a shuffling of feet and a bowing of heads. I keep my gaze fixed forward and try to make my mind blank, but the memories come anyway. An autumn afternoon, like this one, the light bleeding out of the day too soon. A Sunday – Harvest Festival evensong – the steam in the kitchen oily with the smell of the rabbit my mother skinned for lunch. Details come back in fragments, embedding themselves in my flesh like shards of broken glass. The bitterness of the gin, which made me gag with every mouthful. Condensation running down the walls, the windows smudged to pale squares that shimmered and pulsed before my eyes.

My whole body pulsed like one giant heart. My skin, scarlet, wrinkled and papery like poppy petals. The blood whooshed in my ears so that I never heard the banging on the door and was surprised to see Dan Lockett's face looming over me through the steam, like something from a disjointed dream. His voice echoed in the empty spaces inside my head, and cool air curled around my body as he lifted me out of the tin bath.

Then I was sick.

The Last Post sounds the end of the silence, but the memory of how he carried me upstairs, slid my nightdress over my head and laid me back against the cool sheet won't be chased away that easily. He must have tidied up the kitchen, emptying the scalding water out of the bath and getting rid of the gin bottle before coming back up to see if I was alright. It was dark by then. I remember him pulling the blackout before switching on my bedside light.

'I'll marry you,' he said and his eyes were dark and sad in the glow of the lamp.

The men of the 429th begin to place their wreaths against the granite base of the new memorial. With a start I feel someone slide their arm through mine. It's Nancy. I stiffen and have to stop myself from pulling away. Lyle is the last to lay his wreath and together we watch him stoop, then straighten and salute.

'He's a good man,' Nancy murmurs beside me, so softly that I don't know if she's talking to me or herself. The ceremony ends and people begin to circulate, greeting each other in subdued tones. Nancy lets go of my arm but doesn't move away. I can tell that there's something she wants to say and I have the strongest feeling that I don't want to hear it.

'We've had our bad times, Lyle and me. He's like any man – easily distracted, especially by a tight skirt and a pretty smile. But not a single day passes when I don't remember how lucky I am to have him.'

I look at her. She seems frailer suddenly. Less assured. The wind pulls at a strand of her ash blonde hair, showing the white at its roots.

'A lot of men didn't come back,' I say neutrally.

'I'm not stupid, Hope.' Head bent, she smoothes the soft leather of her gloves over her fingers. 'You know, when he was over here during the war I used to pray every day that God would send him back to me. I didn't even ask for him to be in one piece, just so long as he came back.' She looks up at me. 'I guess I never thought that the piece that might be missing was his heart.'

The crowd is thinning now as people drift off in the direction of the pub, where there is a fire and a free bar. I close my eyes for a second, wincing at a pain I can't quite locate, then I take a deep breath. 'No,' I say, on an exhalation. 'He never loved me. I was his distraction from the job, that's all. His heart was always with you.'

It's true. In fact, it's so blindingly obvious as Lyle walks over, his smile freezing at the sight of Nancy and me together, that I feel a little stunned. Lightheaded. He glances at me uneasily as he puts his arm around his wife, as if he is wondering what I've told her, trying to calculate how much he has to explain. Nancy gathers herself, her mask of serenity slipping back into place as she looks up at him.

'It was a moving ceremony, sweetheart. I'm glad we could be here.'

'Me too, honey.' Clearly relieved, he gives her a little squeeze. 'Now, how 'bout we go to the bar and I'll buy you a pint of English beer?'

'After everything you told me about it?' She swats at him affectionately. 'I'll pass, thanks. You'll come, won't you Hope?'

I feel tired and peculiarly disorientated. I open my mouth to make an excuse when something catches the corner of my eye and makes me look again. Something shifts and slots into place in my head.

'Sorry, would you excuse me?' Nancy looks surprised as I embrace her briefly. 'It was lovely to meet you,' I say, and I too am surprised because I mean it.

Lyle follows the direction of my gaze and gives a grunt. 'I recognise that fella…Wasn't he the guy with the weak heart, lived out by the woods? Damned if I can think of the name…'

But I don't wait to see if he remembers the man who took the photograph on that summer's day in 1943. The man who picked up the pieces of me that were left after Lyle went, and offered to be a father to his child.

There was no need in the end. About a week after Dan found me in the bath I woke up with cramps in my stomach and blood on the sheets. I should have been relieved, but I wasn't. I felt like a murderer. Like I'd lost everything and deserved nothing. Maybe that was why I told Dan he didn't have to marry me.

'Dan, wait!'

He is walking away from the square, up the lane past the church. He stops and turns, and his smile is as wistful as the autumn afternoon.

'You don't have to tell me to do that, Hope Riley. I've been waiting for you for almost fifty years.'

I stop. My chest is tight and the breath burning my throat, but it's not just from walking too fast to catch him up.

'Dan, I've been so stupid.' The word spills out of me, like a sob. 'All these years I stayed here, just in case he came back…'

Like Snow White in her glass coffin, waiting and waiting for Prince Charming to come and bring her back to life, so I waited for Lyle. But it turned out that he wasn't the Prince after all; just a charming boy a long way from home.

Dan shakes his head, slowly, his eyes full of an emotion I can't read. I've known him for so long, but suddenly I realise I barely know him at all. And I want to. I really want to.

'And I stayed here in case he didn't,' he sighs. 'But now he has.'

'Thank God, because now I know. I see…' My throat feels raw, like I'm getting a cold, and my cheeks are wet. 'Dan, is it too late?'

The next thing I know he has pulled me into his arms and is holding me, cradling me against his chest, just like he did on that September Sunday so long ago when he called round to bring firewood. The years fall away and the ice in my veins creaks as the blood begins to move again. I can hear his heart, slow and steady against my cheek. Strong. I never did believe that story about the Army turning him down.

We stay like that for a long time. His breath is warm against my hair.

'It's never too late,' he murmurs at last.

Still we don't move.

We have waited a lifetime. There's no rush.

Judy Astley

Judy Astley's first novel, *Just For The Summer* was published in 1990, before which she worked as a dressmaker, illustrator, painter and parent. Her eighteen novels are all published by Transworld and the most recent is *In The Summertime,* a twenty-years-on follow-up to that first book.

Judy's specialist areas are family disharmony and family chaos with a mix of love-and-passion and plenty of humour thrown in, ranging across all generations – love isn't only for the young!

She's been a regular columnist on magazines and enjoys writing journalism pieces on more or less any subject, usually from a fun viewpoint. She lives in London and Cornwall, loves plants, books, hot sun and rock music, preferably all at once. She would claim that being excessively curious about other people's lives and listening into the conversations of strangers is essential in her line of work.

Judy's website is at www.judyastley.com

&

How To Get A Pill Into A Cat

It's not the best start to a neighbourly relationship is it, when the first words you hear on the doorstep of the man who's just moved in next door are, 'Hello! So you're the other cat-lady.'

Catlady? Oh terrific. Not a stereotype at all then. Just because I don't have a resident man on my premises but *do* have a cat (and just one old dozy mog, not twenty pampered furry beasts), it doesn't make me a demented Cat Woman.

I try but fail to regain my cheery-neighbour smile. 'I have *a* cat, yes,' I tell him, handing over my welcome-to-the-street cake and sensing I'm looking as idiotically po-faced as I feel. We exchange a few remarks about parking permits, wheelie bins and over-the-road's amazing monkey puzzle tree and I go home to have a bit of a seethe.

I don't have to guess how he already knows about me. It's obvious that Polly, who lives on the other side of him, has already raced round and introduced herself and given him all the street info. Trust her to get in first, I think, suddenly embarrassed for my humble, and frankly a bit lopsided, Victoria sandwich. She'd have worn a vat of lipgloss and brought champagne. But then she was young and swishily glamorous whereas I was a perpetually flustered divorcée with earth under my fingernails – hazard of working at the plant nursery

– and a teenage daughter stressing over exams and boys. My cat was *not* some man/baby substitute, in fact, poor Boris hardly got a look-in some days. Thank goodness for dry cat food. At least he was always sure there was a meal in his bowl, even though Polly's shameless Burmese called Princess – I ask you – often ran in through our back door like she owned the place and gobbled down his lunch.

'Oh Mum, like chill?' Cassie said, an hour later over supper when I was still grumping about the perceived image of lone women of a certain age. 'He's probably well butters and keeps cages full of minging ferrets in his shed.'

I don't answer that. OK it was a flying visit but I did manage to take in that next-door Nick isn't remotely 'well butters' as Cassie and her teenage mates so charmingly put it. He's quite the opposite actually: an attractive arty-looking grey-eyed sort with frondy blond hair like a slightly past it surfer. He is also without an on-site partner (information from Polly who got it via the estate agent the minute the keys were handed over). I couldn't see any obvious evidence of massed smelly pets either but I had seen a gorgeous brass bed that I coveted the moment I saw the removal men unloading it. Not that I was being nosy or anything. I just happened to be fixing the iffy blind at the front window at the time.

A few weeks later and next-door Nick and I have progressed to being on grumbling-about-the-weather terms and taking in each other's mis-delivered parcels. He tells me he's something to do with music production and I tell him about working on the help-desk giving advice on pruning wisteria and the eternal autumn-or-spring sowing debate when it comes to hardy annuals. He really likes Love-in-A-Mist and I feel a bit flustered and mutter, 'Oh yes, Nigella. Very pretty.'

To which he laughs and says, 'No, not really my type.' And we leave it on a confusion of who-mean-what.

I'm so out of the habit of looking to find anyone attractive that I only realise I fancy him a bit when I'm in the garden on the first sunny day in ages, hanging out laundry. I'm suddenly hesitant about having my underwear dangling on the washing line in full view of his window and I stand there dithering, damp knickers in hand, conscious that they are very much the sort that can only be described as Sensible. I take them back inside and drape them over the sitting room radiator where Cassie takes one look, shrieks in full teen drama *stylee* and orders me to make sure they're 'like, to'ally gone' before any of her friends come round and faint from repulsion.

A knock on the door has me stuffing my pants down the back of the sofa in a panic but it's only Polly – accompanied by Princess who runs past me at the front door, straight to Boris's food bowl – calling in to tell me she's going away for several days and would I mind keeping an eye out for burglars, squatters and any chancer up a ladder claiming to be a window cleaner. I wish her a safe journey and she gives me a naughty wink – which means she's probably not going to see a lot of the great outdoors on this trip, (lucky girl) as she totters off on her sky-heels, followed by little grey Princess who is still chewing my cat's lunch as she goes.

There's something bugging me though, something Polly hasn't said and it isn't till the next morning as I'm retrieving my knickers from behind the sofa and I hear her pink Mini roaring away down the street that I realise what it is. Any other time she's been away for a few days, she's asked me to call in and feed Princess. This time she hasn't. Perhaps, I think, she's taken the cat away with her but that evening as

I drive home from work via the supermarket I see Princess sitting on Nick's garden wall, washing her paws. Then Nick emerges from his front door, tip-toeing towards the cat in a furtive creeping-up way, holding out something in his hand and calling Princess to come to him. I sit in the car for a few moments with the window down, watching him sneaking up on her, trying not to laugh as I hear him softly calling, 'Come on Princess, nice din-dins for you, pusscat.' Princess gives him the look, flicks her tail at him and stalks off. So that's it, I realise, the attack of the giggles vanishing abruptly, Polly has asked Nick to take care of Princess instead of me. I get a twinge of envy. Whatever Polly's up to on this break, she's clearly well onto Nick's case for when she gets back. In my head I'm way down the imagination line, trying on hats for their wedding and holding back tears at the ceremony. Polly of course looks young, slender and stunningly bridal-radiant. Nick looks – as he always does – bloody gorgeous. I'd be tempted to wear green – the colour meant to bring bad luck to a bride and groom – but I'm really not that nasty. Yet.

'Cat care going well then?' I to Nick as I open the car boot and start to haul the bags out.

Nick, all sky blue linen shirt and a sexy little rip over the knee of his jeans, comes down the path and helps me unload and I wish I didn't look so rushed and hot and that the new boy at the nursery had shown some sense of control with the hose pipe while watering the mixed bedding. The left side of me, hair to feet, is still noticeably damp.

'Very highly strung,' Nick murmurs, pulling a face in the direction of the rude rear end of the little cat.

'Polly or Princess?' I can't resist saying.

'Both probably. She has to take pills. The cat, I mean.

Twice a day. Polly only told me that little gem just as she was dashing off – said Princess's paw had been stung by a wasp and the vet's given her anti-biotics. I tried it this morning but the pill ended up down a crack in the floorboards.'

I sympathise. Anyone with a cat knows about the pill scenario. One weekend when Polly went off, she left me with instructions vis-à-vis Princess and some worming tablets. Nice.

We were in my kitchen now, Nick's brought most of the bags in and shopping is spilling out all over the table. 'Would you like some help?' I ask him as I switch the kettle on. 'Two can get a pill into a cat far easier than one.'

'I was hoping you'd say that.' Nick smiles at me, the skin by his eyes creasing appealingly into a fan. I pour cat biscuits into the bowl of the long-suffering Boris, open the back door and wait for Princess to hurtle in at the sound of a spoon tapping against the dish. We don't have long to wait.

By the evening of day four we're on a roll with the pill routine. It's coffee for the morning session and in the evening I pour us each a glass of wine and we get under way with a few skill-sharpening sips before I wrap my old Adam Ant T-shirt firmly round Princess. Nick holds her tight while I try to shove the tablet throat-wards, avoiding her needle teeth. After a bit of a tussle, success gets us clinking glasses and relaxing on the garden sofa in the early evening sunshine, talking and laughing about anything and everything. My staff-discount phlox and tobacco flowers scent the soft warm air and in a giddy optimism I contemplate buying fancy underwear and consigning the pants of shame to the bin.

Polly is due back tonight. Nick comes round at nine in the morning with Princess and her pills. I look at him over the coffee I'm pouring and he's looking at me and I can't help wishing Polly was going to be away for a fortnight, not just this long weekend.

'Right, so it's just this one last pill,' Nick says, watching Princess tucking into Boris's breakfast.

'Yep,' I say, feeling a bit sad. These few days of having him casually in and out of my house have been such a delight. And yes, I know he's only next door but what excuse can I find to get this close to him again?

Nick pulls the tablets out of his pocket, flicks one out too fast from the pack and it drops on the floor, rolling under the table. Just as I go to pick it up, Princess gets there first and pounces on it. We stand there, silent, watching her wolf it down, crunching it noisily.

Nick shifts a bit and I look at him, thinking of all that hassle we've gone to over those days, the T-shirt and the cat-wrapping and the holding and the teeth.

'Er…sorry. I just…um, you know…' He shrugs and smiles guiltily, looking delightfully shy. 'OK, I was enjoying the company.'

'You actually knew all the time that Princess would do that?' I ask him, as some kind of penny drops slowly and very, very pleasingly in my brain.

'Bang to rights. Polly did actually tell me the cat was fine with pills. Thinks they're treats,' he admits. 'So… er… yes, I did know.'

I don't tell him, but so did I.

Kate Harrison

Kate Harrison writes fiction and non-fiction for adults and teenagers, including the bestselling Secret Shopper series, *The Boot Camp* and a trilogy of thrillers: *Soul Beach*, *Soul Fire* and *Soul Storm*. She also writes non-fiction, including *Sunday Times* bestseller, *The 5:2 Diet Book*, and a cookbook, *The Ultimate 5:2 Diet Recipe Book*. Her books have been translated into fifteen languages.

Before becoming a novelist, she was a BBC correspondent and producer, working in news, consumer programmes and documentaries. She loves cooking, writing and beaches, and lives not far from the sea in Brighton with her partner. Find out more at www.kate-harrison.com and www.the5-2dietbook.com She also tweets (now and then) @katewritesbooks

Life of Pies was inspired by a fantastic trip behind the scenes at Sussex-based pie experts, Higgidy Pies, though the flavours and strange goings on in the story are definitely not based on reality!

&

Life Of Pies

I can't say I wasn't warned.

Ron 'Mr Storage' Brown was crystal clear at the interview. 'It's quite a boring job, and the opportunities for promotion are non-existent. But there *are* compensations.'

'Such as?'

He raised a flamboyantly bushy eyebrow. 'Take the job, you might find out. You look like you need feeding up.'

I took the job. I didn't have much choice. Since I got back from travelling, I've had doors slamming in my face, phone lines going mysteriously dead – the average internet spammer gets more responses to their speculative emails than I do.

I really thought I'd come back from my round-the-world-trip with a CV-full of transferable skills. The plan was…well, there was no plan. Dad's will made it clear that he was leaving me 'mad money' so I could leave my tedious accountancy job and see life without spread-sheets.

I booked a one-way ticket to Bangkok and figured I'd make the rest up as I went along. Mum wasn't thrilled. 'You'll fall in love with someone from the Outback, or the Congo, and I'll never see you again.'

I can't pretend that my trip was entirely man-free. But I didn't fall in love with the world's men – I fell in love with its menus. I spent fourteen months on a gastro-tour of the globe. But now most employers are underwhelmed by those new transferable skills: Vietnamese spring-rolling, bagel-boiling, whipping up the perfect crème Chantilly.

OK. I took a chance, to see where life would take me. And life has dumped me unceremoniously on a trading estate two miles from where I grew up.

Day one is going OK. I've had an extensive tour of Ron's storage containers, and now know all there is to know about the different grades of bubble wrap. Ron's wife Brenda has been telling me their life history, from humble beginnings in cardboard boxes. The two of them had hoped to spend their twilight years on ocean cruises, but the bottom has now fallen out of the container market and no one wants to buy the business off them, so they're stuck.

'But the recession's gotta end soon, hasn't it?' Brenda says, squeezing her husband's meaty hand. I can imagine her on an ocean cruise, with her bird-of-paradise earrings and turbo-charged hair.

The Browns are lovely people, but there is no escape. There's nowhere to buy lunch or a paper. Even the brick unit opposite is empty. I wait all day for the 'compensations' to make themselves known, but nothing happens. I go home feeling so depressed that Mum skips the 'you've wasted your life' speech she's given me every other day since I got back.

On Tuesday, the unit opposite comes to life. There are cars and vans and people wearing blue overalls and unflattering hairnets. When I ask Brenda what they do there, she just gives me a mysterious smile.

It's not till after lunch – cling-filmed ham sandwiches, made by Mum, which catapult me twenty years back in time to Springhill Juniors, and not in a good way – that I catch my first whiff. Ron and Brenda are watching me expectantly.

I sniff once, twice. It's yeasty. Toasty.

'Pastry?'

Brenda nods conspiratorially. 'Do you like pies, Rachel?'

'Um. I suppose so.' But not British pies: I don't rate sturdy steak-and-kidney, or soggy-bottomed chicken. No, I'm thinking crisp quiche Lorraine, fresh from a Parisian pâtisserie. Or the velvety pumpkin pie I was served at Thanksgiving in the heart of Texas. Spicy and sweet and… 'Why?'

'The factory opposite?' Brenda says. 'It's the HQ for Life of Pie. Best gourmet pies in the country. Super-expensive if you have to pay full price. Luckily we don't.'

She points out of the window. In the pie factory car park, a stall has appeared, as though it's been picked up by hurricane from a village fete and dropped onto the concrete. Already people are emerging from all corners of the estate, following their noses, like the kids in the Bisto gravy ads.

'Compensations, remember?' Ron says, and I know I should have taken that call centre job. Discounted re-heatable pies are not my idea of a perk.

But still, I follow them downstairs, because it gives me a break from comparing masking tape suppliers.

Outside the sun beats down and heat rises from the tarmac, and I sweat like a New York corn-dog sandwiched between two hotplates. I look up at the blue sky and think about all the other places I'd rather be.

The queue's already twenty strong: there are mechanics, a big guy in overalls covered in sawdust, a gaggle of women who smell of perm solution. Brenda pushes in.

'Rachel, come and meet Anton, the head chef. He's from Paris, you know.'

He looks familiar, but it's only because he is straight from central casting. Checked blue trousers, chef's whites, a stupid tall hat, with black curls escaping along the hairline. Tall? Yes. Dark? Yes. Handsome? Depends on whether you like Gallic arrogance, pouty lips and a large Roman nose.

Brenda's a fan, her cheeks have gone all pink. Anton turns to me. '*Enchanté*,' he says, and holds out his hand. When I go to shake it, he lifts my hand to his lips and kisses it.

I blush, even though what he just did strikes me as ridiculously OTT. And not awfully hygienic, when he's handling food.

'Which of my pies would you like to try?' he asks, in a voice as unctuous as oven-baked camembert. 'They all taste good, but ze appearance is not *parfait*, which is why we give zem away to our charming neighbours.'

There are two piles of wide, flat boxes on the table in front of him. The packaging is classier than I expected, with *Life of Pies created by Chef Anton* written across the front in a swirly design. There are vintage-style photos on the boxes, too: the left hand one has a blonde woman in a low-cut, forties blouse and the right features a farmer with a gappy smile, chewing straw.

'Ploughman Pete and Tarty Lorraine,' Ron says. 'Anton names his pies after people from the estate. Pete works in the plumbers' merchants, and then Lorraine—'

'Is our marketing manager and ze one who gives ze pies stupid English names,' Anton says, pouting. 'I am responsible only for ze recipes. Which remain authentically French.'

I almost don't take one, because he's so full of himself. But then I catch sight of the pie through the steamed up plastic window. It's more like a quiche, golden brown with flecks of pink and white.

I take a Tarty Lorraine and as I walk back to the office, I remember one of the many things I discovered in Paris: that I might love French food, but I am less *enchanté* by the French.

* * *

Mum and I are in pie heaven.

From the crisp short crust, to the custardy filling, Lorraine is spectacular. Even Mum, who normally thinks ready meals are a travesty, is won over. 'Try to keep that job long enough to fill the chest freezer with free pies, eh, Rach?'

Next morning, I sniff the air when I get off the bus but there's nothing yet. The smell of baking doesn't waft in our direction till just after twelve. This time, there's a garlicky top note above the pastry aroma.

'Oh, it's Mickey's Mushroom Medley today,' Brenda says. 'Named after their fork lift truck driver, who goes mushroom hunting at weekends.'

I think back to the glorious autumn day I spent foraging in Tuscany. It was there, picking finest fungi with a grizzled old guide, and then cooking them over a wood fire, that I dreamed of a different life, leading gourmet tours around the world.

A lorry thunders past, making my desk shake. So much for that different life…I glance across the road towards the pie factory, and glimpse a chef's hat silhouetted against a window on the second floor. Is Chef Anton thinking the same thing – *how did we end up here?*

The hat disappears, and ten minutes later, the stall is set up.

When I get to the front of the line, Anton immediately interrogates me about last night's meal. 'So. Ze Lorraine? You liked it?'

I hate it when people fish for compliments. 'It was OK,' I say, watching his eyes narrow. 'But there could have been more ham, so you get some in every mouthful.'

'More ham?' He looks cross. 'Try *champignon*.' He thrusts a box into my hands. 'Ze browning is a little uneven but I think of it as *jolie laide*. Which is what we French call something so ugly it is almost pretty.'

Is that a comment aimed at me? It is true that I'm looking ropey at the moment. My tan's faded to a yellowy hue, though my freckles are as prominent as ever, and I'm way too skinny. Nothing has tasted right since I got back.

Though when I heat up the mushroom pie at home, it certainly smells right. And I wish I'd asked him for two.

* * *

On Thursday the air smells like a brewery – thanks to Bulldog Bill's Beef and Ale Pie.

When the stall pops up at two o'clock, I'm first in the queue.

'Your ugly mushrooms were pretty good,' I tell Anton.

His lips turn up very slightly at the edges. 'Praise indeed. Perhaps you would care to bring your very sophisticated palate to our special tasting next Tuesday. When we develop new pies, we like to try zem out on our most loyal customers.'

'I'll think about it.'

As Brenda and I carry our Bulldog pies back to the office, she looks like she's about to explode from excitement. 'He promised he'd consider naming his next pie after me, Rachel. This time next week, I could be immortalised in pastry!'

* * *

I spend the weekend with old school friends who have great jobs, handsome husbands and bonny babies.

It's almost a relief to get back to the ordinariness of Mr Storage, though my heart sinks when Brenda reminds me that Life of Pies doesn't bake on a Monday. 'But we have tomorrow's tasting to look forward to!'

We're all counting down the hours till Tuesday evening. As we finally cross the road at six, I feel like Charlie approaching the chocolate factory, though Anton is not Willy Wonka and there are no oompah-loompahs on the factory floor. The offices themselves are as boring as ours, but the famous tarty Lorraine leads us through the corridors and upstairs to the 'tasting room' where Ron, Brenda and I sit at a long bench, alongside a couple of lads from the injection moulding firm next door.

Lorraine explains she'll be recording our reactions, while Anton broods in the background. An alarm pings and he pulls a freshly-baked pie out of the oven.

'I present the first in our range of dessert pies for the winter, this is Brenda's Blackberry Clafoutis!'

Brenda shrieks so loud you'd think he'd suggested actually baking her in the pie itself. But she's beside herself with delight. 'Oh, *Anton.* It's an honour. A privilege.'

You haven't tasted it yet, I think.

But it certainly looks the part, with a bouffant golden brown topping that's every bit as bouncy as Brenda's blow-dry. The pastry has big circular gaps, which remind me of Brenda's favourite polka dot blouse, and underneath there's a deep purple fruity base that matches her lipstick.

We're each given a slice and heat rises from the jammy middle. Not the ideal pud for a steamy August day, but it does smell seriously good. Just before I taste the first forkful, I look up. Anton is staring at me. I smile but he doesn't. Surly so and so.

But then I look again: his face is crossed with tension. It might just be a pie to me, but it matters to him.

Ron, Brenda and the moulders are already getting stuck in, and are making funny little contented noises, but Anton is still waiting for my response. I lift the fork to my mouth and close my eyes.

The fruit bursts on my tongue, richer than wine, and the batter is light and airy, with a satisfying crunch at the top. And yet…

Lorraine's ready with her tape recorder, though the others are struggling to move on from Mmm and Ahh.

'I think there's something missing,' I say.

Lorraine's jaw drops. My fellow testers gawp at me. Anton raises a Gallic eyebrow. 'Missing?' he says.

I take another mouthful, and keep a neutral face as I swallow. 'It's not quite as…luscious as I'd hoped. Not nearly as much personality as Brenda has.'

'It's one of France's classic desserts,' Anton snaps.

'Maybe that's the problem,' I say. 'All your other pies have an English element. The pickle and the ale and the—'

'Ze blackberries are British!'

'Cobblers!' I say.

'Blimey,' Ron says, 'bit harsh, Rachel.'

'You should make cobblers,' I repeat. 'Not clafoutis, but blackberry cobblers. Same basic idea, but a bit heartier for the British taste.'

Anton is frowning. 'Lorraine, make a note.'

'So long as it's still named after me,' Brenda says, giving me a slightly dirty look.

'Sorry,' I say, realising that pissing off my new employer so soon might not be the smartest move. 'I was only trying to help.'

* * *

Wednesday smells of chicken and tarragon, but the ugly pie stall doesn't make an appearance and I can tell Ron and Brenda think it's my fault.

On Thursday I think I catch a glimpse of Anton's hat through the window opposite but then someone pulls down the blinds so I can't see. And on Friday, I get a call from a head-hunter offering a temp job in London, at half the rate I used to get before I went travelling. I tell him I'll think about it. I know it'll be a one-way ticket to my old life.

It would have been Dad's birthday on the Sunday, so Mum and I take a walk along Seven Sisters. The last time we came, Dad was in a wheelchair, and we sat together for more than an hour, as the sun bounced off the sea. It looked like the sisters were dancing.

'Bet you didn't see anything that beautiful on your travels, did you, Rach?'

Right now, I can't think of anywhere nicer. 'Was it a mistake, Mum? Leaving my job like that, and ending up back here flogging cardboard boxes?'

'If you want to go back to London, love, you know I'll manage.'

I haven't mentioned the job offer, but she's always been able to see through me. 'If I go back, I'll never escape again, will I?'

Mum turns round. In the sunlight, the greys in her hair shine like platinum and her eyes are periwinkle blue. 'The fact you call it escaping tells me all I need to know. Take your time, Rachel. *That's* all me and your dad ever wanted.'

* * *

On Monday when I get to work, the estate smells of beer, which makes zero sense as *Life of Pies* doesn't bake today.

As I let myself into the depot – Ron and Brenda are on a mini-cruise to the Hook of Holland – I realise the smell emanates from closer to home. Beer is oozing out under the metal doors of the biggest container. When I open it with the master key, it's carnage.

Some scumbag tenant has set up a micro-brewery, but one of the kegs must have exploded, setting them all off. His mobile's ringing out, so it's going to be down to me to clear up. It's going to take me all day – assuming I don't sever an artery on the shards of glass or slip on the beer and drown in a barrel.

If the head-hunter calls me right now, as I wade through a tidal wave of IPA and sticky cherry beer, I'm accepting his offer.

I've been working for twenty minutes when someone starts banging on the shutter at the front of the building.

'Didn't you see the sign?' I call out. 'We're closed due to

an emergency?' But the banging continues. My trainers make a slurping noise as I walk to the control panel and raise the shutter.

I see the legs, first, clad in blue chequered cotton.

Anton.

I try to pull the lank hair back off my face, because I am a beer-sodden, sweaty mess. But he's already limboing underneath the shutter.

'Mind your hat!' I shout out, and when he twists his body straight again, he's clinging onto the thing like his life depends on it.

He looks at me, then the scene behind me. 'What the hell…?'

'A minor explosion, I think.'

He walks ahead of me. 'Shit…I mean, *merde*. See, I am so bilingual I swear in two languages, *non*?'

'Impressive.' I wish he'd leave me to it.

'We will have this fixed in no time.' Before I can argue, he's grabbed the mop and bucket I'd found in stores and is beginning to soak up the spillage like a pro.

'There's no need,' I say, but I don't really mean it.

He ignores me – the right thing to do – and I pick up the dustpan and begin to sweep the glass up behind him.

Which just happens to give me a view of what is actually an unexpectedly taut backside underneath the comedy trousers.

* * *

We make a good team. After an hour, we've cleared all the glass and mopped up the worst of the beer. Anton looks as sweaty and unkempt as me now, though he still keeps his silly hat on.

I put the kettle on and we take a break to get enough energy to pull pieces of metal out of the pockmarked walls. Anton asks for tea with milk – I tell him he can't possibly be a true Frenchman, and he shrugs Gallically and says he's gone native.

'And you, Rachel. What brings you here? I cannot believe your lifelong passion is bubble wrap.'

I laugh. 'Not exactly. It's a long story.'

'I like long stories.' The sneery arrogance seems to have gone – I think he really wants to know.

So I tell him the lot: about Dad's bequest, and the world trip. Even the moment in the forest when I imagined running my own food and travel empire. 'I only came back last month but already it seems like a lifetime ago.'

Anton shakes his head. 'You need to remember how you felt in the forest. That drive. The freedom. There's no reason why you can't do the gourmet tour thing.'

'Except money. And the recession. And the fact I don't really know anything about food except that I like the taste of it.'

He tuts. 'But you've got a great palate. That's the important part. How do you think I got started with my own company? By taking a leap of faith.'

'Yes, but you're a natural born pastry chef. And French.'

'A natural, huh? How come you hated my clafoutis?'

'Ha! I knew you'd taken offence, chef.'

He shrugs. 'At first, yes. My pies are my passion so I can be a bit precious. But I want them to be the very best pies in the world and honesty is very hard to come by when you are giving away food. That's why I came round here. To invite you to another tasting. Savoury this time.'

'Oh. Right, I suppose it's the least I can do after you've saved me from drowning in beer.'

'Tomorrow? After work?'

'The alternative is another night watching *Emmerdale* with my mother and wondering where it all went wrong.'

Anton smiles. 'I'll take that as a yes. In the meantime, do you know what I'd love right now?'

'No idea.'

'A nice cold *bière*?' he says, deadpan, and there's a tiniest pause before we both burst out laughing.

* * *

The smell coming from the factory on Tuesday afternoon is richly savoury.

Umami. I learned that word from a Japanese chef I met in Sydney. It means cheesy, marmite-y, salty mushroomy flavours that make the mouth water.

Mr Home Brew is on the phone, ranting about the fact that I recycled his demi-johns instead of saving the fragments. I let him shout, and let my mind wander. What pie will Anton make later? I saw a different side to him yesterday. And he got me thinking about my own future. If he could follow his dream and make a life from pies, why can't I follow my own dreams?

That must be why I'm looking forward to tonight: he's an inspiration.

When I finally lock up the depot, the estate is deserted

and the factory has fallen silent. I buzz the door and wait for Lorraine to let me in.

Instead it's Anton who opens the door. '*Bienvenue*!' he says and then bounds off up the stairs. When he shows me into the tasting room, it's…well, different. Number one, it's much darker, with the blinds lowered and a couple of candles flickering on the worktop.

'A new approach I am trying,' he says. 'To try to recreate a more homely environment to replicate ze atmosphere in which you would normally be eating ze pies.'

Number two, the radio's on, tuned to Classic FM.

And number three, I appear to be the only guinea pig.

'Where are the others, chef?'

'Ozzers?' he says. Does his accent get stronger when he's nervous? I'm sure he wasn't sounding quite so French yesterday. 'Unfortunately there was no one else available.'

'Hmm.' I try not to think about the fact that I am in a deserted building on a deserted industrial estate with a man who is surgically attached to his chef's hat and gets very jumpy when anyone criticises his short crust…

And then I smell it. The richest, umami-ist smell that my nostrils have ever encountered.

Anton puts a plate down in front of me. The pie has delicate pastry sides, with lattice work over the top. The filling underneath is bubbling with cheese and there are bright splashes of green too.

He cuts the pie into precise quarters , places one on a separate plate and hands it to me. 'You can have ze entire pie. As much as you need to form an opinion.'

'What about your tape recorder?'

He shrugs. 'I have a good memory.'

I cut a small piece, and taste.

It's good. *Very good.* The filling is light and airy, cheddary, spring-oniony, mustardy…all of my favourite things.

I take another bite. And another, and another.

Anton is beginning to look impatient.

'Well, Rachel?'

'You said I could take as many slices as I needed to.'

'*Oui, mais* – '

'OK,' I say, putting down my knife and fork on the plate, which I've left spotless. 'It's the best thing I've tasted from Life of Pies. And that's saying something. But – '

'Don't tell me, zere is something *missing*,' he mutters.

'I was going to say, it's…well, not French at all. All your other dishes are kind of…a fusion between the French and the British.'

'Ah.'

'But this tastes a lot like Welsh Rarebit.'

Anton gives me a curious look. 'Rabbit? *Vraiment*?'

'Yes, really. Maybe that's why it's so good. You are turning British. If you embrace your adopted land, chef, maybe your pies will do even better.'

He stands up straight: his chef's hat brushes against the ceiling.

'*Merci* for the feedback. But I feel…well, in view of your comments, zere is another team member you must meet.'

'Oh. OK.' I don't know why, but I feel disappointed. I'd hoped we might have more of a chat. Maybe a glass of wine. Another pie. Some more advice on how to follow my dream.

'Back *à bientot*,' he says, ducking under the doorframe so his hat doesn't fall off.

I drum my fingers on the bar table and look through the window, at Ron's bright orange illuminated sign:

MR STORAGE – SPACE TO LIVE YOUR LIFE!

My own life since I took this job has got weirder and weirder. But, weirder still, I'm beginning to think of the trading estate as a kind of second home. Somewhere I could even stay, while I save and plan for a future doing what I *really* want.

I hear footsteps in the corridor outside, and when I look up, there's a new guy in the doorway. He's not wearing Anton's chequered trousers but a rugby shirt and jeans. He's smiling nervously. A nice smile, though. Genuine. No chef's hat, just a generous head of chestnut hair.

Maybe he works in the warehouse? Nice of Anton to give everyone credit.

'Hi, I'm Rachel,' I say, holding out my hand and suddenly feeling out of my depth. 'And what do you do?' *Isn't that the kind of question the Queen asks?*

'I'm Tony,' he says, and there's something familiar about his voice. And his eyes. 'I was one of the original team.'

Then I realise.

'You're Tony Barnes, aren't you? From Springhill Juniors?'

His face lights up. He was the joker of the class, who made everyone laugh with silly impersonations of our teachers. All the girls liked him, though he made me feel so shy.

'Anthony David Barnes, settle down this instant or I'll send you to the head teacher.' Even now, twenty years later, he's got our class teacher's voice so spot-on that I feel I should be sitting cross-legged on the floor, waiting for story time.

'God, poor Miss Prendergast. You gave her hell.'

'And I gave *you* scones. Remember?'

Scones. I remember the smell of them, and the feeling of having them snatched out of my reach. 'No. You gave Sharon Smith scones.'

He shakes his head. 'They were meant for you, Rachel. Sharon Smith was just a greedy guts with faster reflexes.'

'You made me *scones*. Wow. If only I'd realised.' I smile at him and something changes as I look at his face: the Roman nose, the full lips. And then I wonder how I couldn't have seen it before. 'Bloody hell. You're *Chef Anton*.'

Tony Barnes blushes. I swear he never blushed once in juniors: he was way too cocky to care what anyone else thought. '*Mais oui*,' he says. 'Chef Anton and Tony Barnes. One and the same.'

'But…why?'

'Lorraine's bloody stupid idea. When we launched, we needed a brand, a story behind the pies. Why people can't just enjoy a nice pie, I don't know, but she was pretty persuasive. And apparently it wasn't going to be enough that I trained in Paris and came home to recreate what I'd seen there. So, poor Tony went off to the pâtisserie in the sky and grumpy Anton was born.'

'Bloody hell.'

'It was fine at first. Bit tedious wearing the wig and the hat, and keeping the accent up outside the factory, but it worked, we got orders off the back of the brand. And then *you* showed up. Little Rachel Marshall, the babe of Year Five. All grown up and prettier than ever.'

'Hardly. You said I was *jolie laide*. And you were even worse to me at school.'

He blushed deeper. 'I was trying to impress you. Didn't you notice I only ever did impersonations when you were watching? I thought it was the only way to impress you. Then when Brenda introduced you, I thought you were bound to see through me.'

'I can't believe I didn't.'

'And as my French accent didn't impress you, I thought I'd try to impress you with my rarebit.' Tony waved at the empty plate.

The taste of it lingers in my mouth. 'First scones, now you invent a recipe for me. You managed to hit on all my favourite flavours, too.'

'Not an accident. I asked Ron and Brenda to take notes on what you brought for lunch. See what you liked.'

'That's…'

'Amazing?' he asks.

'Hmm.' *And slightly odd,* I think.

'Wait till you see the packaging.' He reaches over the counter to pick up a box. 'This is the prototype design.' He sits next to me, to see my reaction.

'Ravishing Rachel's Rarebit,' I read, then giggle. The photo on the box is of me, but as a child. 'You kept that since school?'

'It's the pigtails that did it for me. But you're even foxier now.'

'Right. Thanks.'

'What do you think? I mean, if you hate it, I can take your name off the pie, call it something else, but…it'd be a shame. Because you've been my muse, really.'

Suddenly I understood why Brenda was so excited about the clafoutis – there's something insane, and insanely flattering about having an entire pie designed for you. Not exactly *romantic*, but then again, it is more permanent than a bunch of red roses. Maybe Ron had a point about compensations…

'It's…weird. And wonderful. But mainly wonderful.'

He's closer to me now. He smells of baking.

'I wanted something that captured the essence of Rachel Marshall.'

I'm very aware suddenly of how hot it is in the room. Like an oven. 'Are you saying that I remind you of cheese and spring onion, Anthony David Barnes?'

'No. But you are very, very tasty.'

And as he leans in to kiss me with hot, buttery lips, I have to admit that he's very tasty too.

Louise Allen

Louise Allen is the author of over forty historical romances with Harlequin Mills & Boon and it was the research for one of them, *Forbidden Jewel of India*, that gave her the inspiration for this story. Louise collects Georgian prints and ephemera and is fascinated by the history of London: her walking guide, *Walking Jane Austen's London* (Shire Publications) reflects these interests. A book on travelling by stagecoach is her next non-fiction publication.

She lives on the North Norfolk coast and shares the house with her husband and the garden with a very bossy pheasant, who thinks he owns it, and a muntjac deer who eats all the vegetables. Louise loves to travel in search of ideas for her writing and is currently working on a novel set in Egypt in 1800.

Find out more about Louise's books at
www.louiseallenregency.com and explore late Georgian
London with her at http://janeaustenslondon.com

&

Head Over Heart

The Waterfront, Calcutta. 1809

'Lady Joanna Holt?'

At last. Restrain your impatience, turn from the ship's rail and the green-brown waters of the Hooghly River and raise one eyebrow. *Just so.* 'Sir?'

'I am Sir Alexander Darvell and I have come to collect you and to convey Mrs Atherton's apologies.' Not some callow youth full of excuses but a man – and one it would be no hardship to find beside her at dinner.

Impassive, impressive and not at all apologetic for leaving her on board ship when all the other passengers had been conveyed to shore at first light two hours ago. True, his broad-brimmed hat was respectfully in his hand but his half smile was more rueful than conciliatory.

'The apologies come from Mr Atherton. Your cousin is otherwise engaged.'

'I would not wish to inconvenience Mrs Atherton.' What she did wish, fervently, was to get off this smelly, cramped ship that had lost any charm or novelty it might have had many long weeks ago, and to draw breath again before beginning the whole tiresome, uncomfortable process of convincing her hostess that she wanted to go back to England at the earliest possible moment. At least it was quiet now that the consignment of husband-hunting girls had disembarked.

The breeze – spice and river-scented – ruffled his carelessly cut brown hair and his hazel eyes crinkled into something very like amusement. 'Mrs Atherton is currently being inconvenienced by the arrival of her first infant.'

A lady does not allow her jaw to drop. 'I was not aware that my cousin was with child.' By the time letters had gone back and forth halfway across the globe it was all too possible that Cousin Maria had not known when she issued the invitation. Or that Mama, snatching at the chance to remove her stubborn daughter from the midst of a scandal, had not noticed any delicate hints.

'Is she well? Do things go as they should?'

Sir Alexander's expression was shaded as he clapped his hat back on his head. 'As far as I can tell. I have ordered your luggage unloaded. Where is your maid?'

Joanna gestured to the girl waiting in the shade of a furled sail. 'Madge, my cousin is in childbed. This gentleman will take us to her.'

'No, ma'am. Mr Atherton suggests I should take you to a lady of our acquaintance until this evening. The house is in some turmoil.' He was already pacing towards the gangway

'You are in haste, Sir Alexander.'

'I am Mr Atherton's business partner. His distraction means I must look to an important matter on his behalf today.'

Trade. But it did not do to be snobbish about it. After all, betrothal to the bluest of blue blood had not saved her from humiliating scandal.

Joanna glanced up to a sky already milky-blue in the glare of the sun. 'I prefer to come with you, Sir Alexander, rather than to be deposited with a stranger. I have been at sea for a long time and would welcome the opportunity to see something of this city.'

That stopped him in his tracks. It was always gratifying to surprise a man. Joanna waited for her smile and his good manners to make the decision for him. His expression was impossible to read: a card-player's face, strong-jawed, heavy-lidded.

'There is no room in my gig for your maid. I will have her conveyed to the Athertons' house. Do you have a veil?' *So, a man of decision.* She liked that, even though she strongly suspected the feeling was not reciprocated.

It meant no chaperon, she realised, as Madge scurried away to fetch her things. But then, what good had strict observance of all the rules done her? 'Thank you, Sir Alexander.'

There was a moment of apprehension as the bo's'n's chair swung out, dangled her over muddy water then lowered her into the boat, but that was merely a rational dislike of heights, not doubt about the wisdom of sauntering around an exotic eastern city with a strange man. This was a new world, one where she was unknown. A space to be free, if only for a day.

For a merchant Sir Alexander was certainly athletic. Joanna shaded her eyes as she watched him climb down the ladder to the boat. Giles, the toad, had long legs and trim buttocks as well – she had received a perfect view of *those* when she found him in the conservatory with Amelia Wilkins. But her current escort had the hardness of a man in his prime.

'You are not discomposed by being in a small boat, I see, Lady Joanna.' He settled next to her as her lips curved into a naughtily appreciative smile.

'I am relishing the freedom after confinement on the ship, sir.' It would not do to let him think her flirtatious. Several of the young ladies on board had found themselves betrothed before they had even set eyes on the coast of India and its rich pool of East India Company nabobs and officers starved of eligible brides. She wanted no husband, either from the ship or ashore here. 'And the peace and quiet.'

'You consider this peaceful?' His gesture encompassed the harbour, with small boats swarming like water beetles on a pond, the shouts from the shore, the multicoloured crowd on the landing stage steps.

'After weeks of female voices, I do.' The river edges were lined with people washing themselves, their clothing, their children. Nets were being cast. The vivid colours spilled across the shore like the contents of an upturned jewel box.

'Ah, the Fishing Fleet in full cry, if that is not a mixed metaphor.' Their eyes met and he smiled. 'I apologise, a most pejorative nickname.'

'I take no offence, but then, I am not a member of it. I have no intention of trawling a net through the shoals of bachelors or attempting to lure a widower with a well-cast fly.'

'No? How refreshing, speaking as a widower myself.'

Joanna could find no answer that was neither coy nor flirtatious.

The boat bumped against granite steps awash with slippery weeds. Noise rose around them: bargaining, laughter, a furious quarrel. Flowers and fabrics were heaped in screaming harmonies of orange, purple, scarlet.

'Let me.' Sir Alexander bent and lifted her, stepped from boat to shore with the ease of a farmer carrying a lamb, and set her on her feet among scattered petals on the upper platform. 'Are you certain I should not take you to one of the English houses?'

'No.' *Breathe.* 'This is fabulous, like something from the *Arabian Nights*.' Colour, noise, people with dark skins, black hair, flashing eyes, ignored her, slipping past her as though she were a rock in a stream and they shoals of fish. 'It takes my breath away.' It could be nothing to do with a pair of strong arms and a broad chest, she was surely immune to that nonsense now.

'Most European ladies recoil in horror.'

'Then they have no imagination.'

'My gig is through here.' His arm sheltered her as they forged through the crowd, stopped every few steps by calls of greeting from European traders, a tall Indian with a yellow headdress pleated into a massive cockade, even porters.

'Here we are.' A turbaned groom stood at the head of a bay mare, its ears flickering amidst the swarm of flies. Sir Alexander settled her and swung up himself. 'You think your countrywomen lack imagination? You mean they have no romance in their soul and do not appreciate this exotic scene as you do?'

'You think me capable only of admiring the romantic? I may read the *Arabian Nights* but that does not make me empty-headed.' Most gentlemen treated ladies as though they were decorative nitwits and Joanna had learned to ignore it, but for some reason, from this man, it hurt. 'I think they cannot be looking beyond the dirt and the flies to see both the beauty and the real, hard life behind it.'

'I apologise, that was patronising.'

There was that hint of a rueful smile again. *Rather charming...For goodness sake! He is a complete stranger.* 'Please, do not regard it. Where are we going?'

'To call on an Indian merchant who is helping Atherton to put together a consignment of textiles for London. You should lower your veil until you reach the women's quarters.'

'I cannot meet him?'

'It is not done. But you will be able to watch and listen.'

'I do not speak their language.' Sudden panic that she might inadvertently cause offence sharpened her voice. 'What if I do something wrong?'

'Place your hands together and bow when you meet them. Do not refuse refreshment and eat only with your right hand.'

His calm assumption that she would cope calmed her. 'Very well. Good luck in getting a good price.'

'Luck has nothing to do with it,' Sir Alexander said as he turned the horse between high walls. Ornate gates creaked open, servants ran forward and Joanna twitched her veil into place. It preserved convention and it covered her smile at the calm masculine assurance in his tone. *So very sure of himself!* But, she sensed, with good reason.

Half an hour later, seated on a pile of slippery silk cushions, Joanna saw nothing to change her opinion. She could not understand what the two men seated in the arcaded room below her were saying, but she could read their body language and watch the reaction of Devdan Khan's wives.

Another glass of sherbet, another plate of strange dainties, both sweet and spice at the same time, were offered. She smiled and accepted them. Her hostesses seemed bent on feeding her to death and stays were not garments designed either for hot climates or for folding oneself up elegantly on the floor, but a lady never showed discomfort.

One of the wives – Nadia, she recalled – gave a little gasp and leaned forward to peer at the scene below. Her husband shrugged and the men clapped hands, palm to palm. A deal had been concluded, it seemed. The Indian handed across a small package; Sir Alexander reciprocated.

'Your man,' Nadia said in her halting English. 'He is…clever.'

'He has made a good deal?' She did not feel capable of arguing that Sir Alexander was most definitely not *her man*. Besides, the thought that he had triumphed was rather pleasing.

The other woman nodded. 'Hard man. My lord admires him.'

When she finally managed to escape her new friends and rejoin Sir Alexander in the courtyard she could read the satisfaction in his smile. 'Congratulations. I gather you came off best there.'

'How do you know that, Lady Joanna?'

'I was watching you. You bargain forcefully and I could tell you won. Nadia says you are a hard man and that her lord admires you.'

'Did she, indeed!' He seemed amused.

'What were you bargaining for?'

'Golden silk. Look in the package. Devdan Khan said it was a present for my lady.'

'I am not – ' It was not the sort of conversation that she should get into, even in denial. Joanna opened the tissue and shook out a scarf, shimmering gold, crisp and alive in her hands. 'How lovely! What is the dye?'

'It is naturally that colour. It is from Assam, a very scarce variety of silkworm. Now the most important business is done we will go to the flower market so I can order garlands to be delivered to the Athertons for the birth of the child. Do you mind crowds?'

'Not at all, although as we are driving through a throng that makes the Strand on a busy day look like a village lane, it is a trifle late to ask!'

'The flower market will make *this* look like the village lane, believe me.'

There was no hope of moving faster than a walk. Most of the crowd was on foot, but there were bullock carts and tiny donkeys, only their feet visible under huge loads of reeds.

'Camels! Look, there are camels.' Joanna found she was hanging on Sir Alexander's arm and bouncing with excitement. 'Oh, I do beg your pardon.'

'There's an elephant.' He pointed with his whip and Joanna could only stare as the great beast lumbered past, the tiny long-lashed eye studying her calmly as it went. When they found themselves following its massive backside – crumpled grey leather swaying as the crowd parted around it – her hand was still tucked into the crook of his left elbow. Somehow it seemed awkward to tug it free.

'Why are you here, if not to find a husband?' he asked without preamble.

'Because I discovered my betrothed tumbling a friend of mine in the conservatory during a reception and I would not do the required thing and pretend nothing had occurred. He is exceedingly eligible, you understand. I threw a potted fern at him, everyone heard – and saw – what was happening. Mama decided the only thing to be done was to pack me off to Cousin Maria. At best, I would find a rich husband out here. At worst, I would return in a year or two and everyone would have forgotten.'

'I admire your restraint in only lobbing the potted plant. In your shoes I would have been tempted by the thought of gelding the swine with blunt scissors.'

'What a shocking suggestion, Sir Alexander!' Somehow she managed not to burst out laughing. 'Unfortunately the fern was all that came to hand.'

'You are a woman of sense. Don't stay here.' The amusement had gone from his voice.

'I have no intention of doing so. I will stay for perhaps a month out of politeness, and now, of course, to see if I can help my cousin. Then I will take the first available berth back. There is nothing for me here.' He gave a grunt that sounded like satisfaction. 'But why do you urge me to leave?'

'Because this country absorbs hundreds of people and most of them do not survive the experience. It is no place for delicately reared young ladies, nor for their children.'

'I have seen Europeans everywhere we have driven. You are here, alive and well.'

'You see the men. I have lived in India since I was nineteen and I've caught most of the diseases it threw at me and survived. This…*market* in young brides is obscene.'

There was more behind his words than an impersonal observation. 'Your own wife died young?'

'Yes. With our child. A fever.'

'Alex, I am so sorry.' The name slipped out. 'Oh, I beg your pardon.'

'I do not mind, no one else calls me that.'

His wife did not, that is what he means. 'I meant…'

'I know. It was six years ago.' He seemed to be choosing his words with care. 'She came out with the Fleet. It was not a love match, simply a suitable one.'

But it mattered to him and the hurt was still there, however he tried to hide it. 'As mine would have been.' *Suitable. Love-less.* 'I shall go back to England, become an eccentric spinster and write lurid novels of eastern romance.'

Alex gave a snort of laughter. 'That would be a waste, Lady Joanna.'

'Joanna, please. We are having a day away from the conventions, are we not?'

'I think we must be. Here is the flower market.'

It was an unnecessary observation. Colour spread around them, spilled in heaps, ran in drifts and rivers, dripped from poles. Colours she had no names for, flowers she had never seen, never imagined except, perhaps, in a feverish delirium. A wanton, lavish abundance that filled a space the size of a town's square.

And people were everywhere, shouting, working, tipping out great wicker baskets of more blossoms, sitting creating the garlands and plaques that were heaped around her. A hump-backed cow wandered through snatching mouthfuls as it passed and no one seemed to care. Camels, their legs folded like surveyors' tripods, sat and sneered at her, a goat trotted up and tried to eat the trailing hem of her gown.

'Get off!' Joanna flapped her parasol at it.

Alex snapped a command to the groom who jumped down and shooed off the animal. 'Naresh will stay and guard you. There is no danger, but he will keep the goats away.'

'Why can't I come with you?' She didn't want Alex going off alone into this carnival atmosphere to buy garlands to celebrate the birth of another man's child, not hard on the heels of those few terse words about his loss. Somehow he had changed from a good-looking, chance-met gentleman to someone whose intelligence and humour she admired: someone who mattered.

Alex was already standing beside the groom. Strong, intelligent, self-contained. What could she do to help a man like that? *Be there*, Joanna realised. She didn't wear her heart on her sleeve either and no one had seen past her anger with at Giles to the pain underneath. No one had seen her misery as anything but a problem. Alex had allowed her see into his own tragedy out of his concern for her. Now she owed it to him to distract him from his ghosts.

'Let me come.'

'In those shoes?' he enquired, leaning to the side to look at her left foot. Joanna twitched her skirts: she knew she had pretty ankles. 'What is underfoot here is indescribable.'

'I will throw them away,' she said and held out a hand to him.

Alex hesitated then swung her down. 'On your feet be it.'

They were both laughing as he took her arm and plunged into the mêlée.

'How much does all this cost?' she asked, as he negotiated the delivery of what looked like a hundredweight of garlands to the Athertons.

'*Paise*. Pennies. These people make a living by working very hard. Now, let us get back to the carriage.'

'No, please. I love this – can we not explore a little more?'

'If you are sure. Look out!' Alex took her by the waist and swung her out of the way of a porter, blinded by his load of foliage. His hands lingered for a moment, broad and strong, and Joanna looked up, amused and off balance. What she saw in his eyes silenced the laughter on her lips and yet she felt no shyness about keeping them curved into a smile. Someone bumped into her back and propelled her against him.

Alex's hands slid up to gather her in. 'I…' He cleared his throat. 'I think one of the side alleys would be less crowded.'

'Yes.' Joanna studied his linen shirtfront an inch from her nose.

Neither of them moved for a heartbeat, then he said, 'Here, let me take your arm. We go down here.'

She glanced up. The only evidence the moment had happened if it were not for the heat in her cheeks and the dip of his Adam's apple as he swallowed hard. Best to pretend nothing had occurred. She tugged free to dart across to a heap of weirdly frizzled purple and pink blooms, but he caught her hand and held it.

'If I lose you in here I might never find you again.'

Was it her imagination or were there layers of meaning under the simple warning? 'No,' Joanna agreed and slid her fingers between Alex's. 'I would not want to lose you.'

'Darvell *sahib*!'

Alex guided her to where a plump trader was waving from behind a mountain of roses. Joanna could not understand but she caught the word '*memsahib*' and saw Alex's eyes suddenly narrow. The man bustled out from behind his flowers, a garland of red roses in either hand.

'No.'

'But they are so lovely? May I not accept them? If you could lend me the money…'

'He offers them as a gift.' The flowers were already around her neck. With what looked like resignation Alex bowed his head for his own garland.

'You be very happy, *memsahib*,' the man said. 'Darvell *sahib* is a good man. Give you many – '

'*Band karo!*' The man subsided, grinning sheepishly. 'Thank you. Come, Joanna.'

'What is the matter?' The scent was intoxicating. Not the sweet apple scent of English roses but perfumed and rich. Wicked.

'These are flowers for a betrothal. He thinks we are affianced.'

Suddenly they were out of the market onto the grass of the riverbank. A few feet in front of them the Hooghly swirled, muddy brown.

'But I have only known you half a day.' Joanna heard her own words and scrabbled to retrieve them. 'It is not as though he has seen us together many times to come to that conclusion.'

'No,' Alex agreed, as he swept some dead leaves from a stone slab in the shade and gestured for her to sit. He made no attempt to remove the flowers.

'I thought I would hate India.' Joanna found her hand had somehow curled into his again.

'You do not know it. How can you learn to love…something after a few hours?'

'Love is an emotion, an instinct. I believe it can be instantaneous or it may grow. I believe it finds us and we cannot seek it. I never expected that it would find me.' Beside her Alex had become very still. Embarrassed by her intensity, perhaps. Or was he in denial of its truth? Joanna swallowed the lump in her throat and deliberately lightened her tone. 'I can tell it is dangerous as well as beautiful here. I can see the poverty, I can smell the raw sewage.' She pointed upstream to where a column of smoke was rising. 'They are cremating a body, aren't they?'

'Yes, that is a burning *ghat*. And the remains will be thrown into the river – this is part of the Ganges and so, sacred.'

'It does not make me want to bathe in the river, certainly. But it does not disgust me, if that is what you expected.'

'I do not know what to expect from you.' It was almost a whisper. An angry whisper, as though he had fought against the words and lost. 'I did not expect *you*.'

'Nor I you.'

She turned so she was facing him. 'And you are sorry I am here.'

'Yes. You should go home.'

Joanna's heart lifted. He was afraid for her. But she knew he wanted her to stay whatever he might say.

'I will not. Not this year. And one person's friendship or rejection will not change that: you need not have my decision on your conscience.'

'Friendship?' Alex's smile did not reach his eyes and he turned from her to stare across the river, fascinated, it seemed, by the efforts of a clumsy barge to come alongside a larger vessel. 'In India it is considered very shocking to kiss in public,' he remarked.

The startled breath had to be dragged up from her toes. 'Not unlike Mayfair, then?'

He gave a choke of laughter as he got to his feet. 'I have

never met a woman like you. Come, I have something to show you.'

They did not speak as he led her back through the market, nor when he helped her into the carriage and drove along a road bounded by a high wall on their left. At a gate he halted and Naresh took the reins, impassive as ever.

Where are we? To ask seemed intrusive for some reason she could not fathom. She followed Alex between a pair of low gatehouses and into a garden. Or a shrubbery, perhaps. It took a moment before she realised what it was. 'A cemetery?'

Paths radiated away beneath trees and everywhere were obelisks and columns, small Classical mausoleums. Tombs and monuments. She walked to the first inscription, brushed away dust.

'Read them.' Alex's voice was so harsh that she had to turn to be certain it really was he who spoke. He was relying on these testaments in stone to teach her the harsh truth about India, but she already understood the risks. But not, it seemed, the reality of the heartbreak and the pathos.

'Sarah Bright, beloved wife...aged nineteen years. Jane Maddox...twenty-five.' And lists, no less pathetic for being inscribed in hard stone, of children. One family had lost six. 'Aged one year and three months, aged five months and two days. Aged four days...' There were young men too, dead in their prime: lieutenants, attorneys, merchants. Nineteen years, twenty-four, twenty. 'Cut down in the flower of his youth.'

It was eerily soothing in the deep shade, patches of brilliant sunlight dappling a dome here, highlighting an inscription there. The only sound was the rustle of leaves underfoot and the bell-calls of birds overhead. Perhaps it was chance that brought her to a simple tomb: *Amelia Anne Darvell, daughter of James Hughes of Braughing, Hertfordshire, wife of Sir Alexander Darvell. Died in her 23rd year...and of her daughter Elizabeth aged two months and ten days.*

There was fresh wreath of red roses lying at its foot and Joanna lifted her own from her neck and placed it beneath the inscription. Then she went and sat on a bench in the shade, so still that the little striped squirrels began to chase and chatter around her feet.

In less than twelve hours she had met a man who, against all reason, had stolen her breath and her heart and it seemed he felt something for her also. Had they a future? Down there by the river it had seemed as simple as overcoming his caution by her own decision to stay. Then they would have time to know each other, to nurture this feeling, whatever it was. *Love?*

But now she saw what she asked of him. He had been through this once, had lost a wife, an infant child. Could she ask him to face that pain and heartbreak again?

There was a little fountain in one corner of the cemetery, its water cool. Once she was certain her eyes and face were serene she walked back to the gate and Alex. She stopped in the deep shade and held out her hand and, after a moment, he came to her and took it.

'I could drown in a shipwreck returning to England.' She raised her free hand when he tried to speak. 'No, let me finish. I could break my neck in a fall from a horse. I could catch a fever in London or have a cut go bad and poison my blood.

'In a week you and I may find we mean something to each other or that we have, in fact, nothing in common. I could go back to England and live to be eighty and regret all my life that I did not risk my heart and that I could not ask a man to make an even greater sacrifice and risk his.'

Alex was silent, his gaze focused somewhere beyond her, down one of the dusty paths.

'I choose to stay and to risk it. I know what I am asking you and I will understand if all I ever see of you again is a glimpse of Cousin George's business partner.'

He seemed to come back to her from a long way away. 'We will go to the Athertons' now. You will be tired from this heat.'

She might as well have been discussing a visit to the botanical gardens. She had played and lost. She would not let him see that she felt anything that would be the worst kind of pleading. Training in deportment, honed in the polite shark pool of the London Marriage Mart, came to her aid. 'Thank you, I confess I am a trifle weary now. I appreciate you showing me something of the real Calcutta.'

'It was my pleasure.'

* * *

The baby was so tiny. Far too small for the parade of names his proud papa had pronounced. Joanna met the unfocused blue gaze and smiled. 'Yes, Georgie, it is a big confusing world out here. You go back to your nurse now.'

She handed him to his *ayah* and watched as Cousin George shepherded them back upstairs to where his exhausted wife was waiting. Then she turned back to the open doors that led out onto the veranda.

'You may come in now.' She had heard the soft crunch

of gravel, seen the long shadow fall across the boards ten minutes ago.

Alex stepped over the threshold, hat in hand, and stood studying her gravely. 'They are both well?'

'So everyone says. You are come to tell me not to become too attached to little Georgie, are you not?'

'I came because the Athertons are my friends. I lingered because I was watching you hold the child. I am here now because I have been thinking about what you said at the cemetery. You are right. If we do not have the courage to hope, to risk, what future is there?'

'Is there a future for us?' Strange how hard it was to speak, as though all the air had been knocked from her lungs.

Alex smiled and sent his hat spinning away into the corner of the room. 'Come here.' He held out his hands. 'Let us find out.'

'I thought kissing was considered immoral in India.' She closed her eyes and let her other senses guide her. His pulse was hard under her fingers. She could smell sandalwood and fresh linen and the now-familiar scent of the soap he used.

'In public.' His breath grazed her face as she tipped her head back and opened her eyes and saw the intensity and the emotion in his. 'This is just us, Joanna. Alone.'

I have come home, she thought as his lips found hers, gentle, questioning and, suddenly, certain. *And so has he.*

Nicola Cornick

Bestselling British author Nicola Cornick writes historical romance for Harlequin HQN Books in the US and MIRA Books in the UK. She was born in Yorkshire and studied history at London University and Ruskin College, Oxford. Nicola is also a historian working for the National Trust at the seventeenth-century hunting lodge, Ashdown House. A three-time nominee for the Romance Writers of America RITA award, Nicola has been described by Publisher's Weekly as 'a rising star of the Regency genre'. Her website is www.nicolacornick.co.uk

&

The Marriage Bargain

Bath, England. January 1814

There was a woman in his bed.

Justin Blake lay quite still. This was inexplicable.

He could remember perfectly the events of the previous night. He had been travelling down from London and when the weather had turned bad he had booked himself into Kennards Hotel in Bath. He had not been drunk, he had not purchased the services of a courtesan and he certainly had not won a young lady in a card game. And up until this moment he would have sworn that Kennards Hotel was the very last word in respectability and would never connive in insinuating a young woman into his bed. There was no logical explanation for her presence.

He turned his head against the pillow. The linen was crisp beneath the morning roughness of his cheek. The grey of first light had barely penetrated the bedroom, suggesting that the freezing fog that had gripped the country so suddenly the night before had not yet lifted.

The woman shifted slightly, making a small, sleepy sound like a somnolent kitten. Her back was turned to him and all Justin could see of her was one smooth, bare shoulder, a tangle of dark brown hair braided in a fat plait, and the lace neckline of a pure white nightdress. She smelled faintly of a summery fragrance – lily of the valley or lavender or rose. Justin was not sure. Gardening was not his forte. All he knew was that it was extremely seductive.

He was sure that she had not been there when he had climbed into the bed the previous night. *Or had she?* Justin hesitated. He had not been drunk but he had been damnably tired. He had told Potter not to bother attending to him and had dispatched the valet to his own bed, consigning a wash and a shave to the morning. He had not even bothered to undress, merely discarding his jacket and throwing his boots carelessly in a corner of the room. And then he had slipped beneath the covers and fallen asleep before his head had touched the pillow. The room had been dark, lit only by one candle, and the tester bed was huge and wide; as big as a barn with its high draped curtains. Half of Wellington's army could have been bedded down in there and he would probably not have noticed.

Justin eased away, trying to slide from beneath the sheets without disturbing the sleeping girl. If he could leave the room before she woke he could avoid so many tiresome consequences. If she was a serving girl or a light skirt who had recognised him and decided to seize her chance, he could escape the obligatory pay-off and serve her right for being so sound a sleeper that her quarry had escaped her while she dreamed of fleecing him.

If she was a lady…Justin shuddered. The word 'compromised' seemed to hang in the cold morning air, sending shivers galloping down his spine. Even if he had wanted to, he would not be able to offer marriage to make good her reputation: he was already married. God forbid that his wife should hear of this. Or his mother-in-law.

He forced himself to calm. This could be no lady. No lady would be alone in a hotel in Bath – or indeed anywhere else.

He was wasting time and she might wake at any moment. He slipped stealthily from the bed and stood up.

With the redistribution in weight, the mattress creaked liked a foundering galleon. The sleeping girl rolled over but she did not open her eyes. Her face was serene in repose, her lashes dark against the line of her cheek, her lips slightly parted. Then she gave a small but unmistakable snore. Justin smiled. It was a very attractive noise but it was a snore nevertheless. He was sure she would be mortified if ever she knew.

He inched backwards to the door, watching her all the while to make sure that she did not wake. He grabbed his coat from the back of the chair and his boots from the corner without even breaking step. He was adept at this. He had lost count of the number of ladies' bedrooms he had reversed out of, usually while uttering platitudes about undying devotion and avoiding the hairbrushes and vases aimed at his head. That was all in the past – a long time in the past now – but it seemed that the skill of beating a hasty retreat had not deserted him.

He groped behind him for the doorknob and it slid reassuringly into his hand. He turned the knob and opened the door a crack. There was a sudden loud groan of hinges so excruciating that Justin closed his eyes and almost groaned in sympathy. There was no possibility that his fair companion would slumber on through that: she was awake.

He opened his eyes slowly and saw her sitting bolt upright, the sheets clutched to her breast in the time-honoured gesture of the shocked innocent. Justin's heart sank.

She was a lady. A young lady. Possibly even a débutante. Every inch of her spoke of quality; from the expensive lace edging on the pure white night dress to the sheen of privilege reflected in her pansy blue eyes. She would be most dreadfully shocked to see him there. She opened her mouth. He braced himself for her scream.

'Close the door behind you,' she said, 'and pray be quick about it.'

Justin stared. At first he wondered if she had mistaken him for one of the hotel servants but he had already noticed the way that her eyes had gone to the boots in his hand and from there to linger on the betraying dent in the pillow beside her. She was innocent but she was not stupid. She must realise that his was the telltale demeanour of a man who had spent the night in the wrong bed and was desperately trying to leave before that fact became apparent. The astonishing thing was that she remained so composed: he had assumed that ladies were brought up to have a fit of the vapours in situations such as this.

He took another step backwards. She was offering him a way out, a simple means of escape. He should have grabbed the opportunity with both hands but for some reason he hesitated. It was nothing to do with the entrancing picture she presented – all tumbled and innocent-looking amidst the bed-sheets, the thick plait of chestnut coloured hair resting over her shoulder and contrasting so gloriously with those pansy blue eyes. He assured himself that it was definitely nothing to do with that, nor with the rounded smoothness of her bare arms or the sweet sensuality of her generous mouth.

'What are you waiting for?' she snapped. She had the cut-glass tones of someone who habitually gave orders to servants, although her voice was softened by a betraying quiver of nervousness.

Justin, who had not grown up with an unchallenged aristocratic sense of entitlement, recognised that neither had she; her autocratic dowager act was adopted to hide her vulnerability. He felt a curious sense of affinity with her.

'I'm going,' he said. 'There is no need to nag.'

For a moment a dimple flashed beside the corner of her mouth as she almost smiled, and he found himself smiling back.

'I don't want my husband to hear of this,' she said. 'He is unlikely to be understanding.'

She was married. Justin felt a sharp pang of disappointment, inappropriate since he was a married man himself. It was followed by a sharper pang of indignation and protectiveness: the man was clearly an undeserving brute to leave his wife alone in Bath, at the mercy of any fool who walked into the wrong hotel bedchamber.

'Your husband is a lucky man,' he said.

She raised a haughty brow. 'And you are overstaying your welcome.'

Justin grinned and raised a hand in farewell. He turned to leave and stepped backward into the arms of Potter, his valet. Potter was carrying a bowl of water and had a towel folded neatly over his arm. The contents of the bowl, which turned out to be scalding hot, splashed down Justin's shirt and puddled about his stockinged feet.

'My lord,' Potter began, in tones of deep disapproval, as he knelt on the floor and dabbed at the faded Turkey carpet, 'if you had but waited in your room – '

The door was still half open. Justin could hear the sound of the bedcovers being thrown back, of someone moving about. He experienced a mixture of fear, frustration and extreme discomfort from his scalded feet. *What was she doing?* If only she would keep quiet he might manage to manoeuvre Potter away until she had had chance to make her escape...

Potter looked up. From his position on the floor Justin estimated that he had just been afforded a glimpse of the hem of a white nightdress and a pair of very pretty ankles. Certainly his face wore the stunned expression of a man who had glimpsed something heavenly and doubted the evidence of his eyes. Then the valet's face settled into the 'more in sorrow than in anger' look of disapproval that Justin was accustomed to from eight years' experience.

He could still recall the expression of utter dismay on Potter's face when he had been assigned as his valet. Justin, orphaned young and packed off to school from the earliest age because his distant relatives had not wanted him cluttering up their family seat, had been a bitter and resentful eighteen-year-old stripling when Potter had taken him under his wing. Since then, they had been through much together: the hallowed portals of Cambridge University to the hellish battlefields of the Peninsular. Potter had disapproved of Justin's hell-raising during his student years, he had deplored his recklessness in battle but he had saved his most severe disapproval for the day Justin had married, when he had gone directly from his wedding breakfast to his club and had got roaring drunk. Justin was obliged to admit that it had not been a mature reaction to his wedded state. Nor had been his departure to rejoin his regiment in the Peninsular the very next day.

Justin swung the door closed with a sharp gesture. 'You saw nothing, Potter,' he said. 'Is that understood?'

'Naturally, my lord,' the valet said resignedly. His eye fell on Justin's boots, still clutched in one hand, and his coat still grasped in the other. 'I take it that we are leaving, my lord.'

'Yes,' Justin said. 'At once.'

'The back stairs are that way, my lord,' Potter said, with a jerk of the head down the corridor. 'That is, if you are leaving the lady to pay the bill.'

Justin looked at him. Potter had an uncanny knack for knowing how to make him feel particularly bad without actually saying anything for which he could be reproved.

'Of course I am not,' he said testily, ignoring the fact that that was exactly what he had been about to do.

The door of the bedroom swung open abruptly and both men turned. Both men gaped. In the aperture stood a perfectly attired lady of quality. She wore a gown of sprigged yellow muslin with a pale lemon spencer about her shoulders. Her hair was confined with a matching lemon ribbon. She looked composed and neatly buttoned up: no longer the ruffled siren who had occupied his bed. Justin estimated her age to be about twenty, twenty-one at the most, and he experienced a sudden and violent pull of attraction and a need to get to know both the neat débutante and the tumbled wanton immediately, quickly, and intimately.

If only he were not married already…

'How the hell did you manage to get dressed so quickly without a maid?' he enquired.

He heard Potter give a small groan at the absolute inappropriateness of both his language and the question.

As though on cue, a black-clad Abigail swept into sight. Like Potter, she was carrying a bowl of water and had a towel folded neatly over her arm. She did not have Potter's sangfroid however. On seeing the tableau in the doorway she gave a shriek of shock. The bowl tipped in her hands and its contents joined the rest of the flood on Kennards's Turkey carpet.

Disaster. There was no possible way to maintain discretion now.

'Do be quiet, Truss,' the girl said sharply. 'There is no call for the vapours.' She turned to Justin. 'I will leave you to dress, sir. Good day to you.'

Justin took her hand and raised it to her lips. 'It was a pleasure to make your acquaintance, ma'am,' he murmured. 'I have seldom spent a more enjoyable night.'

She blushed and pulled her hand smartly out of his. 'You are inappropriate, sir,' she said.

'I fear it has always been a failing of mine,' Justin agreed.

It was then that he saw her luggage: three shiny portmanteaux standing in neat ranks to the right of the door with his battered leather kit bag slumped next to them. The only thing that they had in common was the name embossed on them: Blake.

Justin felt his stomach drop.

He looked at her again. Those pansy blue eyes were decidedly wary now and she was biting her full bottom lip in vexation.

It could not be. It had to be.

'*Paullina*?' he said.

* * *

Her husband had spent the night in her bed and he had not recognised her. He had not even known she was there. It was the perfect illustration of their relationship.

'Justin,' Paullina acknowledged. She was not going to pretend that she had not known him. She was not going to pretend to be pleased to see him either. If she wanted to be fair to him – and she did not, particularly – she would have allowed that it was only the fourth time they had met. The first time had been in her parents' drawing room when the betrothal had been agreed. Theirs was a marriage bargain, his title for her money, a common enough arrangement in the ton. He had been distant and civil; she had been tongue-tied and keenly aware that she had been sold.

Their second meeting had been the following night when they had danced together at Lady Swanson's ball. It was difficult to talk while performing the steps of a complex country-dance, and she recalled that they had had very little conversation. Justin had not asked for another dance, let alone the coveted and slightly scandalous third that would have indicated a genuine interest in her. Instead he had drifted away to the card room to gamble on the prospect of her fortune, leaving her to wilt like the wallflower she was.

The third time had been in front of the altar on their wedding day. He had left for his club with the wedding breakfast barely consumed. She had not seen him again. Until now.

He was still as handsome. That annoyed her considerably.

She had hoped that four years in the Peninsular would have dimmed those spectacular good looks, so it was disconcerting to see that he looked even better now than he had when he had gone to war. Four years ago he had been a boy; a little callow, a little brash. Now his authority and assurance felt real. His voice was clipped and accustomed to command. His face was thinner than she remembered, tanned, with lines it had not had before. His eyes – very dark, very direct – were only a couple of shades lighter than his hair.

Deep, deep inside she felt her heart skip a beat. She tried to ignore it. Four years ago she had conceived a foolish school-girl's infatuation for Justin Blake. She had already been half in love with him before they met, her sympathy engaged by his sad history: the death of his parents when he was barely out of the cradle, the chilly relatives who did not want the orphaned child. It had been stupid of her, though, to think that she could offer him some sort of comfort or affection. He did not want her, only her money. It had been very lowering to be hopelessly in love with one's husband when he preferred the company of his regiment.

He was frowning at her. It was intimidating but she was his wife, not a junior officer, so she raised her chin and met his gaze very directly.

'What are you doing here?' he asked.

'I am on my way to London,' Paullina said.

'Did you not receive my letter telling you that I was on my way to Coombe Abbey?'

'Yes,' Paullina said. 'That was why I was going to London.'

Justin did not appear annoyed by her blunt explanation. A half-smile curled his lips. It did curious things to her pulse.

'I see,' he said. 'You are running away from me.'

There was a challenge in that. It quickened her blood.

'Given that you have shown no desire for my company in the past four years,' she said sharply, 'I could not believe you would want it now. And I never run.' She flicked an imaginary speck disdainfully from her sleeve.

He had not taken his eyes from her face. Now he smiled properly; a smile that made her tingle down to her toes. No one had ever looked at her the way Justin was looking at her now. Suddenly she was acutely aware of him: of the intensity of his gaze, his scent and of his masculinity.

'You recognised me this morning, didn't you,' he said.

'Of course,' Paullina said. 'But as you did not appear to recognise me – '

'You thought you would hurry me on my way in order to affect your escape all the more speedily.'

Well, she had to give him credit for quick wits. He had guessed her strategy all too easily.

'The unsympathetic husband was a nice touch.' He sounded rueful.

'I thought so.' Paullina smiled politely. 'And not a word of a lie.'

She looked him up and down with her best impression of a haughty dowager. Anything to keep him from guessing the effect his lazy appraisal was having on her.

'Were there no spare rooms to be had last night?' she asked.

He shrugged his broad shoulders indifferently. 'I have no idea. Either I misheard the room number the clerk gave me or, more likely, he thought that as we are Lord and Lady Blake – ' he put some emphasis on the words ' – he was showing great initiative in directing me to my wife's bedchamber.'

Paullina could see how it had happened. She might even
have found it amusing under other circumstances. When she
had arrived the eager young clerk had asked if her husband
would be joining her later. She had replied, somewhat dryly,
that she considered it very unlikely. The clerk had looked
most sympathetic. He must have been delighted for her
when Justin had strolled in and announced that he was Lord
Blake.

'I shall lock my door in future to deter importunate gentlemen,' she said.

Justin gave her a smile that was so sudden and so wicked
that she caught her breath. 'It's a little late for that, my dear,'
he said. 'You've just spent the night with a complete scoundrel.' He gestured towards the stair. 'Would you do me the
honour of taking breakfast with me before you leave?'

Paullina's heart tumbled to her slippers. For a moment the
disappointment was so acute it stole her breath. It was not
that she wanted Justin to insist she accompany him back to
Coombe – theirs was a marriage of convenience, after all, so
there was no necessity to spend any time together – but it
would have been nice if he had not been quite so quick to fall
in with her plans.

He was watching her. Her emotions felt too naked; she
turned away.

'I insist you dress properly first,' she said lightly. 'I make
it a rule not to take breakfast with gentlemen in a state of
undress.'

He sketched her an ironic bow. 'Then I will see you in a
moment in the parlour.'

Downstairs in the empty dining room she could not settle so she stood and looked from the window. Outside,

Henrietta Street was equally deserted, blanketed in thick fog.

The door opened and Justin came in to join her. With his shirt hanging loose over his breeches and a day's stubble darkening his chin he had looked dashing and dishevelled, the very epitome of a chaperon's warning. Now he was all that was elegant, in a coat of green superfine with a crisp white cravat at his throat. He had even had time to shave.

'I ordered tea,' Paullina said, 'but there is chocolate if you prefer.'

Amusement lit his dark eyes. 'It all sounds frightfully respectable.'

'This isn't the sort of establishment to serve spirits at breakfast,' Paullina said.

She sat down at the table, making a fuss of arranging her skirts, anything to avoid looking across at Justin. He rested his broad shoulders against the back of the chair, apparently at ease, in contrast to her agitation. The hotel servants brought the tea and a selection of rolls still warm from the ovens, with butter and preserves. Silence fell again. Paullina poured the tea in order to give herself something to do. It was too weak because she had not let it brew for sufficient time. She sipped it and tasted nothing but hot water.

She had not imagined that when – if – she saw her husband again they would be encased in this awkward silence. She was shocked how bitter and resentful she felt inside. She had schooled herself to acceptance, of the marriage and of his absence, yet it seemed she had not accepted it at all. Inside she was raging. Words tripped over themselves in her head, angry words, words of reproach. She had too much pride to utter them aloud. Their marriage had not been born out of a love match. She refused to show that she cared now.

Justin was studying her intently. It was disconcerting. The intimacy of the situation, taking breakfast together, felt strange. It confused her. She reached sharply for a bread roll and started to butter it.

'Were your eyes always so blue?' Justin asked. His voice was a little rough.

'Of course,' Paullina said. 'How could they change colour?'

'I did not notice before.' He spread marmalade thickly onto his toast. 'I don't believe you ever looked at me.'

That was probably true. She had been far too shy at seventeen to meet his gaze.

'I could not even see your face on our wedding day let alone the colour of your eyes,' Justin continued. 'Your veil was too thick.'

The veil had been her mother's choice; endless layers of expensive tulle simply to show that they could afford the best. Her over-decorated wedding gown had been another monstrosity, dripping with lace. She had hated it.

'I could have been marrying anyone,' Justin said. It was a tacit apology for not recognising her. It was also the last straw.

'That was rather the point, wasn't it?' Paullina abandoned any attempt to keep the bitterness from her tone. 'You were a fortune-hunter. You would have married anyone with money as long as they had their own hair and teeth, and even on that you were not too particular since you were leaving the country.'

He did not deny it. She gave him credit for that. 'Not my finest hour,' he admitted ruefully.

'Since you were mentioned in dispatches I suspect you kept your finest hour for the battlefield,' Paullina said.

His gaze sharpened on her. 'You were following my career then?'

Damn. She had not meant to give so much away. 'Someone mentioned it to me,' she said evasively.

The smile in his eyes called her a liar. She fidgeted, reaching for another bread roll that she did not want. Her appetite had gone.

'We both agreed – '

'I know,' she cut him off before he could say anything else to inadvertently hurt her. 'It was a business arrangement not a love match.'

'I hated it,' Justin said suddenly. 'I hated humbling my pride to ashes because I had had to go cap in hand to your father for money.'

Paullina had known that too. She had sensed how much it had offended his honour to barter his title for her fortune.

'I suspect my father did not make that easy for you,' she said quietly. 'He had a fine sense of grievance towards those whose birth was more aristocratic than his own.'

Justin reached out and touched the back of her hand, a fleeting touch, instantly withdrawn. Nevertheless her skin tingled.

'It was not easy for you either,' he said. There was a shade of warmth in his tone now. 'You were so sweet and so shy. Too sweet to be used like that. It was shameful. *I* was ashamed.'

It was enough of a shock to bring her gaze straight up to

meet his. There was something of sincerity and regret in his eyes and the sight of it dried her mouth and set her heart pounding.

'I knew what I was doing,' she said. His honesty demanded equal honesty in return. She had made a deliberate choice.

'Escaping your parents?' He gave her a lopsided smile that was rakish and boyish at the same time. 'I suspected that they made your life a misery.'

She did not answer that. The truth was she had always known that to her parents she was no more than a means of social mountaineering. Her father had ached to join the ranks of the nobility he so vociferously decried.

Justin's gaze was moody as it rested on her. 'Did you ever think about me, Paullina?'

She looked up sharply.

I thought about you every day. She certainly was not going to tell him that though. She had too much pride to risk loving him again: an adult love this time, no childish infatuation.

'Never,' she said. Nevertheless her throat was thick with tears for the opportunity they had wasted.

She saw the flare of some expression in his eyes. 'A pity,' he said. 'I thought about you all the time. In all the heat and the dust and the horror of killing I thought about you. It kept me sane.' He waited a moment but when she did not reply he made a slight gesture as though to brush the words away. 'No matter – '

Paullina put a hand out and touched his wrist to stop him. 'It matters,' she said. He had been brave enough to lay his heart beneath her feet. Now she had to be brave too. 'I lied,' she said, with difficulty. 'I never stopped thinking about you.'

He moved so fast then that she was not quite sure what happened. The table toppled over, the marmalade pot clattered away across the floor. She was clasped in Justin's arms very tightly and he was kissing her, and it was delightful – hot and sweet and urgent, and full of promise for the future.

'What do we do now, Justin?' Paullina asked, when finally he released her sufficiently to draw breath.

'Well…' Justin drew her by the hand across to the parlour window. Outside the fog pressed thicker than ever against the glass. 'We could resume our journeys in opposite directions but I do not think we would get very far in this weather. Or – ' he smiled that sudden wicked smile that set her pulse fluttering ' – we could go back to bed.'

'Really, Justin.' Paullina could feel herself blushing. 'We are practically strangers.'

He was drawing her back into his arms, very purposefully. 'Nonsense, my love. Have you forgotten that we are married and we spent last night together?'

Paullina could feel herself blushing all the harder now. Justin bent his head towards her again but she placed one hand against his chest to hold him off. Kissing Justin was delicious and she wished she had realised it sooner instead of wasting so much time, but she was not going to fall into his arms or his bed quite so quickly. She wanted a courtship first.

'I think,' she murmured, toying with one of the mother of pearl buttons on his jacket, 'that I should like to spend some time here in Bath: view the shops, go to the theatre, sample the water at The Pump Rooms. I hear it tastes appalling.'

'That sounds delightful.' Justin was smiling. 'I am told Bath water is particularly good for the stamina. And we should thank that booking clerk,' he added. 'Without him we might have wasted four more years.'

He kissed her again – even more potently and powerfully this time – until Paullina's head spun and her knees weakened and she could feel her toes curling in her silk slippers.

'For shame, Justin,' she said, emerging ruffled and radiant from his arms. 'In the breakfast parlour! Anyone might come in!'

'I am sure they will indulge us,' Justin said. 'After all, we are on our wedding trip. We should savour all the pleasures Bath has to offer.' He kissed her a third time, and it was heated and passionate and very pleasurable indeed. 'We have a great deal of time to make up,' he whispered. 'This, my love, is only the beginning.'

Sue Moorcroft

Sue Moorcroft loves writing about irresistible heroes and dauntless heroines. *Shocking Behaviour* is set in 'her' village of Middledip, as are her Choc Lit novels *Starting Over*, *All That Mullarkey*, *Dream a Little Dream* and *Is This Love?* Middledip came from Sue's imagination so she's intrigued when people say they're sure Middledip is based on a village they know.

Born in Germany into an Army family, Sue has lived in Cyprus, Malta and the UK. By writing novels, short stories, serials, columns and courses, and working as a creative writing tutor, she manages to avoid 'proper jobs'.

Sue has won the Best Romantic Read Award and the Katie Fforde Bursary Award and received several other nominations including for a RoNA in 2012. She's the vice chair of the Romantic Novelists' Association and editor of *Truly, Madly, Deeply*.

Her website and newsletter sign-up can be found here: www.suemoorcroft.com

Twitter: @suemoorcroft

Facebook: sue.moorcroft.3

&

Shocking Behaviour

'O*w*!' Lizzy Parr limped up the stairs to her new flat
on the Bankside Estate. She intended to run regularly now
that she'd moved to Middledip village – much cheaper than
Saturday mornings at the gym. Having blasted her bank
accounts to smithereens to become the proud owner of a
one-bedroom flat, cheap had become good. Essential, in
fact. But she should've warmed up more thoroughly before
setting off instead of assuming that a week of unpacking
boxes would have created muscles permanently ready for
action.

Painfully, she hobbled up the final steps and rounded the
corner. Then halted with a suddenness that caused her a
breath-sucking twang of pain. A man was trying the door to
her new flat. A key was in the lock and the door handle in his
hand.

'What the hell do you think you're doing?' The words flew
from her mouth before she'd had a chance to consider other,
more sensible, options like hobbling quietly off again and
phoning the police.

The man jumped violently. His tousled hair was chestnut,
his horrified eyes hazel and his mouth a perfect O of shock.
Then he managed an apologetic smile. 'Erm…would you be
the new owner? Miss Parr?'

If he knew her name, there was a reasonable chance that he was harmless. Lizzy nodded cautiously. 'Ye-es.'

'I'm the old owner – Jax. Jaxon Cheney.'

'Oh, right.' A whoosh of relief. She'd never met her vendor; his estate agent and solicitor had handled the sale. 'I'm Lizzy.' She glanced at the key that was still in the lock of her door.

He reddened. 'I came to see Rick on the top floor and he still had the spare key to my – your – flat, which he'd kept for emergencies. I brought it down to you but I stuck it in the lock without thinking: force of habit.' He shifted sheepishly as he smiled a warm, contrite smile. And Lizzy felt her tummy dip like a roller coaster.

Wow, what a heartbreaker of a smile! And now she had time to flick her gaze over him – well, he was a pretty heartbreaking package: beckoning eyes, a sexy suggestion of stubble on a sensational jawline and snaky hips in extremely well-fitting jeans. Lizzy was suddenly glad that abandoning her run had at least saved her from being a walking haze of sweat. She could feel Jax's gaze like a weight.

'I'm on my way to the shop for coffee. Rick's run out.'

So Lizzy limped to her holly-green front door and turned the key, conscious of passing close to him. 'Care to try my brand?' Her coffee was only instant – but so was the attraction.

She left him to watch the kettle boil while she nipped into her bedroom to whip off her black joggers and on her most flattering jeans. When she returned, Jax had found a spot on the grey-blue sofa nestled among the stuff that still waited to be found a home. Like a big cat, she thought, finding a comfortable corner and then watching her with compelling, luminous eyes. She reached for the mugs. 'Should we have invited Rick, if he has no coffee?'

Jax's gaze flickered. 'I think he's supposed to be meeting his girlfriend.'

It sounded hurriedly concocted. Lizzy hoped so, anyway. Alone with the endlessly appealing Jax Cheney? She'd learn to cope. She settled herself and her coffee in the other corner of the sofa, propping her leg on a convenient packing box. The throbbing was subsiding to an ache. 'How's your new place?'

'It's bigger and has built-in cable TV but there's something I miss about this one. How about you? Any problems?' And he sounded as if he really wanted to know.

'It's a mixed experience, isn't it, moving? You wait for the right place, endure the formalities, can't wait for moving day. But then you realise how much work there is.' She waved at a pile of plastic-coated chipboard. 'That will eventually be a shelving unit – if the instructions are to be believed – where I can put all the stuff from these boxes. Which will only leave me with too much rubbish for the wheelie bin.'

'How about I give you a hand? I'm good with flatpacks.'

'That would be amazing.' Her heart leapt. 'I'm not even going to pretend to protest, I want it done too much.' After a short search she located her toolkit – four screwdrivers and a hammer – and watched him lay out the lengths of shelving. The muscles of his upper body flexed as the shelves formed themselves up under his capable hands.

The complete unit looked twice as big as when she'd bought it and it didn't take long to distribute her belongings across the capacious shelves. 'I can see the carpet,' Lizzy sighed happily as the last box was emptied.

He began gathering up the rubbish. 'I'll stuff this into my car and drop it at the tip. It's on my way home.'

'You've been such a star. I hope you're very happy in your new flat.' She felt a pang that the afternoon was over and was going to miss Jax's thoughtful gaze. Not to mention the smile and the snaky hips…Would it look totally desperate to thank him with an offer of dinner?

He slid his arms into his jacket and saved her from the decision. 'Could I take you out tonight? If there's no boyfriend on the scene, that is.'

'No.' Pleasure skittered down her spine. 'I mean yes. Yes, I'd like to. No, there's no boyfriend.'

Slowly, he smiled. 'Later, then. Pick you up at eight?'

* * *

He was back at eight, less tousled and more edible in black trousers and a shirt the colour of twilight, complementing perfectly her strappy dress in darkest mulberry. A hungry expression crossed his face. 'You look…amazing.'

When he looked at her like that she felt amazing. It was the beginning of a heart-thumping, stomach-dropping, body-tingling evening when it felt as if time extended itself especially for them as they discovered a shared love of Thai food, white wine even when they should be drinking red and jolly pubs rather than raucous clubs. The air fizzed between them like shaken champagne.

But, finally, after dinner, after drinks, after a late, long, hand-in-hand stroll around the moonlit village so that he could show her the village shop and the pub – both of which she was already well aware of – at last she was opening her front door and stepping into her sitting room, Jax beside her.

'Coffee?' Her voice was husky.

He caught her, pulled her gently against him. 'I'd rather kiss you.'

Her eyes closed as his lips brushed her cheekbones, the corners of her mouth. She shuddered as his tongue ran slowly along her upper lip.

And then her hands were pulling him deeper into the kiss, her body pushing against the hardness of his in a scalding rush of desire.

His arms tightened fiercely.

She let her head fall back as his mouth dropped to her throat and she forgot that she was no first-date pushover and wondered instead whether it would feel seriously weird to him to make love to her in the bedroom that had been his until so recently. It was shocking behaviour.

* * *

The middle of the night. Lizzy drifted out of sleep, Jax's body warm and firm against the length of hers, fairies' footsteps prowling down her naked back.

She squirmed against him. Amazing that the fingertips of such a big man could be so feather-light, flushing her with fresh appetite as they trickled across her shoulders, her neck, down to her ribs.

She kissed his neck, nibbling his throat and flicking her tongue into the hollow below his Adam's Apple. She heard his breathing quicken, felt the feather-light touch vanish as his hands became firmer and more demanding.

* * *

Morning. Lizzy found Jax kissing her awake, giving her one of his magical smiles when her eyes fluttered open. 'Lizzy, can we talk about – ?'

But she was already kissing him back and whatever he'd meant to say was postponed because this was something special, something awesome. Something new.

They breakfasted at noon in a cosy café in Bettsbrough with cane chairs and green chequered tablecloths, eating pain au chocolat and drinking Costa Rican coffee. A sultry day, the pain au chocolat sweet on the air.

Suddenly, Jax beat the space over Lizzy's head. 'Wasp!'

Lizzy grabbed a menu. As the wasp buzzed her she swatted wildly, sweat bursting out on her forehead. 'Get rid of it!'

'Don't panic. Stay still.' The wasp was drunk that late in the summer and Jax was able to do something dextrous with a glass and a menu then release the wasp through an open window.

Lizzy felt stupid as soon as the danger was past. 'I must seem like a wimp, but I go into anaphylactic shock if I get stung. I swell up and have to shoot myself with adrenaline and get to casualty within fifteen minutes. If not…' She gave a wobbly smile.

'Oh no!' he breathed. Colour drained from his cheeks.

She frowned. 'It's OK. The allergy thing's scary but I carry my adrenalin with me.' She patted her bag.

He didn't smile. 'We need to talk about it. I'll settle up and we can walk to the park.'

Puzzled, she watched him cross the room to the till. Was he one of those people who couldn't handle the least mention of medical things? That could be a problem because when the worst happened she had to grab the adrenalin pen and plunge it into her thigh. She didn't have time to mop anybody's squeamish brow.

Jax's phone rang. He'd left it on the table.

'Jax…?' she called to him. But he'd finished at the counter and was just disappearing into the gents. She hesitated, then picked up. 'This is Jax's phone.'

'Isn't he there?' a man's voice said. 'I'm Tom, could you tell him we're meeting at the Pig and Trough in Bettsbrough tonight if he's up for it?'

'Pig and Trough, tonight,' she repeated.

'And did he find Rosie?'

She paused. 'Rosie?'

'Never mind, I'll ask him later. Thanks!'

Jax returned. His colour was nearly normal again and he took her hand as they threaded their way through the tables and out into the sunshine.

She told him about the call. It would be cooler not to ask but she couldn't resist. 'Who's Rosie?'

He halted, his eyes sombre. 'That's what I needed to talk about.'

She waited. Traffic rumbled past, blowing her hair across her face.

'Right. Well. Um…on the day I moved out of your flat, her tank must've tipped so the lid slipped and she scampered off. I suppose she was scared.' His eyes were wary. 'And…look, this doesn't sound good, but when you found me at your door I was going in to see if I could get her back without you having to know. We watched you leaving and I thought I had at least half an hour.'

'Who scampered off?'

'Rosie,' he said. 'My rose hair tarantula. Tom's an enthusiast and I bought Rosie from him.'

'*Tarantula!*' For the second time in half an hour she felt sweat burst across her skin.

He led her over to a stone bench. 'I know I should've been honest but I was trying to protect her. It's not her fault she freaks people out. I was scared you'd buy cans of bug spray and nuke the place. She's probably in the ducts for the air heating. It'll be really bad if the heating comes on – she needs moisture as much as heat – '

She made an inarticulate noise in her throat.

He slid his arm around her. 'It seemed the best way of getting Rosie back safely…But when you told me about your allergy, I realised I had to own up.'

'But that's outrageous!' she burst out, mind racing, face scalding with fury. 'You bastard! You *slept* with me – to get Rosie back.'

He recoiled. 'Absolutely not! I slept with you because you had me absolutely gibbering with desire – '

'Don't touch me!' She leapt up and in seconds was across the road, running as if she had to burn a million calories before nightfall. Her heart felt like mince. His behaviour had been so much more shocking than hers.

* * *

The first text message came through before she'd even driven home:

Pls don't think I slept with u bcos of Rosie. Last night was best ever.

Yeah right, Lizzy replied.

Pls don't nuke Rosie. Give me chance 2 find her. She's black and about 10cms. Don't pick her up, he warned.

Fat chance!

Despite rumours, tarantula bites are only like bee stings.

Bee stings threaten my life! she exploded.

Argh! I'm sooooooo sorry.

She thought suddenly of the fairies' footsteps she'd felt on her naked back during the night. Urrgh! Yuck. Ick. *Ick!*

* * *

That evening, stalking into the Pig and Trough, she found Jax gazing at the footie on the big-screen telly, an island of misery within a sea of cheery men.

His face brightened when he saw her but fell again when she slammed her spare keys on the wooden tabletop.

His mates fell abruptly silent.

'I'm going to stay with my sister,' she snapped. 'You can bloody well find Rosie. You've got four days before I need to be back.'

'Lizzy – ' he tried, eyes pleading.

She cut him off. 'Go find her, Spiderman.'

* * *

It took three days.

Three days to spend with her married sister, Kay, Kay's slightly annoying husband, Niall, and their two daughters,

Melissa and Rhiannon. If she'd thought Kay's house would be a haven in which to sulk peacefully, she'd been mistaken. On the first evening, Kay sent Niall to the pub and got the children into their pretty pink pyjamas and to bed in record time, then flumped down beside Lizzy, clutching a bottle of wine.

'So what's up?'

Lizzy inspected the glass Kay had shoved into her hand. 'Nothing.'

Her sister snorted, taking a healthy slug of white. '"Nothing",' she mimicked. 'The kind of nothing to send you here with a face like a trout? C'mon. Give.'

So Lizzy confessed all: Jax, the instant attraction, the sleeping together on the first date, the spider.

Kay's eyes grew round. 'Lizzy,' she breathed. 'The first date? You were *used*.'

'I know!'

'You should've nuked the flat, anyway.'

'But he said it wasn't fair on Rosie…'

Kay snorted. 'He slept with you to get his spider back. That's really impolite.'

'Well…he said not. He said, "Absolutely NOT!"'

'Believe him?'

Lizzy shrugged. 'I don't know.'

Then they looked up tarantulas on the internet and shrieked at the pictures of the business end of an oversized arachnid. Lizzy went clammy with horror and even Kay looked unsettled. 'You'd better stay clear of *that*.'

On the third day, Jax texted: Hooray! Rosie safey off yr premises. Return any time. Jax xxxxx

Lizzy snorted. He could keep his kisses.

* * *

There was a man outside her flat.

He was sitting on the floor with his back against the door, reading a book.

'What have you lost this time?' she demanded grumpily.

He smiled faintly. 'My place in your affections.'

She let her bags drop to the ground. 'I might not have come home till late.'

'I would've waited. I've been here since six.'

She raised her eyebrows. 'You've spent the day on my doormat?' She was almost impressed. 'Even though you had the key?'

He extracted it from his top pocket and handed it up to her. 'If you'd come home and found me in your flat I think there would've been blood on the carpet.'

She snorted, scraping the key into the lock. 'Don't confuse me by treating me with respect at this stage. I suppose you'd better come in. But you can't be long because I need to do a food run to the supermarket or I won't eat tonight.'

He stood in the sitting room, watching her flicking through her post with cautious, hazel eyes. He needed a shave. It looked really hot.

'I should've told you about Rosie. But people get very freaky about tarantulas; I had to protect her.'

'So you said.'

'Once we got together, I didn't want anything to spoil it and half the time I wasn't thinking straight. But I want you to be very clear that what happened between us was no scuzzy plan on my part to gain access to my spider. Lizzy, I'm so attracted to you.'

She felt tears prickle the backs of her eyes. Her voice came out low and furious. 'Then you shouldn't have made me feel like a convenient moron.'

'I didn't mean to.' He twisted a painful smile. 'I just wanted you a lot.' Silence. 'And you wanted me,' he added, softly. 'Before you knew about Rosie.'

She shrugged, trying to look as if she couldn't remember.

Slowly, he fished his car keys from his pocket and made for the door. Lizzy willed herself not to blink the moisture out of her eyes and down her cheeks. He turned back. 'Oh yeah.' He hesitated. 'Well, it probably won't happen.'

'What?'

'It's just…sometimes, if tarantulas creep away like Rosie did it's because they're about to lay their eggs.' He frowned. 'You've got my mobile number if you see any spiderlings. Ring me and I'll come round and…well, do my best.' He looked as if he had no clue what this might entail.

Lizzy curled up her toes. 'Would I be able to see them?'

He opened the door. 'Well, there would be about three thousand.'

'*Three thousand?*' Her heart began to thump out of her chest and she had to clutch the kitchen counter at the thought that in her heating system there could be three thousand eggs all ready to hatch into three thousand baby Rosies.

In a moment he was there, pulling her into the safety of his arms. 'You'd better come to my flat while we decide what to do. I can cook you dinner and we'll look up how long it takes for tarantula eggs to hatch.'

'But you've got Rosie at your flat,' she wailed. Then

stopped. 'Hang on!' She pulled back to regard him narrowly. 'For a girl spider to lay eggs, doesn't there have to be a boy spider involved? Did you send Rosie to stud or something?'

He bit his lip. 'Um, I'd "forgotten" about that bit.' He tried a smile. 'I was going to suggest you came to my place until we were sure yours was clear. Rosie's boarding at Tom's indefinitely.'

She stared. 'You've sent Rosie away?'

He frowned. 'Of course. I've looked up anaphylactic shock – it's really dangerous, Lizzy. I'm not exposing you to a health risk like that. You could die, you know.'

'I do know! Why do you think getting stung freaks me out?' But Lizzy's glare softened at his sincerity. And suddenly she was melting inside. 'You must be lonely in that big flat all alone.'

His eyes gleamed with sudden hope. 'I am, incredibly. Even though Rosie wasn't a great conversationalist, I liked having her around.' Slowly, he dipped his head until he could brush her lips with his. 'But I'll send her a "Be Happy in Your New Home" card – if it means you and me can be together.'

She flooded with sudden heat. 'You'd give up your spider for me?'

'Tom's a bit shocked but, yes. In a heartbeat.'

She sighed as she slipped her arms around his neck. 'That's the kind of shocking behaviour I can deal with.'

Alison May

Alison May was born and raised in North Yorkshire but now lives in Worcester with one husband, no kids and no pets. There were goldfish once. That ended badly.

Alison has studied History at the University of York, and worked as a waitress, a shop assistant, a learning adviser, an advice centre manager, and a freelance trainer, before settling on 'making up stories' as an entirely acceptable grown-up career plan.

Alison has been a member of the Romantic Novelists' Association since 2011, and won the Elizabeth Goudge Trophy in 2012. She has a degree in Creative Writing and now writes contemporary romantic comedies. Her debut novel, *Much Ado About Sweet Nothing*, was published by Choc Lit in November 2013.

You can follow Alison on Twitter @MsAlisonMay, and find out more about her at www.alison-may.co.uk

&

Feel The Fear

Eleven hundred hours. Situation review: I can't see it. It's not in its place by the skirting board. I pull my feet onto the chair and scan the room. A movement catches my eye. It's there. It stops close to the wall between the fireplace and the TV stand. I think it's looking at me.

I take a deep breath. I can do this. It's not watching me. It's not taunting me by being here. I imagine Neil's voice, 'It's more scared of you than you are of it.'

I try to forget that Neil lied about everything, and pretend that, on infestation issues at least, he was an upstanding and reliable purveyor of truths. I pull a flip-flop off and take careful aim. Bravery is what is required here. I lower my feet onto the floor and lean towards it. I launch the shoe as hard as I can towards my captor. It lands four inches short. The thing scuttles along the wall towards the TV. As soon as it moves, I jump back into my chair and pull my feet into the safe zone.

Situation review: Line of sight to the thing? Check. Still breathing? Check. Number of shoes? One. The thrown flip-flop is lying out of reach, deep in no-man's-land. Only a fool would go back for it. I hug my knees and look at the clock: 11:04, Saturday morning. That's good. I'm not at work until Monday, so I can totally just stay here. It's fine.

There's a magazine on the arm of the sofa. I lean out of my

chair and grab it. See. This is OK. I'm having a nice relaxing Saturday morning, chilling out, reading my magazine. I try to concentrate on the fashion spread. It's tricky when one eye is on permanent watch duty.

The thing is still for a clear thirteen minutes but that doesn't mean I can relax. It wants me to relax. It's waiting for me to let my guard down.

Making as little noise as I can, I drop the magazine, and put my hands on the arms of the chair. I push my weight up onto my arms and lean forward so that I'm squatting on the seat rather than sitting. Thing still in sight? Check.

I turn towards the sofa. What's the best way to do this? Slow and stealthy or as fast as possible? Slow and stealthy has worked this far. Very carefully I stand up on my chair and start to move. I just need to edge along the sofa and then I can hop straight into the hallway. Freedom.

As I take the first step over the arm of the chair and onto the sofa, it moves straight towards me across the middle of the room. Slow and stealthy is out the window. I bounce across the sofa and leap through the open door. Forgetting the plan, I dash across the hallway and out the front door.

In the communal stairwell I stop, jamming my foot in the door so it doesn't lock behind me. I breathe.

Situation review: Thing? Out of view. Must be assumed to have taken control of all territory inside the flat. Me? Standing on communal landing in shortie pyjamas and one shoe.

'What are you doing?'

Voice behind me? Unfamiliar.

I turn round. The speaker is in his early, or maybe mid, twenties. He's holding a dining chair, and, to his great credit, trying really hard not to stare at my boobs or legs. In fact, he's looking very intently at a spot about three inches to the left of my ear. I notice that the door across the hall is propped open with a box.

'Moving in?' I ask brightly, deciding not to dwell on what I'm doing.

He nods, puts the dining chair down and holds out a hand. 'I'm Adam.'

I shake the hand. 'Hannah.'

'Right.' He pauses, allowing his eyes to skim across my clearly-not-leaving-the-house attire. 'Well, I'll let you get back inside.'

'Good. Great.' At this point I could still come out of this looking normal. I could simply have been checking the post or taking some rubbish out. That would not be totally insane. All I need to do is walk back inside and I'll still look like a functioning grown-up.

I push the door open further and peer into the flat. I can't see it. It's not there. It must still be in the living room. Or not? There's a cupboard in the hallway and a coat stand. It could be behind either of those. Waiting.

God! I wish Neil was here. No, I don't. Neil's gone. That's good. He's dealing with some other girl's crises now. I don't need him. In my mind I list all the things I've done on my own since he went: I got the car serviced and successfully argued about the price when they ramped it up to little-woman-who-doesn't-know-cars levels; I tiled the bathroom; I made tea for my sister while she retiled the bathroom. But that's fine because tiling ability is not a key indicator of independence.

I'm still not technically inside.

'Seriously, are you OK?'

Same voice. Same guy.

'I'm fine.'

He shoots an eyebrow upwards. 'You don't seem fine.'

I don't answer.

'OK. You're the quiet type. Am I allowed to guess?'

I lean myself against the doorframe where I can look at him and still sneak glances back into the flat in case of sudden movement. It's ridiculous, but so long as he's guessing I don't have to go back inside. I nod.

'Right. You're an assassin who's been sent to take down the owner of this flat – '

'Why would I be in pyjamas?'

'Good point. You're not an assassin. You're a supermodel, shooting a nightwear campaign – '

'So why aren't I being photographed?'

'You snuck out to find food, because your manager only lets you have one grape and a celery stick per week.'

I laugh, and then I remember that I'm not supposed to be enjoying myself with men because I'm sad about Neil. Then I remember that I'm not supposed to be enjoying myself at all until I've worked out how to regain possession of my flat. I stop laughing.

'I'm not a supermodel.'

'Shame.' He grins. 'So you actually live here?'

I nod.

'And you've got a horribly misjudged one-night stand in there who's refusing to leave?'

'No.'

'No one-night stand. Boyfriend then?'

I shake my head.

'Husband?'

I shake my head.

'Girlfriend?'

'No.'

He sighs. 'I could've helped with the one-night stand.'

'How?'

'By pretending to be your very jealous boyfriend.'

I'm not sure what to say to that. I scan my eyes back across the hallway: still no movement. That doesn't mean anything. It's in there somewhere.

'You're really not going to tell me?'

I shake my head. I'm dealing with it on my own.

'But you do live here? I don't need to call the police or anything?'

'I live here.'

'Right. Well, I'd better get back to unpacking.'

He heads back down the stairs. He must have a van outside. That gives me about a minute, probably, to be out of the stairwell before he comes back. Being caught like this once was OK. Twice was eccentric. Three times might burn bridges.

I push the door completely open and force myself to take a big step into the flat. Straightaway I see it. It runs from the living room right out into the hallway and stops about a metre in front of me. I'm genuinely stuck here now. My brain tells my feet to back out into the hallway. Then it tells them to move against the wall and edge past it. My feet overrule my brain.

'Seriously, are you OK?'

He's behind me again, in the doorway. I don't turn around. I just lift one arm and point very slowly at the spider. I can feel his breath on my neck as he looks over my shoulder.

'Don't laugh.'

He laughs.

I try to keep my voice as low as possible, in case shouting might make it come at me. 'It's a phobia. It's not weird.'

'OK. What do you normally do?'

'Neil deals with them.'

'Neil?'

'Doesn't live here anymore.'

'Right.'

I feel him step away. 'Don't go.' I hiss the words.

He's leaving me on my own.

A few seconds later he's back. He moves slowly to stand alongside me. 'Hold out your hands.'

I do as I'm told. He places a pint glass in one hand and a postcard in the other.

'What am I supposed to do with these?'

'Glass over the spider. Card underneath. Take the whole lot outside and let him go.'

'It's not a "him". It's an "it".'

'Whatever.'

'Can't you do it?'

'Sure, but what about next time?'

He's right. I really hate him for it, but he's right. 'Neil used to kill them.'

'Neil sounds like a jerk.'

'You know nothing about him.'

'Tell me something.'

I can only think of one thing. 'He cheated.'

'See. Jerk.' He puts a hand on the small of my back. 'Is that OK?' His touch is warm and I realise it's the first time I've felt something that isn't anger or fear for a very long time. I nod. Very gently, he edges me forward. 'Off you go.'

I step out of my remaining flip-flop. Bare feet will be quieter on the carpet. My steps are tiny, tentative, but the spider doesn't budge. I'm about a foot away now. Close enough to lean over and drop the glass onto it. I hold my breath, lean as far forward as I dare and drop. The glass goes clean over the spider. I breathe again.

His hand moves away and a tiny round of applause breaks out behind me. 'Keep going.'

I kneel down next to the glass and peer at my hostage. Trapped under glass, it looks remarkably placid. I place the postcard on the floor next to the glass and start to slide. It goes under easily. I have the spider ready to be taken far far away.

'Now pick it up.'

I'm less sure about this bit. I'll actually have it in my hands. The thought makes me feel sick, but giving up isn't an option. If I only learn to get this far, I'll end up with a flat full of trapped spiders and nothing to drink from.

I slide my fingers under the edge of the card and grip the glass with the other hand. As soon as I've got it off the ground I run for the open kitchen window and hurl the whole lot outside. I hear it smash on the pavement below.

'Oh my God!'

I lean out of the window. There's no one around, just a lot of broken glass on the floor.

'I'm really sorry.'

He's laughing a big laugh that goes all the way from his mouth to his eyes. He swallows twice before he can speak. 'It's OK. You just got a bit carried away.'

'I'd better clear that up.'

He nods. 'Maybe put some clothes on first.'

'Yeah.' I'd sort of forgotten that I was wearing next to

nothing all the time that his hand was on my back and his breath was on my neck.

'I'd better get on.'

'OK.' My insides are all swirly, which I'm completely sure is from the excitement of overcoming my fear. I add that to list of things I've achieved without Neil. Life is actually going on. I'm managing. I'm independent, which, apparently, isn't the same as on my own.

'Adam?'

He stops. 'Yeah?'

'I'll pay you for the glass.'

'It's just a glass.'

'But – ' be brave ' – I could help you unpack or something. If you want.'

'Cool.' He smiles.

And I smile too.

Situation review: Improving.

Jenny Harper

Jenny was born in Calcutta – hence her fascination with this buzzing city – but she now lives in Edinburgh, Scotland. She's seen all sides of the publishing business as a commissioning editor, journalist and novelist.

Her published books include *Face the Wind and Fly* and *Loving Susie*, a children's novel and a number of books on Scotland and Scottish themes. Her history of childbirth, *With Child, Birth Through the Ages* (written as Jenny Carter), is used as a reference by many historical novelists. It's still available on Amazon!

Awards

Jenny was runner-up for the BBC *Woman's Hour/Woman's Weekly* Romantic Novelist of the Year and winner of the RNA's Elizabeth Goudge Award, as well as being awarded numerous awards for feature writing and magazine design.

RNA

Designed the RNA magazine *Romance Matters* 2006–2012, and *Fabulous at Fifty*, the RNA memoir

Oversaw the RNA rebranding

Novels

Face the wind and fly

Loving Susie

http://www.jennyharperauthor.co.uk/ Or go to Twitter
@harper_jenny or find her on Facebook
http://novelpointsofview.blogspot.co.uk/

&

The Eighth Promise

Scorn is a double-edged knife. You can retreat, mortally wounded, from its thrust, or turn it aside by meeting steel with steel.

When Edward Massinger – smart as a whip in his new uniform – looked at me with his dark eyes and said, 'I feel sorry for you,' a fuse began to burn towards all the anger I held within me. Besides, it was the second time I had met him and the memory of the first encounter was still livid.

* * *

I sailed to India in the summer of 1939 with a rebellious heart and absolutely no intention whatsoever of looking for a husband. This was no 'fishing trip'. I was twenty-two years old and bright as a silver button. No mere man was going to come between me and my ambition.

'I work for *Vogue*,' I repeated to everyone on the ship who was foolish enough to ask me about myself. 'Yes, in the fashion department, *naturellement*. I look after the photographers. Yes, it's so exciting I can hardly bear to leave it even for a short break.'

In truth, my job was a lowly one. I was a general assistant, a gofer, a dogsbody. I made tea, ran errands for the photographers and made sure that the demands of the models were accommodated. I didn't divulge that, naturally, and in any case, it didn't really matter because I was learning the trade. I was young, pretty, starry-eyed and happier than I could ever remember being.

The letter from my mother would have been rapturously welcomed at any other time in the preceding dozen or so years. Arriving, as it did, in the midst of the hectic run-up to Ascot, I read it with dismay.

Frank and Jean Arbuthnot
The Palm House
Ronaldshay Road,
Alipore
Calcutta

13th May, 1939

Darling Cecilia,
At last we have made provision for you to come and see us! Your father and I have waited so long for this day to come. We are now in Calcutta. Out in the sticks we felt so isolated it did not seem right to ask you to give up your life in the bright lights to join us, even for a short visit.

Father has been appointed headmaster of a very good school in this fine city. A house comes with the job – a big one at that – so you see, there is plenty of room for you.

Of course, we understand that you have obtained employment in London. However, my letter to your superiors has elicited the response we sought – you are to be given a three-month period of leave! Your ticket for the passage awaits you at the P&O offices in Cockspur Street and you will sail in June.

We are so excited about having you with us once more, even for the shortest of times.

Your ever-loving Mama

I had barely seen my parents since I was nine years old. Everyone knew that the intolerable heat of India, with all the inevitable disease it brought, made it a poor place to raise children, but even so, the shock I experienced at being sent to a boarding school in Perthshire was considerable.

The food there was appalling, the conditions spartan and the freezing winters well-nigh unbearable. I suffered chilblains on my toes and gained a lifelong aversion to rice pudding and outdoor games. I endured crippling homesickness for a year, and then spent my remaining eight years at school raging at my situation. By the time I was due to leave, I felt estranged from my parents – who had managed to visit me only twice – and I had no idea what I was going to do or where I would go.

It was Great Aunt Edie – my father's aunt – who was my saviour.

'I have found you a job, Cecilia,' she wrote from London, just before I was due to leave St Margaret's School for Girls in Crieff. 'As an assistant at a magazine. You can stay with me in Cadogan Square.'

The thought of staying with Great Aunt Edie was daunting, to say the least. I had only met her once, years ago, and had a dim recollection of slenderness and elegance, of scent and the rustle of taffeta. I eyed my school blazer and despised green woollen skirt with embarrassment.

Cadogan Square, though, turned out to be a very smart address in central London and Great Aunt Edie a wise, funny and extremely well-connected woman. She was in her seventies and childless, and she was itching to spoil me. She bought me a whole collection of smart new clothes. She introduced me to the concept of elegance and modishness. And, joy of joys, the magazine where I was to work turned out to be *Vogue*, the grand arbiter of fashion.

My mother's summons to Calcutta, just when I was settling in nicely was, therefore, far from welcome.

My friend Lottie was deeply envious. 'Think of all the men you'll meet, Ceci. That's where every girl goes who wants to find a husband. Everyone knows that. They're desperate for pretty girls out in India.'

'But I don't want a husband,' I protested. 'I want a career. And how can I achieve that if I'm shoved off to Calcutta?'

'It's only until September,' Lottie said reasonably, her thick dark hair crimped and curled to within an inch of its life, her lips sweeping arcs of crimson. I thought Lottie the epitome of fashion and tried to copy her style, but I found that my own fine, blonde hair refused to hold a wave, and crimson against my fair skin looked like blood in the snow. Still, I was slimmer than Lottie, and I knew I was cleverer and I was happy to accept these trade-offs.

In the end, I had no choice and I suppose curiosity and the faint memories I still had of India and of my parents also acted as enticement. I sailed from Southampton at the end of June and it was impossible not to feel the excitement as the huge liner edged away from the quay to the cacophonous accompaniment of a dozen horns, a thousand ragged cheers and a cascade of coloured streamers.

I discovered a sport I did enjoy: flexing my charm muscles. By the time we sailed past Gibraltar, I had flirted with almost all of the men under thirty. By Malta, I had broken the hearts of those under forty. When we reached Port Said, I abandoned interest in all of them and became fascinated instead by the half dozen wealthy and darkly handsome Egyptian businessmen who came aboard with their retinues.

For some reason, I didn't come across Edward Massinger until after we had sailed out of Colombo and were making our way up the east coast of the Indian sub-continent. I was at the captain's cocktail reception in the imposing Grand Saloon. Great Aunt Edith had made me a parting present of an outrageously expensive gown, which I had donned for the occasion.

'Balenciaga,' I was declaiming to a circle of women who were clustered around me, admiring the dress, 'is using soft blue this season. Chanel prefers coral. For myself, I'm more partial to the blue.'

There were appreciative murmurs, not just from the women but also from my usual group of hangers-on and hopefuls.

A voice came from the back of the crowd, deep, but dry as fine sherry. 'I should have thought that khaki is more likely to be the colour next year.'

I craned my neck and spied a tall stranger with dark, slicked-back hair and fathomless eyes. Irritated at my flow being interrupted, I repeated, puzzled, 'Khaki?'

'I believe we will be at war within a few months.' The

man had caught the attention of the group, which turned towards him as one. Immediately fashion was forgotten, I was ignored, and the conversation had changed to politics and the international situation.

I pouted with irritation. This man – who was he? – was undeniably good looking, but I certainly did not appreciate my thunder being stolen. 'Women,' I said loftily, raising my voice above the murmur of discussion, 'would never be seen dead in khaki.' But I had lost my audience. My fragile blonde prettiness and Balenciaga gown could not compete with the topic that was on everyone's mind, the shaky state of the peace in Europe.

In the days that followed – to my utter frustration – Edward Massinger proved polite but consistently uninterested in my looks, my conversation or my company.

* * *

'I'm bored,' I said to my mother, sitting up in my lounger and tossing aside my book. I yawned ostentatiously to underline my point. 'Bored, bored, bored.'

In September, just as I was due to sail for London after a visit that I had found tedious to the point of numbness, war had been declared and all civilian shipping stopped immediately. To my utmost horror, I found I was stranded in India. What started as a mildly irritating duty visit turned into a nightmare with no discernible end.

'The *dhirzee* is coming this afternoon,' Mama replied, fanning herself wearily in the hazy heat of the morning sun. 'You could ask him to make up a new dress for you. I'll buy you some cotton lawn.'

'Oh, the *dhirzee*, the *dhirzee*,' I parroted impatiently. 'Who cares about the *dhirzee*? At *Vogue* – '

Mama frowned. Her interest in my work at the magazine had long since evaporated.

'There's a reception at Government House tonight,' she said, clearly more in hope than in expectation I would agree to attend. She knew I hated the way she lined up men for me to consider as a husband.

I yawned again and drawled, 'Terrific. Another boring do with more boring people.' Then, as much to my astonishment as Mama's, I added, 'I suppose I might go. Anything is better than sitting in this dreary place.'

I was being unkind and I knew it. Calcutta was far from dreary: the city teemed with life and colour and every day brought new sights and new experiences. It was just that I had set my mind against them all. I longed for London and for the world of high fashion. Mother's candidates did not attract me because I had no wish to marry, not in India at least.

I spent the late afternoon in the bazaar. I had little money for shopping but the smells and sounds and the blaze of colour generally lifted my spirits. I might find some trinket to adorn my hair, perhaps, or at least watch the glass blower at work and admire the pretty coloured baubles he coaxed from the end of his pipe. Here was the potter, his brick-red platters and bowls stacked high outside his shop. In this corner was the silversmith, using his bellows to fan the fire in his floor hole to heat his tongs. I stopped to watch him.

'The process is called annealing,' he told me in his old-fashioned, curiously lilting English, in response to my questions. 'When I hammer the silver it goes hard. I have to heat it in the furnace to make it workable again.'

I had no money for his wares but I stopped at the tassel shop to finger the silky cords that hung there: white, green, magenta, gold. Why, I wondered in a rare moment of introspection as I stroked some intricately embroidered trimmings, was I so cantankerous all the time? I held a scarlet ribbon up next to my face and studied myself in the mirror the tassel seller held up for me. A small vertical line had developed on my forehead, like a reproach, and my lips seemed to have become tighter and thinner.

'I'll take this,' I told the wrinkled, nut-brown vendor hurriedly, waving the mirror away.

The truth was, I hated being in Calcutta – and it was beginning to show.

* * *

The reception was in honour of a new regiment that had been recruited. Already troops were beginning to move through Calcutta and the atmosphere was increasingly sombre. In August, a friend of Mama's had called a meeting at the Lighthouse Cinema to form 'The Ladies General War Committee'. Mama had tried to persuade me to attend, but I had been stubbornly resistant. This war would be over in a few months and I was going back to London, and to *Vogue*. Why should I care?

I had taken some trouble over my appearance, donning another of Great Aunt Edie's gifts, a daring scarlet gown, which I set off with a smart bow among my soft curls. The silk ribbon I had purchased was a vivid weal against my fair hair, but suited my present mood. I thought of Lottie and outlined my lips in bright red lipstick. It seemed appropriate: a bloody colour for the bloody war that was keeping me from England.

At the reception, I accepted a glass of tepid gin and bitters and managed to discreetly separate myself from my mother's overbearing clutches.

Sir John Herbert, the new governor, bore down on me, clearly trying not to look too directly at my rather low neckline. 'Ah, Miss Arbuthnot, delighted, delighted,' he said. Then, making a gallant effort to engage me, he caught a passing soldier by the elbow and boomed, 'May I introduce Captain Massinger? Or perhaps you know him already? I believe you sailed out together earlier this year.'

I turned and found myself staring into familiar inky black eyes. 'Oh. It's you,' I said abruptly, disconcerted by the amusement I read in his gaze.

'Honoured.' He took my hand and bent over it, curiously formal, as Sir John's attention was drawn elsewhere. 'And how are you finding Calcutta?'

'Utterly tedious,' I replied with rash honesty.

'Really? I should have thought there would be a great deal to do here. Calcutta's going to be an important hub as this war unfolds. My friends tell me lots of women are already working hard to put support in place for those of us who will be on the front line.'

'I don't fancy knitting socks,' I said, aware, even as I spoke, that the words sounded churlish. I had been distracted because I had just realised that a uniform did something to a man. Edward Massinger, accountant, had been handsome but irritatingly pedestrian. Edward Massinger soldier, though, had another aura entirely. On the ship I had seen him merely as a challenge. Now I felt the stirrings of real interest. Perhaps there might be something in Calcutta for me after all.

'I concede the tedium of knitting socks,' he smiled, 'but I should have thought there would be other openings. The Messenger Service? Red Cross Supplies? The Censorship Office? What do you do with your time, by the way?'

I bridled. Was amusement turning to contempt? 'I'm extremely busy,' I lied.

'Really? I suppose there is a certain amount of work necessary to maintain one's looks – even for such a natural beauty as yourself.'

The compliment was so backhanded that I felt my breath leave my body. 'Oh!' I gasped, my hand fluttering to my heart. Tact was not my strongest suit, but I expected more of it in others.

'Boredom,' he added more gently, observing my upset, 'should be a word in nobody's lexicon. I apologise for my rudeness, Miss Arbuthnot, but I feel sorry for you. I believe you grossly underestimate how long this war will last and I do believe you might find some interest in some form of useful work.'

He took my hand to shake it farewell, but failed to release it. His eyes drilled into the core of my being and I felt my heart lurch absurdly. 'You've been given many gifts, Cecilia,' he said in a low voice, as if trying to address my very soul, 'but you have only one life. Don't waste it.'

His touch seemed to sear my skin like a branding iron. I felt that he was patronising, and I hated that – but something in a dusty corner of my mind must have registered the wisdom of his words. I had never felt so confused. I wished he would stop looking at me with that amused, gentle gaze, but at the same time I wanted nothing more than to sink into his embrace and dance with him into paradise. In that moment, I sensed a current of electricity arcing between us and knew that he felt it also.

Then he released my hand and was gone.

* * *

I joined the St John Ambulance Brigade and started my training as a nurse the very next day. There was little thought in my head either of self-fulfillment or of contributing to the war effort, the act was merely a settled determination to show Captain Massinger exactly what I was made of. I chose the St John, if I was honest, because the white dress and short veil offered the smartest uniform of all the volunteer services in Calcutta, and because I had a mental vision of myself as tender heroine, an angel of healing, adored by all. What I had completely failed to consider was just how grim the job would be.

Sister Crawford tried to instil in us the qualities we were expected to show. 'We wear on our breasts the eight-pointed cross of Malta,' she told us briskly on our first day. 'Each point carries a promise assigned to it by the ancient Knights of St John: Loyalty, Perseverance, Tact – '

Commitment and determination I had in abundance, discretion I knew I needed to learn. She went on. ' – Dexterity, Observation, Explicitness, Gallantry – ' She explained what each would mean to us as nurses. ' – Sympathy.'

Here I struggled. Years of boarding had toughened me to the point of selfishness. I persevered, though. Anything was better than sitting at home with Mama, whose efforts to secure me a husband had intensified. The lectures on First Aid and Home Nursing and the examinations were dull but easy enough. Reality bit when I went on duty at the hospital. I experienced the humdrum of hospital routine and suffered through endless, sleep-deprived nights on duty. A month in an operation theatre began a gruelling process of hardening my soul to the sight of human bodies being sliced open, the flow of crimson blood and the nail-biting tension of emergency surgery. The operating theatre was just the beginning of it. In the wards, I had to steel myself against the hideous stench of gangrenous limbs and suppurating abscesses. I dealt with tuberculosis and venereal disease as a matter of routine.

I thought of the silversmith in the bazaar. 'Hammering makes the silver hard,' he had told me. I felt as though my mind and my senses were being constantly hammered. These things offended me but they didn't touch my heart.

One day, a distraught mother arrived at the hospital with her baby, who had been appallingly scalded by an accident with a cooking pot. The mother's wails were tortured, but the child seemed to be beyond screaming. She stared at me with terrified brown eyes. A single tear trembled on her cheek. I caught my breath.

'I can't bear this,' I whimpered to my colleague as she started to dress the burns.

The nurse looked at me, irritated. 'Just be glad that we are able to help,' she said curtly. 'And for God's sake, get me some more liniment.'

It was a turning point. I forgot the hours of tedium spent in rolling bandages in the early days of my training or in staffing the first aid tent at sweltering gymkhanas. I saw how useful the work I had done protestingly at the baby clinic and the women's outpatient department had really been.

Like the silver in the bazaar I had been plunged into the fire, and my compassion was finally unlocked. I went through the process of annealing, becoming hardened to the sights, smells and sounds of injury and disease, and softened by compassion for those I tended.

It had been almost a year since I had seen Edward Massinger at the governor's party. I dreamed of him often but the searing memory of his taunts had been set against the grim reality of my daily experiences and had faded into nothingness. I only wished I could tell him.

* * *

I met Edward, for the third time, at a party on Christmas Day, 1940. I had arrived, hot and weary, and still dressed in my white uniform dress with the eight-pointed St John Ambulance cross embroidered in black on the left breast. In the saddlebag of my bicycle there was a pretty floral gown and some sandals.

Above me was an open window and I could hear Christmas carols being sung. 'In the bleak midwinter, frosty wind made moan,' was being lustily chanted by a dozen mildly drunk voices, and floated through the humid evening air. I started to laugh. The incongruity of song and place and time, compounded by exhaustion and the emotional intensity of the experiences of the day, proved too much for me. My laughter turned abruptly into hysteria and I flopped helplessly to the grass. My bicycle toppled and started to fall and through my tears and wails I had the sense of it being caught by a strong hand, and steadied.

'Here,' said a familiar voice, 'let me.' The bicycle was swiftly parked against the wall, a khaki-clad figure folded easily onto the grass beside me and a clean cotton square was produced for my use.

'I'm so-so-sorry,' I sniffed, when I was able to catch enough breath. 'This is silly.'

An arm came round my shoulders and I felt a hand tilt my face upwards so that I found myself looking into a pair of eyes as dark as the night.

'Oh, it's you,' I said, as I had once before.

'You became a nurse, Miss Arbuthnot,' he said, surveying my white dress with its eight-pointed cross: Eight promises, the eighth of which is love.

I smiled shakily. This was not at all how I had imagined our meeting. 'You dared me. I was so angry with you for patronising me I went and volunteered the next day.'

'Good for you.'

I looked at him sharply. In the bright, clear light of the stars I could see in the flesh the straight nose, the thick, dark eyebrows and strong chin that I had seen in my dreams for so long.

'Are you being condescending again?'

I'd long since got over my anger. It had not been Edward's fault that I had been packed off to boarding school half a world away from my family and it was not his fault that I was trapped here by the war. And – though I hated to admit it – he had been right. Working had been good for me, not just because it kept me busy to the point of bone weariness, but also because becoming a nurse had taught me about love.

'If you thought I was being condescending, I'm sorry.'

The carollers above us trilled energetically into the night air: 'Angels and archangels may have gathered there.'

I'd imagined my feelings for Edward Massinger were based on anger and had refused to countenance any other possibility. I'd longed to meet him again so that I could brandish my achievements in his face and prove that his opinion of me had been false. I'd wanted to thumb my pert little nose at him.

Now, under the stars, I was overcome by an ineluctable torrent of desire. I wasn't angry with him, I realised – I craved his approval and I wanted only his love.

Another strain drifted towards us: 'Worshipped the beloved with a kiss.'

I didn't think about whether what I was doing was right or wrong – or, indeed, what the consequences might be. I simply lifted my hands and cradled them round his face, pulling his mouth towards mine, my hunger for his touch overwhelming.

'Still bored, lovely Cecilia?' he whispered, when at last we surfaced for air.

London seemed a world away, *Vogue* a ludicrous indulgence. Even if I returned to England after the war, I knew I would never go back to the magazine. Sympathy, Compassion, Love – the eighth promise. I looked deep into Edward's eyes and saw that he already knew the answer to his question.

I pulled him closer again and we kissed until my breath ran out and my lips became blissfully numb.

'Yet what I can I give him,' came the voices from the window above us, drawing the carol to an end, 'Give my heart.'

Nikki Moore

Nikki Moore lives in beautiful Dorset and writes short stories and touching, sexy contemporary romances.

She has been a finalist in several writing competitions since 2010, including Novelicious Undiscovered 2012. A member of the Romantic Novelists' Association, she has contributed to their magazine *Romance Matters*, has far too much fun attending the annual conferences and has also chaired a panel and taken part in a workshop at the Festival of Romance.

She blogs about three of her favourite things – Writing, Work and Wine – at www.nikkimoore.wordpress.com and believes in supporting other writers as part of a friendly, talented and diverse community.

You can follow her on Twitter @NikkiMoore_Auth and she invites you to pop in for chats about love, life, reading and writing.

&

A Night To Remember

'Oh, bugger! Oops, excuse the language.'

The teenage girl huffs out a breath as she accidentally rams the side of my bulky wheelchair into the doorframe, something metal clanging beside me. Luckily I have learnt to keep all limbs inside its frame; she is not the most graceful of creatures. Mind you, neither am I. It's still hard to believe that I was stupid enough to trip over our new puppy on the way into the garden, fracturing my shin as I fell onto the cold hard patio slabs. What an idiot.

And now here I am stuck in this stupid thing: a nuisance, an inconvenience. Bloody great. Attempts to wheel myself around have been met with appalled expressions. 'No,' everyone keeps saying. 'You always take care of everyone else, now you have to let us take care of you.' Hmmph. Is it the fact I'm a nurse that makes me such a bad patient?

'Stupid thing!' Pulling me back and then realigning, 'Hang on,' she pants, before finally lurching us forward into the large airy room, my plastered leg sticking out in front of me.

A loud cheer erupts from a cluster of people nearby who have been watching our antics with amusement. I crane my neck to see my blonde helper stick her tongue out and a finger up at them in response, though she retracts both upon realising I've noticed. She blushes and they cheer again and laugh good naturedly, audible even above the rock band in the corner. The music being played is so loud that I can feel its beat in the pit of my stomach, the thrum of the bass in my blood: *thump*, *thump*, *thump*, *thump*.

It looks like this is going to be one heck of a party. Gold and white balloons hang suspended from the ceiling in tightly woven nets. A few stray balloons have already escaped and fallen to the marble floor, floating and bouncing around as people talk and drink and dance. Long tables covered with pristine white tablecloths and gold runners form an orderly line against one wall. Sprays of waxen lilies are arranged in bulbous vases full of clear glass beads. They look stylish but I wish they hadn't used those particular flowers. Funeral flowers. They always remind me of death and decay. Maybe it's because I see enough of those in my day job to last me a lifetime, to colour my dreams and make me all too aware of how precious every moment is. How quickly those moments can be taken away.

God, I am maudlin tonight. I'm at a party. *Cheer up, woman,* I tell myself, *enjoy the atmosphere, even if it's from the seat of this silly construction of bars and bolts.*

Right. I refocus and see that on the tables there are also twinkling candles floating in lazy circles in bowls of water, and sparkly table confetti is scattered liberally around on the cloth. Gold and silver helium balloons anchored to the centrepiece float and bob in the air. It all looks divine. The scents of slow cooking food and beer and sweat and flowers mingle to form a kaleidoscope of smells, which is not unpleasant.

As well as the band there is a DJ, and I feel momentarily disoriented as the coloured lights on his deck splash a rainbow of hues across the room – bright sky blue, deep ruby red, clear sunny yellow, fields of England green – washing over people's faces. I clutch the blanket on my lap tighter as a shiver runs through me, and pleat the waffle of the material nervously between my fingers.

Nerves are soon forgotten as my gorgeous helper wheels me forward, trying to avoid the mass of smart leather Oxfords and glamorous high heels. Some of the party guests crowd round me to say *hello, hi* and *how are you*, touching my shoulders and arms in greeting. Being patted, especially when at waist height to everyone makes me feel suffocated, claustrophobic, but I say nothing, I simply give them a tight grin. If they are so pleased to see me then who am I to ruin their fun?

And it's nice to feel wanted, even if I don't recognise them all. Although thinking about it some *are* vaguely familiar. Perhaps they are distant relatives who carry a strong family resemblance? It would explain why their faces are those of strangers but oddly known.

As the group around us dissolves away, I spot a white banner hanging from between two pale columns that seem to hold up the roof. HAPPY GOLDEN WEDDING ANNIVERSARY the sign declares in huge gold lettering.

But whose anniversary is it?

I frown. Golden – that's fifty years isn't it? Robert and I were married in the springtime four years ago, pink apple blossom spiralling around us in the faint breeze as we stood outside the tiny church in my home village. The way he looked at me that day, so adoringly, still moves me. His brown eyes were so gentle yet at the same time glowing with heat. His smile was crooked and indulgent. It's the way he looked at me the first day our eyes met across the surgical ward of the local city hospital. It's the way he has looked at me every day since then. I hope with everything inside me that he never stops looking at me like that.

Searching for my handsome husband's presence, I can't find his dark hair or dimples anywhere. There is an old silver haired man standing a few feet away that I recognise: nice of my father-in-law to make an effort to attend a family event. Perhaps he's coming round to the idea of me after all. It would be good if we could settle our differences before Robert and I have children. Apparently Daniel thinks I'm a bad influence, an inappropriate woman for his son.

On the sole occasion I have convinced Robert to share his father's concerns with me – he'd resisted up until then because he didn't want to hurt my feelings, but I pinned him down playfully and insisted seriously that he reveal all – he told me two things.

One, that my father-in-law thinks I am far too headstrong for my own good. Why? Because I don't automatically agree to everything that Robert suggests, don't obey my husband without question, the way I am expected to. Daniel is old-fashioned that way.

Two, that I'm selfish, not a good wife because I want to build a career and see a bit of the world before becoming a mother. He thinks it's unnatural for a woman to feel that way, but surely it's better that I'm honest about these things rather than staying quiet and then being resentful towards my children when I have them and my freedom is curbed, my hopes and dreams curtailed? I am sure that it's the children who suffer when their parents are frustrated and bitter, feel that life has passed them by. I think it's more responsible to be sure, to know with absolute clarity that you're ready for them.

So sod Daniel. I know that my husband loves me, that I'm my own woman, different to others he's known. I know that he has told his father that fact. His dad doesn't respect his choice of bride, but he does respect his son and his occupation, so he leaves us alone for the most part.

Robert is a doctor. We met at work. He was such a charmer, with his sparkling eyes and white teeth and lovely bedside manner, one that I was instantly eager to try out in a very unprofessional way. But I didn't make it easy for him, I played it cool and made sure we got to know each other and that I was the only one for him before we –

Anyway, Robert says he is happy if I'm happy and that we can have fun practising making babies until I'm ready. Daniel is just going to have to accept that his only child is an adult and that when we start a family is entirely up to us. He'll come to terms with it I'm sure. I've got about forty years to win him over. Let's hope that's long enough.

The girl leans over my shoulder and interrupts my thoughts, which seem to be hopping around randomly tonight. 'Where do you want me to park you?' she asks directly into my ear, making me wince. Her face is pressed close to mine, hair tickling my neck, fresh spicy fragrance drifting up my nose. I know it's ridiculously loud in here, but still, does she think I'm deaf or something just because she's a few years younger than me? Yet when I glance up into her clear blue eyes, they are warm with affection, nothing else. It makes me smile, so I scan the room rather than question her volume.

'Over by that table,' I point to one furthest away from the band, 'and then can I have a gin and tonic, please?'

She seems surprised, hesitating, but shrugs. 'Sure, why

not?' Rolling me over to the designated table, she sets me next to it without incident and pops the wheelchair's brake on. 'I'll be back in a minute.'

'Thank you.' As I watch her walk away, hoping she won't trip and hurt herself given how accident-prone she is, a young man with messy brown hair catches my eye. He starts to make his way towards me purposefully. I hope that I'm not going to have to fend him off. When Robert and I first started dating – going to the cinema and restaurants and on long walks – I used to get a lot of attention from other men. He found it frustrating; I found it amusing. Even now after a few years of marriage, he feels insecure about it. He's got nothing to worry about, but it's endearing in someone normally so confident. I would never take advantage of that vulnerability though, and so I tend to flash my wedding ring at admirers so that they know to back off.

I look down at my lap, at the modest diamond engagement ring and gold band on my finger. I frown. The gold looks smudged and scratched. I'd better make sure I polish it before my next shift. The silver disco ball spins rapidly above me and the reflected glittering spots of dancing light make my hands look strangely pale in the darkness. I shrug. I need to take some time off work, try and find some solace in the British sun, however weak it may be.

'How are you, man?' Apparently unperturbed by lack of eye contact the young man has crouched down in front of my wheelchair, avoiding my outstretched leg carefully. The plaster on it is starting to drive me crazy. There's a recurring itch right down inside the cast. Perhaps I can lay my hands on a pen to scratch it? Or a spoon? Maybe a fork?

Remembering my manners, I register my new companion's odd greeting. 'Man?' What is *that* about? And what is he wearing? I seriously dislike the whole baggy jeans and loose T-shirt style. Can't he try any harder? I raise an arched eyebrow at him. My patients say it's my 'I'm not impressed' look. When he seems distinctly unaffected by it, I waggle my fingers to draw his attention to my wedding ring, this time noticing how thin my fingers are. I've been on a diet to lose a few pounds to fit into my fabulous new swimsuit, but surely I've not lost that much weight already?

'So?' The stranger ignores the waggling to peer at me. 'I asked how you are?'

'Hmm?' I respond absently, wondering again where Robert is. Perhaps he's on call or has been drawn away to attend an emergency at the hospital. There seem to be a lot of those at the moment. It feels like I haven't seen him in an age, even though we share a home.

'Are you OK?' he repeats, appearing worried.

'I'm fine, thank you,' I murmur, attention captured by my father-in-law sitting down next to me. I'm surprised he's doing so and am not sure what to say to him. So I risk a quick glance over to try and assess his expression in the darkened room, the whirling lights my only illumination. Is it my imagination, or does Daniel look sad? If he's regretting having been so standoffish with me over the past few years, the only thing that has blighted my happy marriage, he's going to have to apologise in a big way. On the other hand, I could show him how mature I am and make peace with easy dignity. We'll see.

'I was wondering,' the man at my feet persists, butting into my thoughts again, 'what's it like to have been married for fifty years?'

'I don't know! Why don't you ask me in forty-five years or so?' I shoot back. What a stupid question.

Daniel winces, probably thinking that my tone is rude, and turns his head away. No doubt he is hoping that my marriage to his precious son won't last too much longer. He will have a long wait if that's the case. Robert and I are forever.

I'm starting to feel irritated, not just with this guy's questions but the way he's addressing me is familiar and intrusive. Even the music that is playing relentlessly within the confines of the heaving room is an annoyance.

I fan myself as a flush rises up my chest. Thankfully the fair angel looking after me returns and sets my drink down on the table beside my elbow. What a good nurse she'd make, I think, if she could just be a little more careful. We wouldn't want her plastering the wrong limb or losing an instrument inside someone's wound. But that's a thought for another day. I really must try and concentrate on enjoying this party, whoever's it is.

'Thank you,' I mouth at her.

She smiles straightaway, mouthing, 'No problem.'

The bloke at my feet stands up beside her. 'All right?'

'Yes.' She throws him a look I can't read, flitters a quick glance at Daniel's face before turning back to him. 'Any luck, Chris?'

'Nope.' He shakes his head ruefully. 'Maybe later.'

Goodness knows what they're on about but whatever it is they're intense, heads bent together as they murmur back and forth. I tilt my chin down, ear cocked towards them to try and hear better, but they catch me at it and fall silent. I drop my chin back down and pretend to be extremely interested in twirling my loose wedding ring round and round my finger: another strike against me. Daniel thinks it a vulgar habit.

When I look up once more he is gesturing to the bar. 'Come with me to get a drink?' he asks my aide.

She gives my shoulder a quick hard squeeze, gazes down at me. 'Will you be OK if I…?'

I'm not sure I've ever seen such a lovely face. How lucky I am to be surrounded by such beauty. It reminds me of a poem I read once, something about daffodils and shepherdesses.

'So?' she prompts.

'Of course I will.' Drat, my mind wandered again. Why does it keep going off on these silly little tangents? Whatever these little white painkillers are that they have me on for my leg, they must be pretty strong.

'Great. I'll be back soon.' The two of them slope away through the heaving crowd, replaced a moment later by a good-looking middle-aged couple.

'Hi, how are you today?' The woman deliberately enunciates each word, her cornflower blue eyes very familiar. I don't answer the question, trying to place her. Is she a member of staff at the hospital? A friend of a friend?

Turning to her partner, an unreadable look passes between them. He reaches down, clasps her hand reassuringly. The thoughtful gesture makes me smile. How romantic. It's the kind of love Robert and I have, a supportive relationship full of mutual respect and understanding. I'm glad that this woman, whoever she is, has found it too.

'Mum? Dad?'

My eyes jerk up. Her attention is focused on me and my father-in-law. I glance over my shoulder, wondering to whom she's talking. I don't see any likely suspects. People are either on the dance floor, propping up the bar or deep in laughing conversation.

'Mum?' she mutters brokenly.

'Shh,' her companion says. 'Give her a minute.'

Who, why, what for? What is happening?

As I swing bewildered eyes up to them, the overhead lights go on and the band finishes their tune. The DJ puts on some background music and announces that food is served and that everyone should help themselves. The music is turned down but the beat of the pop song still feels too loud, sending a *doosh*, *doosh*, *doosh* through my body. It makes me feel sick and jars my head.

I blink against the harsh glare of the overhead chandelier and turn to complain to Daniel that a headache is forming. He may not like me but he would not be impolite enough to ignore a woman in distress.

I stop, realising something as I see the man next to me properly for the first time. He isn't Daniel. The features are similar but they aren't haughty and sharp. The dark eyes are tender and warm and…hopeful?

A gauzy fog, one I was unaware of, starts clearing, fragmented pieces of faces and conversations crowding my mind.

He reaches down and lifts my hand to his lips, sparkling eyes crinkling at the corners, dimples denting his whiskery cheeks, silvery hair falling forwards over his brow. As his mouth brushes the skin of my wrist, it ignites a magical spark that courses through my veins, prickles hotly along my nerve endings.

'Robert?' I gasp, as with a moment of lucidity I remember. *Everything.*

Memories flow back in a rush, flashing through my head like a series of scenes from a film: a doctor in whites, stethoscope dangling from his neck, hands sure at my waist, excitement fluttering in my stomach as he leans in for a special first kiss in the supply cupboard. Blossom twirling on the wind, my fitted white lace dress clinging to me as my father walks me into church past a row of daffodils and gives me over to the man who will become my husband in the next few breaths. The day I am promoted to matron and we celebrate with a bottle of cheap dry cider that ends up on our clothes and in our hair and later on our naked skin as we make love, hands clasped tight and sighs filling the room.

The images flicker by faster.

Our first tiny but comfortable house and the decision to upsize a few years later when my mornings begin being punctuated by nauseous retching over the toilet bowl, moisture beading my brow as my stomach turns and swoops.

The moment some months later, when I hold our first and only child in my arms triumphantly, a beautiful precious baby girl. Her father's hand resting on mine on top of her downy head after he's been let in to our bedroom

Faster, quicker, spinning round my head.

The endless fraught and sleepless nights when I thought I would never know rest again, the first steps, the first run, the first perilous climb up the apple tree in our garden. Yellow stumpy pigtails, Peter Pan collars on dresses, scraped knees, the first broken bone. I smile. The teenage years, riddled with a mixture of angst and challenge and anxiety and fierce love, the need to protect stronger than the need to let go, time marching on resolutely so that five minutes later it seems we are waving her off to secretarial college in London, wishing only the best for her, wishing her skirts could be a little longer and more modest. But hey, it's the fashion, she tells us.

The decision to downsize when she calls us a year later to tell us she is happy in the city, she is never moving home again. The villa bought in Spain, the glorious sun, the muggy heat, the heartbreak of having to sell at a loss when the cost of living rises and the bottom drops out of the market.

The phone call in which she tells me she's met the one, '*her* Robert,' and a while later their gaudy and vibrant wedding at the registry office and then down the local pub which we disapprove of but enjoy anyway because she is glowing with happiness. Then the birth of our first grandchild, such a proud joyous time.

It's a merry-go-round, I can't keep up. They are moving so quickly, at the speed of light. I close my eyes, reopen them.

With all these memories, shock, anger, regret, love and longing sweep over me in a tsunami of emotion. And with these, I regain my identity.

I have lived my life and I have rediscovered it.

I know who I am.

Thinking back over the evening I recall the strange but familiar faces, the behaviour of everyone around me: every remark, every touch, and every look. I think about the changes to my body, the way my mind has flittered around, like a butterfly unsure of the safe haven upon which to land.

And I understand.

I realise the ugly truth. This is not the first time I have been lost to those around me, or to myself.

How many times before has this happened? How often do I wander into my own world, a realm where others cannot find me?

I am devastated, choked. But I know one thing. It must be so much worse for them, for my family. I am guessing that when I am lost I do not know it. But they do. I can't lose *this* moment. I must make it count.

So I force myself to smile up at the blonde woman despite the despair that grips me.

'Hello, my darling, how are you?' This is my daughter Gail, her husband Peter. The young man was my grandson Christopher – calling me 'Nan' not 'man' – and the teenage girl is my lovely granddaughter Amelia.

Gail gasps, leans forward and wraps her arms around me, holding me tight. 'Fine, Mum,' she cries before stepping back to her husband's side, who puts an arm around her shoulders and squeezes. 'I'm fine now.'

I nod at him. *Take care of her when I can't.* He nods back. I think we have an understanding.

'Good,' I murmur.

I turn to Robert, squeeze his hand and bring it to my lips. The wrinkles on our faces are a testament of the years that we have spent together: raising a family, battling through good times and bad. *This is my husband, whom I love.* Maybe my diseased mind fools me into forgetting him sometimes, but I am comforted by the fact that somehow my heart will always find a way to recognise him.

Love *does* overcome.

Focusing on the banner above our heads, I realise that tonight is a celebration of fifty years of our marriage, commemorating the day that I chose to spend the rest of my life with my best friend and perfect lover.

'Happy anniversary, darling,' I whisper.

The corner of his mouth quirks up and the movement

spreads until it is a huge grin across his face, a happy light making his eyes twinkle. 'Happy anniversary, my love. Thank you for coming back to me.'

'Always,' I reply fiercely, tears burning my vision.

But I smile bravely.

Because for now, for this moment, for this night, I am his again.

Rhoda Baxter

Rhoda lives in the East Yorkshire, where the cake shops are excellent. When she was choosing her A-levels, she wanted to take English as her main subject, but her parents suggested that she study science – so that she could get a 'real job' – and write in her spare time. Which, funnily enough, is what she does. So it turns out her parents were right. Again.

She writes romantic comedy with a touch of cynicism. Vik from this short story is a character from her next book, *Doctor January*, which will be published by Choc Lit in 2014.

You can find out more about Rhoda, her books and other obsessions on her website, www.rhodabaxter.com (which is home to the Inheritance Books blog feature), or you can catch her on Twitter (@rhodabaxter) or Facebook.

&

The Truth About The Other Guy

Aasha sat in the back, slightly out of breath, and tried to do her lipstick while the car was moving. In front her mother was fussing, her bangles clinking as she searched in her sparkly peach handbag for the party tickets. Her father muttered under his breath about how many times she'd asked him about those bloody tickets.

Out of the window, she saw people setting off for a fun night out. Her old friends would be going out about now. So would Greg. And his glamorous new girlfriend. She'd never realised how many of her friends were Greg's friends first. Well, now she knew. They got to go out while she got to spend New Year's Eve with her parents. Going to a Sri Lankan party in London. Great.

She looked over at her father's silhouette and felt fourteen again. She put the lipstick in her clutch bag and sighed. If she'd known then, that ten years later she'd be sitting in the back of her parents' car, going to the same party she'd been to every year until she'd left home, she'd have committed suicide. This was crap. It couldn't get much worse.

'I'm glad you could come,' said Ammi.

'Me too.' May as well be nice. Ammi had been so thrilled when Aasha accepted the invitation, it had been quite touching.

'Did the new shoes fit?'

She stretched out a foot. The shoes were dainty and the perfect red for the sari she was wearing. The high heels made her feet look long and feminine. It made a change from the Doc Marten boots she usually wore. She wished she'd taken the time to paint her toenails. 'Yes,' she said. 'Thank you. They're lovely.'

Her train had been late. So, instead of having lots of time at home to get changed, she'd had to brazen her way into the station hotel's toilets, get changed into her sari and run back through the concourse just in time to jump in the car.

'Actually, Aasha, there's something I need to talk to you about.'

Aasha tensed. That tone of voice never heralded anything good. 'Yes?'

'There's someone at the party I'd like you to meet.'

She closed her eyes and groaned. 'Not again, Ammi. I told you, I don't want you to find me a husband.'

Jewellery tinkled as Ammi turned in her seat. 'You haven't already got a boyfriend, have you?' She looked more hopeful than worried. Aasha wondered whether she would feel the same if she'd known about Greg. Probably not.

'No.' Aasha blew out her cheeks. 'Of course not.' Greg was scruffy, not Sri Lankan and, possibly worst of all, a smoker. Ammi would have had a fit if Aasha had ever brought him home.

'So, you need some help.' Ammi settled back in her seat. 'He's a nice boy. I met him at the temple a few weeks back. He's – '

'Ammi. I don't want to meet someone "suitable".' She

made quotes marks in the air. 'I want to meet someone I like. OK? I don't need you to line people up for me.'

Despite Aasha living in London all her life, Ammi still insisted that she should have a suitable Sri Lankan man, which wasn't exactly a realistic thing to expect. Aasha's solution had been to keep her boyfriends and her parents well apart, living a sort of divided life. Since the whole fiasco with Greg, this separation began to bothered her. She rationalised it by thinking of it not as proper lying, just as omitting a few things.

Ammi wasn't finished. 'You'll like him.'

'You don't know that.'

'I know you and I know you'll like him.'

She hated it when Ammi did that 'I know my little girl' thing. 'Thathi – ' she began.

'Don't ask me,' said her father. 'This is between you and your mother. I just drive the car.'

No wonder Ammi had been so pleased. She'd seen the chance to do some matchmaking, as though Aasha were a piece of furniture that needed to be sold off. If there were an eBay for Sri Lankan brides, Ammi would have put her on there. She was about to say something about it, when she realised that there probably were online 'meet a bride' sites. Best not to give Ammi ideas. Oh god.

'I don't want to meet him.'

'You don't know anything about him yet,' said Ammi. 'I've spoken to his parents, they seem very nice.'

Aasha folded her arms and glared out of the window. Ammi had been so sure of Aasha's feelings that she'd sorted everything before Aasha had even met the guy! Well, not if she had anything to do with it. 'I won't speak to him.'

'I've told them you'll be there and I'll introduce you,' said Ammi. 'So you have to speak to him.'

She pursed her lips. She'd see about that.

'You look so beautiful in that sari and those shoes, he's bound to fall in love with you, instantly.'

She'd see about that too.

* * *

The party was in a council hall somewhere in the suburbs. By the time they got there, the car park was almost full. Thathi found a space at the far end.

'Come on,' said Ammi. 'And don't pout. It makes you look ugly.'

Aasha's scowl deepened. How dare Ammi treat her like she was ten years old? She had no intention of going along with this plan. The first thing to do was to get out of this ridiculous princess get-up.

Halfway across the car park, she said 'Wait, I forgot my phone. Thathi, give me the car keys a minute, I'll be right back.'

Thathi shot Ammi a quick look, then tossed Aasha the keys.

'We'll be waiting for you,' Ammi called after her.

Thankfully, they were too keen to get into the warmth to come with her. Aasha opened the boot and in the dim light, located her Doc Martens. There wasn't much she could do about the sari, but the shoes could go.

She needed an excuse for changing into them. She could lie, but if she didn't want other people to lie to her, she couldn't lie to them. A quick search revealed the toolkit

Thathi always kept in the car. She pulled out the spanner. Grabbing hold of one of the lovely red shoes, she whispered, 'I'm sorry,' and brought the spanner down on it. There was a satisfying crack as the heel came away from the shoe.

She pulled the laces tight on her boots and let the sari fall over them. It was so much warmer wearing these than the high heels. And more comfortable. And far less elegant. She grabbed her clutch bag, locked the car, and marched to her parents.

* * *

Ammi was standing by the coats, talking to someone Aasha didn't recognise. The breeze through the door made their saris flare, bright against the drab seventies brickwork. Aasha shucked off her fleece and hung it up. She immediately felt cold and vulnerable, like a butterfly longing for the safety of its cocoon. She wished she hadn't let Ammi talk her into wearing a sari.

Ammi spotted the boots immediately. She grabbed Aasha's arm and steered her into the hall. 'What happened to your shoes?' she hissed.

'One of the heels is broken.' It was true.

Ammi narrowed her eyes. 'Hmm.' She stopped and looked around the room.

The hall was decorated with Sri Lankan flags, batik prints, and, incongruously, notices about the Girl Guides. Baila music played from a sound system in the corner, loud enough and jaunty enough to make people tap their feet unconsciously as they talked. Ladies in saris and sparkly *salwar kameez* mingled with men in hideous jumpers and teenagers in the latest from Topshop. Kids chased balloons around islands of adults. It was like being zoomed straight back to her childhood.

'There they are.' Ammi gripped Aasha's hand a little too hard. 'Now, be nice.' She set off, like a galleon in full sail, with Aasha trailing in her wake.

The group included of one Ammi's friends and two young-ish men. One of them was tall and wore his shirt buttoned up to the top. The other guy was slightly shorter and was in jeans, a shirt and a blazer. There was an aura of suppressed amusement about him, as though he was about to laugh. He looked at her from head to toe, spotted her shoes and looked up again. Aasha looked away.

Ammi's friend greeted her with a kiss on the cheek and a lavender scented embrace. 'Aasha, so nice to see you again.'

'Hello, aunty.' The nice thing about all older ladies being called 'aunty' was that it didn't matter that Aasha couldn't remember the lady's name.

Ammi took up introductions. 'This is Sanath,' she said, indicating the tall guy. 'He's a banker.'

'Hi. Nice to meet you.' He spoke with a slight South London accent.

'You too.'

They shook hands. There was an awkward pause. Aasha looked at Ammi. No one introduced her to the other guy. He gave her a friendly nod and resumed his conversation with the person standing next to him.

'So,' said Sanath. 'I hear you work for a law firm.'

'That's right.' Aasha looked around for a means of escape. The bar was impossibly far away. Besides, she didn't drink alcohol in front of her parents, although she was never sure why not.

Sanath cleared his throat, preparing to speak again. Thankfully, the doors opened and the food arrived, distracting him from whatever he was going to say. Caterers brought in enormous pots and laid the buffet on a long table. A queue formed almost immediately.

Ammi and Aunty engineered things so that Aasha was standing next to Sanath in the queue. From behind him, Ammi was making encouraging head movements. Aasha sighed and turned to see who was on the other side of her. It was the other guy.

'Hi,' he said. 'I like the shoes.'

She looked down at her scruffy boots peeking out from under the folds of the sari. 'Thanks.' She lifted her gaze and saw the corners of his mouth twitch. 'I'm Aasha.'

'I know,' he said. 'I'm Kaushalya, but most people call me Vik.'

'Vik? Sounds like something you rub on your chest.'

He smirked. 'I live in hope.'

She giggled. This guy was more fun than Sanath. And talking to him annoyed Ammi. Bonus.

Aasha sneaked another glance along the queue to Ammi: she was now eyeing up the food. The smell of chicken curry wafted over, making her stomach rumble. The food was the best thing about these parties.

Vik handed her a plate. She mumbled her thanks.

The smell of spices drifted up as lids were lifted and tureens stirred. Aasha heaped on a spoonful of cashew nut curry. Delicious. The chicken curry looked red and fierce. She took a more cautious portion of that. She didn't want to talk to either of the guys. She just wanted to be left alone.

'What sort of lawyer are you, then?' Vik said, suddenly.

'I'm not any sort of lawyer. I'm a paralegal. Family law, if you must know.'

He held a lid open for her while she served herself some rice. She really wanted to turn away and sulk, but there was something about his twinkling eyes that made it difficult to look away. Eventually, she said, 'What about you? What do you do?'

'I'm a student. I'm doing a PhD.' He followed her to a table and sat beside her.

'So, basically, you're clever, but you're broke.' She was being rude but she didn't really care. Oddly, Vik didn't seem to mind.

He grinned. 'Yep. How about you?'

'Me? I'm mediocre. And broke.'

'My ideal woman, then.'

Aasha couldn't help laughing. She glanced across the table and caught Ammi watching her. Good. Vik was the complete opposite to the sort of guy her mother would choose for her. In fact, he wasn't much like the sort of man she usually chose for herself, but she was enjoying his company. He was making her laugh. She'd done precious little laughing over the past year. It was nice to be lifted out of the dark.

'How come you're here?' she said. 'At a New Year's do, I mean.'

'I have no friends.' Then, noticing her expression, he added, 'My two best friends started going out with each other a few months ago. I'd normally hang out with them, but now…it didn't seem appropriate. So when Aunty asked me if I wanted to come to this, I thought, why not.' He smiled. 'I figured the food would be good and I might meet a pretty girl.'

'Oh yeah? How's that working out?'

The look he gave her had a strange intensity. To her surprise, she felt a fluttering in her stomach. She hadn't felt that in years. Not even, she suddenly realised, with Greg.

'Dunno,' he said. 'It's too early to tell.'

Aasha dropped her gaze from his. She didn't want him to see the confusion in them. Her flirting with him was only meant as a ploy to annoy Ammi. She wasn't supposed to actually mean it.

Once the food was cleared away, someone turned up the music. The dance floor filled up with little kids, teenagers and drunken uncles. Aasha stuck to the sidelines in case she got dragged on to dance. She didn't want to step on anyone's toes in her big boots.

She looked around for her parents. Ammi was talking to someone while keeping a wary eye on Aasha. Thathi was sitting with some other men, having an animated discussion about cricket, probably. Aasha sighed. At least they were having fun. This was their world. She didn't really belong here. Her world was…her world was the one she'd known with Greg. She didn't belong there any more either. So where did she fit in?

She scanned the room until she spotted Vik, who was listening politely to a couple of aunties. She had spent the whole meal talking to him. It had been…fun. He took her prickly comments with humour. And he laughed. A lot. When he did, his face lit up from the inside. There was something about him that made her feel safe. As though nothing in the world would ever hurt her again. She could get used to that.

Now that she was able to observe him properly, she realised he was quite handsome in a slightly mussed up way. She watched him, enchanted, until he looked up and spotted her. He smiled. She looked away, her face suddenly hot.

It got closer and closer to midnight. This time last year, she'd been outside, huddled into Greg for warmth. He'd had his arm around her. She'd known that, at the stroke of midnight, he would kiss her. This time last year seemed like a lifetime ago now. This time last year she'd been about twelve hours away from heartbreak.

She looked at her watch: 11:40. All around her people were preparing to toast the New Year. The room was sweltering. It was surreal being here in this sweltering room, surrounded by saris and spices. This was not how she was supposed to see in the New Year. She was supposed to be clutching a glass of champagne, staring squiffily at the crisp black sky, waiting for that first gong. This was wrong. This was just another way the world could tell her what she'd lost.

Ammi had gone to the toilet. If she was going to escape, this was the time to do it. Aasha made for the door and slipped out into the car park.

It was freezing outside. Her sari was completely inappropriate. Hairs stood up on her bare arms. The cold bit the inside of her nose. She knew she should go back inside, but couldn't face it. She wrapped the sari tighter around her shoulders instead. It didn't make any difference. She shivered.

'You'll freeze.' A voice behind her made her jump. 'I saw you sneaking out,' Vik said. He offered her his jacket. 'Here.

Take it. Saris aren't meant to be worn in near zero temperatures.'

She took it and slipped her arms into the sleeves. The warmth was a relief.

'Are you OK?' he asked.

It had been one thing talking to Vik in the crowded hall, under Ammi's annoyed glare. Then she had been able to relax and let his infectious good humour flow through her. She could even eye him up without getting too close. Things were different out here in the frosted night. Here, she felt suddenly shy. The pause was awkward.

Vik cleared his throat. 'Are you enjoying the party?'

'Yes, thanks.'

Another pause.

'What will you do in the new year, Aasha?' He put his hands in his pocket and leant against the wall behind him, his face turned up towards the sky.

She gave a little snort of laughter. 'Same old, I should think. Work. More work. How about you?'

'Finish my PhD, if I'm lucky. Get a real job.'

'If you're luckier.'

He glanced at her sideways and grinned. 'Exactly.' He looked down and drew a breath. 'Aasha. I'd like to see you again.' He looked up at the sky again and then back at her. 'You know, in the daytime.'

Her heart skipped. 'Like a date?'

This time, he looked at her properly. 'Like a date.'

She hadn't been on a date since Greg. She hadn't enjoyed anyone's company since Greg. Until now. Until sweet and charming Vik. 'I'd like that.'

His smile was lovely to see. 'Can I have your number? I'll

call you.' He pushed away from the wall. Now that he was standing straight, he was close enough to feel the warmth emanating from him.

She fished her phone out of her little bag. 'Why don't I call you and you can save it to your phone.'

'Ah. I left my phone at Aunty's house.'

'What's your number then? I'll put it in my phone.'

He looked sheepish. 'Would you believe I don't know it?'

'Seriously?'

'I don't phone myself that often.'

'What do you do when people ask for your number?'

'I usually take theirs and call them so that it comes up on their phone…' The laugh caught his voice mid-sentence.

Aasha laughed too. 'This conversation seems to have gone round in circles.' She pulled out a pen. 'Have you got a piece of paper?'

He checked his pockets and found nothing. 'I could go and get a napkin…' He turned as though to leave, then turned back. He pulled up his sleeve and presented her with his bare forearm. 'Write it on there.'

She raised her eyebrows at him.

He raised his back.

With a sigh that she hoped sounded exasperated, she steadied his arm with one hand and wrote on it with the other. In the cold night air, his arm felt warm and comforting. She finished the number with a full stop and looked up. He had been watching her write. His face was close enough for her to look into his eyes. The want in them made her catch her breath. They stood there for a moment, too close for friendship. And then he closed the gap between them.

It wasn't a long kiss, but it was kiss to be remembered. She felt giddy, as though the world had tilted on its axis. Her blood roared and her whole body felt liquid. Aasha brought her hand up to his face, her fingertips stroking the high cheekbone. His breath caught at her touch. He slipped his arm around her waist and pulled her closer, until their bodies were pressed together. She could feel the heat of his skin through the thin material of her sari. A glow started somewhere in the depth of Aasha's stomach and warmed her up from head to toe. When they drew apart, she no longer noticed the cold.

Vik started to say something but was interrupted by the sound of a door opening.

'Aasha?' Ammi's voice cut through the night.

Aasha jumped away from Vik. He stepped back and disappeared into the shadows.

'What are you doing out there, child? You'll freeze.'

'I just needed some fresh air.' Aasha went back in, hoping that Vik had the sense to stay outside and not set off Ammi's gossip sensors. She'd have a field day if she found out that instead of talking to the nice, well-groomed Sanath, Aasha had been snogging the scruffy student. Ammi's plan had gone wrong. It couldn't have gone more wrong, in fact. She would be disappointed when she found out. Aasha almost felt sorry for her. Almost.

'What were you doing out there?' Ammi sniffed. 'You haven't been smoking?'

'No!'

'Whose jacket is that?'

Jeez. Ammi was like a Rottweiler when she was suspicious.

'It's mine.' Vik stepped in, shutting the door behind him.

Oh great. Well, that just ruined everything. What was he *doing*?

'We were talking,' Aasha said quickly. 'He lent me his coat. Wasn't that kind? Look.' She pointed to the coat, hoping that kindness would soften the blow.

Ammi turned towards Vik, who was looking uncomfortable. He shifted his weight from one foot to the other and looked apologetic. Perhaps he was feeling sorry for Ammi too. Except her wasn't looking at Ammi. He was looking at Aasha.

'Actually,' said Vik. 'There's something I need to confess.'

His eyebrows were knitted with worry. The eyes that had looked at her with such hunger a few minutes ago, looked wary now. Frightened, almost. Asha had a flashback to last New Year's Eve. Fear clamoured in her head. What could he possibly have to confess? He was married? He had a girlfriend he was cheating on? At least he was confessing now and not leaving his girlfriend to find a sexy text from the other woman. Was there something wrong with her that meant she could only ever fall for men who lied? Aasha felt her heart slide into her Docs. The cold outside was nothing compared to the chill she felt now.

Ammi turned back. To Aasha's surprise, she was smiling. 'I knew it would work. See, I told you I knew what sort of man would be ideal for you.'

Aasha blinked, her thoughts momentarily derailed. Ammi was less painful to deal with than Vik. She moved her focus. 'Ammi, what are you talking about? I didn't like Sanath.'

Ammi waved a hand. 'Oh him! He wasn't the person you

were supposed to meet. I knew you'd be stubborn and refuse to talk to whomever I introduced you to, so I arranged a decoy.'

'A decoy?' Aasha looked at Vik. Realisation dawned. She had been set up. 'Was that what you wanted to confess? You were in on it.' She looked directly at Vik. He nodded. Annoyance and relief battled it out inside her. 'But why?'

'If we hadn't, you wouldn't have talked to him,' said Ammi. She was still smiling. 'Now come on. The fireworks are about to start.' She bustled back into the hall.

Vik touched her arm. 'Are you OK?'

She didn't know what to think. He had lied to her. But if he hadn't, they wouldn't have chatted and had that kiss…that kiss would never have happened. 'You lied to me.'

He winced. 'Only a little bit. And I came clean.' His hand moved down to take hers. 'It was the only way to get you to talk to me. At least that's what your mother said.' He raised his eyebrows, ruefully. 'And she can be a very persuasive woman.'

This thawed her completely. She knew exactly what Ammi could be like and she'd had a lifetime to learn how to deal with it. Vik wouldn't have stood a chance. 'She can.' A smile threatened to rise to her face. She tried to suppress it.

'Am I forgiven then?' He touched her hand, hesitantly.

The thrill of his hand in hers took Aasha by surprise. It was as though her heart and body had worked something out well before her head had done.

'I wanted to tell you, but we got talking and then it was too late,' said Vik.

So, he'd lied. A bit. So, she'd been set up. All it really

meant was that this man she liked was a man her mother approved of. Anyway, he'd not actually told a real lie. Just left some stuff out. Was that so wrong?

Besides, if just the feel of his hand was making her buzz like this, what would it be like to kiss him again?

'I – ' he began.

She interrupted him with a kiss. Her lips pressed firmly against his. He kissed her back and the world tilted again. That was not wrong. Oh no. Nothing that made her heart pound like this could ever be wrong. When they parted again, he had a huge smile on his face.

'Just don't lie to me again,' she said, in her most severe voice.

'I promise.' He grinned. 'Shall we go and face the fireworks?'

Aasha handed his jacket back to him and re-entered the room. The smile that had been battling to come out finally made it. As she made her way across the hot room to her parents and the big glass window, she felt, rather than saw, Vik follow her in.

Thathi put a drink in her hand. Surprised, she took it. She stood with her parents as the countdown to the new year started. She thought about Vik's kiss and her lips tingled at the thought. It promised to be an interesting year.

Ammi was chanting the countdown. On impulse, Aasha leaned down and gave her mother a hug. Ammi touched a hand to the side of Aasha's head and kissed her cheek. To her surprise, she saw tears in her mother's eyes.

She had been distant from her parents lately. She'd never told them about Greg, which meant there were huge swathes of her life that she'd had to keep hidden from them. In the new year, she would be different. She would make more of an effort. She would call her parents more often.

She sneaked a glance across the room and caught Vik's eye. He came to stand next to her. Her father noticed and gave him a nod of acknowledgement. Vik smiled back. As Thathi turned back to watch the fireworks, Vik stood next to Aasha. His fingers touched hers, but he didn't put his arm around her or show any other sign of ownership, like Greg would have done. He understood the need for discretion. It would be a refreshing change to go out with someone she could tell her parents about. Vik's fingers gently stroked her palm, making a thrill run through her. Oh yes. In the new year, things would be different. Very different. Aasha looked across at Vik and smiled.

The clock struck midnight and the sky above her exploded into coloured sparks.

Sophie Pembroke

Sophie Pembroke has been dreaming, reading and writing romance ever since she read her first Mills and Boon as part of her English Literature degree at Lancaster University. So getting to write romances for a living really is a dream come true!

Sophie lives in a little Hertfordshire market town with her scientist husband and her incredibly imaginative four-year-old daughter.

She writes stories about friends, family and falling in love, usually while drinking too much tea and eating homemade cakes. Or, when things are looking very bad for her heroes and heroines, white wine and dark chocolate.

She keeps a blog at www.SophiePembroke.com which should be about romance and writing, but is usually about cake and castles instead.

&

The Fairy-Tale Way

'You need to – ' across the table, Karen made hefting motions with her hands ' – boost them up a bit. Shorten the straps, that should help.'

'Where in your book, exactly, does it say that every fairy-tale princess needs to wear a Wonderbra?' Glancing around to make sure no one was paying me any attention, I attempted to adjust my bra straps under my dress. Not an easy feat at the best of times, and made considerably more difficult by the fact we were sitting in one of London's newest and hottest bar-cum-restaurants.

'Rapunzel, maybe. But with boobs instead of hair,' Karen replied, after a moment's thought. 'No, wait! It's clearly Cinderella. Making the most of yourself before meeting your prince.'

I gave the book sitting on the table between us my filthiest look, usually reserved for men who tried to grope me on the night bus home. 'Let me guess. This makes you my fairy godmother.'

Karen beamed. 'You should be grateful I haven't sent you out to find a pumpkin and six white mice.'

'No, just a Wonderbra, a short skirt and a couple of gin and tonics. I can't help thinking that fairy tale standards are slipping.'

With a frown, Karen picked up the book and held it close to her—also Wonderbra enhanced—chest. 'Really, Donna. *The Fairy-tale Way* got five stars in *Fresh Start* magazine, I'll have you know. They said it's – '

'"The new bible for the newly single,"' I finished for her. 'I know. You emailed me the review. Then called and read it out over the phone.' While I was trying to finalise a work document. I just hoped I hadn't given my manager a personnel report on Sleeping Beauty.

'I don't know why you won't take it seriously.' Karen placed the book lovingly back on the table, one hand still caressing the picture of Cinderella and Prince Charming on the cover.

'It's about fairy tales,' I pointed out.

'It's about love!' Shaking her head, Karen reached for her gin and tonic. 'I think that's the real reason you won't give it a chance. You're too scared to fall in love again.'

Which was patently absurd. Who could be scared of love? Love was wonderful: hearts and flowers and fluffy things. Making a fool of yourself with someone you *thought* loved you, only to find out that, actually, they weren't that fussed – now that was something to be afraid of.

'I'm not scared. I'm just not in a hurry for another relationship.'

Karen drained the last of her gin. 'Well, I am. And I need a wingman. Or wing woman. Or whatever. It'll be more fun if we do it together. Besides, it'll be good for you to get out there and get to know new people.'

Given how awful the last person I'd got to know turned out to be, I wasn't sure I was entirely ready for new people. Three years with a guy suffering from self-diagnosed commitment-phobia – at least, until he upped sticks and got engaged to a Swedish model – was enough to put you off people for a while. Even princes.

I checked my watch. Gone eleven, and no sign of Prince Charming. Still, it was Friday night and we were supposed to be having footloose and fancy-free single girl fun, not moping about waiting like Rapunzel in her tower. 'One last gin and tonic?' I suggested, and Karen nodded.

The queue at the bar, which had stretched to the loos and beyond earlier in the evening, had died down now, and only one lonely bartender was serving. I waited for him to finish mixing cocktails for the guys in suits at the other end, then smiled widely at him as he approached me. I once got a twenty percent discount on my drinks for smiling at a bartender and, while it's never happened again, I figure it's always worth a try.

'What can I get you?' he asked, grinning back. He had a great smile, I realised. The sort that made his eyes crinkle and his face lighten.

'Two last gin and tonics before bed, please.' My brain caught up with my mouth a moment too late as his grin grew. 'Bed for me, I mean – Not you. Because you'll probably have to close up here – Not that, if you didn't, I mean – ' I paused for breath. 'Just stop me. Please.'

He took pity on me. 'I do, in fact, have to stay and close up tonight: peril of owning the place. When no one else can do it, it always has to be me.'

I watched his tanned hands measure gin into our glasses, and boosted myself up onto the bar stool.

'You're the boss, then?' Even sitting up high at the bar, I had to look up to meet his eyes. Tall, then. Taller than me which, at nearly six foot in my heels, was a rarity.

Putting down the bottle, he reached across the bar. 'Luke Malone.'

His hand was dry and warm in mine as we shook. A perfectly respectable, ordinary handshake, but something about the brush of his fingers against my palm made my arm tingle.

Dropping my hand quickly, I fished around in my brain for a response. 'Wow. It's not every day I get to meet the owner of the bar *About Town* magazine gave five stars to,' I gushed. 'My friend read the review out to me to persuade me to come and try your gin and tonics.'

'It's less glamorous than it sounds,' Luke said, dropping ice into the gin. 'And I wish they'd told me they were going to print that beforehand. I'd have got some extra staff in.'

'Been busy, huh?'

He gave me a tired smile. 'Manic. But, you know. That's good, too.'

Luke topped the glasses up with tonic, garnished them with lime, and pushed them across the bar to me. I started to fumble in my bag for my purse, but he shook his head. 'Those two are on me, as long as you toast my surprise success.'

I bit my lip. 'Thanks. That's very kind.'

He shrugged. 'Well, since I can't help you to bed as you suggested…'

Laughing, I glanced over at Karen. Engrossed in *The Fairy-tale Way* again. Surely she wouldn't notice if I talked to Luke for a few moments longer.

'Looks like your friend's already wishing she was tucked up with her book,' he said, following my gaze.

I groaned. 'Oh, that book,' I said as I took off my cardigan and lay it over the bar stool next to me.

Luke raised an eyebrow at me. 'What is it? The latest big thing that everyone's reading?'

He had a good read on Karen already, it seemed. 'It's a new dating manual for women looking for Prince Charming. All about how to use fairy-tale rules to play the dating game.'

'That sounds…absurd.'

'Pretty much.' I looked back again; Karen was still reading. 'But…Karen's divorce only came through a couple of months ago, and she's convinced she'll never find love again so I'm humouring her as much as I can.'

'You're not interested in finding your prince?'

I shrugged. 'I kinda thought I already had. But apparently not.'

'Ah.' He winced. 'That's tough.'

'Yeah. I'm ready for a bit of a break from love, to be honest.'

'Sleeping Beauty?' he suggested. 'Asleep in your castle, waiting for the right prince to find you?'

'Actually, for the time being, I'm happy playing the lady in waiting.'

'Being a good friend, then.' Luke smiled. 'Which fairy tale is that from again?'

'You'd have to ask Karen. I'm still avoiding reading the book.'

'Ask Karen what?' Karen's sudden appearance beside me made me jump. 'And what happened to our drinks?'

Luke pushed one glass towards her with a smile. 'Sorry for the delay. Your friend was telling me all about the book you're reading, and I found it fascinating.'

Karen gave him a disbelieving look. 'Really. Well, I'd love to stay and discuss it with you, but I'm afraid it's getting late.' With a very obvious look at her watch, she widened her eyes and said. 'The Cinderella rule, Donna. Remember?'

I picked up my drink and slid off my stool. Apparently my conversation with Luke was over. 'Um, not really?'

'Always leave before midnight.' Karen shook her head. 'I'm just going to have to buy you your own copy, aren't I? Anyway, drink up. We've only got ten minutes.'

As I followed her back to our table, I stole a glance back at Luke, watching us go. He raised a hand to wave goodbye, and I smiled.

Maybe, if his bar stayed as hot and happening as *About Town* promised, I could persuade Karen it should be our new regular watering hole.

* * *

As part of Karen's 'getting back in the game' plan, she'd booked up my Saturday nights for the next month and a half. So the following night I found myself struggling into another Karen-approved dress, ready for some party at a pub halfway across London. I was almost considering reading the damn book if she'd let me stay in with a box of chocolates and a bottle of wine to do it.

'I'm going to freeze in this,' I pointed out, surveying my bare arms in the mirror. 'It's November, Karen.'

Karen put down her wineglass and started rooting through the pile of clothes on my bed again. 'So put a cardigan on. Where's the silver one you wore last night?'

'It should be on the chair.' I looked over at the overladen

seat. There lay last night's skirt and top, but no cardigan. 'Unless...I had my coat last night. And I took my cardigan off at the bar...'

Rolling her eyes, Karen flopped back onto the bed. 'Fine, we'll pick it up on our way. But, be honest, did you leave it there on purpose so you could talk to that bartender again?'

I hadn't. But probably only because I hadn't thought of it. 'He's the owner, actually.'

'Really?' Karen shook her head. 'Doesn't matter. He's a total Buttons.'

I stopped brushing my hair. 'Buttons? Are we veering into pantomime territory here?'

'Buttons is the best friend. The guy you're fond of, that you like talking to, who fixes you good gin and tonics. But he's also the guy you drop in a heartbeat, when you meet your prince.'

I met her gaze in the mirror. 'You think I was Richard's Buttons, don't you?'

Karen looked away. 'Well, it does fit the pattern – '

'Or, it could just be that he was an utter bastard who kept me hanging on hoping until he met someone he thought was better.' I started brushing my hair again, rather more vigorously. 'I'd never do that to someone.'

'Of course not,' Karen said, soothingly, as she pushed my glass of wine closer to my hand. 'Which is why you don't want to get too close to bartender guy.'

'His name was Luke.'

'Which would be important, if you were going to waste any more time on him. But instead, we're going to pick up your cardigan, then never go near there again. Right?'

I stared at my refection for a moment. With my hair

brushed out around my face, and my eyes brightened by the wine, I looked almost fierce. Definitely a woman who could make her own decisions. 'We'll see.'

As it happened, it was a moot point. The bar was fully staffed and Luke was nowhere to be seen. One of the staff fetched my cardigan from a back room when I asked politely. I unfolded it to put it on while Karen hailed a cab outside, and almost missed the small square of paper that fell out from the material. Picking it up, I turned it over in my hands, studying the bold lettering, and the slashes of black ink.

It was just a quick sketch: trailing leaves and thorns covering a wall, and a figure with a sword in one hand and a cocktail glass in the other, about to fight their way through. Sleeping Beauty's prince? I smiled, reading the words he'd written below: Ready when you are.

'Definitely not a Buttons,' I murmured, as Karen waved manically at me through the window, one foot already in the taxi. Apparently we had a carriage to our ball.

I spent the party stuck in the corner, next to an overgrown, spiky, dragon tree plant that laddered my tights in several places, being bored stupid by an accountant from Surrey. Karen, on the other hand, spent it deep in conversation with a good-looking guy in a suit. Dark hair, loosened tie, just the right amount of stubble: absolutely Karen's type. She smiled a lot, and for the first time since her decree nisi came through, it actually looked genuine. So I nodded politely at my accountant, tried to rearrange the spiky leaves of the dragon tree plant, and looked around desperately for more gin.

'He's just…I think he's a prince, Donna!' Karen announced, as she fell into the taxi home, just before midnight.

'How on earth can you tell from one evening's acquaintance?' I asked, still smarting from my boring evening.

Karen gave me a shocked look. 'Would you ask Cinderella that? Or Snow White? Snow White woke up from almost-death to find her prince kissing her, and knew she'd live happily ever after.'

Well, if all you needed was a guy who could kiss, I reckoned princes had to be a lot more common than I'd always believed. 'So did this bloke kiss you?'

'His name's John. And, no, not yet.'

'So the prince thing's still up for debate.' I wondered if, by this new definition, Luke might be promoted to prince, instead of Buttons. I couldn't say for sure, but I'd spent quite a lot of the night before staring at his lips. I'd place money on him being one hell of a kisser.

'But only until Friday,' Karen said, one triumphant finger raised. 'I have a date for dinner with him on Friday evening, and I bet he kisses me then.'

'I'm sure he will,' I said, just grateful to have a night off from having fun, while she was out with her potential prince.

'Actually…' Karen gave me that smile she always wore right before she told me something I wasn't going to like. Half apologetic, half charming. And entirely false. 'He's got this friend…'

My head clunked against the headrest of the taxi's back seat. 'I don't want to be set up.'

'Please, Donna.' Karen clasped her hands together and begged. 'He's got this friend staying next weekend, and he can't leave him home on his own. So I said I'd find him a date. Please, Don, I really think this guy could be my prince.'

There simply wasn't any way I was getting out of this one.

'Fine. But after this, I get to choose my own dates, OK? Princes or not.'

'Of course!' Karen gave a little squeal of drunken delight. 'And besides, maybe John's friend could be your prince! Think how great it could be. I can just see it now – '

Luckily for me, the cab pulled up at my flat before she could start planning our double wedding.

* * *

I had a late, very dull meeting at work on Friday afternoon, so I packed my dress and heels into a bag and got changed in the ladies at the office. I missed the glass of wine to get me in the party mood, but it was considerably more peaceful without Karen's running commentary. And it meant that she couldn't object to the outfit I'd chosen, or try and talk me into something shorter and shinier.

She called just as I was smoothing down my knee-length navy dress. Sophisticated, but with a hint of cleavage. It felt much more like me than last weekend's outfits.

'We're meeting at the Parasol Bar round the corner from you,' Karen said, voice raised over the sounds of the pub. 'Then John says he's heard of some great restaurant we just have to try out.'

'Let me guess. He read a review in *About Town*.' I checked my reflection one last time, then swivelled my lipstick back into the tube. 'Maybe you two *are* made for each other.'

'Very funny.' The sounds of conversation and clinking glasses faded, only to be replaced by the noise of passing traffic. 'I've been chatting to your date, by the way,' she said, which explained why she'd left the bar. Privacy to gossip.

'And?' I asked, not that it really mattered. Apparently I was Sleeping Beauty – taking a break, waiting for my prince. I had a hundred years or so before the right one would come along. I slipped the lipstick back into my bag and felt the edge of a piece of paper sticking out of the pocket: Luke's sketch. *Well, maybe…*

The pause on the other end of the phone wasn't at all encouraging. Maybe I could just go home and curl up with Friday night TV instead.

'The thing I want you to remember when you meet him…You know the story of Beauty and the Beast, right?' Karen's tone was upbeat and encouraging. I closed my eyes and tried to think of a way out of this.

'You're telling me he's a beast?'

'No! Just that…well, you might need to look a little deeper to get to know the real him. I'm sure he must be a great guy, really. I mean, he's friends with John, after all.'

Since all I knew about John was that he read restaurant reviews and it was his fault I had to go on this double date in the first place, I wasn't feeling encouraged by this.

Still, I reminded myself as I set out for the bar, it wasn't as if I'd expected this guy to actually be my prince, or anything. Perhaps he'd be a perfectly nice man who I could have a pleasant dinner with then never see again. It didn't matter if I wasn't attracted to him, or even if he bored me stupid. It was one evening of my life, so that Karen got a shot with her prince. I could do that.

By the time I'd finished my pep talk, I was standing at the entrance of Parasol Bar, wishing I was at Luke's instead. With a sigh, I straightened my shoulders and walked in.

I couldn't miss Karen, perched on a bar stool at one of the

high tables in the window, flame red shoe dangling from one foot. She was tossing her dark hair and beaming at a guy I vaguely recognised as John. And making up the third point of their triangle was a short guy in an ill-fitting brown suit. A very short guy.

Past experience had taught me that a lot of guys were intimidated by my height. From the expression on my date's face when Karen waved at me, he was one of them.

'Sorry I'm late,' I said, sliding up onto the fourth stool. 'I got held up at work.'

John shook his head and smiled. 'Don't worry about it. Now, Donna, this is my very good friend Harold.'

I turned my best smile in Harold's direction but I think he was too busy scowling at John to notice. I'd place money that they wouldn't be such close friends by the end of the night.

'Well, she's here now,' Harold said, dropping down from his stool. God, I wished I'd worn flat shoes. The guy barely came up to my shoulders. 'Let's go.'

I collared Karen as we exited the bar, trying not to be too grumpy that I hadn't even got a gin and tonic. 'I'm feeling more like Snow White than Beauty and the Beast here.'

Her eyebrows crinkled. 'Snow White?'

'With my very own dwarf.'

Karen clapped a hand over her mouth. 'Oh, that's mean,' she said, but she was laughing behind her fingers. 'I'm sure he's a lovely man.'

'A lovely man with a complex about his height?'

She winced. 'Possibly.'

I let out a sigh as we followed the men down the street. John appeared to be getting quite the haranguing.

'The problem with fairy tales,' I said, 'is that they make every man want to be a prince. And they expect their princesses to be petite and soft and pretty. I'm not sure I fit the mould.'

'Maybe you should have worn flats,' Karen said and, even though I'd thought the same thing earlier, the words rankled.

Why should I have to wear flat shoes to avoid making a guy feel intimidated? Why should I have to be less, to make him feel better? The unfairness of it bubbled up inside me until I realised my fists were clenched.

'Are you OK?' Karen asked, concern in her wide blue eyes.

I relaxed my fists. It wasn't Karen's fault. It was mine; for ever wishing I could be something I wasn't.

'It wouldn't have made any difference,' I said. 'The flats, I mean. I'd still be taller than him.'

Karen surveyed our dates, walking ahead. 'Probably. Sorry.'

I shrugged. 'Is John still a potential prince?'

Her grin spread across her whole face. 'He is.'

'Then let's get on with this dinner then.'

The guys stopped walking right in front of Luke's restaurant.

'He really does read the same reviews as you,' I muttered to Karen, trying to pretend that my heart hadn't suddenly kicked up a beat. I was on a date, for heaven's sake. I couldn't go flirting with another man. Although, it might signal to Luke that Sleeping Beauty was ready to wake up at last. Was that what I wanted? I wasn't even sure.

Karen gave me a dark look. 'Just behave, you.'

'When do I do anything else?' I asked, only half joking.

We'd not eaten at Luke's on our last visit, so I was eager to see if the food lived up to Karen's review. That, I told myself, was the only reason for the smile I couldn't wipe from my face, and the way my body hummed with anticipation.

The food. Right.

Still, my improved mood seemed to have a mollifying effect on Harold, who even pulled my chair out for me at the table. Shame for him that my sudden enthusiasm for the evening had more to do with the food than the company.

At least, until our waiter arrived to take our drinks order: Luke.

'Escaped from behind the bar this evening?' I asked, as he handed the wine list to John for him to study.

The blandly innocent look in his eyes gave me hope that perhaps he had exerted boss's privileges to take over our table for the night. Would he do that just to see me? He had given me that sketch, after all…Maybe, I decided, not even caring when John ordered something red, even though I only ever drink white.

'And a gin and tonic for you?' Luke asked me, and I grinned.

'That would be lovely, thanks.'

As Luke nodded and retreated to the bar, I turned my attention back to Harold and the return of his scowl.

'You've been here before, then?' he said.

'Oh, but only for drinks,' Karen jumped in, smiling widely at John as she spoke. 'Such a treat to come here for dinner.'

'Don't you like red wine?' John asked me, frowning a little.

'Gives me a headache,' I admitted.

Harold raised his eyebrows, lips twisted into a superior

smile. 'I do think an appreciation of fine wine is an excellent indicator of sophistication in a woman.'

'Really?' I asked, wishing my gin and tonic would arrive already. 'I find that knowing what you want is a far more attractive trait.'

Karen's smile wobbled a little but she gamely launched into an anecdote about a wine tasting she'd attended once. I had no idea if it was true or not, but it seemed to improve the mood of the men, anyway.

My gin and tonic finally arrived, delivered by the waiter who'd shown us to our table originally. While the others went into raptures over the depth of flavour in the wine, I glanced over at the bar and spotted Luke waving his hands about as he talked on the phone. As I watched, he slammed the receiver down and disappeared into the back room. His evening clearly wasn't going much better than mine.

The food was, as *About Town* had promised, utterly sublime. The company, however, was sadly lacking. While Karen tried to keep up the good humour, and John seemed inclined to go along with her, Harold kept puncturing every joke, every story she told, with cutting barbs. I tried to start a conversation once or twice, and every time he talked over me. In the end, I gave up and concentrated on the food instead.

After the mains were cleared, and after Harold had informed me that it was very bad manners for a woman to order dessert on a first date, I escaped to the bathrooms, Karen trailing behind.

As the door swung shut behind us, we both leant against the sinks and stared at the tiles.

'So, is this the worst double date you've ever been on?' Karen asked, a touch of hysteria in her voice.

'By far,' I confirmed. 'And how on earth is ordering dessert bad manners?'

'I'm so sorry.'

'Don't worry, I'm ordering the honeycomb cheesecake anyway.'

'Good.' Karen straightened up, turning to inspect her reflection in the mirror. 'That's the right attitude. I think the thing to remember here is – '

'If it's a fairy tale, I might cry,' I warned, but she ignored me.

'The story of the Frog Prince.'

'Oh good grief.'

'No, really. You have to kiss a lot of frogs to find your prince.'

'I think this one might be a toad.'

'But the next one – '

'Actually,' I interrupted, looking at my own reflection. 'I'm not sure I'm looking for a prince at all.'

'You want to be single forever?' Karen asked, disbelievingly.

'No. But I don't want to be some princess who needs to be saved from her tower, either. I don't want to wait for some prince to kiss me to wake me up.' I thought of Luke's sketch, and the gin and tonic in the prince's hand. Maybe I'd been getting it the wrong way around all along.

'Then what do you want?' Karen sounded frustrated now, so I tried to find a way to put my confused thoughts into words.

I didn't want Harold. And I didn't want to wait around for someone else to make a move for me. 'I want…I think *I* want to be the prince this time.' Even as I said it, I knew it felt right. Pushing away from the sink, I pulled open the door to the restaurant again, Karen following behind.

'You can't be the prince,' she said, flatly. 'You're a woman.'

I didn't even look towards our table. Instead, I scanned the bar and found Luke at the end, hanging up the phone again, looking half asleep as he ran his hand through his hair. Then he looked up, saw me, and smiled tiredly.

I smiled back. 'Yes I can. And I'm going to employ the Sleeping Beauty technique, right now.'

Ignoring Karen's splutter of objection, I covered the ground between me and the bar in long strides, until I stood looking up into Luke's eyes.

'Hello,' he said.

'Hello.' I bit my lip. 'Ready to wake up?'

His smile widened. 'Definitely.'

'Good.'

And you know what? As my lips met his for the first time, I even found myself believing in fairy-tale magic again.

Discover more romance at

www.millsandboon.co.uk

- ❤ WIN great prizes in our exclusive competitions
- ❤ BUY new titles before they hit the shops
- ❤ BROWSE new books and REVIEW your favourites
- ❤ SAVE on new books with the Mills & Boon® Bookclub™
- ❤ DISCOVER new authors

PLUS, to chat about your favourite reads, get the latest news and find special offers:

- Find us on facebook.com/millsandboon
- Follow us on twitter.com/millsandboonuk
- ❤ Sign up to our newsletter at millsandboon.co.uk